THE ASSISTANT

AMANDA REYNOLDS

Boldwood

First published in Great Britain in 2023 by Boldwood Books Ltd.

Cover Design by Nick Castle

Cover Photography: Shutterstock

A CIP catalogue record for this book is available from the British Library.

Paperback ISBN 978-1-83751-360-4

Large Print ISBN 978-1-83751-356-7

Hardback ISBN 978-1-83751-355-0

Ebook ISBN 978-1-83751-353-6

Kindle ISBN 978-1-83751-354-3

Audio CD ISBN 978-1-83751-361-1

MP3 CD ISBN 978-1-83751-358-1

Digital audio download ISBN 978-1-83751-352-9

Boldwood Books Ltd
23 Bowerdean Street
London SW6 3TN
www.boldwoodbooks.com

For Hayley and Kate

LEXINGTON GARDENS

PILOT SCRIPT – FIRST DRAFT

FADE IN:

EXT. LOCATION #1 – A GRAND LONDON STREET IN BELGRAVIA – 1 APRIL – DAY

A line of icing sugar Georgian townhouses of grand proportions shimmers in the spring sunshine, a light dusting of unseasonable snow making them glitter. The camera pans down the street until it lands on the number 56 painted in neat font on a white pillar of a house near the far end of the exclusive street, then up to the glossy black front door where a mature woman's hand tentatively lifts the polished brass door knocker and releases it. We don't see her, just the hand, devoid of rings, the skin aged, a slight tremor detectable.

NARRATOR V.O

It was late 2022 when I first met Gail Frost. An unremarkable woman. Eccentric even, in that great British tradition. Socially awkward, prickly, defensive, but I was soon sloughing off my preconceptions which were purely superficial and based mainly on her unkempt appearance and reduced circumstances, as well as those terrible photos printed of her and salacious headlines. I interviewed her in the dank bedsit she was renting in Reading. An awful place, mould on the walls. She was lucid, intelligent, and entirely compelling throughout the lengthy interview process.

The camera watches the grand door as the unseen woman waits for it to open, her breaths ragged, sounds of her clearing her throat, then the camera looks up to the very top floor and a roof terrace, lingering there until it snaps back to the door. She knocks again, louder this time and then we hear sounds of footsteps approaching from the other side. A figure is visible through the small sliver of obscured glass, someone is unlocking the door.

NARRATOR V.O

Gail and I were to meet many times over the following weeks and then months. I quickly set aside the opinion I had formed of her based on what I'd read in the tabloid press. I would ask you to do the same. Come to her story with fresh eyes. Come to her story with compassion. As this series airs, I would ask you again, Gail, to be in touch. We care about you. We want to help you.

SCREEN FADES TO BLACK AS GAIL'S QUOTE TYPES, ONE WORD AT A TIME...

"We are rarely brought down by a nemesis exacting revenge. Those scenarios exist only in stories, bad ones at that. No, the dispiriting but prosaic truth is… we are our own worst enemies."

Gail Frost November 2022

SCENE ONE

The large front door to Lexington Gardens opens... we see the two women meet face to face for the first time.

1

INTERVIEW WITH GAIL FROST – SUNDAY 2 OCTOBER

What do I remember of that time back in April? Well, everything, of course. As if it were yesterday. How the icy air funnelled into my nose and mouth and shocked my lungs. And the grate of a metal gate being opened to the residents' gardens across the road, a very ugly dog pulled through it, and my first glimpse of the long row of five-storey mansions. And how very beautiful that spring morning was. And so quiet. A slice of blue sky as the snow clouds cleared above Lexington Gardens. As if even the weather, on the first day of April, knew better than to play the fool at the home of Larissa Elroyd-Fox, or Ris as you probably know her better.

Number fifty-six was within thirty, maybe forty paces of me, but I do have a short stride. Not that I've measured it, but I've been told so, repeatedly in my younger days. Although wouldn't every child walk slowly compared to an adult?

Sorry, where was I? Oh yes, Lexington Gardens. One of London's most magnificent Georgian terraces, right in the heart of Belgravia. The home of the rich and powerful. And imposters. Like Ris. She was thirty-two when she met a multi-millionaire twenty years her senior. Not the twenty-something ingenue you might have assumed from the lurid headlines and paparazzi photo ops. A cocktail waitress turned pseudo-celebrity turned influencer, whatever that means. The bimbo who'd somehow bagged Miles Fox, of the Fox Hotel Empire. A handsome man in his fifties. Lured away from his family by the fake smile and the fake lips and the fake boobs. Head turned by trickery.

Number fifty-six cost the newly-weds twenty million pounds just over two years ago. Not an improbable amount for one of the most prestigious addresses in London, but even so, would you spend twenty million on a home for two people? It's obscene, in my opinion. Think of the good you could do with that kind of money. How much difference it would make in the right hands. Most people won't earn a fraction of that in their whole lives. I certainly won't. Lord only knows what it's worth now, with all the effort and money lavished on it. The transformation of house and owner chronicled in prolific and excruciating detail via Ris' social media accounts. Because did it even exist if not? The ultimate irony in a tale which could very much be subtitled 'be careful what you wish for'. For notoriety has brought Ris what she always wanted, but was it what she needed? Oh, don't look at me like that, as if I don't know what I'm talking about. I've witnessed that same condescension on other journalists' faces. The ones who came before you, knocking hard at the door I opened for you this grey Sunday. Don't make me regret that decision. Casting doubt on my words as they did, twisting their meaning to make me out to be a fantasist, or losing my marbles. I am just about to turn fifty-seven, not a hundred and seven. I have all my faculties. And I am the only one who saw what happened, first-hand.

We both know what wealthy people are capable of. The rich, especially the nouveau riche, are not only entitled, but they are careless. And they stop at nothing. The likes of you and I, we are... inconsequential. But we are ignored at our peril. Am I right?

Of course I am.

* * *

You know I lived in during the week whilst I was in Ris' employ? The flat came with the job of executive assistant. Another basement, yes, but it was *very* different to here. Pristine. Not a spot of mould in sight. Nothing grand, mind you, but a bijou, pleasant abode, and the perfect location to observe and plan. Both talents I have honed over many years. I may not have a university degree, or a decent employment record, but I have other transferable skills. The ability to melt into the background, for instance, as I did that first day. No doubt immediately forgotten by the only observers to my arrival, that ridiculous dog and its owner, a sulky teen who dragged it through the park gate. I was of no import, and certainly no interest to either of them. The reverberating sound of metal clanging shut as the gate closed. The gardens locked at all times.

Security of course, is always a concern, but especially somewhere as desirable and monied as Lexington Gardens. The lower-level windows are grilled on most of the houses, ensuring no vulnerable point of entry, but not at fifty-six. It would 'spoil the kerbside appeal' according to one of Ris' mid-renovation posts. A rather unwise share, wouldn't you say? But people give away all manner of information without even thinking.

And all the houses have sophisticated-looking alarm systems.

The code to number fifty-six will likely have been changed by now, if Ris has any sense at all, which is debatable. But I'm sure *Hubs*, as she always so horrifically referred to him, will have taken the necessary precautions.

The alarm made a horrible sound that one time I set it off. Ear-splitting. Not something I'd care to repeat. But any noises were distant as I approached my future home that crisp morning: the hum of traffic, the far-off drone of a pneumatic drill, a snatch of birdsong then a siren wailing, but muted, in the distance. As if the city knew its place as much as I felt mine.

Other than an occasional passing van or car, the only sounds came from me. My breaths short and staccato: an internal mantra keeping time with my heartbeat. *Don't-go-back. Don't-give-up. Not-now. Not-now.* And of course, a flutter of delight as I spotted the two pillars framing the door, as well as the pristine coir mat, and an ornate metal boot scraper found in Portobello Market. All so identifiable from Ris' doorstep snaps. The covered porch cloistering the entrance is imposing enough to repel all but the most persistent of callers.

The door is also very impressive. Hard to explain unless you've been there, but it looms over you with its deep gloss black. The mirror-shine gold knocker catching the sun and my eye, a catch in my heart too as I imagined the imperative sound it would make. The attention it would draw. I must admit my hand shook as I lifted it and let go, so hesitantly the sound was barely audible. Watching the sliver of etched glass at eye-level for any signs of life.

I'd pre-empted that moment many times, planned it to the point it had already happened a thousand-fold in my imagination, but as I contemplated the majestic lion head, my scowling reflection distorted in its polished surfaces, it struck me I could simply turn around and go home. Back to the safety of a life half-lived. Maybe not even half. The life I'd grown used to, but which had become of late, for many reasons, a compromise too far.

Like a game of Knock Down Ginger, I must have considered the option of walking away. Been tempted by its lack of jeopardy, the ease of anonymity calling to me. Another evening spent in my own company. A bowl of cereal. A trawl through the internet. Notes updated with every tiny detail of my visit, plans revised to incorporate an aborted attempt and ideas jotted down of how one day I would see it through to its conclusion. The thrill of having been so close would have sustained me for a few more weeks, even months. But inevitably, I would have been drawn back. There is little worse in life, after all, than being ignored. A daily occurrence for a woman of my age and means, but something that's never easy to endure.

I lifted the heavy ring in the lion's mouth again and dropped it much harder this time, before I could overthink it. The loud thwack of metal against metal surely announcing my presence.

For good or evil, I would no longer be hiding behind a screen. Unseen. Unheard. That part of my life was over. Time to become a part of the story.

2

INTERVIEW WITH GAIL FROST – SUNDAY 2 OCTOBER

So sorry about the milk, and the biscuits. I can't keep anything here, not with the damp, but the landlord won't do a thing about it. I suppose I should move on, but it's not quite that simple, not with my financial situation being as it is.

I'm really not up to looking for work, you see. Not that anyone would have me, not after those headlines, and any money I was paid by those hacks... well, let's just say what little there was is no more. Not that I'm hinting, I know you won't be paying me for these interviews. It's never been about the money; it's about getting the truth out there.

So where was I? Oh yes, at her door!

It was probably only thirty or forty seconds before I heard footsteps and saw a figure approaching in the small window of etched glass. It distorts the view, so you can't make out who, but I could tell someone was there, turning the lock, the door easing open.

Those were the last few moments I had to re-evaluate the wisdom of my intended strategy and panic was truly setting in. I might have worked out a way to inveigle myself into Ris' home and the intention contained in that, but I had no idea whatsoever of the practicalities. My 'plan', such as it was, can be summed up as a vague notion of due diligence whilst building mutual trust. It was a little more involved than that – I had bullet points; planning is my *modus operandi* – but fair to say I would be winging it to some extent. There were so many variables, unknowable factors I could not incorporate into my scheme without the risk of abandoning it before it was begun. I had to be ready to flex, pouncing on chances as they arose, and making them happen if they weren't readily available. Opportunities to bring Ris down from her falsely won place of immense good fortune. But first, I had to get inside. So much expectation riding on that single aim of dethroning an unworthy imposter.

It had been almost three years since Ris had first blipped on my radar, those headlines sensational and entirely compelling. The photos even more so. A scantily clad waitress pressed to the wealthy entrepreneur's side as they spilled messily from one of his trendy hotels, the disparity in their ages and situations jarring. And not only to me. Social media exploded, as did the press. And the under-the-line comments... I'm sure you've read them too. The words 'cunning' and 'fox' featured heavily.

It was all so seedy. So... uncouth. I was appalled and yet I couldn't look away and neither could anyone else. Her rise from nobody to somebody, swift. And embraced by Ris to the max.

They had been married for two years and one month when I knocked that door. I had already waited far too long, but I'd been hoping for a firm plan to form and I suppose it was like all good ideas: as soon as it came to me, I wondered why I hadn't thought of it sooner. It was so obvious. The only appropriate justice was a reversal of that meteoric rise. A slither back down the snake.

Ris must be *cancelled*.

* * *

I'd expected a housekeeper or some such to open the door. Maybe in a recognisable uniform, although as I'm sure you've noticed from Ris' Instagram posts, at least before the account was deleted, staff were never a feature. The lady of the house very much centre-stage, and invariably flying solo. It shouldn't have therefore been quite such a shock when a familiar face appeared, blinking into the sunlight.

As I recall, which I do – my memory is pretty much photographic – Ris had her hair scraped back, and she wore only subtle make-up. Other than those jet-black brows; symmetrical arches sculpted monthly by a process bizarrely entitled 'lamination.' Are you familiar? Yes, I suppose a woman your age would be, but it was not something I'd heard of. Fashions change of course, and bushy is back, but only for eyebrows, not... Anyway, I digress. It was Ris at the door and I was completely thrown by her presence. My mind emptied. As if I'd gone into a room and momentarily forgotten what it was I needed in there. I could have walked away but that would have looked very odd. Even odder than the fact I was rendered mute by those authoritative dark eyes beneath the dark brows, surveying me with scepticism and simultaneous disinterest. I simply could not summon the words I'd practised many times at this very table, talking to the wall rather than your good self. Not one of them came out. Not even an excuse to turn around and leave. I was turned to stone by that look of hers. You know the one? No, I don't suppose you would, and not the mirror face she shared on Insta – that was bizarre, wasn't it? All that pouting and posing. No, this was a dead-eyed but penetrating stare, the slight tilt of her head to the right indicating not curiosity but impatience. And she was chewing gum, only pausing in her constant jawing long enough to expel a single dismissive syllable. 'Yes?'

I'd felt pleased with my appearance as I left home, the unseasonable late fall of sleety snow only dampening my spirits a little as

I exited Paddington station and walked across Hyde Park. My outfit, what I'd deem smart office wear, more than adequate for the role I was about to play, but my artificially inflated sense of self-worth dropped several notches in comparison to the woman facing me. A particularly caustic bout of self-hatred filling the void and tainting my throat with acid bile. Although, I'll admit now, it was perhaps more a case of petty jealousy. A quick sharp bite rather than the slow burn of envy I'd lived with for years, corrosive in the gut like an ulcer.

My feelings of inadequacy in her presence irritating in the extreme, but not profound or as ultimately disabling as I'd feared.

It's worth saying at this point that, with Ris, even when I knew her better, I was always on the back foot. A deliberate and blanket strategy on her part. Not that she had any reason to doubt me on our first meeting, or at any time I was in her employ, but her default position is haughty standoffishness.

That's what money does, of course, amongst other things. It buys you disdain. And her wealth was certainly on show in her signature 'casual' look. From the laminated brows to the designer jeans and soft cashmere lounge top, which exposed one angular shoulder; it was high-maintenance masquerading as the opposite.

I willed the rehearsed words to spill out, but when they finally came they tumbled so fast they were barely decipherable. She frowned and I tried again. 'Sorry, I'm here about the role of assistant? My name's Gail Frost. The agency should have been in touch with my CV?'

I unzipped my shoulder bag and thrust a printed version of my *curriculum vitae* towards her, jabbing the six inches or so of tanned toned flesh she'd left deliberately exposed between jeans and cropped sweater. When you've put in that much effort – a hundred stomach crunches per day – I guess you want to flaunt the results at every opportunity, but it felt too... brazen. Her navel winking at me.

Maybe I'm being prudish. The thought of exposing my flabby midriff is abhorrent but that's more an age thing, I suppose. Five years post hysterectomy, the four small surgical marks are fading, but the emotional scars... although in my younger days, I had a twenty-six-inch waist and a stomach that was... in fairness, it was never flat. But I was attractive. I was told so. By more than one man. Anyway, it seemed I'd done a reasonable job with my CV, the diligent preparation I'd put in saving me from a slammed door in my face.

Ris unclipped some fancy looking glasses from her sweater and read the printed sheet, both sides, nodding and remarking on my experience, lack of family ties, maturity. And she even pulled out some tiny but clever embellishments which I'd thought would appeal, like complete flexibility on hours and duties. A contrast to her recently fired executive assistant whom Ris had tweeted was, 'Never around when I needed her.'

The full circumstances of the previous EA's departure were unclear, but I imagine that Ris' insecurities about her husband's wandering eye were a major factor in the attractive young woman's dismissal. She must have got her to sign a stringent non-disclosure agreement because I checked thoroughly and she's never even as much as sub-tweeted, but she left a vacancy which I very much hoped to fill for multiple reasons: financial, personal, moral. Although, I'm not going to wrap it up in issues of feminism and socialism. This was not a crusade, at least, only a personal one, but there were wider injustices, I suppose. It was very much a win-win situation. Ticking many boxes. At least, that was the hope.

Ris then informed me I'd have to make another appointment, thrusting the crumpled sheets at me. 'I'm busy; and I didn't know you were coming. You'll have to speak with the agency.' Fair enough, but I couldn't allow myself to be defeated quite so easily. The door was closing, and with it a very small window of opportunity. I needed to act fast, deploy my fallback position. I always have one of those. As I said, planning is my forte, and in my experience, absolutely key. I'm sure it's the same in your line of work. I mean, journalism is a slapdash industry at the best of times, but 'investigative journalist' has a very different ring to it.

Anyhow, in my desperation I recalled a little something I had tucked away in a metaphorical pocket, ready for just such a situation.

I nodded, turned as if to leave and then turned back, finger raised, and gestured to a point across the park, somewhere equally well-heeled, the rooftops just visible in the next Georgian square. Ris looked non-plussed, as she might, but I explained how I'd come straight from an interview at a property in that street. That she might know the woman. Then I gave Ris a name.

One I'd conveniently landed on a month before.

You might well know of her too. The wedding was featured in the clickbait press last summer, in one of those magazines that pays for everything in exchange for an exclusive. Column inches Ris had similarly dominated in the heady days of her affair with her future husband. This Italian lakeside extravaganza was the subject of a very splashy exclusive, both grotesque in its excess and enthralling in its star-studded guest list. A three-day spectacular to which Ris had very much *not* been invited. And believe me, I had checked and double-checked. Especially as the happy couple lived nearby, in a similarly excessive home, and Ris would definitely have made the most of the photo ops on her socials had she been present. She had clearly never connected with the woman. And she was the kind of friend Ris would have made a point of making and then sharing all over her carefully curated timeline. The kind of woman Ris had hoped to be. Who lunched and laughed with other well-heeled wives like her. Who attended charity balls and film premieres and called her acquaintances 'dear friends'. Ris was, in that respect, as much of an interloper as I was. Ostracised by the rarefied slice of London society she aspired to join but was totally excluded from.

The woman's name left my lips and floated between us in the frozen air. A spiky breath of ice well aimed, but also my last hope. It could have gone either way, my future resting on Ris' hesitation as she looked beyond me to that other woman's world, just across the park. To the lifestyle she'd coveted and thought she'd won, but which still eluded her. So near and yet so far.

An expression passed across her hard features, one that I would witness many times after that. A visible manifestation of the fear of something she wanted, or might want, slipping away from her. She wavered. Panic manifesting as a drumming of long nails against the black paint as she held the door, still barring my entrance. I was counting on her coveting something she might not be able to have. Like a child denied sweets at the checkout. My apparent popularity making me an instantly more attractive prospect. She couldn't join that particular closed circle of friends, but she could snipe something one of them wanted.

Just as a side issue, but I think it shines a light on that moment of indecision and how it might have gone either way... I'd been rather pleased with my raincoat, a rare find in my local charity shop and freshly dry-cleaned by its kind benefactor, the ticket still safety-pinned to the label – which I discovered on the train journey home, cheeks burning at my oversight – but I could tell Ris was unimpressed by my pre-loved find, her lip curling as she looked me up, and down, deliberating her verdict.

Much in life hangs on the smallest of things, doesn't it? A memory, a phrase that still stings. A decision made. A choice taken. Not least by those two women who faced one another for the first time across the threshold, deciding if they might be colleagues, maybe even friends. Although little was as it seemed. On either side. And she hated my coat; bought me a new one in the end.

Luckily, depending on which way you now view it, Ris' expression then changed from thoughtful – or if I was being a tad unkind, resting bitch face – to that practised smile she reserved for her Instagram reels. The one where all her white veneers were on show and her eyes sparkled, hair glossy as a pony's, the dewy glow of her skin so covetable that the previous autumn I had blown a whole month's food budget on a pot of her 'must-have' recommended face cream and spent weeks surviving on cold baked beans. That's the power of being someone like Ris. A power she wielded with little thought for those drawn to her, moths to a flame. And I count myself amongst those misled by the thin sheen of glamour, my smile as wide as hers as she opened the door and invited me into her beautiful home.

3

INTERVIEW WITH GAIL FROST – SUNDAY 2 OCTOBER

Have you ever been inside one of those enormous Belgravia townhouses? Neither had I before that moment. They are of course very impressive. But number fifty-six was *something else*. From the moment I went through the door, the scope and grandeur were breathtaking.

The hallway was perhaps the most arresting part of the house, with its marble flooring and glittering chandeliers and the sweep of the staircase. As though you'd entered another world just in those few steps up from the pavement. A palatial promise of more to come, so much more. Such a short residence, sadly, and yet I felt immediately as if I was meant to be there.

The hall is painted white, as is the rest of the house. Although one wall, to your right as you go in, is tiled in mirrored panels above a console table. The myriad reflections created an unsettling feeling of visibility. One I could most definitely have done without.

I looked, as I'd intended, non-threatening to the point of bland, but also nervous, and apologetic. Fifty-six is no age, and yet I carried every one of my years into that pristine hallway. Whilst Ris, even without full make-up and in her mid-thirties, was what my late mother would have termed 'striking'. It was not a compliment Mum ever levelled at me, but I understood it to mean there was attractiveness, but little natural beauty. A hard strike, I suppose. Arresting, but not pretty. Which left me with an initial impression of Ris as possessing glamour but with little if any warmth. Her ostentatious home was designed to astound, which it did. In spades. And in fairness, so did she, but there was an emptiness to both.

Ris indicated I should leave my wet coat on a bench seat strewn with the fluffy sheepskin of a large but long-dead ewe.

She waited whilst I disrobed. Watchful, as though I might defy that initial instruction and defile her home if left to my own shoddy devices. Then she requested my shoes should be slipped off, the toes of my tights darkened with damp which I sincerely hope she did not mistake for perspiration as it was in fact a combination of wet weather and worn shoes. Her feet were bare, red-tipped toes splayed on the cold tiles beyond the doormat. She has large feet, size eight. Long and thin, the bones visible, a bunion on one from always wearing heels. I laid the coat down with care. It felt a significant moment, a flag placed in the ground. I was there, at last. The sheep's sacrifice, and mine, interwoven. Within touching distance of everything I'd coveted for so long. So close I could taste success as I followed her across the brightly patterned rug on the promise of 'a coffee and a chat' in the kitchen.

She was at pains to convey a spontaneous but professional approach and I did my best to reflect that back. Although I was hyper-aware of my every movement as I took those first few stockinged paces; walking becoming a conscious action. I tripped on the rug and she spun round, asked if I was OK, but her tone indicated not being so would be an annoyance. I assured her I was perfectly fine, although my heart was pounding and cold sweat covered my back. The reassurance I gave her of normality was my first outright lie, other than the invented job offer, yes, and a wildly fabricated employment history. But put yourself in my shoes, or rather tights. I was hardly going to concede my inner turmoil. My chatter, should I have allowed it to leave my thoughts, giddy to say the least, and her irritation at my clumsiness was not aiding my composure.

It's silly, isn't it, how certain people unsettle us so. The censorious teacher whom we can never shake off, the parent whose critical voice follows us into adulthood, even from beyond the grave. I can generally hold my own, but Ris had that effect on me, right from the start. Like I said, I was always on the back foot with her. The physical chasm in our situations, clearly seismic, would be disconcerting for anyone. Although, as I moved deeper into her home my initial reaction turned from stunned awe to – how shall I put this? – *comforting familiarity*.

Very odd, I agree, but I'd liken it to travelling to an iconic location, somewhere you've seen in films, read about, looked up on Google. You recognise what's before you, and yet you can't quite believe you're there. And it felt as if everything had slowed down, allowing me to experience my new surroundings in micro-detail. Not exactly *déjà vu* but yes... *familiarity*. I don't suppose it's that surprising, given I'd avidly followed the renovations since Ris had found her #ForeverHome two years earlier, just after she was married, yes, but I was on unfamiliar territory. I so rarely visit London, let alone Belgravia.

That teddy over there on my bed... yes, the one with the Harrods 2007 on its foot... that was bought for me on a rare sightseeing trip with a friend, but I could count on one hand the times I've ventured into 'Town' as Mum always called it. I find London noisy and dirty. My skin always feels grimy after I've been there. It might only be twenty-two minutes by train, as you say, but you and I meeting on a Paddington-bound trip was a very fortunate coincidence. Like I said to you at the time, I rarely have reason to go into the city. But I did love living at Lexington Gardens.

It's so incredibly luxurious, although not entirely to my taste, with splashes of Ris' rather ostentatious choices creeping in here and there – the pink velvet sofas, a peacock head on the sitting room wall – but thankfully she'd relied heavily on the better judgement of professionals. A long and expensive process, the redecoration chronicled in overly zealous detail on Ris' social media. Every designer who couldn't fulfil her 'vision', or builder who traipsed dust across the newly restored original floorboards, named and shamed. She went through them at a similar rate of knots to assistants. A new one praised and then gone before I'd had time to fully research their backstory. For a while it felt as though Ris' Instagram content had morphed into an episodic version of one of those awful makeover shows which proliferated back in the day. But the work was eventually completed and aside from occasional extravagant purchases – or 'pieces' as Ris pretentiously referred to them – she returned to her favourite subject: Ris. And her loyal followers were rewarded for their supportive comments during the renovation with guided tours of each finished room. All eighteen of them, if you include the basement.

I think some of those videos are still available to watch on YouTube. You should check them out if you haven't already. Ris filmed them herself, phone held aloft, and narrated in her trademark hyperbolic manner. Everything is 'amazing' or 'fantastic'. From the suntrap roof terrace, where a bit of 'naughty' nude sunbathing took place when the weather allowed, to the 'cute' basement quarters where her procession of assistants moved in and then all-too-quickly back out again, myself included.

I miss living there, of course I do, but that's not why I feel the need to avail you of the facts. This story needs to be told. Properly this time. I don't think it's overstating the case to say a woman is unaccounted for. Worst-case scenario? I'd rather not think about that right now. But I suppose we must, and we will, and soon. I know your visits are of necessity weekly, but we must act.

Anyway, to get back to that first visit, it was incredible to be immersed in it all. A house I knew intimately but had never set foot inside before that moment. It was overwhelming, as I'm sure you can imagine. My familiarity with it disconcerting. I had clicked on the shared links, of course, logged and stored and even dreamt of those purchases in those swampy nights of insomniac sweats and menopausal wakefulness, but then there I was, close enough to reach out and touch the vase on the console table or stroke the hand-painted silk cushion on the chair beside it. Not that I did. I simply stared, most likely slack-jawed as I allowed it all to sink in.

And the hallway smelt divine. It always did. A heady mix of the lilies in the vase and the diffusers placed either side of the gorgeous flowers. Expensive diffusers, of course, nothing *too* tacky. Other than her. Ris might have lacquered over the past, but her provenance was there for all to see. Plumped lip curled as she waited for me to catch up after my unfortunate trip and follow her into the kitchen. I then clambered up, or tried to, onto the stool she'd offered me, taking the opportunity to grab onto the kitchen island for support whilst Ris turned her back to see to the offered refreshments.

The same island where she'd once given a long tutorial about how to make a Pornstar Martini 'to die for'. It truly was a sensory overload. The long but narrow room filled with every designer gadget and top-of-the-range appliance you might imagine. A world I'd coveted and studied and lived vicariously every day for the previous two years. It seemed ridiculous it had taken me this long to work up the courage to come here. This long to devise a way to not only be at Lexington Gardens, but also take what was rightfully mine.

Let me give you an example of what I mean by that. It might illustrate my purpose more effectively for you.

The vase I mentioned, on the console in the hall, it is very pretty. Pale blue with impressions of white fluffy clouds circling it, and it's always filled with those long-stemmed calla lilies, petals like creamy champagne flutes... you know the kind, often found in wedding bouquets and hotel lobbies? I'd imagine they cost at least five pounds a stem, maybe twice that. Possibly more, I have no idea, but the price was obviously not an issue; a new bunch delivered weekly, the old ones tossed away by the cleaners unless I managed to salvage them first. The flower shop is only a few streets away, door painted lilac and surrounded by baskets of blooms. Hand-tied bouquets upwards of fifty pounds, and that scent... if I pass a florist, any florist, it takes me straight back to those beautiful lilies. Such a contrast from the damp smell in this place. Anyway, the vase cost seven thousand pounds. *Seven thousand.* You know my weekly budget for food? Fifteen pounds. That vase could feed me for almost ten years. One vase. A vase I could have tipped and smashed with a glancing blow any day as I walked past. A vase that Ris, I'm convinced, barely ever noticed. So if I wanted to turn the tables, finally, and dethrone the imposter, then no, I don't think that was so wrong of me. What you have to ask yourself, as I did, many times... why her? Why should she get so lucky? Why not me? That's the premise I began this journey with, and although I may have failed in some respects, I will not give up on what has now become so much more than a simple balancing of the books. For this is not driven by envy, or retribution, or whatever else is going through your head as I begin to explain what's really happened to that missing woman. It's about so much more than that. It's about a crime so heinous, and yet so unbelievable, that it seems I am the only one who can expose it. With your help, I hope.

EMAIL SUBJECT: INTERVIEWS WITH GAIL FROST

DATE: THURSDAY 6 OCTOBER

Hey, so nice to e-meet you the other day and thanks for offering to take a look at my notes from Sunday. I had no idea you and I had a mutual script agent and you were also looking for a 'true crime' project. And thanks so much for the feedback on the first interview with Gail, we plan to meet up weekly. She says there is some urgency but won't be drawn on exactly what that means. I have to keep on with the day job at the magazine, so you know… boundaries, can't be with her all day every day.

She's my jumping off point for this story, but a good one I think. I find it fascinating what she chooses to tell me and, even more, chooses to leave out. Very much an edited and, in some ways, I suspect, fantastical version of what happened between her and Ris at Lexington Gardens. Gail is adept at glossing over her misdeeds and justifying her actions every which way. But she's not your typical conspiracist either. Or even the hacked-off ex-employee turned tattletale the tabloids have made her out to be. She's a bit odd, for sure, but I haven't written her off as a complete nutjob, not quite yet.

She's certainly not motivated by money, thank goodness, as I have no budget. This is my pet project, not for the magazine. My editor's not interested and I'd rather keep it as mine. Especially now we're talking scripts, always an ambition.

It's very early days, as you said yourself, and maybe Gail's all those things and this will be less revealing than hoped, but I don't think so.

And thanks so much for agreeing to read more. I must admit, when I was subbing the idea to our agent, after I met Gail on a train of all places and my boss had told me it was a non-starter, I had no idea he would send it to you with all your amazing connections and previous projects. I've been such an admirer of your drama-documentaries. What a stroke of luck. Scriptwriting has been my back-burner project for years, a dream of mine, but the day job is editorial copy. Let's hope the stars align. I saw it more as a deep-dive long read, but your vision for it is much more exciting, so yes, of course I'd love to explore the idea of bringing it to a wider audience.

And I totally get your point about diluting the message, but I do think I need to go as wide as possible in my research.

I'm tracking down all the major players who were at 56 Lexington Gardens when Gail was Ris' executive assistant – from early April to the night of the infamous book launch party on the sixteenth of June, for corroboration as well as background. I am also, as you advise, very much taking Gail's words with a mighty pinch of salt. She has her own agenda. That much is abundantly clear. She's making some wild claims then failing to either substantiate or fully reveal them. Heinous crimes, a missing woman... intriguing but who knows?!

I'll hang in there for the ride but appreciate any steers. What do you envisage as next steps?

Best wishes,

Ax

4

SECOND INTERVIEW WITH GAIL FROST – SUNDAY 9 OCTOBER

Sorry about the tea. It's impossible to keep anything in this place... the damp spores. Don't feel you have to drink it.

So, where was I when we ended our interview last week? Oh yes, Ris and I were in the kitchen and she was making coffee, well, dropping a pod in a machine, but she must have noticed me looking around, drinking in my surroundings as well as that delicious aroma as it dripped into the cup, because she took it upon herself to then explain the renovations. How the house was Grade II listed, and that the work she had overseen needed to be in-keeping, *naturally*. I didn't care for the patronising lecture, my knowledge of her home encyclopaedic, but I hope I looked suitably enthralled, despite the fact I could have recited the sales brochure to her word for word:

A complete renovation will be required, but once completed, fifty-six Lexington Gardens will provide the owners with a stunning family home in one of Belgravia's...

That would have freaked her out, wouldn't it? So useful when documents remain online in perpetuity, don't you think? For you too, I suspect. In your line of work.

And as a side note, the only garden – a small courtyard, very high brick walls and dominated at its centre by the most magnificent magnolia tree – is only accessible via the basement flat, where I would soon live.

I hadn't had a garden in years, and I loved it. Used to open the patio doors every morning, rain or shine, and step out barefoot onto the cobbles, coffee in hand, the damp or warmth settling on my upturned face beneath the dappled shade of that glorious tree, eyes closed, heart full. Such lovely memories.

Anyway, getting ahead of myself again... we were the kitchen and nothing had been decided, but it was looking very hopeful. I was balanced on one of the two teal leather-backed stools, the only pop of colour against the bank of floor-to-ceiling white cabinets, my feet finding the footrest moments before Ris handed me my hot coffee. A glass of filtered water poured from the tap for herself – she avoided caffeine and refined sugar – her long slim wrists swathed in bangles and, of course, sporting the ubiquitous smart watch. She owned three of them. One on, one charging, and a spare. Everything she did had to be tracked, you see, even in her sleep.

She slid onto the stool beside me with ease, her legs so much longer and lither than mine, laptop opened up, fingerprint recognised. Lean thighs crossed, red-varnished toes pressed to the side of the island like dots of blood spatter in a crime scene. The overpowering scent of her favoured Jo Malone perfume, Pomegranate Noir, suffocating me. It's a beautiful scent, I agree, but she always sprayed herself in clouds of it. I begged for a freebie at the department store concession when I was sent to buy more, but the tiny sample ran out after barely two pumps. I confess to then helping myself to the odd spritz of hers, but I'd hardly describe it as theft. Not when she sprayed it round like air freshener. A new bottle purchased each time they'd almost ran out. I kept the leftovers, squirrelled them away in my bathroom cabinet, but I'm sad to say I left them behind. Not the only casualty of a hasty exit, but still rather a sad loss.

She often sent me on errands to the beauty counters nearby, not only for perfume but other cosmetics, as well as requests for packs of gum, tights, cans of diet energy drink. Anything that popped into her head. There was a large Boots chemist close by, or the department stores in Kensington. Very convenient. I was the dogsbody, but I rarely minded. All part of the remit as far as I was concerned. And far from the worst part of the role. Plus it got me out of the house, which was a blessed relief at times, particularly towards the end.

Anyway, that first time, at the kitchen island, I sipped the black Americano – far too bitter for my taste, I prefer a drop of milk, but it had felt the right choice – and Ris donned her Prada reading glasses then angled herself and her laptop away from me and read from what sounded like a pre-prepared script. A series of questions and prompts she recited robotically and between which the words I'd rehearsed slotted in reasonably well. I was quite impressed with myself, especially as I had no physical aide-memoire as she did, relying on the fading grey matter and caffeine hits alone. It wasn't easy, mind. There were so many distractions, not least her constant gum-chewing – dazzling veneers causing a slight crowding of the mouth so some of her sounds weren't crisp – plus I kept noticing details around the room I recognised from her posts. The row of 'gifted' cookbooks above the hob from which she'd begun her 'clean eating' obsession, and the photos of her in various exotic locations hung gallery-like on the wall behind her. The bikinis she favoured cut so high they bordered on obscene. I must have hesitated in one of my responses. I don't recall over which question in particular, but she frowned and then we continued on regarding my education – I went to an all-girls' school – and work experience – secretarial then personal assistant to various, well-to-do employers, too numerous to list them all – and hobbies – mainly reading, knitting, walking – the kind of neutral interests that wouldn't impact a potential employer. It was a melting pot of truth and invention, as all the most credible accounts must be. Although, I do recall improvising an interest in skiing when a photo of Ris in a vivid pink all-in-one at the top of a mountain caught my eye. I was banking on the fact by ski-season I would no longer be in her employ, my plan executed by then.

Yes, I had some fun along the way, but mainly it was a demonstration of the art of flattery getting one through most situations. None of us is immune to it, and Ris lapped it up. Me playing my part as a well-travelled spinster dedicated to the cause of satisfying her future employer's every whim and whimper to an absolute tee.

Call it exaggeration if it sits with you better, but I'm not alone in massaging the truth to gain a job. Everyone does it to a greater or lesser degree. I'm sure you have too.

I meant no harm, not in that regard. I simply supplied what she needed: her ideal executive assistant, at least on paper, with the added incentive she would be swiping me from the clutches of one of the Belgravia set who'd so royally snubbed her on account of her husband-stealing reputation.

Rather unfairly?

You think?

Perhaps...

As you say, she had only 'stolen' a husband that once, and there was no cause to think she would do it again, but there are no second chances, or I suspect first chances either, with the likes of the first Mrs Fox and her chums. Trudy had made sure Ris was *persona non grata* from the first whisperings of Miles' affair, having something of a head-start in the race to win friends and repel enemies. Trudy was from old money, you see, of many generations, and whatever anyone would rather believe, that kind of pedigree still counts amongst the top strata of British society. To put it succinctly, Trudy had completely obliterated her successor's aspirations of joining the Belgravia set. Revenge no doubt sweet and cold.

Another interesting detail you might want to include in your article is that the Prada glasses Ris wore, the ones she popped on at the door and again as she interviewed me in the kitchen – and often featured when she posed for selfies at her desk in the upstairs study – were made of clear glass; no prescription required. I found that out when I tried them on whilst 'borrowing' her laptop one day shortly into my employ, hoping they might magnify the figures on screen, which of course, they didn't. Not a jot. The glasses were purely for show! Although, I have to say, the frames worked well with her angular features, but of no practical value whatsoever. Appropriate, wouldn't you say? And a fitting allegory for their owner.

Yes, I studied Ris carefully during that interview, comparing the social media version with close-quarters actuality as she talked at length about herself, something she enjoyed very much. It was almost as if she was a little girl play-acting at being the boss, and I was taking the part of her dull interviewee.

My initial observations? Of her appearance, you mean?

I was shocked by how thin she was. And despite the bluster, I'd say she was nervous. She's always been portrayed as overly confident by the press, right from those first sightings beside Miles Fox, but I discerned an unexpected anxiety. Barely there, but it lent a chink of vulnerability. The crack in the vase that let in some light as the saying goes. Maybe it was that which had secured her a relatively healthy fan base even back then. Roughly 100K on Insta I think... although after she leaked her 'amazing news' it ballooned very quickly to double that. And in the aftermath of the book launch party and my interviews with the tabloids, it briefly hit the lusted after seven figures before she then deleted all her social media accounts. That must have been a painful moment for such a publicity whore.

Sorry, I've lost my thread, which is ironic as I've just recalled I did much the same at the time, zoning out as Ris waxed lyrical about her 'Brand'. Which was an unfortunate lapse on my part as the brand was very much her thing. A nebulous product which she promoted at every opportunity, as though she was adding value to the world beyond monetising her good fortune even further. But I should have been paying more attention. It was central to my prospective employer's hopes and ambitions, and therefore by extension, also to mine.

How to define Ris' 'Brand'...

It's tricky as she rarely explained without overuse of idealistic platitudes. As if clarity might weaken its tenuous potency, but the idea was propped up on the linked premises of 'Lifestyle' and 'Beauty'. Basically anything which pertained to 'Being Ris' which was coincidentally, or maybe not, also the title of her ill-fated *Lifestyle & Beauty Bible*. The trouble was, as the wife of a multi-millionaire, most of her purchases were far beyond the means of us mere mortals. The vase very much a case in point. An extreme example, but there were many.

Her daily consumption of eye creams, serums, perfume, would have soon mounted up to the debt of a small country. Although she did have some restraint regarding *shares*. She would never have boasted on social media about the vase for instance; that was too extravagant. Although the 'must-haves' were still hugely aspirational. A conundrum which weirdly seemed to work in her favour, at least with her most-devoted fans, as though wanting and having could co-exist in an odd co-dependency of yearning. It was a perplexing dichotomy, the coming together of a 'Have' with so many 'Have-Nots'. Ris' ability to flaunt yet endear – posting another three-grand handbag or hundred pounds a pot neck cream – a definite if questionable talent.

If I'm brutally honest, I think it was morbid curiosity that drew the majority of people to her. It was different for the die-hard fans – they seemed to love her unconditionally – but for the majority of us it was that persuasive mix of envy and fascination. The daily torture we all like to inflict upon ourselves... the 'If Only' scenario.

If only I were thinner, richer, younger... a carrot dangled close enough but then again far enough out of reach to drag you along in its wake; a glittering prize you never, or would even want to, reach. Isn't that what drives social media on the whole? You don't have to be liked to be followed. Frequently quite the reverse. You simply have to produce more and more content. Whore out every aspect of your perfect life.

It was certainly my experience of Ris via Instagram, Facebook, Twitter, even TikTok, God help me! The hours I wasted equivalent to the full-time role I was applying for, except this time I was hoping to be paid handsomely. The amount as yet undisclosed. I was dying to ask, my financial situation as bad back then as it is again now, well almost, but we weren't quite there. Ris was still in full flow on her favourite topic: herself.

I smiled, but inside I despised and derided my host for her inflated sense of her own worth, as well as her condescension and the artificially plumped top lip. Her inability to empathise was breathtaking. Her self-absorption monumental. Planet Ris. Population of one. She had no interest, concern, idea, or curiosity about me, other than in relation to her. If she had paid me any attention at all maybe she'd have noticed something was amiss: that my smile didn't reach my eyes, that I drove a thumb nail into my palm to keep alert, that everything she told me deepened my hatred, if that were even possible.

It's human nature, I suppose, to critique. And we women can

have a cruel streak. But she did herself no favours. It was all about *her*. Or rather *Ris*... a concoction of reality and fantasy. Maybe she believed her own hype? It's very difficult to present an entirely honest account of oneself, even if you are trying to, which neither of us did that day, but her self-delusion was on another level and strangely fascinating in its way.

I'm an avid observer of people, always have been. Their quirks and ticks particularly illuminating.

For instance, as Ris lectured me on her 'Brand', she continually smoothed the dome of her scraped back hair, pointed nails combing her scalp, wedding band and enormous diamond engagement ring, both slightly loose, catching the bright lights, a glimpse of that tattoo creeping from the cuff of her sweater as she smoothed the glossy ponytail. An intertwining R and M, as I recall. Cherry blossom curling in and out of the connected initials on the soft slightly paler flesh of her right inner arm. I'm not a fan of 'ink' in general, but fair enough, if you like that kind of thing.

The repetitive move with her hair, however, was an annoyance. It happened too often and was so clearly deliberate.

Comfortable, confident people don't feel the need to continually preen. They are understated, contained. Self-possessed. Ris leaked her insecurities like a colander and I capitalised on those, drawing inner strength from them so I could at last shrug off my nerves and face her as I had originally intended: confident and more than equal to the role. Equal to her. And why shouldn't I be? At least everything I have, sagging and worn as it may be, is God-given.

Oh yes, work had most definitely been done!

The boob-job for starters, which in fairness she'd owned up to, and that ski-slope lip, but I must say she had exercised enough restraint to remain a relatively normal-looking if highly groomed thirty-five-year-old. I'm not going to say there hadn't been other 'procedures' I'm not aware of, but she was not *odd* in the uncanny valley way some of her ilk can be. But those, who, like her, shall we say come from *humble beginnings* do unfortunately show their roots in their questionable choices. The greying gum then prised from Ris' jaw with nails like pincers, and pressed into the wrapper of the replacement slice, which she folded in. The veneered smile, infrequent and insincere, way too white. Dark eyes flinty, impenetrable beneath far too long lashes. It was all very... false.

That reminds me, there was one expression of hers I quickly learnt to spot. The displeased but outwardly smiling Ris, eyes narrowed. When the shutters came down and I was in the presence of the former cocktail waitress who would no doubt have ignored me if I'd been stood at the bar waiting for service. Not that I can afford to go to those type of places. And nothing wrong with bar work, done it myself, but I suspect serving drinks wasn't always the full extent of it in Ris' case.

But we women have had to adapt, haven't we? Make the most of what we've got. And I suppose Ris was no exception. Some of that journey was to be admired, potentially, but a lot of it more dubious. And we all carry round our pasts in our personal baggage, and that manifested in Ris via certain affectations. Like when she would suddenly clasp a hand to her breast, bangles jangling on impossibly thin wrists, nails splayed like five glossy talons, ready to strike their prey. It was her killer move, practised to the finest detail, and very compelling. It would convey shock, or hurt, and it always stopped any protests dead in their tracks. In fact, on this occasion I almost toppled from the stool when she concluded the interview with the flourished hand-to-heart move and declared I had got the job.

I recovered my seat, and then, rather boldly, now I look back on it, reminded her that I wasn't in a position, however much personally I would be honoured to be her executive assistant, to accept. I had given my word to another. And with that I removed myself unsteadily from the stool and made my way back to my snow-wet coat in the hallway. The mousy woman returned in those mirror tiles.

I threaded a fist down one sleeve and then another, tying the waist belt and settling the collar, hoping Ris would follow me out and beg me to stay. Had I pushed her too hard? Ris was no fool, and I was desperate for the job, would have done pretty much anything to get it. I watched the kitchen door through sideways glances as I pushed damp feet into damp shoes, exhaling my relief as I saw Ris just the other side, watching me.

The white teeth dazzled once more as she walked towards me, red toenails on the colourful rug, silver bangles jangling as a hand was extended to take mine, and breath minty as she leant in and whispered, 'How much will it take to keep you as mine, Gail?'

5

SECOND INTERVIEW WITH GAIL FROST – SUNDAY 9 OCTOBER

Do you know what, I've just realised I've misrepresented myself! I'm fifty-six, not fifty-five. Oh, did I say fifty-six? I always get muddled about my age. And next month I'll be fifty-seven! Gosh, how time flies, but birthdays have never been a big thing for me. I rarely had parties as a child, which is why I was never invited to them. I'd imagine any decent therapist would have a field day about that, but it was honestly not a big deal. You don't miss what you've never had. And I've never been one for 'talking therapies'. Counselling certainly hadn't helped Ris much, her posts always very 'open' about her 'mental health journey'. We all have mental health, good and bad, and despite the therapy, long over by the time we met, she remained a narcissist who threw money at whatever she wanted.

I was a commodity and no doubt would have been tossed aside had she had the chance to tire of me. Not that we got to that point, but like the vase in the hallway, I am certain my presence would have become less shiny, less covetable, if events hadn't overtaken us and ended our short time together long before that.

The arrangement, much as having an assistant in the first place, signalled status to Ris. And an EA poached from a woman who'd excluded her from every clique she'd hoped to join when she'd married Miles Fox, was a personal *fuck-you* to the Belgravia set. I'm surprised she showed enough restraint not to flaunt me on her 'feed', but of course social media posts were exclusively about Ris.

Her desire for visibility made perfect sense to me after I met her, but it would be unfair to characterise her only as a vacuous publicity whore. Gullible, greedy, entitled? *Yes*. And, given what's happened, capable of unspeakable deceptions in the name of getting what she wanted, but as I said, she was no one's fool, least of all mine. Ris might not have had a grasp of good grammar or even good manners but she was street smart. A hustler who'd married into money and was determined to make the most of it. Not least by securing a book deal off the back of her talentless good fortune.

You've got to admire her endeavour.

I would go so far as to say there were days when I almost liked her. Not in the way you like a dog or a child, not that uncomplicated kind of adoration, but more of a platonic crush on the girl at the school disco in the coolest outfit. Yes, there was definitely something that drew me to her, despite the loathing that underlined every one of our transactions.

Ris certainly deployed some very well-honed techniques designed to charm and engage in that hallway negotiation.

Such as? Let me think... using my name with regularity, accompanied by a light touch to my coat sleeve, non-threatening eye contact. Although after she'd doubled the competing salary figure I'd plucked from thin air, she dropped her hand and said, 'I put in 110 per cent and I can tell that you do the same, Gail. You'll earn every penny, don't worry about that.'

I resisted the urge to point out that a hundred per cent is the most anyone can be expected to deliver; anything else a mathematical impossibility. I was literally – and again I use that word advisedly and in its proper sense – biting my tongue as Ris leant in, pointed talons digging in my clasped hand, and delivered her next line. 'The thing is, the best does not come cheap, does it, Gail?' Then, still barefoot but towering over me, she stepped back, spun on her heel, and headed back towards the kitchen.

Her graceful move put me mind of a prima ballerina. It was impressive. I followed, her elbows digging into the island, her body bent at the waist so I could see down the neck of her jumper to a lacy bra. She straightened up and lifted the bouncy trademark ponytail, running it through her palm before placing it lovingly on one tennis ball sized breast. Like a... what's the word? *Familiar*. Yes, that's it. I truly imagined it with eyes, boring into me, hissing teeth. Distrustful like the waterfowl by the Serpentine when I'd walked through Hyde Park that morning. Or an urban fox, getting into the bins.

Anyway, enough of my overactive imagination. Ris never wasted much time on small talk and she didn't that day either, the charm offensive suspended in favour of a machine-gun approach as she explained about the rhythm of her days. How she saw her personal trainer, Veronique, weekdays at ten, and some lengthy instructions about mixing up protein shakes and keeping on top of her inbox. The funny thing was, Ris was talking as if I'd accepted her offer when I hadn't actually agreed to anything. That's what entitlement teaches you, I suppose: that everyone has their price and she'd doubled mine. And she was right. I could be bought, probably at a much lower rate than offered, but that wasn't my primary reason for being there.

Although I needed the money, can't deny that.

Ris hadn't come from wealth either, but she'd quickly become accustomed to it, and the power it gave her to improve, acquire, change. Power she wielded with little to no humility, or caution.

You only have to look back at the *before* photos to note the rapid assimilation which took place. The physical metamorphosis alone is startling. Teeth, hair, boobs, but it's more fundamental than that. Her deportment too. It's not just a case of a young-ish woman maturing well in that period; she carries herself better, her walk has changed. A haughtiness, I suppose, which most definitely wasn't there when she was waiting tables in one of Miles Fox's central London hotels. It clearly doesn't take much time to adjust to that level of wealth, and of course no one wants to go back, having tasted what's on offer, even by association.

No, not even me. That's true. Although it was never my style, I lived it by reduced proxy and for all too short a time. But you're right, it's incredibly seductive.

In her continuing assumption of my acquiescence, Ris then explained my main priority as her EA would be running her diary. I would be on call when needed, work the hours she did – 24/7 – and travel if and when that suited her.

I have what she said written down in my notebook. I would pop down to the basement and update it whenever the opportunity arose. In fact, I have several quotes from that time. Just need to find the right one, and my glasses.

Ah, here you go! Obviously, I've paraphrased, but this was the gist of it as she made me stand in her kitchen whilst she laid out her terms.

'Your role will be to make sure I'm OK, Gail, as in untroubled by the logistics, so that means sourcing cars – I prefer electric vehicles if available, black cabs are fine, but I *never* go in an Uber – and booking my regular appointments: hair, make-up, nails, etc.... I don't expect you to take time off without prior agreement and of course, you will sign a very stringent non-disclosure agreement which will cover everything you see or hear whilst in my employ, especially regarding my private life. My husband is often away on business, but when he's here our time together is private so you will be asked to either take annual leave or confine yourself to the basement flat.'

The NDA was the only issue for me. I wasn't ever going to sign up for that, but fortunately I managed to avoid it, although it hung over me the whole time I was living there. One of those obstacles waiting in the fog for which I couldn't pre-legislate. I resolved I'd either outright refuse if it came up, on the basis it was an affront to our mutual trust which I'd hopefully built up enough by then, or agree to sign but suggest I scan it in myself, causing further delay and confusion. I soon discovered, however, that Ris was terribly lax about admin, which she hated with a passion. I never signed so much as an employment contract, let alone a legally binding vow of silence. And as I say, the rest of her demands were much as I'd expected. I assured her I had no ties, free as a bird. If I took the job, I'd be entirely at her disposal.

I've just noticed this note I made under that list of demands. It brought a smile to my face at the time, I must say.

I expect you to be efficient, professional, and as much as possible, invisible, Gail. Is that doable?

Invisibility, the super-power of the middle-aged woman. How ironic.

Anyway, business concluded, she led me back to the front door, my tacit approval taken for granted, Ris' right hand proffered once more. An awful inclination to wipe my palm dry before taking hers, thankfully resisted. Ris' palm was chalky and cold, the skin-to-skin touch leaving nothing behind, neither heat nor chills. But the deal was sealed. Well, almost. Just a small token of good faith required as we said our goodbyes. A welcome breeze cooling my brow as she leant towards me and whispered, 'So, between us girls, Gail, what was she like?'

I had no idea to whom she was referring, then I caught up and followed her eyeline across the gated residents' gardens towards the houses beyond. They were larger, more impressive, if that's possible. I walked that way back to Paddington and smiled at my artifice. I'd chosen so well.

I gave Ris what she wanted... inventing something rather risqué, shall we say, about her Italian wedding nemesis. She pulled back, and I feared it was too much, but then she smiled. She knew the woman well, she claimed, which I knew to be a lie, but it was still a chancy move on my part. The bluffs were layering up. I was in danger of losing track. And the house was only two streets away, although it might as well have been the moon. That's the trouble with measuring oneself against others. There is always another door to get through, another rung up the ladder. Ris, in that sense, was just as much of a trespasser as I was. Little wonder she'd ruffled a few feathers. Anyway, my invented gossip did the trick. She said she'd follow-up on the referees I'd given on my CV and be in touch 'super-soon'. I left my fate in her hands, imagining there was only a twenty per cent chance I'd get away with it. It had been fun at least, whilst it lasted. But that would never have been enough.

* * *

Ris called the number I'd supplied for my referee only an hour later, her voice jarring as I answered my recently purchased 'spare' mobile phone. The one I binned when I reached Reading. My delayed train was just about to leave Paddington station, that handshake still an impression on my shaking palm as I tentatively said hello. It was quite funny, in an absurd way, although terrifying at the same time. Heart in mouth I asked her to wait whilst I 'transferred' her around the supposedly capacious Highlands home of my previous employers. I was convinced the train announcer would blow my cover or one of my fellow travellers would explode into laughter as I attempted different accents and voices. It really was most absurd. But I got away with it.

I passed it all off as an audition when, heart hammering, the call ended and I looked up to too many interested stares. The clutch of passengers within earshot congratulated me on my excellent performance and wished me good luck in securing the part. Like I say, the most convincing lies are always closest to the truth.

It all fell into place with such ease I should have known I'd pay the price later on. How heavy a personal cost, of course, I still had no idea, the ripples from that dropped pebble radiating far beyond my expectations and far beyond me.

6

THIRD INTERVIEW WITH GAIL FROST – SUNDAY 16 OCTOBER

You know the tabloids called me, amongst other things, a confidence trickster? Not that I'd ascribe to their limited portrayal of a cartoonish and two-dimensional villain, but in one sense the description was correct. I was brimming with confidence after I left Ris that Friday, the easily won position of executive assistant filling me with a false sense of security. I'd done it. My audacious, somewhat shonky plan had worked. I was elated by my brinkmanship. I could pull off anything, including the intention that had taken me so far already. I would succeed. I would depose the imposter.

And yes, in answer to your frown, which I assume is an expression of doubt or even disgust, I felt, and still do, entirely justified in that endeavour.

There's much more to it than the disparity in our relative financial circumstances, but don't you agree it is unfair to flaunt such unjust good fortune? I mean look at all the so-called celebrities trading off their minuscule talent to secure book deals and TV shows. That must annoy you as a talented writer and serious journalist.

Like I said, my plan wasn't as nailed down as I'd have liked, but it felt as though the sky was the limit now I was going to be working, and also living at Lexington Gardens.

I returned the following Monday morning to a sky still painted blue but also filled with scudding clouds, them and I bouncing happily along Lexington Gardens. My scruffy wheeled case in tow, wheels squeaking.

If I could give my former self one piece of advice, shadow of her that I now am, it would be to never take anyone or any situation for granted. But everything was shiny and new, except the case. Only three days since my interview, the magnolia in the courtyard garden directly outside the basement's patio doors shedding petals like discarded love letters as I unpacked my few belongings and quickly stowed the case under the bed before Ris had chance to clock its shameful state of disrepair. I was ebullient, if not a little light-headed. The cost of my peak time single fare from Reading to Paddington necessitating meagre rations over the weekend.

I know I'm not the only person in the world who has to make choices like that – eat or buy a train ticket, eat or heat my flat, eat or replace worn shoe leather – far from it, but it might have been nice if Ris had thought to offer me some kind of advance on my wages to cover my expenses. It wouldn't have occurred to her I'd be so compromised, of course, and in fairness, why should it? I'd spun a history of well-paid jobs and invented a swanky home in an exclusive development in the centre of Reading, which I could never have afforded in a million years.

You can just about see it if you run back up my steps; have a look on your way out. It catches the sunlight if there's any out there today. Tall, glass, very modern. Made me chuckle to think of the actual resident of the penthouse opening the offer of employment letter which Ris sent as a 'formality' and I 'strangely' never received.

Like I say, she liked to play at being a proper boss. And my subterfuge was a necessary part of the illusion. Problematic at times, but essential. I had to strike a careful balance between appearing of sufficient status to represent Ris and her 'Brand', whilst subservient enough to require paid employment. But I had arrived. The harder part, I hoped, behind me. Like I say, if I could have a word with my former self... but it was a beautiful spring day as I hung up my two skirts and three blouses, then dropped a toothbrush in the glass on the shelf above the small but stylish sink.

The three-roomed basement – bedroom, bathroom, and combined workspace/kitchenette – was accessed internally via a precipitously steep staircase located behind a semi-concealed door in the hallway. The door when closed matched the wall, the paint and architrave fitting exactly so you might never have known it was there other than the discreet handle. I liked that, as if I was occupying a part of the house that was hidden away, which I suppose was the point. And despite being semi-subterranean it was in sharp contrast to this place, the basement at Lexington Gardens light and bright, mainly on account of the patio doors to the courtyard.

The sun slanted across the floorboards that glorious morning in early April, illuminating the brand-new crisp white bedding – of excellent thread count – and further improving my already sunny mood.

A personal touch, which did surprise me, was the bunch of yellow daffodils arranged in a glass vase on the tiny half-moon table next to the patio doors. That's where I also found the loaned laptop, plugged into the wall and fully charged. There was also a plentiful supply of loo roll and fresh towels in the shower room and some sunny yellow cushions on the small couch. I was therefore feeling happy with my lot as I went back up those steep stairs, notepad in hand, then up the next flight from the hallway, a flutter in my tummy, as well as audible hunger pangs.

Ris was, as she'd told me she would be, in her study. An airy room on the mezzanine. The study faces out onto the street, two large windows giving an unobstructed view of the private residents' gardens across the road. I walked over to the left-hand window and looked out, my wandering gaze taking in the high railings and thick hedges, then the neat borders planted with colourful spring blooms and, at their heart, an empty bench.

It was then I spotted the telescope at the other window, trained on the exact spot where that bench sat. I guess I must have stepped back, or in some way shown my alarm as Ris took off the useless glasses and laughed as I asked, voice stuttering, if she ever spied on her neighbours or the gardens. The telescope was a 'design element' she explained, the lens revealing only a black circle when I placed my eye to it, to be certain. A relief as you might imagine, swiftly replaced by nerves as my boss had grown impatient, as she so often did, patting the chair she'd moved to the same side of the desk as hers. Like I said, she was never one for pleasantries.

I'd been worrying myself silly over the weekend about what might be expected of me, and topping up my admin skills online as best I could so I might be equal to whatever tasks Ris assigned me, but that first morning was really rather dull. A lot of listening and nodding and note-taking. It didn't seem as though I would have much to do at all. As I suspected at the interview, my role was more to add weight to Ris' notions of grandeur than borne of necessity. She wasn't in any way fully occupied, so how could I be? I was there to handle the kind of life admin most of us deal with ourselves and without a second thought. Hardly taxing. I must have looked less than enthusiastic as Ris shared her screen with me, the pair of us still cheek-by-jowl at her cluttered desk three hours later. I was tired by then. It was approaching lunchtime and the mental and physical exhaustion of packing a case and leaving Reading on an early train, then dragging said case across London in the freezing cold, was starting to take its toll. I'd assured her I didn't need to stop for lunch, out of politeness rather than meaning it, but thankfully Ris then insisted, opening the enormous fridge in her pristine kitchen and telling me to take whatever I fancied, just this once as I hadn't had a chance to go shopping. I was grateful for that. My hands shook with hunger as I reached in.

Ris talked on and on through our working lunch of microwaved noodles, taken back at her desk. Explaining about her twice monthly nail infills and weekly blowouts; apparently what blow dries are now called. I might have even yawned, although I sincerely hope not. But it's a definite possibility.

Ris sighed heavily as she put down her phone – a rare event – turning to me, so close I could catch the garlic on her breath as she delivered 'The Platform' speech.

You must have come across it? It was plastered all over her social media in varying forms. I got the long, sanctimonious version. Let me find it in my notes.

Ah yes, here we go, or as close to as recent memory served. I used to write my notes up in the evenings mostly, unless I got a sneaky moment in the day.

'I suppose my social media platform might seem to you rather frivolous, Gail, but I'm not a wannabee influencer. I'm a business-woman who utilises my audience to create opportunities. If I were a man I'd be congratulated for that, but because I care about my appearance and share details about myself and my home, people make assumptions about me as a person. That I'm stupid, or selfish, spoilt. So be it, I'm used to that, but as I say to everyone, you included, Gail, don't ever underestimate me. That would be a *huge* mistake.'

I don't know why I got the lecture at that point, but she was always on the lookout for any dissension, and contrary to my early preconceptions, I was actually kept surprisingly busy in my role.

Particularly towards the time of the book launch just before my departure, but that was still over two months away.

The delivery of that early reprimand over our bowls of noodle ramen was, even by Ris' standards, somewhat self-righteous. I recall reluctantly setting down my spoon as I listened, the content of her monologue unpalatable, as was the food. Hardly a filling lunch, or particularly nutritious, a limp prawn floating on top of a brackish broth, chopsticks clearly not my forte and hardly suitable for soup. I soon set them aside in favour of a spoon. I can guarantee, although it's not in my notes, Ris also had a three hundred calorie bowl of ramen. It might have been chicken, or tofu, but it would have been with noodles. She had the same every single day. The unappetising portions were delivered in recyclable cartons on Tuesdays, dropped by van to the door, enough to last the week, which often led to wastage, the ethical credentials of the ingredients and sustainable packaging rather undermined by the fact half were thrown away, best before dates religiously observed, which everyone knows is ridiculous. The wastage criminal, despite the watery contents.

I pushed mine away and assured her, when she finally drew breath, I had in no way meant to give the impression I underestimated her platform's power, quite the reverse. I was simply concentrating as I got to grips with her 'Brand'. Then I added something about my social awkwardness always being a bit of personal concern and she immediately softened, might have even apologised. She definitely said it was important to her she be 'fully inclusive', whatever that means.

Her enthusiasm for the microwaved noodle soup had also waned, but I knew it would be all I'd eat that day, the cupboards bare in the basement, so I offered to clear the lunch things and took everything down to the kitchen where I slurped the cold broth from both cartons before I threw them into the recycling bin.

* * *

I upped my game for the afternoon session, but her next gripe, ironically, was my lack of in-depth knowledge regarding her social media channels. An obfuscation on my part, of course, but you appreciate why? Not least because Ris had become the victim of a vicious troll in the weeks before I joined her.

Everyone has their detractors, par for the course these days and in many ways Ris was asking for it, parading her wealth in times when so many are struggling, but this soon became more personal than that. I needed to ensure there was never a whisper of suspicion I might be the rather prosaically titled Becca2004xxx.

Let me clarify here. I do not in any way align myself to or condone Becca's online behaviour. Yes, there were times our opinions may have coincided, and she might have been of some help to me, fanning the first flames of the early conspiracy theories, but to be clear… I am not a troll and Becca is not me.

I realise this denial will not deter you entirely from jumping to the easy conclusion, but I assure you, it is the truth. Anyway, despite my extensive knowledge of Ris' social media, I said something along the lines of realising I am an anathema these days, not connected to my phone 24/7, but that didn't mean I couldn't admire her clever use of the platforms. 'If only it had been around when I was in my twenties, maybe I'd be in your position now.' That kind of thing. And I assured her, in case it was still an issue, that I was of course familiar with the main sites, just not a great user of them. Which is a bend in the truth, rather than break. I'd describe myself as more of a lurker than a user, so it's arguable, but I'd say I erred on the side of the truth.

She seemed happy with my explanation, asked if I'd looked her up, her nails pastel pink that day. She must have had them redone over the weekend, and the rose colour reminded me of the unopened buds on the magnolia. A comforting thought. The hopefulness those buds brought of warmer spring days and cosy nights ensconced in the luxury of Lexington Gardens, buoying my flagging concentration in that post-lunch graveyard shift.

Fortunately, Ris then suggested we break for a coffee and take a tour of the five floors, both suggestions much appreciated.

It is such a lovely house. Hard not to feel empowered and inspired whilst there. From the lowly basement right up to the spectacular rooftop terrace with its stupendous views of the London skyline, reminiscent of a favourite childhood film... you know the scene I mean? In *Mary Poppins* when they jump from roof to roof. Although there are railings in place around the brick walls that surround the exposed terrace, solid iron ones with spikes on. As tall as me or I'd never have ventured out, even with Ris' assurances that it was perfectly safe. You have to climb up a rickety steel half-staircase to get there. She went first and was looking over the front elevation and pointing out the highlights of London on the skyline as I emerged. She was laughing when I told her to be careful, leaning out to terrify me further and threatening to climb over the railings to sit on the narrow ledge. She said she'd done it once before, as a dare.

The terrace is furnished with two enormous, cushioned loungers – apparently re-assembled up there as the stairs were too narrow – and it's festooned with strung fairy lights that come on via a sensor when anyone steps out. It's only big enough for the loungers, definitely an adult space, but the previous owners had young children so as a precaution they'd added the railings.

I tiptoed towards but not right up to the edge. It must be a sixty-foot drop down to the cobbled courtyard another five storeys below.

I had to duck a little as we went back into the sloping guest suite, and I'm only five feet three in my bare feet, but that's the only floor, other than the basement, that doesn't boast high ceilings. The eaves angle down either side of the large guest bed as well as on the one side of the sumptuous en suite above a whirlpool bath. There's also a gym up there – mirrored wall, complicated looking apparatus and mats, plus those big plastic balls you sit astride.

I suppose I might have felt disgruntled I wasn't offered the top suite as my accommodation; it is much larger, and the views are to die for, but I liked the basement just fine. It's entirely self-contained, and I could cook meals on the two rings and stow my essentials in the larder fridge. Not that I did. Cook, that is – crackers or a bowl of cereal the extent of it. But I would always take my first coffee of the day *en plein air*. The metal patio table beneath the magnolia tree spattered with rain or drenched in sunlight, the gnarled trunk a full two hands round when I tried. The high walls absorbed and retained any warmth, the yellow-tinged London Stock weathered and patinaed with lichen, so I would lose myself in their forms and find faces and mythical beasts as I placed a palm to the blood temperature brick. I used to do something similar as a child. The floral wallpaper by my single bed coming alive as my parents fought downstairs. I got so good at it I could tune out all but the worst crashes and bangs until the forest or sea or castle enveloped me and I could slip away into my imagination.

I loved those quiet dawn hours in the courtyard garden, coffee in one hand, the walls protecting me and my secrets as I touched them with the other. As if I owned fifty-six Lexington Gardens from the ground up. I had claimed my home in it at last, just a small stake, and I worked hard to preserve that for as long as I could. It mattered to me, greatly, that I be there. I had a right.

No, I didn't leave voluntarily, but I suppose that's evident from those awful photos in the tabloids. They must have had some better ones of me; they just wanted me to look like a mad old bat!

I shouldn't be surprised, especially after the coverage I endured in the weeks that followed, but it's so disappointing that fellow humans would be so lacking in... humanity.

I suppose I should be keeping a low profile now the press interest has finally died down, but as you know, I'm pinning my hopes on you being rather different. 'A purveyor of truth', isn't that what your Twitter profile says?

Of course I've looked you up.

* * *

Anyway, there are five floors and we toured them all. From the guest suite, down a floor to the master suite, and opposite it a room I assumed would be another office, or maybe a small bedroom, although Ris didn't open the door on our tour. Then the mezzanine where her study was and another bathroom and bedroom, maybe two? I've lost count, is that five floors? Yes, with the ground floor where the kitchen, dining and sitting room are and then the basement. It's a vast property, over three thousand square feet.

Tour concluded, we resumed our places at her desk with coffees and I cemented my supposed ignorance of social media by asking Ris how many followers she had. She claimed she hadn't checked lately, but thought it was a little higher than my guess. The largest number on Instagram, where it had reached six figures.

'My platform is massively important, Gail. I need to protect the content and that takes a lot of my time. The book deal requires constantly updated content, but more than that, my followers depend on me for an awful lot. For some, I'm their only friend.'

That word – 'protect' – came up a lot. Protect her privacy, her 'Brand', her time with *Hubs*. It spoke so clearly of her fear of losing it all. And as such, alerted me to her weak spot. We all have those, don't we? The place we can't go to, even in our darkest imaginings, lest we tempt fate. Fear of loss, fear of exposure, fear of dying. Fear of being friendless. Unloved. Alone.

My fears? Well, that would be telling, but I'm sure, given time, you'll work it all out. Maybe you already have. That is your job after all, but don't disappoint me and go for the obvious. That would be insulting to us both. The important thing was finding Ris' darkest secret and then taking advantage of it. Which I would soon do.

In fact, I had already touched on a nerve. I just didn't know it.

7

THIRD INTERVIEW WITH GAIL FROST – SUNDAY 16 OCTOBER

I feel like I'm getting to know you a bit better now, do you feel the same? A glint in your eye when I say something that excites you. Or a crinkle in your brow when I'm boring you. I suppose it's the chase for the story that first ignited your interest as we chatted on the train. Two strangers, exchanging pleasantries and then phone numbers. Sorry if I was wary of you, but I've been so badly treated at the hands of other journalists. I'm not saying you're like them. You work for a serious publication. I would never have invited you into my home if you were a hack for one of the tabloids, but you and I, we understand the dance, don't we? The transaction that's taking place. We're not friends. I know that. But, as I say, feel like I know you a little better than when we began our... what shall we call them? Chats, maybe.

* * *

That first working week with Ris passed remarkably quickly. She had, as claimed, a packed diary, and despite my initial doubts, it was pretty much a full-time job keeping up with it, and her. I maintained a low profile, resisting the urge to question her husband's absence or the reason for it, or feed her insecurities about the women she followed on social media who didn't follow her back; pretending not to notice their posts of shared lunches on her screen when I returned from my lunch of a bowl of Special K.

I never passed comment on the fact she didn't seem to know anybody who was not in some way in her employ, or that she never saw any friends or family. That would have been petty and I am not that, and besides, there was no mileage in annoying my boss and risking my job. In fact, the dissonance between her public profile and reality would most likely play into the public sympathy should I draw any unwanted attention to her rather pathetic and lonely existence.

Poor Ris, she has no friends.

Oh please, don't you feel sorry for her too!

She wanted for nothing, although it was painfully obvious that aside from the maintenance of her appearance and the house, and of course her social media accounts, Ris led an entirely pointless existence. Such a modern condition, the pure consumer. Not that I'd call Ris pure. She was fake and a liar. What I needed, however, was proof of that. Not on a basic level, but something unequivocally damning that had been buried deep in the fabric of her past. Something so bad, no one could condone it, not even her most ardent fans whom she collected like Whimsies.

You don't recall those? You're too young, of course.

Awful trinkets, another preoccupation of my childhood. I'd line them up on my windowsill, polished and cherished, like a gang of friends. The analogy being, if you haven't already spotted it, these fans of Ris were not real friends any more than those brown pottery animals were mine. But we both collected them with religious fervour and refused to part with them until they were prised from our clutches.

Ris would lose hours replying to comments, validating herself – and the source, I suppose – with a ping-pong of mutual adoration and gushing praise. And no one seemed to question her insincerity, or their own. Very odd.

Ris' Instagram tiles were also an ongoing fixation. She talked about them incessantly. The *grid layouts* and *flat lays* and *reels* and *stories*. How this or that post was pleasing, or not. How much *engagement* each one attracted. The only reason she contemplated getting a designer puppy was because they 'really pull in the likes'.

I found it incredibly tedious, the endless staring at the screen and tuning me out: posing, snapping, deleting, round and round. Even when she was happy with a photo, the text that went with it was meticulously edited. I couldn't tell you exactly what was involved, I only saw the end result, once I was back in the privacy of the basement, thumb and forefinger expanding each image, combing through the text underneath for ammunition: a falsity that would trip her up, a breadcrumb trail to a clandestine lover or sex-worker past, but it was all fluff. No substance, or as my mother would have said, 'No meat on the bone.' I was living with Ris now but had fallen back on social media to provide the clues, which it hadn't.

Other than the intricacies of an exhaustive and ongoing process to achieve the illusion of perfection, I'd learnt nothing. Only confirmation it was an illusion. And that she must be lonely, and bored, and like me, frustrated. There were no real friends, no family, only a mother she'd disowned after the wedding. No husband either, with constant excuses of business taking him out the country. It was just her. And then me, of course. Unlikely pair that we were.

Only once did she ask me to take a photo, passing me her mobile and telling me the pin code as I hesitated and the screen then went black. Naturally, she hated the result. Not up to scratch, although I thought it a perfectly passable representation of her seated at her desk, glasses on, affecting deep concentration, laptop open as if she was running a conglomerate single-handedly. She spent a while photoshopping it before she frowned unattractively and made a sound in the back of her throat and told me she'd deleted it. Then reminding me to check her next Botox top-up before she dismissed me from her presence.

Her regular appointments provided the structure of our day, the rest filler, if you'll excuse the pun. Although Ris seemed to be under the impression the constant maintenance of her appearance was all part of her *job*, and therefore mine. She didn't have a job, but she treated the self-imposed regime as a mission. A quest for an ideal version of herself. That was the drive, and as I say, it kept us both remarkably busy as well as all the high-end beauticians within a ten-mile radius of Lexington Gardens.

* * *

Her personal trainer arrived at ten most mornings, Veronique's voice penetrating the whole house even though Ris' efforts were confined to the gym on the top floor. The music was high energy and judging by the thudding that travelled down through the yoga mats and stripped floorboards, and Ris' sweaty face afterwards, Veronique worked Ris to her limit.

Ris would emerge with a hand towel and an exaggerated colour, her chest heaving, sweat pouring as she declared it was so good to get the toxins out and the endorphins flowing, although the photos and videos she shared were always taken pre not post workout. A slight glow the most she'd distribute to her followers.

No, I wouldn't say it's worth interviewing Veronique.

She was barely in the same room as us and certainly never privy to anything of note. And her Instagram posts are all about *PBs* and *carbs* and her meat-head boyfriend who is possibly worth a look simply out of curiosity. How someone achieves that rather grotesque level of muscle tone is beyond me.

Anyway, Veronique would run down the stairs at eleven, always at high velocity, and slam the front door behind her without a word to me. Then Ris would text for a protein shake that I'd mix to her exacting recipes, weighing and blitzing in the prescribed order before placing it ready for her on the kitchen island. Disgusting concoctions they were. Chia seeds, blueberries, kale, spinach, some kind of dust that came in packets, very odd. Then she'd shower and we'd reconvene in the study to run through the diary again and tackle any emails and DMs. Not that there was much of substance.

The direct messages were usually from chancers looking for a free endorsement, the emails to her 'business' account, mostly spam. The only ones she was interested in discussing were those from her book publicist.

Other than that, the only presence in the house that first week were the interchangeable agency cleaners who came every morning at nine. Their pink van would pull up outside whilst Ris was still in bed, bringing two, sometimes three women in pink tabards. They were very efficient, silently performing their duties.

They'd see to the master suite once Ris was with Veronique on the top floor. Although sometimes she'd text the agency and ask them not to come at all, or come later, and they always obliged.

I've worked as a cleaner on and off over the years. It's hard graft, but reasonably well paid compared to some other casual jobs. I've no idea why people look down on it so much. As if scrubbing someone else's toilet bowl makes you less of a person, when of course the inverse is true. But it really was money for old rope at Lexington Gardens. At least, when it was just Ris and me there to clean up after. And I saw to the basement. I'm a naturally tidy person, always have been.

* * *

The afternoons were often spent in the back of cabs and that first week was no exception. I'd accompany Ris to her many appointments via a zigzag route around Kensington and Chelsea: fake tan salons, hair and make-up stylists, a pedi or mani or both, although the one she already had still looked immaculate. I would invariably wait in the cab, double-checking everything was OK for the next appointment – woe betide there be any inconvenience to madam – whilst ensuring I was home in time for orders she'd requested be delivered without a thought to the logistics: food, wine, flowers, beauty buys, clothes... in fact, it was one afternoon later that week when we were circling between salons that the puppy idea first came up. We cooed over Maltipoos and French Bulldogs for an hour or so, and I even made a few calls. You know they start at three grand, those designer breeds? And some were quoting me up to ten thousand! Of course it wasn't the price that put Ris off in the end, but that's another story entirely. One I'd much rather forget.

Wherever we were – in a taxi, a salon, or shopping – Ris was always on her phone. The only time she wasn't checking her updates or posting something was the time she spent sleeping. She did a lot of daytime napping; on account of her insomnia, I assume. Not something she spoke about with me, or online, but I heard her nocturnal wanderings and the calls she took, in the early hours, when her errant husband would finally ring her back.

I could never partake of those daytime naps, much as I needed them, or sleep much at night either. I couldn't relax, not for a second; instead I would endlessly check through my notebook, updating it then popping it back under my pillow or in a drawer, berating myself for my lack of progress, although I had managed to cross off one bullet point when I'd procured the pin code for her phone. That was something.

Yes, I found my feet during our first week together. A routine established and a good working relationship, based on my subservience and endless gratitude and praise of my employer. It was a one-way street, but fine, I could live with that, the hope being that soon the ground would move, cracks appearing. Because no one's life is *that* perfect.

I would find those fissures and open them even wider. It would just take longer than I'd thought.

Although, whilst we are on the subject of Miles' late-night calls, it did seem as though *Hubs* didn't prioritise her as a happily married man would. Her excitement when he did contact her, or return one of her frequent messages, causing such elation it struck me as either pathetic or tragic, depending on my mood.

I recall late one night that first week, must have been the Thursday, catching her breathy gabble through the closed door to the master suite, her prattle punctuated with short pauses when presumably he was allowed to speak. She missed him, she repeated, ad nauseam, but my ears did prick up when she mentioned me. 'Told you I'd find somebody good to replace her... yes, of course I checked this one out thoroughly, called the last employer myself, couldn't speak highly enough of her, and she's really hard working... for an old gal.'

Can't say I was thrilled with the 'old gal' part, but at least it meant all my hard work those first few days had been worth it. She was pleased with me. Which was important, not only to secure my continuing presence at Lexington Gardens, but to win her trust. Essential if I was to implement the next phase of my campaign to topple her from her unearned seat of privilege.

My week one plan had been to keep up with the job, get some security codes or passwords, and gain her trust. All of which were ticked off my list by the end of play on the Friday. A good start, but I'd need a lot more than that: email passwords, bank account details, something incendiary in her past no one knew about, that kind of thing. I had done well, but not that well. Besides, the phone was never out of her palm so having the passcode was of little to no value.

* * *

It was around five on the Friday afternoon when I discovered, rather disappointingly, the expectation was I would spend my weekends not resting in the lovely basement flat in Lexington Gardens, but back here, in a condemned, or should be, bedsit in Reading.

A misunderstanding between us, or as Ris termed it, an assumption of mine.

Either way, not the most enticing of prospects, returning to squalor after living in luxury all week.

Fortunately, I suppose, I hadn't given notice on this place, just in case things didn't work out, and to be honest I was shattered, unused to the demands of learning a multi-skill set as well as the mental stimulation of being at Ris' beck and call the whole time. With the lack of sleep and mental exhaustion, I accepted my fate reasonably well and went downstairs to pack and book a train ticket.

It would do us both good to have a breather, I reasoned. I'd tiptoed a little too close to the mark a couple of times and seen Ris bristle at my subtle insinuations of marital disharmony. It was a rich vein, but a couple of days alone to mull over my next move would not be a bad thing. I needed to clear my head. Being in her company was demanding. I was constantly running up and down those blessed flights of stairs; whatever she needed always seemed to be on a different floor. This place might be damp, cramped, everything Lexington Gardens isn't, but at least it's on one level.

I used the last of my extended overdraft limit booking a seat on the six o'clock train and galvanised myself for the prospect of a long walk to Paddington station, dragging my wobbly-wheeled case behind me for the crowded rush-hour train. I was almost looking forward to a couple of days on this saggy sofa of mine with my bowls of cereal, some mindless drivel on the TV. A chance to ponder the possibilities for an orchestrated and preferably public take-down. Forty-eight hours to recharge and regroup was most definitely in order. And a blessed break from the endless, 'Would you mind?' and, 'You couldn't be a doll could you...?' All I had to do was find Ris to say my goodbyes and the pretence could stop, at least until Monday.

I found her in the master suite, throwing things into an open case, the enormous king-sized bed littered with clothes and shoes. She was wired and somewhat agitated, neither of which were conducive to a well-packed weekend bag, nor the conversation I'd intended to broach before my departure. Taking an educated guess, I asked if she was going away somewhere. She'd told me barely ten minutes before she was going to 'hunker down' for a weekend of pampering and Netflix after her 'exhausting' week. Cleary her plans had changed.

It transpired *Hubs* had called whilst I was in the basement, proposing an impromptu romantic weekend, '*A deux en Par-is*'.

Ris peeled off another layer so she was in an increasing state of not only animation but also undress. She hadn't showered after her workout that morning, in a rush to get to her waxing appointment, her hair still up in a topknot, face bare, the silence on social media no doubt attributable to her unkempt appearance. I caught a whiff of sweat and stale perfume as I picked up the discarded leggings and socks and asked if I might be of help in any way, hoping not as I was pushing it for time as it was.

A flurry of activity ensued as I booked her flights, a car to Heathrow, and a suite at The Ritz.

The Ritz, Paris, yes. Three thousand euros a night, just for a place to sleep.

I suspected the trip was her suggestion, although she sold it to me as a romantic gesture on his part. I averted my eyes from the lacy underwear she was packing, only for my gaze to land on a silk negligee laid out on the bed. She snatched it up, asking me to check how long the driver would be. I confirmed he was due in fifteen minutes.

She glanced at her watch in that way of looking at it rather than reading it and half-heartedly offered to drop me at the station on her way. I'd just about have made my train if she did, and I accepted gladly, but she immediately retracted the offer, saying she wasn't sure there'd be time; would I mind? There was another train straight after, right?

I'd have to pay to change to a later one, which was potentially a big issue as, *zero funds*, but I told her it was fine, I'd stay and help her pack and then I could grab a cab myself. 'I'm in no hurry.' Although I did raise the subject of my expenses as she gathered designer outfits together. I'd thought she'd be more amenable after my generous offer to miss my train, but my hints about ticket costs and London prices were brushed aside as they had been the previous times when I'd to discuss my incurred costs.

It wasn't as though she couldn't afford to reimburse me. The carelessness of not needing to worry about money blinkering her to my desperate need, I guess? Or she simply didn't care?

I'd spun a tale of a comfortable life, but nothing akin to her prosperity. It annoyed me intensely. She was thoughtless and wasteful. Not just with me, but generally. I'd witnessed her, even in those first few days, throw away food, clothes, make-up, a book she grew tired of. Maybe she saw me as equally dispensable and as such an irritant as she rushed to get ready. For whatever reason, she again ignored my request, muttering how hard it was to know what to pack, and how men had it easy compared to 'us girls'.

I find that pseudo-inclusive girlie chatter entirely disingenuous and totally *ick*, but I was annoyed with her already so not entirely receptive.

She sent me into the en suite for her bristle brush and that's when I saw her, reflected in the mirror as she surreptitiously removed the recognisable branded box from a Boots carrier bag, the receipt swimming to the floor. The unopened, freshly purchased box of tampons stuffed quickly into her case beneath other items.

It was evident that not only did she want to hide their inclusion from me, but also from anyone who might glance inside her case. The question was why? I mean, man and wife, and it's a natural thing, surely she wasn't embarrassed about needing them? But maybe not the vibe she was hoping for on a romantic weekend away. Although *interesting*. I mean, only mildly at that point, but it was of note and I had duly noted it. Why all the subterfuge? It was only a period.

I've never stayed somewhere as posh as The Ritz, but even if, as you say, they might unpack for you, then no amount of superficial concealment would help.

When I returned with the brush, Ris had begun to decant products from her dressing table into a velvet make-up pouch. I took my chance to surreptitiously pocket the receipt which was on the carpet and when I got the chance, found it pre-dated my arrival by several days.

Ris then lost patience with the packing and threw the make-up pouch on the bed, products spilling out. She ignored the mess, turning her attention to a barrel-shaped device she'd pulled from her bedside drawer. My cheeks turned scarlet, but it wasn't one of those. Although I must admit that's where my mind went too, which would have been mortifying. No, it was an epilator, and she needed me to find the charger. As I began to search, opening dressing table drawers stuffed with more products – make-up, brushes, creams, serums – Ris pulled her vest top over her head, revealing a sports bra. And to quote her directly, she announced, 'God, I stink!' Bra and knickers then removed.

I was rather taken aback. But what could I say? *I'd rather not see you naked, you're my boss?* But that was the point: she *was* my boss. And to make matters worse, Ris then remembered the charger could well be in the en suite and sent me back in there to hunt for it whilst she simultaneously 'jumped in the shower'.

I was on my knees, rooting through the cupboard under the dual sinks when she stepped back out, dripping wet. I saw her pink toes beside me first and the recollection of that scene reminds me now how quickly I was privy to not only every part of Lexington Gardens, even areas you'd consider sacrosanct like her bathroom, but also Ris herself. Such an exhibitionist! Maybe she was comfortable in her own skin, as you say, or simply in a rush?

I know she loved an audience, that was a given, but it was only me there. A nobody, invisible and inconsequential. Dispensable. Although, she worked hard for that body; perhaps it was her taking another chance to show it off, even though it was just me there so see it? I looked away, rifling through the cupboards, but as I glanced up – gosh, even the memory is making me blush – I was eye level with her pubic hair, or rather a complete lack of it.

Is it normal these days, to have it all removed? No, please don't answer that! It certainly took me by surprise. She was plucked like a chicken, a hairless, naked woman, inches from me. I honestly wouldn't have known what to do with myself if it wasn't for the task

I'd been given but Ris seemed not to notice my discomfort, and crouched beside me, still naked. I handed her the located charger, my hand shaking, and she slotted it into the epilator before straightening up to connect it to the shaver point by the enormous lit mirror to give it a 'quick juice'. Not a jot of embarrassment on her part, or any recognition of mine. Then – as if I were the instigator of this whole cringe-worthy performance – Ris asked if I wouldn't mind leaving her alone so she could dry herself properly.

My face was on fire, palms hot and clammy as I closed the bathroom door behind me. Rather too late by then, but I guess better late than never. The thing is, I hadn't caused that situation and yet it was me, as Ris emerged many minutes later wrapped up in her monogrammed robe, who felt apologetic. But time was not on my side, the car due any moment. If I was going to make anything out of the opportunity presented by her impending absence, it was now or never.

I cleared my throat and made my suggestion, couching it in terms of *me* doing *her* a favour rather than the other way around. Suggesting a couple of uninterrupted days to get on top of the admin whilst the house was empty – update those spreadsheets and catch up on all those outstanding emails, never know who might be offering some amazing partnership ops – would be a great idea. For her. Not me.

She paused in her preparations, moisturiser stroked onto her legs despite the imminent arrival of her lift to the airport. Her attention returned to the make-up pouch as she tried again to shove everything inside and failed. Frustrated, she inverted it, the contents clattering down onto the bed, a foundation leaking onto the duvet cover. The churlishness of a child.

I took over, slotting the lipsticks and eyeshadow palettes in neatly, like a game of Tetris, the zip sliding across with ease, and she was delighted, asking whatever would she do without me.

I was flattered, of course. Her effusiveness was hard to resist. But she still hadn't commented on me staying in the house over the weekend. Her reluctance soon evident when she asked, 'Couldn't you work from that lovely apartment of yours, Gail? I'm sure you're dying to get back there.' I pressed my cause as she shrugged off the robe and donned a red lace thong and push-up bra.

Despite the distractions, I explained it would be just this once; it had been a crazy week and travelling back to Reading when the London house would be empty seemed a bit of a waste of my time... but obviously if wasn't convenient...

I stopped talking, waiting for her decision. I find it's often best to shut up and leave space for a reply in these moments of indecision.

I was honestly as concerned about the train fare as anything else. My ticket was non-refundable and it really was the least she could do after making me miss it, but she remained adamant. The arrangement, she insisted, although I felt not explicit, had been for me to work Monday to Friday only. She saw no need to change that, talking, or rather shouting this to me from her walk-in closet. I tried to avoid her exposed bum cheeks in the thong and stared instead at the rows of identical black stiletto heels lined up on the shelves to her left. It was difficult to know where to look to be honest, mirrors on three sides of the brightly lit carpeted room. Her figure was lean rather than curvy, other than the unnaturally enhanced boobs in the push-up bra.

I accepted my fate and was about to take my leave, hoping I might get away with my existing ticket if I avoided the conductor, when a plan came to me. The opportunity provided by an overheard one-sided conversation that morning as Veronique, on her phone, hurtled down the stairs. The words 'tight' and 'bitch' snagging my ear as I made my way to the kitchen to mix Ris' post-workout smoothie.

I told Ris she was right, the payments could all wait until

Monday. Veronique really had no right to involve me in the first place, chasing up her fees.

Ris was clearly incensed her PT had gone behind her back. And yet still she hesitated. Reticent to hand over her whole house to, let's face it, a relative stranger. She was holding a pair of the red-soled heels, one in each hand, the spikes pointing upwards, weighing up her options.

She'd dressed in jeans and a sweater and shoved the Louboutins on her feet, glancing at her watch again as she pulled on a dark blazer. Still no response as she returned to her suitcase, the silence becoming heavy. She zipped it closed and only after another long beat then expressed a wish that I'd mentioned this sooner.

I almost lost my composure at that point, my fists curling at my sides as I swallowed my anger, best as I could. It was Ris who'd made *me* late. *Her* selfishness causing me unforeseen cost and not inconsiderable concern. I'm afraid I bit back, just a little, which of course I shouldn't have done. I don't recall my exact words, but it was something along the lines of… I'd hoped she'd have dealt with any outstanding invoices professionally and promptly herself or brought them to my immediate attention to action for her. It's not what I'd been used to, at my level. Chasers landing in my inbox late on a Friday. 'I am only offering to stay on and tidy up, in my own time.'

She jerked up from her phone, meeting my stare. It could have gone either way. A swift rebuke for my insolence, or compliance in the face of the implication she was out of her depth. She could have even called Veronique, and therefore my bluff.

Instead, she drew in a deep breath and said, 'I don't think, Gail, this is the right moment to tackle this. I'd need to log on, talk you through all my passwords and accounts. Like you say, it can wait until Monday. I'll be back before you, my flight is early. I can message Veronique when I get a moment, apologise. She's not usually worried about a few days. I'm not sure why she's making a fuss now.'

What you need to understand, as I recount this debate, is my perilous financial position, already compromised, was by that Friday night hanging off the edge of a cliff. I had no cash, no further means of credit, and a most-likely useless train ticket. I'm not trying to elicit sympathy, but the fact was I had nothing waiting for me here and no means at my disposal, even on credit, to buy so much as a pint of milk. A concept Ris would never have been able to fathom.

I was looking at a weekend spent either wandering the streets of London, or... well, there was no immediate fallback. The bench in the residents' gardens, maybe? If I could push through the prickly hedges? It was cold at night, recent snow. Not really an option. I'd have to break back into the basement, a set of keys not as yet provided, although I'd asked, more than once. I believe it was due to 'issues' with the previous assistant, but for whatever reason Ris was on her guard concerning access.

I had never been left in the house unsupervised for a minute, so a whole weekend was clearly not going to be acceptable.

A hostel? The thought made me shudder. The injustice of it cutting too deep to go down without a fight. Not least because the reason I had no cash flow to draw on was largely down Ris.

I've always lived hand-to-mouth but I've been careful and managed, just.

However, in Ris' company, that had become impossible. Between the daily almond-milk decaf coffee run to the chic little café down the road, my heart in my throat each time I used my card, and the charity collector who'd explained to Ris at the door that no, he didn't carry a card reader, the last note teased from my purse before I'd had the presence of mind to claim I never carried cash either, and the out-of-pocket expenses I'd incurred to look presentable enough to be in her daily company – tights, a lipstick, a couple of charity shop blouses – I found myself completely without funds.

She'd stated any expenses incurred would be added to my wages, but Ris' brow had wrinkled unattractively whenever I brought it up, as if it was crass to even mention it. So nothing had been agreed, or paid, and now it seemed, wouldn't be until at the earliest Monday when I reported back for duty at nine. The doorbell rang and I left Ris squashing her iPad into the front pocket of her designer case.

I instructed the driver to go upstairs and retrieve the luggage, maybe a tad brusque as he gave me a look but did as asked. Ris came down as he went up, all smiles as she advised me to take the weekend off, go home, chill out, I'd earned it. I thanked her and said I'd grab my wheelie case from the basement and be right behind her. What else could I do?

The trouble was, even setting aside my lack of means, it was far too good an opportunity to pass up. A whole weekend alone in the house. I'd have been a fool not to take that chance, however dicey. Not when I could achieve in one weekend what might take weeks with Ris around. And what other option did I have? Quickly stealing a pair of Louboutins to sell on?

As Ris ran out the front door, I ran down to the basement, ostensibly to grab my case. As I heard the car drive off, I think I whooped! I'm sure you can imagine my delight. I had the run of the place, at last!

8

THIRD INTERVIEW WITH GAIL FROST – SUNDAY 16 OCTOBER

I'm not proud of this, but the first thing I did after Ris left the house was sift through the kitchen bin. I managed to salvage some out-of-date calorie-counted ramens thrown in there, and a net of satsumas, largely intact although one was squashy so I threw it back.

Not going to lie, I experienced a dip in mood as I caught my reflection in the shiny lid when it dropped back down. Nothing like facing one's unguarded expression for a reality check. But I was soon back to my kitchen pilfering whilst singing at the top of my voice.

Yes, I made the most of the freedom Ris' departure had gifted me.

The freezer yielded slim pickings: a pint of almond milk and a sliced sourdough. The fridge, salty butter, two eggs and some dodgy-smelling orange juice. I knew Ris wouldn't notice if I 'borrowed' a few things, not with an Ocado delivery due on Monday, the ramens Tuesday, but it was unfortunately meagre rations. That's the trouble living with someone who counts every single calorie, but Ris wasn't quite as virtuous as she liked to make out.

What I really wanted were the fat olives she sent me to buy from the deli. And the paper-thin slices of salty prosciutto, and the pots of oily anchovies her pink-tipped nails dug into greedily of an evening once I'd gone to bed and the wine was poured. Chilled white in those enormous glasses she filled carelessly as I crept up from the basement and hovered at the top of the stairs, or the black-currant red she splashed into even larger glasses, jammy rings left on the white kitchen island for the cleaners to scrub at the next morning. But most of all I wanted one of those ice-cold bottles of champagne lined up in the wine fridge. The deli bounty might have been thin on the ground, but the champagne was not. An abundance of it. Ready for a special occasion which may or may not arise. Wasn't it special enough that I had a whole weekend to myself in a twenty-million-pound Belgravia mansion? Two full days to comb fifty-six Lexington Gardens for damaging evidence that would smash apart Ris' faux-perfect world.

I'm not sure exactly what I thought I'd find that weekend. Maybe the usual suspects that trip up the unworthy. A secret lover sending emails to her laptop, or a nude photo in a saved file, or even better, a video from her shadier days. Something unwise that I could allow, anonymously, to resurface.

Not my finest hour, I'll admit, but I am trying to be completely honest with you, and these were the frenzied thoughts running through my head as I helped myself to supplies. And before I lose all sympathy, assuming you had any for me in the first place, may I advise you there were mitigating circumstances. *Extremely* mitigating. This woman deserved to be taken down, and more than a peg or two. So yes, fizz was definitely in order. Ris would be unlikely to miss one bottle, even two. It was the very least she owed me.

I made toast and sat at the island, allowing the crumbs to fall, butter running down my chin as I greedily filled my empty stomach, then I was ready for a drink.

It had been years since my last sip of the good stuff. I grabbed my notebook and laptop from the basement and skipped back upstairs, spirits lifted as I stowed the freezing bottle under my elbow, crystal flute in hand.

I was actually looking forward to the weekend. Which, without wishing to play the sympathy card, had not been the case in years. And whilst I cannot blame Ris for everything, her sudden and continuing good fortune had most definitely coincided with my misfortune. If not vindicated, I would go as far as to say I felt more than justified in both my actions and the delight they gave, frivolous as they were.

Dropping everything on the king-size bed, I spritzed some of Ris' expensive scent from her dressing table on my neck and décolletage, then lay back on her pillows, my phone held aloft to take a photo.

No, I wasn't that stupid! Of course not.

It would have been both foolish and gratuitous to provide potential evidence of my misdemeanours, the kind of mistake that easily catches one out, although maybe tempting... but I had already broken one of my cardinal rules. I had acted without a plan and the consequences of that thoughtlessness induced a cold dread which rapidly spread through me so I sat bolt upright, adrenalin pumping hard as the stomach-churning realisation of my utter stupidity began to sink in.

I don't know if you saw an American TV show, years ago, might have even been a drama, can't recall the name of it, pretty lowbrow to be honest, that depicted the consequences of home surveillance? A rich family had set hidden cameras to watch their nanny, to catch her out. You see where my thoughts had taken me?

I stowed the unopened champagne bottle behind a pillow and stood up, po-faced, which was ridiculous. If Ris or Miles were 'tuned in' to my shenanigans, the game was already well and truly up.

I'd been such an idiot, especially as I'd broached the subject with Ris earlier in the week, enquiring about the security system, should I ever be required to set it. Were there codes I should know? Cameras?

Ris hadn't batted an overly long eyelash, looking up from her phone and telling me the cameras were linked to the alarm system, but they only came on when it was set, and as I was never there alone, I needn't worry. 'No one is watching you, Gail. I promise.'

The alarm wasn't set, I knew that much. She'd rushed out and left me to it, saying she'd activate it remotely later on, a detail I'd somehow forgotten in my glee, and clearly so had she, but one that rushed at me as I paced her bedroom.

It may surprise you what I decided to do next.

I suppose by then I was past caring. My thinking along the lines of... I might as well be hung for a sheep as a lamb. You don't know that phrase? One of my father's. In reference to my mother's acid tongue regarding his drinking. Anyway, I think I was as much in denial as he always was, kidding myself that Ris would forget to set the alarm all weekend much as she would neglect to message an apology to Veronique. Which also meant no cameras. I opened the bottle clumsily, fizz spuming across the duvet. My lack of recent experience showing. I drank a glass of champagne straight down, the hit of alcohol adding to my conviction she'd totally forgotten about the alarm.

It was only a few minutes later when the beeping began.

I ran downstairs to the control panel by the door, not that I knew the code, but I began jabbing wildly at the keypad. I took a breath and tried Ris' date of birth, then 1234, when the most terrible sound started up.

An ear-splitting racket. The sound unbearable, which is of

course, the whole point.

I've no idea how I managed to send Ris that message, let alone make it coherent enough for her to text me the four-digit code. The silence after I managed to key in the correct sequence, blessed, although my ears were ringing.

Then she called.

I don't recall the exact exchange, I was half-deaf with tinnitus, but the gist was, 'Why are you still there?! I waited an hour, Gail. Surely you'd have left by now?'

I told her I had just been sorting out a few final bits and was about to leave. I must have sounded agitated as she told me not to panic, and that it was bit more complicated than just putting the code back in when I left, but not to worry as she'd set it remotely as soon as I messaged her I was out the house. But soon. She was about to board. I could hear announcements in the background. The chimes and tinny voice of an airport tannoy. It seemed I would have no choice but to go, and soon. I ran upstairs to cover my tracks but then a text arrived which changed everything.

I've been called for my flight, but I've managed to disable the whole system, somehow. It should be fine for the next couple of days. There are rarely break-ins. Feel free to leave whenever you're ready. And have a lovely weekend. x

Emboldened by my good fortune, I downed the rest of the bottle.

* * *

A whole bottle when you're not used to it... hardly surprising I felt rather disinhibited. But when I look back now and see myself having my little party for one... Shameful, but fun!

The LEDs were triggered in the walk-in wardrobe when I staggered in, the racks of shoes, bags, jackets, jeans, shirts, and dresses lit up. Ris' feet are enormous, although her waist is tiny. The physique of a catwalk model. It's not necessarily what men want, but I think it's what most women covet. A walking clothes horse. She was able to wear anything with ease, whilst I have what I believe is known as an *apron* of menopausal flab. The concealment of which dictates my every choice of outfit. We really couldn't have been physically more different, but by feeding my arms carefully through the narrow opening to sleeves, or slipping spaghetti straps onto my sloping shoulders, I was able to get an impression of wearing each frock, had they been mine. And by ignoring the old-lady face and messy grey hair, and the gaping apertures at my back where the zips wouldn't do up, faded bra strap and back fat on show, I managed to swish and sway; fabrics rustling in an exhilarating fashion as I paraded before the wrap-around mirrors. Silks and satins rippling like liquid silk against my gooseflesh thighs.

I half-closed my eyes and a fuzzy image replaced the reality as the high heels my feet slid around in lengthened my legs and raised my expectations. I could be her, given half a chance. But of course, I couldn't. Not even close. I toppled into the mirror and staggered back, almost ripping the Gucci midi that pooled at my feet. I've never owned a single designer label. The extent of it a lucky charity shop find or high street knock-off. I could wear pretty much anything in my youth and feel sexy... but no point dwelling on the past. That's what I told myself. Although the bittersweet memories had dried my mouth. I needed another drink.

The next hour or so passed in a blur of rabid exploration and a second bottle of fizz. There wasn't an inch of fifty-six Lexington Gardens I didn't poke around as I sank glass after delicious, ice-cold glass. No drawer unopened, no dark recess left un-rummaged. I couldn't say what I was looking for specifically, other than something incriminating against my new boss. Something private I could make very public.

I found vibrators and lubricant, but everyone has those in their bedside drawer. Hardly scandalous these days. Nor the old passports, photos, Valentine cards or the many personal effects that waylaid me. Of mild interest, but not useful.

Hours passed with nothing gained except increasing drunkenness. I was disappointed, of course, but there was one compensation. As I'd searched, I'd found cold hard cash. Notes and coins. In the crevices of the pale pink velvet sofas, stuffed into the purses and bags on the lit shelves in the dressing room, and deep within *Hubs*' suit pockets, his cologne still clinging to the lapels. And with my spoils jangling in the pockets of one of Ris' cashmere lounge sets, the bottoms stretchy enough to accommodate me, just, the top clinging whereas it swamped Ris, I walked to the deli, my exposed stomach grumbling, the aromas making my mouth water as I opened the door.

It was almost ten – thank goodness for London hours of opening – just enough time before closing to buy a feast for *my* consumption: the olives and anchovies I'd coveted, and a croissant, day-old stale, and a lone lemon posset, deliciously tart, plus punnets of fat raspberries and finally, bright-purple blackberries, overripe and shiny with juice, which, as I piled them sloppily into one of those pretentious wicker baskets, dribbled a wavy purple line behind me on the glossy tiles.

The assistant, with an exaggerated eyeroll and pronounced underbite, looked at me as if I was rather a trial. I *was* a bit drunk, maybe more than a bit, but she counted out the notes and coins as if they were no longer legal tender. Then she asked if my purchases were for Ris, clearly recognising me from my previous visits through the week. 'She has an account, you know? You can charge whatever you like.' I could have kicked myself, not only as I'd parted needlessly with the cash, but because I wasn't meant to be in Belgravia. I should have left hours before.

I told the surly assistant I had no idea whom she meant, rushing out, my purchases held tight to me so the cashmere lounge set was stained by the time I was back inside. My heart was still thrashing in my chest long after I'd recovered from the sprint home, hands plunged in cold water as I rinsed the cashmere under a running tap and then binned it. Ris had so many, she never noticed.

No, as I said I didn't have a key.

I'd left the outside basement door unlocked, which was a bit risky, but fine. And as it happened, it wouldn't have mattered if the deli assistant had told Ris she'd seen me, but I wasn't to know that at the time.

That's why I keep detailed notes. To cover all eventualities, especially when you potentially mess up as I had, more than once that Friday night. And it was about to get so much worse than a triggered alarm and a vague worry about a shop assistant and some ruined cashmere. But before that, I still had the whole of Saturday, a glorious day.

Not that it began in the best of health, the morning dawning too bright and too early for a woman of a certain age nursing a hangover.

I'd actually slept surprisingly well. The king-size in the master was so much more comfortable than the bed in the basement. I'd been imagining myself in it ever since Ris had posted one of those *American Beauty* type poses, wrapped in silk sheets rather than covered in rose petals, the angle a little wrong as she'd taken the photo herself. And despite my previous circumspection, it appeared I had tried to recreate it somewhere north of midnight. The results, in the cold light of day, were utterly humiliating. I deleted the resultant image and threw back the soft sheets and goose down coverlet, then climbed into the rain shower, the same one I'd watched Ris step out of just the day before. It was very restorative, much better than the dribble I was used to in the basement. And much needed. I wasn't used to alcohol. I'd abstained for my health for years – it doesn't mix that well with my medication – and the rich food was also a shock to my deprived digestive system. Some of the evidence of this over-indulgence was still in the toilet bowl and sink. But I had a whole cabinet of vitamins and probiotics to choose from. Some of which I recognised, some not.

After I'd cleared up, I downed a few supplements that looked appropriate for a hangover, along with a tall glass of water and a couple of paracetamol and I soon felt well enough to resume my search, this time with a sharper focus and clearer goal.

Ris had taken her iPad with her to Paris, as I told you, but her pink, or as she called it, 'rose-gold' laptop was on her desk in the study, and fortunately I had finally committed the password to memory from all the times I'd sat beside her. I attempted a log on and got past the first screen. It was momentarily exciting, any remnants of a headache evaporating with the buzz of it, but I soon hit a brick wall as I needed a passcode to get any further on her banking app. This would require some lateral thought.

A very carefully composed email message was eventually sent.

I explained that a chaser invoice had come in from Veronique that morning, Ris' out of office (*out of office?? Ha!!!*) citing me as a point of contact. Should I pay? It seemed urgent.

I knew it would enrage her that Veronique had involved me, again, and the reply came back immediately.

Shit! That's so crap of her to do that. Could you deal, Gail?! Your such a doll! Rx

Y-O-U-R not Y-O-U-'-R-E. But we'll let that go. For now.

I replied that I was of course happy to oblige, if she could send the passwords for her personal bank account via WhatsApp, which was the safest method.

You never know who might be trying to hack into your accounts.

She thanked me profusely.

Your a lifesaver, Gail. Merci beau-coup!

The use of French – no doubt with the use of Google Translate as Ris could barely spell in English – took the edge off my good humour. I was eating a stale croissant whilst she was likely quaffing from a tray delivered to the suite I'd booked. Soft, warm pastries covered in a silver cloche, freshly squeezed orange juice, hot coffee, that kind of thing, if the website photos were to be believed. But at least I had access to her bank account, and a valid reason for going there. Two minutes later, as if she had read my thoughts, another message came through.

Gail, whilst your at it, transfer your owed wages/expenses for last week.
I trust you to work out the amount! I'll pay you monthly from now on.
Ris x

I paid in what I was owed, plus a bit extra, for the delay. Which I think was fair enough, especially after I saw some of the purchases and withdrawals she'd made. It seemed as though she had a monthly allowance from *Hubs*, which was so generous she would never miss my modest transfers, her disinterest in 'admin' as she called it, again to my advantage.

I was in desperate need, and she was so very clearly not, her account balance in six figures. I paid Veronique and sent apologies via DM to her Instagram account.

The PT's indiscreet reply was almost immediate.

Thanks, Gail, she's so fucking tight! I'd been meaning to chase, but it's awks, isn't it? I'll come to you directly in future. V xx

You could say I was lucky, but I prefer to think of it as judicious planning achieving the required result. I was solvent again and with the alarm sorted I could relax and review my bullet pointed plan. First job, trawling Ris' Mac for anything of interest: emails, search history, that kind of thing.

I was disappointed at first; it all seemed very much as I'd expected. Even the emails were the ones she'd shared with me. Invitations to product launches which she'd turned down on the basis they were beneath her, a discount code for this and that, which she never bothered to use. Oh, and that's when I tried on the glasses and discovered they are completely for show, when I was transferring the funds. Then I stumbled upon an email folder of exchanges between Ris and *Hubs*.

The Paris trip as I'd suspected, was all her idea. She'd pleaded for it multiple times before it was agreed last minute, Ris' missives to *Hubs* verbose, his responses curt, as if he was busy and she were a nuisance. There were a few things I noted down, mainly tonal observations regarding the state of their relationship. Nothing concrete, but fascinating to read the subtext of a marriage crumbling after barely two years. Their relationship by then less than three years in total. I read them all twice and jotted down my thoughts.

Her browser history was also illuminating. Her Google searches in particular. She really should learn to clear her cache; I do it as a matter of course. I'd recommend everyone do the same, but with Ris... it was all there.

She was clearly obsessed with Miles' ex-wife, Trudy, and their twin daughters, images of them clicked on as well as articles that mentioned their names: Coco and Lily. But most of the sites she'd visited were related to infertility issues and ways to cope with that, from IVF to adoption and even surrogacy. The picture I built up was one of insecurity and desperation. An entirely different take to the one which she'd shared with her followers, expressing sadness but acceptance of the end of her journey to try and get pregnant.

Hubs and I are blessed to have one another, and that's enough.

Clearly Ris was still actively searching for ways to have a child.

My last stop was to check on her social media posts. I'd neglected Ris' feed that past week, which was very out of character. It had been a somewhat obsessive preoccupation, whole days lost doomscrolling. But I'd been in her company all day every day, my curiosity dampened by the proximity of her 'in real life', or #IRL as Ris would post. But I remained inquisitive, not least to compare and contrast what I'd witnessed first-hand with the content she'd chosen to share with her followers. The seductive lure of the waiting dopamine hit hastening my pace as I shut down Ris' Mac and went back up to her bed, the loaned work phone in hand. How far apart would reality and make-believe stand? What had made the cut and what, possibly more telling, had she decided to keep private?

Notepad and pen beside me, I lay back with a glass of something rather nice beside me. It was still early, but you know five o'clock somewhere, and it was a delicious wine. Claret, I think, although red wine is much of a muchness to me. A bit cheeky, granted, but let's not pretend I'm living by the usual rules at this point. Those had been cast aside around two a.m. when I was belting out the *Titanic* theme at full pelt, holding a pink rubber bunny-themed vibrator as my improvised microphone. I'd definitely crossed a line, but it's quite funny when I look back now. Like I was a different person. Which I suppose I was.

Anyway, I plumped the pillows – they were actually very hard, over-stuffed – then began my overdue scroll through Twitter, Facebook and finally Instagram, which was always Ris' favourite. I sipped the blackcurrant wine and put it down, zooming in on every detail of those touched-up recent photos, paying particular attention to anything I might have missed in the background, a note of concern creeping in.

I was looking for an inadvertent cameo from me, of course. Which might have put rather a crimp in my plans. I was not, after all, exactly who I'd claimed to be.

I'd been watchful whenever she was taking a photo or recording a video, and on the one occasion Ris had asked my permission to introduce her 'fabulous new EA' to her followers, I'd trotted out the excuse of an amorous ex-employer I'd rather not alert to my new location. 'Gosh, you're a dark horse, Gail.' So she knew I was camera-shy, and there was always plenty of warning when she was taking a photo – Ris did a kind of mating dance for the camera, chin up, eyes down, hips this way then that before, tap, tap, tap, then checking the results, delete, delete, before an image was even considered suitable to share: her ramen lunch, her green tea, her new nails, her fabulous new body-con dress, perfect for transitional wear between seasons – but you never know, I might have been snapped, which was why I checked.

Many posts had gone up over the previous five days. But as she had suggested at interview, I remained, to my great relief, invisible. As far as Ris' social media was concerned, it was as if I'd never set foot in Lexington Gardens. Which was perfect.

But I *was* there. Unsupervised. And I would use the remaining time well. The trouble was, I actually had much less time left than I thought.

9

THIRD INTERVIEW WITH GAIL FROST – SUNDAY 16 OCTOBER

It was the sound of the car drawing up in the quiet street which first roused me from a deep sleep that Sunday morning. My head pounding as I lifted it tentatively from the overstuffed pillows. Snippets of the previous night returning to me as I slowly regained consciousness. Recollections soused in the surfeit of red wine I'd drowned my sorrows in. My frustration that my second and more thorough search of the house, which took all of Saturday, had proved entirely fruitless, leading to another night of drunken excess. No dirt, literally or figuratively to be found. I'd checked every bit of paperwork in her desk and every drawer and cupboard. Not a court order, or even evidence of points on her licence. Not an unpaid bill or a letter from a lover. Not an old VHS sex tape. Not a little black book. Not a hidden child or a mad relative. Not a drunken fight in a club toilet or a hushed up un-PC comment. The best I'd come up with were my suspicions about the impact of her infertility on the Foxes' crumbling marriage. A subject more likely to elicit public sympathy than condemnation.

Yes, infertility is, quite rightly, one of those 'triggering' subjects, as you say, so I had to accept I would have to steer clear of it. And yet I could not ignore a gut feeling there was something there I might put to good use. If only I knew what.

Anyway, I desperately needed a wee, so I headed towards the en suite and quite by chance, lifted the edge of the blind on my way. It was then my bleary eyes snapped fully open, a full bladder the least of my worries as I took in what was unfolding at street level.

Directly below me, so close he'd have met my startled gaze if he'd thought to look up, a man in a dark jumper and trousers was wheeling Ris' heavy suitcase up the path, his efforts to bump it up the stone steps distracting him from my presence at the bedroom window. And Ris was right behind the driver. Preoccupied, as always, by her phone. Thank God.

I drew back, scalded, but still rooted to the spot by sheer terror. It was only the sound of a key slotted in the door that jump-started me into action.

To provide some background here, you should know I was wearing a pair of Ris' silk pyjamas and when I looked back at her bed, the evidence of my drunken night was all over it: work laptop with her Insta page open, emptied wine bottle and balloon glass, notebook and pen. The detritus of snacks strewn amongst the tangled duvet and pillows far too much to hide in the moments it would take for Ris to come upstairs. I ran into the en suite where I ripped off the silk pyjamas and wrapped myself in her monogrammed robe. I'm not sure why I felt that was preferable, but I did and I think that was the right call. No time to use the toilet as I heard an exchange of voices on the landing and heavy footfall running back down the stairs before the front door slammed. I cinched the robe and stepped out at the same moment as the bedroom door opened, the silk pjs thrown under a pillow in the very nick of time.

Ris was wheeling her case through the door, palmed phone still distracting her, an agonising pause before she looked up and screamed.

I suppose anyone might have taken a moment to absorb what was in front of their eyes, but it felt like an age before Ris uttered her first word. 'Fuck!!!' Followed swiftly by, 'Gail?!'

My heart was throbbing so hard against the underside of the embroidered robe I was afraid she might hear it, but I also felt the repeated and increasingly urgent need to pee, amplified no doubt by the situation I found myself in, cheeks flaming, sweat sticking the towelling robe to my back. Goodness knows what I must have looked like. Bed-wild hair, lips stained red from the claret, and grinning inanely as if I was happy to see her as I clamped my thighs to assist my weakened pelvic floor.

Her expression darkened as I said something stupidly obvious like I was surprised to see her back, hadn't she been due home a day later?

Ris' initial confusion was lifting, leaving behind unadulterated rage. She dropped the case which fell to the floor with a thud, then stepped over it and, arms folded, demanded to know what the fuck was going on.

I'd messed up. No doubt about that. My idiocy confounding me before I'd begun. I would no doubt be fired, but that might be the least of my concerns. The police would be called, my past catching up with me, another reason I'd hoped for anonymity. But none of that mattered, not really; it was a deep sense of shame and disappointment that felled me. After almost two years of working out a way to establish myself in that house, then finally getting there, everything laid out before me, ready to go, I'd ruined my chances through drunken excess. I was a sixteen-year-old stood before my mother after the school disco, vomit down my new boiler suit, semen in my M&S knickers. Except I was old enough and ugly enough to have known better, and to add to my utter humiliation, I was about to wet myself. A grown woman of fifty-six. Hideous.

My bare exposed feet were twitching, my thighs still pressed hard together, although it was reaching a critical point, my bladder painful. I squeezed tighter as she demanded to know what the fuck was going on. Why was I in her bedroom, in her robe? Had I... 'Oh my God, you slept in my bed, Gail?'

I'd managed to throw the duvet across the bottle and glass as she walked in and slam the laptop shut, but my notebook and pen and the closed laptop were still visible. It was pretty damning. I had no idea what to do or say. I had to think on my feet. And fast.

'Well?' she demanded and it was then I knew I had to run. I pushed past her and darted downstairs, across the hallway and at breakneck speed down the flight of steps to the basement, some pressure already escaping so I could feel the wetness running down my legs. Ris came after me, calling my name, demanding I stop and explain myself, but I couldn't.

I slammed the door to the tiny bathroom and sat down on the toilet not a moment too soon, the relief palpable despite the fact Ris was on the other side of the door hammering hard with a fist and shouting that I better tell her what the fuck was going on or she'd been calling 999.

I took those few moments to think, ignoring her tirade, relieved to have dealt with the immediate issue. And she was being over dramatic. I was her assistant, not an intruder.

I emerged contrite and avoiding eye contact. I was feeling unwell, could I please have a moment to gather myself? Then I would of course, explain.

'I'm not happy, Gail,' she said, stalking out, but then she turned back. 'Five minutes, then come find me. We need to talk. I hope you're OK? It's not catching, is it?'

I assured her it wasn't, then used the time to quickly get dressed and throw the robe in the laundry before I crept up to the master suite again. Ris was in the shower, the bathroom door closed, case thrown on the bed, narrowly avoiding the concealed glass and bottle. I lifted the case to the floor, stripped the bed and gathered up everything in the sheets, running down to throw them in the corner of the laundry where I could deal with them later. I just made it back up as Ris emerged, a towel wrapped tight around her body and another wound turban-like around her hair, lips pressed firm when she saw me at her bedroom door. Brow knotted, she demanded to know what possible explanation there could be for this... gross misconduct.

'You said you were leaving, Gail, when you've clearly been here all weekend! It's... it's unacceptable! Gail?'

She started shouting again, swearing in fact, and even though I was in fight or flight mode, I do recall thinking it was a good thing she had a regular Botox appointment booked. Strange how our brains work in those heightened moments. Off on little trips here and there and taking up valuable space on inconsequential matters. I rather unwisely reiterated that I'd thought she was back the following morning – change of plans? The question did distract her, momentarily, her expression flickering between doubt, sadness, and then back to fury.

She clearly wasn't happy with me – understatement of the year – as she eyed the stripped bed. 'I'll ask again, and you better answer me this time... what is going on?'

Of course, I immediately put paid to any suggestion I'd slept in her room. That would have been game over. No one wants a stranger in their bed. I explained that I had arrived early and been changing the bedding prior to her return, after the make-up mishap when she'd been packing. I'd then felt somewhat unwell after the exertion of my efforts, particularly my energetic scrubbing of the shower. Which was why I'd stripped off. 'You can really only clean a shower properly when you're in it.'

She shook her head in disbelief and pointed out that the cleaners take care of the bedding, and the bathrooms. I was supposed to be in Reading for the weekend. Had I come back early or did I stay the whole weekend? 'You did, didn't you? You were in my robe!!! I deliberately haven't given you a key. It was too soon. All that rubbish about the alarm. It was all lies! You wanted to stay so you did!'

I feigned outrage. 'Do you honestly think I would do such a thing, Ris? You spoke to my previous employer, you saw my employment record, it's unblemished. If you just let me explain...' I was buying time and I think we both knew it.

Ris said nothing, arms folded defensively. Then she barked at me, 'This had better be good, Gail! The truth this time, last chance!'

I muttered something again about coming back early, but I could see it wasn't going to wash. She was right, I had no key. The only logical explanation was that I hadn't left at all.

It was only my acceptance of that which saved me in the end, and the choice of direction I then decided to travel. As suggested, towards the truth. Not all the way, clearly. A full confession would have been disastrous. But I explained that she was right, I didn't leave on Friday night; I couldn't.

It was a risk, but what else could I say? My garbled excuses, even to my own ears, inadequate. She closed her mouth and raised her eyebrows, waiting for me to go on, her body language defensive, bordering on aggressive.

I then confessed I'd been terrified by the possibility the unalarmed house would robbed and it would be my fault for being such an idiot. Almost making her miss her flight when the alarm went off. My fault, of course, as I had been such a dilly leaving. Then she couldn't reset it remotely. Also my fault, of course, but I'd forever blame myself if her beautiful, perfect home was broken into and vandalised. I even invented a story about my penthouse flat in Reading being broken into a month before and how upsetting it had been. Excrement on the new carpet. She baulked at that part of the story and raised her hand to stop me. 'And my robe, and my bed?'

I explained how I'd worked all Saturday in the basement, paying bills and sorting emails. Then once that was done I'd tried to make myself useful around the rest of the house to salve my guilty conscience for still being there, against her express wishes. I emptied the fridge of old food, stripped her foundation-stained bed, or had begun to. Then I was scrubbing the shower because the cleaners never did it properly, did they? And to be honest, I'd felt a bit faint at the end of all that. I'd got so hot and sweaty in the shower. I'd had to rinse myself off too. Menopause, awful.

I even dropped my chin to my chest in a gesture of shame as I apologised for grabbing the nearest thing to hand, her robe, when I heard her come in. It was quite the bravura performance if I do say so myself. 'I'm so sorry for any embarrassment caused. I was so startled by your early return, Ris, as you could no doubt tell. I do hope everything is OK with you and Mr Fox?'

When I dared to look up, her brow was most definitely still furrowed.

Another lecture ensued which I was expected to endure in silence, or with the odd 'mm-mmm' to agree with it all. She hadn't sanctioned a stay; in fact, she'd refused my offer several times. At the very least... the *very* least... I should have let her know. And I shouldn't ever go in her bedroom without her express permission, especially when she wasn't home. I had no cause to be in there, let alone use her shower, unless she invited me into her room. Was that clear?

I apologised, again, and reiterated my social awkwardness that had been such a plus before. Then, heart in mouth, throat pounding, impossible to swallow, I waited for the final verdict. I'd thrown myself on her mercy, explained, apologised, use my age, an invented trauma, but had no idea what she might do or say next, her expression hard to read, my fate once again in her hands.

'The thing is, Gail. I need to trust you, and this is such a huge breach. I honestly don't know if there's a way back from this and it's been such a shitty return after what should have been... I understand you were trying to help, but...'

I nodded, then hung my head again, looking down at my bare feet. I'd pulled on a skirt, blouse, and knickers after I'd used the basement toilet, but hadn't had time for my usual Natural Tan thirty denier. I didn't want to ladder another pair. Easily done when in a panic. But my toenails were shameful, in need of a lot of TLC. I curled them in and noticed the hairs on my big toes. I used to shave them, back in the day, but left untended for several years, they'd got so much worse.

The silence stretched out, and I didn't think it was my place to fill it. But then something unexpected happened.

Ris started to cry. Huge fat tears pouring down her face. Silent at first, then gulping sobs as she threw herself face down onto the stripped bed. I didn't know what to do at first. The mood had changed in an instant and it took me far too long to catch up, but eventually, when the hysterics didn't stop, I stepped over the case, by then opened, contents spilling out, and sat beside her prone figure, tentatively patting her back. I might have also said something comforting; I hope so.

She sniffed and rolled over to face me. 'Sorry, Gail, it's just you asked if everything was OK with Miles and me, and it was, I think, but then he had to leave... yesterday, on business, and I know I should be more understanding, but we spend so much time apart... and now more than ever... I couldn't bear being in that hotel room alone. There's a particular sadness in a suite for one, isn't there?'

I nodded, unsure whether I should comment. Instead, I remained there, beside her, feeling even more awkward. She was sniffing again and rubbing the heel of her hand under her nose.

'God, I'm so hormonal, Gail. I'll be all right in a mo. Are you OK? I didn't even ask. You said you're menopausal. Is it awful? God, what do we girls have to go through, eh? It never stops.'

Without waiting for my response, she went into the bathroom to 'clean up' and emerged, tissue in hand. I asked if she was feeling better.

'Much,' she told me and then launched into a lecture about how next time she'd appreciate my honesty if I had a concern. 'Trust is vital with staff, Gail. You should know that with your years of experience. You can't just... you have to respect my authority, but please do feel free to tell me if you have a problem in the future. I'm not just your boss; we're friends now.'

I sensed it was best to cut my losses and promised to return post-haste with fresh bedding. Always nice, I commented, hopefully quashing any further concerns that I'd slept in the bed myself. The cleaners changed them twice weekly, but Ris probably didn't know that.

She mirrored my parting smile, both of us half-heartedly. It had been a rollercoaster and I was ready to get off but then apropos of nothing she stopped me to say that the weekend had been 'amazing', but Miles had to fly back to the States unexpectedly for a huge project he'd been working on for 'literally' months, that was all. 'Nothing to worry about.'

It felt as though there was, or why make a point of it? But she was then complaining of a headache and needing rest. I said I'd be straight back with the clean sheets. I grabbed what I needed from the cupboard by the study and returned to make up the bed, thankful to find the room empty again, the en suite door closed as I shook out the laundered sheets and pushed in a fresh duvet, my chamber maid days coming in very handy. But then I do find everything in life eventually pays dividends, even the shitty jobs you take just to get by.

Ris emerged as I was finishing, in her favourite pyjamas and with a matching eye mask raised to her forehead, the dressed bed waiting for her, cushions piled high, throw smoothed, hospital corners on the flat sheet. Everything as neat as a pin.

We were fine again. In fact, she looked at me with what might be described as affection as I turned back the covers and patted the spot where she could slide in. I genuinely believe she was pleased to have my companionship, grateful for it even.

Something had wounded her in Paris, their romantic weekend cut short for reasons other than those given, I was sure of it. Anyway, my antics in her absence were clearly now the least of her concerns, any reservations about me set aside as she thanked me for my diligence and although she didn't go so far as to apologise for doubting me, she was much more appreciative than usual. I was still only The Help, but she was glad to have me there, I know that much. She told me so as she closed her eyes and asked me to pull the blinds and switch off the light although it was only eleven thirty in the morning.

* * *

That Sunday proved to be a watershed moment. Her weekend in Paris, and whatever had transpired there – which I would not learn more of until the following morning – coupled with her clear malaise, deepening our bond.

She stayed in bed for hours and complained of a cold when I found her snivelling in the darkness mid-afternoon.

I brought soup on a tray to her, thrown together from store cupboard ingredients. Then when she ventured down to the sitting room in the evening, I rustled up soft poached eggs on toast for supper, her rawness making her ripe for an onslaught of motherly TLC. I gladly smothered her with my care, keen to make up for any lost ground and win back her confidence.

It was an evening of comfortable domesticity, watching a favourite romcom together. A façade, I recognise that, but we both needed it and she lapped it all up. I had no idea what was on the horizon and how much everything was about to change, but that Sunday was an oasis of calm after the storm. Ris tucked up in bed again by ten, me at the kitchen island, coffee before me, triumphant. Not only because of the near-escape and my mastery in slipping out of a tricky situation relatively unscathed, but that despite my lack of specific knowledge, and with only the previous email exchanges to base my theories on, and Ris' low mood, it was becoming increasingly obvious all was not well between husband and wife, the brief reunion in Paris only making matters worse.

When I tapped on her door an hour later to say I was going to bed, I found her properly sobbing into her pillow. She made light of it, said it was the film we'd watched, it always did that to her. Then she patted the bed, taking my hand in both of hers.

She said it had clearly been a shock, finding me at home, but she knew she'd made the right choice, following her gut and appointing me as her EA. She even boasted how she had a good instinct for people; she knew straight away I was the right woman for the job, and we should put it all behind us now. We were a team. Equals. 'Honesty on both sides from now on, though, OK, Gail?'

I bowed out with a genuine smile on my face. Some people really are incredibly stupid, aren't they? And such two-faced liars.

EMAIL SUBJECT: INTERVIEWS WITH GAIL FROST

DATE: WEDNESDAY 19 OCTOBER

Hey, how's things? I hope you are well.

It was so great to catch up by phone the other day and wow, talking scripts and casting ideas already! I mean, I know it's all theoretical, but still so exciting for a newbie like me. Stuff of dreams! I love the idea of a dramatisation of the real events, and the working title!

Just to bring you up to speed, I've been to see Ris today. Or tried to. I called round to Lexington Gardens this morning before work, knocked on the door of number fifty-six. It was tipping it down – great British summer! – so I pushed a card through with a note on the back saying if she ever wants to put her side of the story, I'm the one to talk to as I'm also interviewing Gail. Fingers crossed that rattles her into a response (might have already done so, see below). Bloody horrible weather, like I say, pouring down! And mud all over the step and a skip outside full of rubbish so I guess they are having some work done, just not answering the door. Although there's a small window of etched glass in the door, and I swear I saw someone pick up the card.

I've also caught up with Veronique, Ris' personal trainer. She's a hoot, would be a great talking head on camera if we go that route, although she's concerned about breaking client confidentiality which is clearly important in her line of business. Kept quoting these weird 'manifestations' to me from a journal she keeps of clients' progress – would love to have a peek at that! Even tried to sign me up to one of her bootcamps and is spamming me with emails about it.

I'll keep in touch with her, and of course needle away at Ris because I'd imagine she must want the chance to dispel a few rumours that do not want to go away. Although, I also suspect it's Miles Fox who is silencing her. Especially as I'd had a delivery whilst I spent a soggy morning in a field on magazine work! I don't know for sure the package was from Ris; it came anonymously. Delivered to me at the magazine's offices in Soho. Padded envelope, handwritten to me. I've interrogated the intern who helpfully has no recollection of which company, if any, delivered it, just that it was a woman, so I can't even follow-up that way. But it feels like a bit of a coincidence after my card was pushed through this morning, wouldn't you say?

The envelope contained a diary – well, at least the torn pages from what I assume was once a diary. Bit mixed up, chronologically, and some entries are of no interest, but I'll sift through them all when I get chance. They're handwritten and illegible in places but I'll do my best. I've attached the first transcribe to kick things off. See what you think. No names mentioned, but wow, the author, whomever she is, is certainly a woman scorned! And after that card was picked up, with my work address on, I'm assuming it's a safe bet to assume Ris sent the pages? The woman who wrote the diary and then 'kindly' shared it with her lover's wife, if my theory about Ris is correct, sounds younger than Ris, mid-twenties at a guess, cabin crew, so presumably glamorous… certainly amorous. All a bit galling to receive, I'd imagine. Especially as Ris is probably feeling very unglamorous and extremely vulnerable as a new mother. And Gail has hinted *Hubs* has a wandering eye and that a Paris trip was cut short so he could catch a flight to the US. I don't think it's a huge leap to assume Ris' suspicions were correct and he was leaving Paris to be with the woman who wrote the diary, the author sending Ris this account to taunt her into finally confronting him? If so, I'm hoping the fact Ris sent these pages to me means she will soon want to talk about not only her husband's affair (interesting background, but not really our focus) but also the conspiracy theories and Gail's wild claims. It all comes down to the revelations that came out the night of the book launch party, which of course I'm dying to ask Gail about, but she is adamant her story will be told in her own way, and in her own sweet time. If I have to spend many more Sundays in that damp basement drinking weak tea made with mouldy teabags… But the price of getting to the truth where others haven't, I suppose. I need to win her trust.

Let's catch up soon! I know you're juggling projects, as always, but nice place to be.

Best wishes,

Ax

DIARY ENTRY #1

Cologne wafts towards me as the passengers move through the cabin to take their seats. The lucky ones in the first few rows have leather recliners so they will be able to lie flat after meal service and close their tired eyes. First Class is a much preferable option for them, but also us, the cabin crew. The rammed section at the rear of the plane not my responsibility for this flight, thank God. I feel I've earned the easier ride after months in the dreaded Economy. Not that I'm in charge today; that dubious honour falls to my male colleague, Perry, who grins an insincere welcome to every passenger as they file past. All except one, who receives Perry's most dazzling welcome.

'Miles Fox,' Perry whispers after the handsome man in a pale-blue shirt and linen jacket has barely taken three steps down the aisle to his privileged place. 'Fox Hotels. Work your charms, dah-ling. I am not queuing again to be turned away at the door of Mr Fox's oh-so exclusive new Greenwich Village club. I have a feeling I'll have more than earned a New York night out after this flight.'

Boarding complete, Perry makes the usual checks, a lewd gesture behind Miles' back indicating I should do whatever it takes to get those VIP passes.

Perry's attention is then turned to the newlyweds who've called him over. They were bumped up from Economy and plan on making the most of it by the looks of them.

Perry's performance has made me smile, which then catches Miles Fox's attention as he stands to remove his jacket. I step forward and offer to hang up the silk-lined, pale beige, checking the label as I slip it onto a wooden hanger in the galley. A make I've never heard of, but clearly expensive. Mr Fox is tucking his shirt in when I return, his stomach flat in a tailored, crisp, cotton shirt. He catches my stare, letting me off with a quick smile, raking his broad hand through his hair, the kind of foppish move that only works in conjunction with a ten-grand watch and a light tan, his skin pale gold. He's good looking, but oh doesn't he know it. I force myself to stop staring and turn back to the galley. Losing myself in my work.

After boarding is complete, Miles Fox accepts a hot towel as I proffer it, tongs poised. So much theatre in First, but that's what the passengers love: the notion of a hierarchy. Priority boarding, attentive staff, the swish of a red curtain. His blue eyes hold my gaze long enough for Perry to notice.

'So?' Perry asks, taking the fold-down seat beside me for take-off.

I shake my head. 'I'm married, remember?'

'Well, I'm hardly his type, dahling,' Perry says, nudging me in the ribs as the engines roar. 'But I'll do my best.'

Fellow crew's antics are always a good antidote to the tedium of long-haul. But in all honesty, I'm not in the mood today. And Miles Fox's trendy club isn't my idea of relaxation. I'd been relieved when we were turned away last time. Head pounding with the jet lag I never quite get on top of, my body clock screaming that it was almost morning at home, feet aching in heels and the return flight only twenty-four hours away. So much has happened in the last month, and none of it good. Although it's been a long time coming: the end of my marriage.

'He's not anyone's type,' I reply as we leave Heathrow. 'Happily married, I believe.'

'Well, married, at least,' Perry observes. 'Have you seen his wife? Hard-faced bitch.'

We start drinks service as soon as the seat belt sign goes off, Perry's first port of call Miles Fox, the newlyweds ignored as Perry takes his time chatting to the man he believes holds the VIP passes, whilst I have to pick up his slack. I set up the tables in the galley and cover them with white cloths. The tables have wheels but are a nightmare to pull through the cabin and anyway, its more personal to serve the food individually.

I move through the passengers, handing out menu cards. When I reach Miles Fox, I pause, waiting for him to decide between boeuf bourguignon and pasta. The coverage of his wedding a few years back comes to mind. I love the glossy mags, read them avidly – they're good research too, we get loads of celebrities on board – but why that wedding has remained with me, even vaguely, I'm not sure. Maybe it was the bride's dress? Not to my taste at all, the posed images showcasing her more than the groom, which I guess is usual. All that fussy lace and the dress was very low-cut – not what I'd have chosen. And there was something else about her I didn't like, beyond the dress: a smugness I think, whilst he seemed much more approachable. She was hard-faced, as Perry said, even as she smiled for the camera. Although isn't that kind of coverage considered the kiss of death to any relationship? Tempting fate. Must have been her choice; not like they needed the money. Miles Fox is opening up hotels and clubs all over the world. Whilst his wife is one of those 'mildly famous for being famous' types.

I've always had a fascination with the ultra-rich. Wondering whether I'd be happier if I had limitless wealth or be much the same. I'd still have worries, I guess. But would it be better? Probably, particularly at the moment. Where I'll live once the house is sold, I have no idea. It's a definite concern.

'I'll take the seafood pasta, thanks,' Miles tells me, the easy charm that only successful, handsome men find effortless cutting through my thoughts of home and what's going on whilst I'm away. The house half-empty by my return. Miles' good looks are distracting though. I return the smile. God, what am I like?

'Let me know if you need anything else, Mr Fox.'

A beat as he reads my name badge aloud, then tells me, 'Call me Miles.'

He works for an hour. Then he sleeps, eye mask on. A handsome repose. No drooling like my soon-to-be-ex. The thought jars, like a false step in a dream that wakes you up with a start, a heavy heart when you remember why you are sad. It's not like it isn't what we've both agreed, but there's a hole in my life I need to fill. And not just the furniture he'll have taken. I'm used to being part of a couple. I don't want to go back to ready meals for one or dating. I want to fast-forward to the dream I've recently lost.

I'm in the galley when Miles Fox passes me on his way to the bathroom, flashing me that smile again, igniting a wick I'd thought my failed marriage had burned down. A low hum set alight, warmth spreading from within; a dull ache, forgotten feelings.

It happens of course: casual encounters between passengers and crew. Both thousands of miles from home – as if that offers a guilt-free pass – but that's never been my style. I guess there have been happy endings to those hook-ups – if cabin crew gossip is to be believed – but it's always struck me as a sordid way to begin a romance. Although I must admit the attention is nice. Been a while since I had that flutter in my stomach, cabin-bloating the usual extent of it. The wide-girthed businessmen I regularly fend off hardly tempting. But Miles Fox is in good shape.

I am facing away from the aisle, serving coffee, when he places a warm palm in the well of my back. I step aside to allow him to retake his seat and he thanks me, eyes bright despite the recycled air, his breath close enough to inhale, pleasant and yet earthy. I offer him a coffee and he declines, asks for a top-up of his mineral water if it's no trouble? He's a pro, knows it's important to stay hydrated and keep alcohol and caffeine to a minimum, unlike the honeymoon couple behind him who are still making the most of the free bar. Their behaviour borders on offensive. Time to cut off the supply.

The newlyweds laugh raucously as I approach. Miles raises an eyebrow and I return the gesture conspiratorially. They'll burn themselves out soon, sleep the second half of the journey. I lean in to share this, but the buck of the plane as we hit turbulence is unsteadying. Miles grabs me, my wrist pleasurably gripped by his strong hand. We're so close I can smell his skin. That expensive cologne. An image of his fingers running through my hair flashes past.

'I'm sorry, Mr Fox,' I tell him, straightening up. 'Just turbulence. Better fasten your seat belt.'

'I told you, call me Miles. And yes, it's fine,' he says, clipping the belt across his lap as I attempt to avert my gaze. 'I'm a frequent flyer.'

A call from two rows back jolts me out of the moment. Perry is gesturing to a scowling businessman at his side. American, rude, done nothing but complain. I've neglected 7B, but Perry gets paid more than me for just this kind of shit.

Later, I will realise this is where it began. These small lapses in my usual conscientiousness that led to larger ones. Resentments building amongst colleagues who are looking for opportunities to leapfrog me to promotion. But as I walk towards Perry and 7B, all I can think of is Miles Fox, watching me from behind. I know he is. And I can't help but smile, and sashay, just a little. Sensing where it may lead.

10

FOURTH INTERVIEW WITH GAIL FROST – SUNDAY 23 OCTOBER

I suppose at this point it's worth discussing Ris' infamous troll.

Everyone who is anyone apparently has one, and Ris was no exception. In fact, she had her fair share of critics, but Becca stood out as the most prolific, and also the most insightful.

Becca2004xxx as she was known on Instagram, certainly knew how to push the right buttons. More than once I found Ris distraught after reading Becca's comments. Which makes it especially ironic that the mysterious troll became a kind of anti-hero, revered in some quarters – and by that I mean the darkest recesses of the web where conspiracists ply their wares – known for being the first to call Ris out.

Yes, there are obvious comparisons to be drawn between Becca and I, which I would strenuously resist. We were saying much the same things about Ris, granted, but the ways we went about it were entirely different. When I spoke up, I did so in a respectful manner, sticking to the facts, and yet I am vilified as the ultimate backstabber, my claims discounted. Although the tide may be turning.

And yes, I was aware of the trolling long before I met Ris. It would be hard to miss, even on a cursory tour round Ris' social media platforms. She certainly had her detractors, but Becca stood out as the harshest and the most prolific. Especially towards the end.

I can't recall specific examples – I tended to skim over the comments – but most of the early stuff I saw, after Ris met and married Miles, was aimed at her appearance – that she wasn't ageing well, she was too thin, a fake bitch – and grumbles about the unfairness of her good fortune. It was all reflecting what many would have thought, myself included, I hold my hands up to that, but to reiterate... I am not a troll.

I prefer to keep my head well below the parapet. Which hasn't been easy of late, but as you no doubt have seen, my social media profile is non-existent. Not like Becca, always piping up whilst hiding behind that fuzzy profile picture, her input increasingly unpleasant, especially after Ris publicly announced her 'Big News'.

It was early on the Monday morning, the day after Ris returned early from that fateful Paris trip, when the first hint of trouble began. We'd had our perfect Sunday together after the shock of her early return had subsided, and I'd expected us to fall back into the routine I'd learnt the previous working week: Veronique, protein shakes, a whizz round Knightsbridge, that kind of thing. And despite my frustration at not finding anything helpful to my cause, matters had moved on to a certain extent. I'd gained access to Ris' bank account, for example. Not that I would abuse that privilege, quite the reverse, but I was feeling more comfortable financially, and with the job; settling in for the long game as a new week began.

I was waiting for Ris to trip up, I suppose, which I knew she would, given enough rope. The signs were already there. I just never expected it would happen so soon.

I'm an early riser as a rule, and my mind was too active to sleep in as late as Ris often did. So I took my coffee – instant, all I had – into the small courtyard garden, bare feet on the cobbles, the magnolia dripping with delicate creamy petals painted pink at their core. I recall them so clearly, their appearance as if the branches had bled into them, capillaries cut. They would soon wither and the petals swim to the ground, the fallen blooms becoming a nuisance; collecting in browning heaps, the brick walls too high for them to be carried away on the breeze, but I did love them. And the garden.

The walls are at least ten feet high, and somewhat claustrophobic in that small space. I would sometimes look up to the vertiginous top floor terrace and wonder if Ris had really climbed over the railings as she had claimed when she'd taken me up there, imagining which wall she'd hit if she fell or if she'd land amongst the branches. But that bright sunny Monday morning the soft petals brushed my feet like velvet as I sat at the small metal table beneath the huge tree, a welcome distraction whilst I raked over the near-miss I'd had with Ris less than twenty-four hours before. I was no doubt torturing myself: the usual self-flagellation. Not that I'm religious, but I do have an unfortunate tendency to worship at the church of What Ifs. I didn't used to be so guilt-ridden, but there we go... older but apparently no wiser. And I was, as always whilst at Lexington Gardens, somewhat on-edge. Much as I coveted that house, absorbed its energy, it was never my home, although I hate to admit to that, even now.

It had been raining overnight, that April mizzle that settles on everything. I'd had to take a hand towel and wipe down the wooden slats of the folding chair before taking a seat, phone then raised, and squinting against both my short-sightedness and the early haze as I scrolled Ris' Instagram page. Little did I know what was waiting for me there.

Ris would often post updates late at night, long after I'd gone to bed. Then I'd be up early and she would sleep in so I would use that time, before Veronique's arrival, to catch up on Ris' late-night online activity. Which is when I first saw the infamous Paris Ritz photo.

You must be familiar?

The romantic trip had already been voraciously chronicled by Ris of course, her posts popping up from the moment she left the house on the Friday night. As if we cared about her pre-flight Bellini and the book she was going to read. I suppose some people did, the boomerang of her cheers-ing thin air in the First Class lounge somewhat ironic, and not a mention of her abrupt return.

It was therefore with little initial interest that I clicked on this new image of the happy couple outside The Ritz. In fact, I almost didn't spot it, lost amongst the myriad others as I swiped through the collection of Mr and Mrs Fox wrapped around one another, or rather Ris wrapped around him, his greying hair a reminder that they were twenty years and a million miles apart. The chasm between the reality of their separate lives and those romantic snaps, frankly laughable.

Anyway, this particular pose must have been captured on the Saturday – some passing Parisian commandeered or maybe the hotel staff were persuaded to help – the outfits matching with others from that day she'd already posted... the usual tourist traps, Miles not featured that heavily, Ris as always, the focus. But unlike the other sporadic and staged moments of marital bliss which had been received by her followers with enthusiasm, this was causing a flurry of wider attention. It certainly grabbed mine, my coffee stone-cold by the time I gave my abandoned mug a second thought. Because if the photo was announcing what I thought it was, this would change everything.

The tabloids used it a lot. The cream canopy of the hotel behind

Ris and Miles, the iconic gold insignia of The Ritz above their heads.

I remember that logo from years before when Princess Diana stayed there with Dodi. The grainy CCTV of them in the tiny lift, Diana's Sloaney blazer and slacks, the trademark blonde flicky hair. So poignant after what was about to happen in that Paris tunnel. She had class, that woman. Unlike Ris, who had so clearly orchestrated the whole scene. Her bony bejewelled hand falling to her stomach in a classic 'I'm pregnant!' pose.

I gasped when I saw it, unable to compute the full impact at first.

Miles was looking directly at her, his overcoat undone, head inclined towards his wife, both of them smiling, his grey hair mingling with her dark wind-blown locks, a red scarf at his neck, also tugged by the breeze. Clearly oblivious to his wife's straying hand and the lie it conveyed.

Oh yes, I knew straight off it was a lie.

She wasn't pregnant, despite that well placed hand. I'd spent the weekend trawling her search history, remember? Infertility, surrogacy, adoption... and the tampons she took with her? I hadn't forgotten those...

I was blindsided for a minute or two, though, I'll admit that. Panicked by the thought it may be true. A pregnancy would make Ris untouchable. There was no way I could discredit her if she was carrying a hard-won child. She would be reborn. Respectable, deserving, not least because of their struggles to conceive. The failed cycles of IVF already shared, as was the 'sad' conclusion to that journey, on her content-hungry feed. This news would be a triumph, offering hope to other women in her position.

All the possibilities ran through my head as I'm sure they do yours now. Of course they did. Could there be an explanation for those searches? Maybe she'd come back with a full box of tampons? Their inclusion in her suitcase merely a precaution?

Perhaps that pose meant nothing at all? A slip of the hand. Although the inference was clear. Especially as the caption read, #TheBestNews!

I abandoned my coffee and dressed quickly, pacing the basement. Ris would usually send a message to my work phone when she was ready for me, but it was almost time for her session with Veronique and my patience had worn thin. I only had a small window in which to raise my increasing concerns, and how I might do that I honestly had no idea. I mean, how do you ask if someone is pregnant? It's such a no-no and could be taken as a huge insult by someone as body conscious as Ris. And you have to remember I'd already messed up with her only the day before. I couldn't afford to do so again. Not so soon.

I found Ris at the kitchen island, still in her pyjamas. The cleaners working around her. Which was all very odd. She rarely ventured downstairs before her post-workout smoothie. Also, despite her late night – I'd heard her prowling the house above me in the early hours – she appeared to be wide awake and visibly upset. None of which did anything to calm my racing nerves. Thoughts of morning sickness crossed my mind. Although the half-empty bottle of wine on the island and lipstick-stained glass the cleaner whisked away spoke of a rather different evening than one which might befit the early stages of a pregnancy. Some reassurance.

I ignored the pink tabarded cleaners, as did Ris, and enquired if she was OK, although plainly she was not. She wiped her nose with the heel of her hand, a rather disgusting habit of hers, and sniffed, eyes red and puffy as she claimed a brewing virus. She'd cancelled Veronique, she told me. 'Not feeling up to it today, Gail.'

I shooed the persistent cleaners out and closed the kitchen door before asking if she needed a doctor, was she sure it was just a virus? It was a ridiculous question; she no more had a cold than I did. I was fishing of course, hoping and also dreading the confirmation of what the photo so clearly indicated; her hand placement, plus smiling face, and the caption, #TheBestNews leaving little if any doubt. That's certainly the meaning taken by everyone who'd left a comment.

Ris shook her head and closed her laptop. 'I actually don't think it's a cold, Gail.'

My heart dropped to the base of my stomach, if that's a thing. It certainly felt like it was. I'd convinced myself it must be a lie, but the prospect it might not be taunted me. She patted the stool beside her and opened up her Mac. I couldn't have been more desperate to know, or afraid to hear.

She swivelled the screen towards me, the Ritz photo filling the central square. And I'll never forget what she said: 'I thought it was a good idea when I posted this last night, Gail, but Miles is furious!!!'

She trailed off then, her expression hard to read although she'd stopped crying, her hand covering her mouth. I think she'd given away more than she meant to. And for the record, I believe she knew exactly what she was doing when she allowed her hand to fall to her stomach for that photo. And she also knew what she was doing, despite the wine, when late on Sunday night, still smarting from her husband's abandonment of her twenty-fours before, she went ahead and posted the photo she'd previously held back, with the caption, #TheBestNews! In fact, I'd go so far as to call it entrapment.

It didn't stop Miles leaving her in Paris, no, but that was the battle lost, not the war. She was just getting started.

I asked her outright if the photo was announcing what it seemed to be, but it was as if she wasn't listening, her attention held by the increasing number of likes and comments. Her number of followers similarly rising. But I had to know for certain. So I asked again. What was the best news? I'd love to know. Were congratulations in order? I think it was a fair question as I was her right-hand woman. It would have affected me too, in regard to my future employment.

She blew her nose and wiped under her eyes, her finger touching the place on screen where her hand had tenderly cradled her midriff, and then she looked at me, any trace of a cold or tears most definitely gone, and after a split-second's hesitation, she smiled.

The deception, I'm sorry to say, had begun in earnest. And oddly, I think she was already believing her own lies.

11

FOURTH INTERVIEW WITH GAIL FROST – SUNDAY 23 OCTOBER

As you can imagine, I have plenty of theories about that photo and Ris' decision to share it. Her distress when I found her in the kitchen that Monday morning, simply a case of remorse after realising the huge impact of what she'd done.

There was certainly no doubt she'd been drinking when she posted the photo and accompanying caption #TheBestNews the night before, the wine bottle and glass still there on the kitchen island the next morning. Hardly the right message if she was hoping to convince me of a pregnancy. But she didn't care about my opinion, did she? She was hung-over and regretful, *Hubs'* anger at what she'd shared with her followers a contributing if not major factor in her distress. What I thought was of no more import to Ris than the opinion of those nameless, faceless cleaners working around her.

Interesting then that she chose neither to confirm nor deny the announcement, either to me or her followers. Quite the reverse, in fact. She revelled in the attention her ambiguity courted. The speculation as well as the huge number of likes and comments both gratifying and I'd imagine terrifying in equal measure. A behemoth unleashed. Her sly smiles as she scrolled through them distasteful on an empty stomach. I left her to it, commenting sardonically that I hoped her cold, or whatever it was, was soon gone. Not that she heard.

I kept a very close eye on the Insta post after that, enthralled when the caption #TheBestNews! was removed an hour later, although the photo stayed up. I think it's fair to assume *Hubs* asked her to remove the caption, if not the post. She'd said he was furious and he's known to be an intensely private man. It was an absolute joke, but in the worst taste.

That's all it was meant to be initially, there's no doubt in my mind. A prank. Another of Ris' cries for help after her husband's early departure from their romantic weekend. A provocation. Revenge. Call it whatever you like... I don't pretend to understand what would make her behave so childishly, but clearly she was desperate.

I was also desperate... to ask more, but I had no means to question her further without risking another fallout. That enigmatic smile was the only answer I was going to get for now. But it didn't add up, not any of it: the recently purchased box of tampons she'd so carefully concealed in her packing for Paris, the continued and excessive drinking, her admittance her husband was furious, and the declaration of previous infertility. Not to mention the subsequent retraction of the caption, and that inconclusive smile she offered me to a direct and obvious question as well as her silence online. I was keeping a rising tally of evidence in my notepad. For a woman who'd declared herself infertile and barely saw her husband, it was nothing short of a miracle.

If she'd just told *Hubs* the news of a longed-for pregnancy, in Paris, the city of love, wouldn't he have wanted to stay there with her, whatever his plans, to celebrate the happiest of news in such a romantic location?

But of course it wouldn't have been the happiest of news, would it? Not for him. The marriage was all but over. He was furious.

And let's not forget Ris was paranoid about the possibility of another woman, and maybe she had good cause. He had left his first wife to be with her; why wouldn't he tire of her in the same way? The writing was on the wall.

They both looked joyful in the photo, but appearances, of course, can be deceptive. I know better than most, the camera almost always lies.

The possibility the news was real, however, still tortured me that Monday morning, despite my gut feeling she was lying and the evidence I'd amassed. I paced the basement until I was summoned at last by a WhatsApp.

Ris was in her study, seated at her desk and staring at her Mac, stroking the trackpad with one hand, the other laid across her lap, echoing her pose in Paris. My gaze fell to her stomach, washboard flat in a close-fitting jersey dress, but yes, women do show in different ways and she hadn't said how far along she was supposed to be. I was thinking of asking just that when she tapped the trackpad, a pointed nail then drawing my attention to a particular comment under the Paris photo. I leant over her shoulder and read the reply to the post.

Becca2004xxx Food baby I'm guessing? Or is it twins? Only joking!!! You're positively anorexic, hun!

Why Ris highlighted that to me, I'm unsure. We all tend to focus on the negative, ignoring praise, that's true, but it was a peculiar move. Like the killer returning to the scene of the crime; flaunting their deceit. Irresistible perhaps?

Becca's obvious inference was that #The Best News! was not what it appeared to be. And that gave me hope. And validation. If I wasn't the only one doubting Ris' word, then surely my gut feeling was correct and she was making it all up, the photo an elaborate hoax that would likely soon backfire. Which would be incredibly helpful.

What had felt like game over could in fact be game on. It was a horrible thing to pretend to be pregnant, and we all know posts can never truly be removed. They live on in screenshots and memes. *Forever.*

I played along, of course, asked Ris what she was going to do about Becca's comment; said it was a terrible thing to say. Ris pulled a face and gave a shrug of disinterest. I couldn't fathom her reaction at first, but then I saw the pile-on from her fans who'd rushed to defend her. Ris was awash in it, the support bringing a genuine smile to her lips. I urged Ris to report Becca, get the account removed. 'That's slander or libel or something, isn't it?'

It seemed the obvious move, but she told me, 'Never feed the trolls, Gail. My lovely followers are dealing with her, look!'

There were more supportive responses arriving even as we talked, many of them congratulating Ris on her fabulous news despite the fact she'd still confirmed nothing. The consequences were ballooning with each new engagement. It wouldn't take long for word to spread beyond social media. The pregnant former cocktail waitress turned wife of a multi-millionaire was surely worthy of a few column inches in the worst of the British press? If Ris was lying, as both Becca and I agreed she was, it was going to become hugely messy. Not least with her 'furious' husband. If I ever felt sorry for Ris, which I didn't, then that would have been the moment. But she was enjoying her fans' defence of her far too much for me to experience more than a modicum of sympathy for the time bomb she'd set ticking.

I could have said more. Drawn up a chair at her desk and used Becca's comments as a start point for a heart-to-heart. Maybe we would have dealt with it together, another exercise in bonding, but why on earth would I? It was the stroke of luck I'd been praying for. I was hardly going to help her fill back in the hole she'd so successfully begun digging, was I? It was a golden opportunity. And I was sure by then that she had invented the whole thing.

Although, I still had my moments of indecision to come. I'll admit that.

Had I extrapolated the evidence I'd found to fit my desired outcome?

Was there a reasonable explanation for it all?

I questioned my thinking just as you do again now. As any reasonable person would. But I remained, and still do, convinced. She duped everyone, except me. And Becca. And few of her less vocal but doubting followers. But worst of all, she'd also duped her husband. The conflicted but well-meaning father-to-be. What a terrible thing to do to the person you claim to love.

Ris was still scrolling through the comments, smiling at the encouraging words and emoticons totting up. She was even starting to quote the more complimentary replies, whilst I was feeling sick to my stomach and keen to leave the study. Dishonesty has never sat well with me, and the quotes she chose to read aloud were especially saccharin.

You're so slim, Ris. Wish I had your figure.

You two, so in love, what a cute pose!

Hardly Shakespeare, or even that genuine in my opinion, but she loved them all. It was her blind spot: attention, engagement, flattery. She craved it. Maybe stemming from her childhood? Not exactly tragic, but dysfunctional. But then whose isn't? And there comes a point in adulthood where you have to move on. Accept that your parents, as Larkin said, fuck you up, but that you are a grown woman with agency and choices. Although I don't blame Ris for cutting her mother out of her life, and I suppose that goes some way to explain why she increasingly looked to me, an older woman, for support in her time of need, but the fandom-thing was very sycophantic. I was disappointed she fell for it. I was there for her, admittedly with my own agenda, but the only one physically by her side. She never gave me credit for that; no one did.

Ris closed the laptop with force, halting me at the door with a comment about how the press loved to resurrect all the old stories from when she'd met Miles. 'His marriage to Trudy was already over when we fell madly in love. I'm not a homewrecker, Gail.'

Her mind had gone where mine had; the press getting hold of the news. Then she said the most curious thing. 'I guess the fact we don't have kids is my punishment for stealing him away.'

An admission of the lie at last? I took it as such, the inference clearly that she wasn't pregnant. I honestly don't see how you can read it in any other way, although people have. Saying it was her voicing what she feared the press would say. That I was the liar, twisting her meaning when she was only referencing the long and arduous journey to motherhood. I neither saw nor heard it that way. Quite the reverse. It sounded as though the struggle was ongoing rather than recently overcome. I was about to drill down into that, maybe even work up to a more definitive, 'But this is a happy ending, isn't it?' when she announced she was feeling crap and going back to bed. Our tête-à-tête concluded on her terms, of course, as always. She pushed past me, forcing me to step aside.

I reminded her as she went upstairs that she had a four o'clock meeting at the publishing house, which surprisingly had slipped her mind. She'd been looking forward to it ever since the previous Wednesday when it was arranged, excited to see her publicist's plans for her beauty and lifestyle bible, *Being Ris*, which was due out in a few weeks' time. She stopped mid-step, brow furrowed as she hesitated, then she asked me to arrange a car and wake her half an hour before it arrived.

I'd thought that was it, conversation over, but she paused again, leaning over the banister to address me in that cloying tone she adopted when she wanted something. 'It would be so nice if you could come with me, Gail. Into the meeting, I mean. For moral support.'

* * *

The taxi was early but Ris was late, although I'd woken her as requested. It was five to four when she finally appeared and despite the gorgeous outfit, skinny jeans, and a loose cream silk blouse, Ris looked like death. I asked if she'd rather cancel, I was genuinely concerned, but she pulled on a pair of Ugg boots – although it was the second week in April and sunny – then slid on oversized sunglasses and a beautiful camel cashmere coat and walked out the door ahead of me.

At a quarter past four we were still sitting in traffic along Victoria Embankment, Ris pasty and unkempt, chewing gum and tapping on her phone, the Paris photo on screen. The likes and comments were stretching down the page by then. Something she remarked upon in the rare moments she spoke on that tiresome journey. I still couldn't work her out. Was she ever going to address mine and her followers' obvious question? It was hanging there, the elephant in the black cab. The pregnancy suggested heavily, but still not confirmed. Despite the many, 'Are you pregnant?' comments.

Becca had upped her game and in her inimitable style hit the nail on the head.

Becca2004xxx So, tell us, Ris, you preggers or just a lying fake skinny bitch?

* * *

At the publishers' offices, a tall gleaming glass building overlooking the river, we were shown by Fleur, Ris' publicist, to a small round table in the meeting 'hub' on the top floor. The room was unbearably hot as the late afternoon sun penetrated the tinted windows and flooded the cramped space. Despite the heat, Ris was still wrapped up in her coat and wearing the oversized dark glasses which made her appear appropriately diva-ish, especially as she said nothing as the introductions were made. The fourth seat taken by the book's editor, Phoebe.

Then Ris excused herself to use the bathroom. And when I say excused, she stood up and left the room with barely a word.

The whole meeting was turning into a nightmare before it had begun, especially as we'd arrived so late.

Fleur – a very sweet girl who wore floral dresses and white trainers and had fabulous hair – did her best to inject some positivity into proceedings as we waited for Ris to come back, but after fifteen minutes the question was raised of whether she was maybe unwell? Or if she might have left the building? Phoebe made her excuses at that point, apparently called away to another meeting, but I suspect her patience with Ris had finally run out. I was about to go and check on Ris, maybe suggest we reconvene another day, when she returned, wordlessly taking her seat and inserting fresh gum. Glasses and coat still on, snapping at me that she was fine. 'Just fine.'

I wonder now, looking back, if Ris had an inkling beforehand that the meeting would be tricky, and that's why she'd wanted me there. But I don't think the book factored into her posting the news on Insta. She'd forgotten the meeting was happening until I reminded her, remember? And the bathroom visits were on account of a heavy period, I'm sure of that now. Well, as sure as I can be.

Anyway, Fleur started to explain that a very similar beauty and lifestyle book was publishing the same day as Ris', and the sales of *Being Ris* were likely to be cannibalised by the competing title. Why they couldn't co-exist was discussed, as well as the fact this hadn't been mentioned to Ris before, but the gist was this other 'author', and I use that term lightly, was a bigger celebrity, her claim to fame being that she'd shagged a fellow contestant on an awful reality show the previous summer which to my shame I had watched, appalled. Ris petulantly pointed out, 'My platform is huge. Over a hundred thou on Insta and growing by the day. And I have a blue tick on Twitter.' Ris' phone pinged with alarming regularity throughout the entire thirty minutes or so we were in that vivarium. And with no sign of Ris muting it, or her dedicated followers leaving her alone, the atmosphere, as you can imagine, grew increasingly tense.

Ris would only occasionally glance up, capturing Fleur's wide-eyed smile and my scowl reflected in her dark glasses; two silent observers to the carnage unfolding somewhere in the ether as she fed the ravenous monster. God knows how she saw anything on her screen with those shades on, but she must have. I checked later and she'd been posting comments the whole time we were in that meeting.

And I have to say, Ris really didn't look well: shifting in her seat, a hand occasionally straying from her phone to rest protectively on her stomach. I was beginning to worry that if she *was* pregnant – a possibility I did not believe in but still could not entirely rule out – then should I insist we leave? Get her to a doctor? If it turned out she was suffering an early miscarriage and I had ignored that... the potential consequences flustered me. I felt responsible for her as the more mature party in the room.

Fleur also appeared concerned. She must have seen Ris' Paris Ritz post on Insta. Most likely before the caption was removed. It was part of her job, keeping an eye on her clients' social media. All this was running through my head as I sat there, boiling in my raincoat – nervous of the kerfuffle I might cause if I stood to take it off – and contributing little other than offering the occasional encouraging smile. I still had no concrete confirmation of what was going on either in Ris' uterus or her head. All I knew was I was extremely hot and bothered.

Fleur, bless her, then threw Ris a bit of rope and conceded that 'Yes, 100K is a nice number' but it wasn't going to be enough, unfortunately. 'Not on its own.' To which I nodded, regretting my allegiance as Ris shot me a look.

Fleur tried her best to explain. 'It's about being current, Ris, hitting the zeitgeist of those key demographics in such a competitive market.' The words felt second-hand, no doubt gifted by the now absent Phoebe. It was crunch time. Do or die. 'The Brand', and I suspected therefore also the book's future success, hanging in the balance.

In what I can only imagine was utter desperation Fleur then turned to me and asked if I had any thoughts. I certainly had nothing of value to contribute, but I unwisely began to broker a more peaceable discussion, looking for positives, if any. What might I do to help? Were there other avenues we could explore? Ris stopped tapping her phone and again looked up, finally removing her dark glasses and surveying me with a less than complimentary gaze. Her eyes were red and puffy and the faux smile did not reach them. I took my cue to shut up and sat back.

It was so important to Ris, that meeting, or at least it had been. The book meant everything; she'd already planned its launch, or rather her look for the launch, down to the minutest of details. Dress, hair, nails, a total 'glow up' as she called it, everything described to me ad nauseam from the moment we began working together. Press had been invited and influential bloggers. So why the stonewalling when all Fleur wanted was something fresh she could use to promote the book? And Ris had exactly that to offer. What was going on in Ris' head? The answer to that of course was that she didn't have anything. Except a lie that was already so out of hand, she was terrified by it.

Ris put her dark glasses back on and Fleur gamely picked up the baton, choosing her words even more carefully. 'Well, it's of course totally your call where you draw the line between private and public, Ris. That has to be your choice. But we do need something new, something different. Any thoughts? This book is very much about you. Your face, beauty regime, body issues...'

The elephant loomed again, and larger than ever, taking up all the space in that stuffy glass office. Fleur was so obviously referencing #TheBestNews! and Ris finally took the plunge, removing the glasses again and asking, 'Would it make any difference... if I... engaged with the speculation?'

I suppose in that response, even before Fleur had replied, Ris had made her choice, one that she had been pondering in her silence, the potential consequences of it huge. But she was fearful of losing so much. Book sales, of course, but more than that, much more... her sense of self, and most importantly, her marriage.

It was total idiocy, of course. A short-term solution to a long-term problem that I had no doubt would come back to haunt her, and soon. Another enigmatic smile her offering, for now, the glasses back on.

Fleur smiled, reiterating that Ris mustn't to do anything she wasn't comfortable with. It was her call, totally her decision. We both looked at Ris: impenetrable. All I could see was my own unflattering reflection. I have no idea what was going through Ris' mind, the bomb ticking louder than ever.

We left soon after, Ris walking ahead of me and not so much as a goodbye to Fleur which was horribly rude. Fleur was a sweet girl who'd done nothing unprofessional at all. I had a quick word with her before I left, a mini heart-to-heart whilst Ris went to the bathroom again, some motherly advice I know was helpful.

The silence in the back of the car remained unbroken on the return trip. The traffic a nightmare. Ris ran inside as soon as the black cab stopped outside fifty-six Lexington Gardens. She must have gone straight up to bed. There was certainly no sign of her as I paid the extortionate fare.

* * *

I didn't see her until the next day. But I had my answer by that Monday evening, and so did all her followers. Ris was overjoyed to announce that it was early days, hence her reticence, but yes, she and *Hubs* were delighted to share the news they were expecting a baby in October. I very much doubted Miles was delighted; in Ris' own words, he had been 'furious'.

Her publisher, on the other hand, was ecstatic, immediately adding their congratulations to the many others, supplying a link to the book, and promising lots of extra content to tie in with the happy news.

You'd have thought Ris would have been pleased with that result, but that's certainly not the impression I got, her mood definitely not buoyant. Especially after a long but mostly inaudible call from *Hubs*, frustratingly conducted behind two closed doors: the bedroom and en suite. I could hear her sobs when I pressed my ear firm to the smooth wood. Her entreaties to him to please listen, she loved him, pathetic to say the least. But distress is never easy to bear witness to, even when it's self-inflicted.

EMAIL SUBJECT: INTERVIEWS WITH GAIL FROST

DATE: TUESDAY 25 OCTOBER

Hey! Glad to hear you're keeping well. The interviews with Gail are really ramping up, aren't they? Seems like your/our hunch on her being pure gold as an interviewee is spot-on. The way she leans into her theories about the fake pregnancy, certain from the beginning that Ris was lying when she freely admits she can't possibly have known for sure. It's hard to empathise with her viewpoint, but I guess she has her reasons, as yet, undisclosed.

It's Gail's unswerving dogma during the initial press attention that first piqued my interest. She's very compelling, but it's hard to understand her motivation. Money, maybe, she's told me she's broke, but her obsession with Ris and that Paris photo runs incredibly deep. Is she just an odd character with a grudge against her ex-employer? She claims no interest in material things, only justice and truth.

Not sure what I think about her conspiracy theories myself, but like you say, best to keep an open mind; that Paris photo is definitely an image that stays with you. Be great to include it if possible? It's been widely used in the press, so I'm assuming it's fine even though the accounts are long deleted. I'm also fascinated to know what Miles' take was on all this. When did he first hear about the pregnancy? Did she tell him in

Paris before he left? Did he believe his wife? Why was he so furious about the announcement? If Gail is to be believed – jury very much out on that one – he was backed into a corner at the point he was planning on leaving the marriage. Gail's even gone so far as to call it entrapment. By the way, I haven't mentioned the possibility of an TV adaptation to Gail as yet. Not sure she'd be on board with it to be honest. I sold the interviews to her as research for a deep-dive opinion piece for the magazine and she's very anti anything she deems lowbrow. Not that this would be, not suggesting that for a second, quite the reverse, just not sure how she will take to the change in plans from a 'serious account of the truth' as she refers to it, and as nothing is decided as yet, I'm going to keep quiet about the script development. Don't want to stop her talking. Not now we're getting closer to the nub of it all. I have to resist asking her about the night of the book launch party every time. But soon...

Sometimes, when I'm with Gail, just the two of us, I get a really bad feeling. It's so intense, being in her thoughts and memories as she relives them. I mean, I like her, and she's utterly convincing, or at least she has convinced herself, but there's a ruthless side to her which scares me. Like when she talks about Ris in callous terms, justifying her responses with phrases like 'mitigating circumstances' and 'extreme provocation'. There's more to it, I know there is. I'll keep plugging away, digging deep. Just wanted to share some thoughts.

Another diary extract transcribed and attached. I've been wondering whether the pages might have been sent by Veronique? The tone is similarly youthful and flowery. Her emails are a bit like that. Anyway, I messaged our PT, asking if she had met Miles, and she made the leap and basically told me to take my suspicions and go away, but not as politely as that! She's only met Miles once and says he gave her 'the serious creeps'. Quote: 'He's a sleazy old man who couldn't take his eyes off my tits!' At least I won't be getting any more Boot Camp invites from her. Dragging a tyre around Clapham Common is not my idea of a fun Saturday morning. I think it's therefore safe to eliminate Veronique from my list of 'The Other Woman' candidates.

I've also been trying to trace cabin crew called Rebecca, Becca, Becky, to tie in with our troll, Becca2004xxx, but as you can imagine, it's like looking for the proverbial. I've tried a couple of the big airlines, but they all came back with the same response about staff confidentiality.

Anyway, whoever The Other Woman is, it's pretty steamy stuff. Enjoy the attached extract and then we can discuss the who/why theories and potential points of view for the script. Heads up, the extract certainly shows Miles in a less than flattering light, which is why I briefly flirted with the idea of Veronique. But aside from anything else, our PT has never been cabin crew.

Gail has reiterated that Ris was convinced he was having an affair and it very much looks that way. The question is, with whom? And does this feed into the pregnancy being faked as a form of entrapment, or not? I still think it's most likely Ris sent me the diary pages, just not sure why she's done that. Maybe she's the one out for revenge? Or maybe the diarist found me another way. Feels like too much of a coincidence they arrived at my office after I put that card through Lexington Gardens with my contact details. Unless there was someone else there when I called round? The someone I saw through the glass could be a woman other than Ris, I guess? I'm going to go back as soon as I have time, ask Ris about the diary pages.

Best wishes,

Ax

DIARY ENTRY #2

Our descent into JFK is smooth. Our pilot knows this route as well as he knows his way round most of the female cabin crew, his propensity to party legendary. Nigel walks a very fine line between unacceptable behaviour and lovable rogue, but we adore him nonetheless. You can't help it, especially as he's the one who gets us into Miles' club that evening, his repartee with the doorman, who is clearly charmed – 'Oh my God, I love your English accents!' – granting us VIP entry, the length of red rope unclipped as we are ushered past the long and vocal queue, every person we pass hating us. It's fun.

The retro tracks transport me as we launch ourselves onto the dance floor, the thudding disco beat twirling me round, as does our pilot. I don't need the lines of coke on offer or the overpriced cocktails. I just want to lose myself for a while, forget about the return flight and how much my feet ache. Forget that my husband is currently packing up the last of his possessions and leaving his set of keys on the kitchen counter. Forget the emptiness waiting for me at home and the double bed I'll only half-fill.

By midnight, I'm ready to go back to my hotel, Nigel's protests that I'm 'boorrr-riing' ringing in my ears, or maybe that's the price of standing next to a speaker for the last hour nursing the youngest member of our crew.

Her first layover and she is messily drunk.

'I need to get her out of here,' I tell Nigel as I manoeuvre her liquid limbs towards the exit and out into the street.

I finally get her into a cab, our flirty pilot appearing too late to be of help, and only to ask me if I need a chaperone back to my hotel. I'm not staying in the same hotel as rest of them, and it's almost two a.m., and it always feels so dark at night in Manhattan, the street lamps lower than the UK, and my dress is very short.

I'm tempted by Nigel's charms, no denying it, but I'd never go there. Far too many rumours about his numerous conquests to accept his 'kind' offer.

'Thanks, I'll be fine. Only a couple of blocks. Don't worry; I'm a big girl.'

I walk into the night, hyper-aware that I am now alone. And it's cold, the wind biting as I pick up my pace and wrap my coat around me. This will be the way of things, striking out solo; may as well get used to it.

The hotel is actually five blocks away, the streets empty of pedestrians, but I'm in good shape, almost enjoying the walk when I tune in to the sound of footsteps behind me, heavier than mine, and they are gaining ground. I daren't look over my shoulder, even when they call after me.

'Hey! Stop!'

I speed up again, but my stalker's pace matches mine so I'm running as his hand reaches out. I spin round, bag held aloft. 'Get off me!'

'Hey, hey!' He holds his palms up protectively, his face washed white by the passing headlamps. 'It's me, Miles. You just left my club. I was on your flight. I called to you as you started walking away; didn't you hear?'

'Sorry, my ears were ringing. I didn't know it was—' A siren interrupts us. He glances at my raised bag and I lower it. 'Sorry, I thought someone was following me.'

He laughs as a yellow cab drives past, illuminating that thousand-watt smile. 'I was.'

I'd craved sleep, but now Miles is here, wearing a tight-fitting shirt and expensive-looking jeans, and I don't feel tired at all. He looks, and smells, so good. I might even go as far as to say, irresistible. We'd be great together; I know that much. But then again, so does he. I decide to take him down a peg or two. 'Sly old Mr Fox.'

'Not so much of the old.' He smiles, parts his lips, and then clamps them round a cigarette. A strike of a match as he lights it, the open packet offered to me. 'But sly... Maybe?'

Good response, self-deprecating, and flirty. I shake my head. 'Dirty habit.'

'Fair enough.' He pockets them and drops the lit cigarette on the pavement. It rolls into the gutter, sparks fizzing as another empty yellow cab sails by. 'And for fuck's sake, call me Miles. Mr Fox makes me feel ancient!'

I could be back in my hotel bed, alone, within minutes. But the street has flipped from threat to promise. I'm in a Meg Ryan movie. I'm in fucking New York with a handsome millionaire. I feel daring. 'You wanna get a coffee, Miles? There's a place open just across the road.'

It's perfect; the kind of diner you see in romcoms, pseudo-Italian and very New York, a beacon of light as we jog towards it across five lanes of sporadic cars and cabs. Manhattan always feels so alive, and yet dangers lurk around every corner, as well as unexpected encounters. The reassurance of his hand to my back as he guides me over, more than welcome.

He orders at the counter from a sullen dough-faced man in a dirty T-shirt. Maybe this place is a dive, but I don't care. I check my phone, work out the time difference. No messages. As agreed. I tuck it back in my coat pocket as Miles returns with thick espressos, which seems like a mad idea at this time of night. I'll never wind down enough to rest, especially as I'm jet lagged. He smiles and it's as if I've already sealed my fate. But I'm not quite there yet, still trying to resist. I tell him that my ex is packing up and leaving our home, quite possibly as we speak, and he confesses he's unhappy with his wife. The exchange of confidences out the way, it's time for choices to be made. The unspoken acted upon. Miles picks up on my smile this time, returning it. I know what he's thinking and I nod, fingertips touching across the sticky table, electricity pulsing between us, as if he's bringing me back to life. The remnants of hot coffee burning as we gulp it down, keen to get going. Enough of talking.

We hail a cab, and slink into the achingly cool Meatpacking District hotel, the staff deferring to him as we cross the foyer, a key to his suite supplied by the front desk before he's even said his name. 'Your room key, Mr Fox.'

I thought he'd have an apartment in New York, but he says he likes to see how the machine works from the inside. The concierge avoids my gaze. No introduction or explanation given for my presence, or required. This, above all else, unnerves me. How is Miles so confident the staff won't gossip? Does this mean he's done this kind of thing before? Often, maybe? Surely his status doesn't discount the chance of scandal getting back to his wife? Or maybe he doesn't care? He said in the café he's had enough of being married, needs to make the break before it's too difficult. He also said they've been trying for kids. Her choice, he's not so sure; he explained there've been a few false alarms which have made him realise it's not what he wants... that his heart really isn't in it. It's been a tough road, really affected his wife's mental health. He blames himself for the marriage failing, said his business takes him away too much; they lead different lives. She'll be better off once they've both moved on. It's cruel to prolong the agony. I told him it's much the same for me. Flying is antisocial, it wrecks relationships. His wife is very... appearance led, he said. They have little in common. He's stayed in the marriage longer than he should have, through guilt mainly. I get the impression they married in haste, and he's clearly regretting it. I know her type. She sounds like a cold bitch. She certainly looked it in the wedding photos.

My concerns, however, do not end with his wife. Fraternisation with passengers is deeply frowned upon. Plus I'm mid-break up. Hardly a wise move to sleep with a high-net-worth frequent flyer.

He orders champagne to his room and we walk towards the lift.

I pause, his finger to the button, the 'elevator' on its way down.

'I'm sorry, Miles, I like you... but I should go. I could get into trouble with the airline. And I need to stop drinking, I've a flight back tomorrow, there are rules, so maybe we should call it a night?'

He takes my hand, rubs his thumb deep into my palm. 'If that's all that's stopping you, I can cancel the champagne.'

It should be off-putting. As if my concerns aren't valid, my job of no import. He's clearly never had to worry about earning enough to pay the bills, or where he might live when the shared home has to be sold, his wealth a buffer he's used to, protecting him from realities the rest of us deal with all the time. But maybe he is simply trying to offer me a solution that works. Either way, when the lift door opens, I step in ahead of him.

We're at the ninth floor when he presses me to the mirrored wall, his body pushed firmly to fit every part of me, a muscular leg parting mine, his lips seeking out a tender but urgent kiss. There's no space for thoughts of the flight home and the loneliness I know is coming, no aching feet in heels, no fear of guilt or repercussions. I can get another job, another home, another life. None of it matters. I am, for once, living purely in the moment. It's a drug.

Even as I take my first hit, I know it will be addictive.

He's inside me seconds after the door to his suite clicks shut.

12

FOURTH INTERVIEW WITH GAIL FROST – SUNDAY 23 OCTOBER

It must have been about three days after confirming the pregnancy news on Instagram when Ris properly rallied, marching into the kitchen where I was eating my lunch at the island. I thought she'd be annoyed to find me tucking into in my tuna melt focaccia, a treat I'd grown rather addicted to since my bank account had gone from overdrawn to a modest amount of credit. It was a very oozy sandwich, delivered on the back of a moped, and Ris had caught me mid-bite, mozzarella stretched between the greasy bread and my clenched teeth. I'd broken an unwritten rule, the invisibility I'd agreed to at the interview compromised by my presence in an area deemed off-limits except by invitation, but as she'd spent the previous three days in bed, I'd felt justified in venturing out from the basement.

I'd taken to chatting to the cleaners for company during Ris' self-imposed, bedbound absence, although the conversations were stilted due to their lack of English, and in fairness, my lack of any alternative. That lunchtime, however, I was alone, the pink van having driven away an hour before. I wiped my hands and closed my laptop, standing up as I waited for the anticipated reprimand.

She really was quite the harridan for a relatively young woman, but also unpredictable. I'd checked on her regularly, concerned for her health and my job, but this was our first proper conversation since that horrible meeting at the publishing house on the Monday.

Ris predictably ignored my greeting and grabbed one of her cartons of ramen from the fridge, ready to 'zap it' in the microwave before changing her mind and returning it to the shelf. Then she spun round, looking not at me but through me, thoughtful. I was wiping my chin with one of those ineffectual paper napkins takeaways provide, spreading the oily mess around and braced for a lecture about the unacceptably fishy smell, or simply my unauthorised presence in her kitchen, but instead she surprised me by saying, 'Let's go out for lunch together, Gail? You and me, doll, what do you say?' Her eyes were bright. Almost manic.

I wasn't in a position to say no, or much at all, juggling the napkin and sandwich as well as my surprise, but I guess I must have smiled as Ris beamed back and clapped her palms together, silver bangles jangling. 'Yay! It'll be such fun!'

She had ignored me for three days. It was presumptive to say the least, but I'd barely begun my sandwich so I wrapped it in the napkin and dropped it into the open mouth of the bin. Then I held up greasy fingers, asking if I might have a moment or two to get ready.

Ris was immaculate, sporting a tight denim zip-up jumpsuit, hair and make-up done, whereas I was barefoot and in my usual blouse and skirt, and I hadn't as much as combed my hair. She frowned and enquired how long I needed. I asked for five minutes and she said she'd walk slowly, her beautiful trench coat billowing at her back as she left the house.

* * *

I finally caught up with her at the entrance to Harvey Nicholls in Knightsbridge, her impatient WhatsApps advising me she had been there for ten minutes. It's an iconic building, in a prime location, I'm sure you know it, but also an odd mix of old and new. I suppose the constraints of being an architecturally important landmark impose certain limitations, but I found it a rather confusing layout inside. Escalators that only run to certain floors and a very retro feel to the design, particularly in Ladies Wear. Put me in mind of an un-PC sitcom my mother loved in the seventies, set in a not too dissimilar if comparatively downbeat department store. I doubt that show has withstood the test of time, full of uncomfortable clichés, but 'Harvey Nix' as Ris called it, evoked that retro-vibe. Although the ground floor was extremely modern, an assault of brightly lit beauty counters stretching as far as the eye could see. Ris led the way, of course. She was my invitation into that world. With her, I almost belonged. But in some ways that only made it worse. I followed her around like a dutiful aunt as she drew lines of lipstick on the back of her bony hand, diamond engagement ring glinting like the rock of Gibraltar under the LEDs. She dripped money, assistants drawn to her only to be rudely dismissed. She seemed dissatisfied with everything, including me, but she bought plenty, the stiff white bags with black lettering shoved at me as we moved from Dior to Chanel, Charlotte Tilbury to Acqua di Parma, Ris spritzing her wrists with so many competing scents I had soon gained a headache. Then she turned her attention on me, pulling at the lapel of my coat and asking how long I'd had it. Before I'd had time to answer she said, 'I can't be in the daily company of this sad little imitation. It reflects very badly, Gail.'

We travelled on the juddering escalator to the first floor, then took a flight of stairs to the second, the Burberry concession Ris' aim, although I didn't know this, not until I saw the iconic check-print lining hanging on shiny silver rails. Ris had the first coat off the hanger and onto my shoulders before I'd had a chance to work out if she was offering to buy it for me or expecting I should shoulder the cost to save her from the insult of my 'sad little imitation'.

I'm not one for designer stuff, but it has always been a dream of mine to own a Burberry trench. Such a classic. But I'd never thought... not in a million years... Ris was wearing one at the time, and another hung in her dressing room, maybe two, but I hadn't dared try those; I knew they cost a small fortune and they were in a tiny size.

Disappointment soon followed as even the largest one on the rail didn't fit me, nowhere near. Ris went in search of an assistant, elusive on the upper floors, and whilst she was gone, I checked the price tag. The number stared back at me, bold as brass. A figure well in excess of the recently bolstered balance in my account. There was no way I could afford it. And even if Ris was paying, it was an obscene amount for a raincoat. I resolved to suggest we try somewhere a little less designer and tucked the tag back in.

Ris returned with an assistant in tow, the younger woman shorter but with the same angular features and dark, severe brows. She also had red lips but hers were drawn outside her own, and the lipstick infilling those dark pencil lines was much lighter, which was rather distracting, as was her use of the word 'Pacific' when she meant 'specific.' I was mesmerised by the pale moving lips and the ridiculous malapropism, used several times, but it was her surly attitude as she expressed doubt they stocked 'the Pacific size' that might fit a normal human woman like me which took my breath away. It was as if they didn't want Ris' money, or mine.

The sales assistant eventually agreed to 'go see'. We waited, Ris agitated, the thrill of leaving the house and looking at stupidly expensive coats already wearing thin for us both. But I wanted the coat. I really wanted it. Isn't that revealing? How seductive it can be, and so fast! I mean, I'm not saying I hadn't coveted Ris' extravagant lifestyle for a long time, and I loved those coats, but my impatience as we waited for a larger size, and the utter relief and exhilaration when I was holding the bag containing that exquisite purchase, paid for on Ris' card without a second thought, was heady indeed. A rollercoaster ride from a tuna melt to a tissue-wrapped piece of heaven.

* * *

At the promised lunch, Ris drank the best part of a bottle of Vino Verde. Make of that what you will. I know I did. Hardly compatible with the early stages of pregnancy.

The pair of us were seated in a cramped corner of the store's rooftop café, the confinement doing little to improve Ris' low mood. It was much too damp a day to sit on the terrace, Ris' preferred option, but I popped out to admire the rooftops of Chelsea and Knightsbridge whilst Ris argued with the front of house about the poor table. It was a Thursday, he kept telling her, as if that explained everything.

I kept my thoughts very much to myself, especially regarding Ris' wine consumption, commenting only on how lovely the restaurant was, not at all your typical department store café. Definitely not the sort I recall sitting in with my mother, Formica tables and teapots that couldn't pour straight, although I'd known to expect something more upmarket from the links Ris posted. It was a favourite haunt of hers, but she usually lunched or cocktailed alone. And on the terrace, or at a table with a better view. She was a very grumpy companion but I had my new coat and a small glass of wine so I was prepared to overlook her rudeness and keep the conversation going as best I could.

Ris was typing on her phone as I chatted away, replying to her followers' comments I assumed, which I have to say were mainly supportive whenever I had a chance to look. A tricky subject to be taking on in any way other than positive, especially as it had been 'such a journey', but it wasn't only Becca and I who were suspicious of this miraculous news. There were a few mutterings about how it had happened 'so suddenly' after her IVF attempts which had ended only a few months before. Not that anyone outright called her a liar, but I sensed some early dissension amongst the ranks.

A very lovely waiter took our food order and soon the imbibed alcohol had mellowed my skittish host. The temptation to raise the subject of recommended units in her supposed condition, hard to resist, but as I say, it really wasn't my place, not when I was being treated to expensive coats and lunches. The small glass I enjoyed was delicious, although Ris was not happy, saying it wasn't a patch on the bottle they'd had in Porto when she and *Hubs* had stayed there in January. She reminisced about the second honeymoon and the hotel and the amazing custard tarts, her nostalgia deepening as she reached the bottom of another glass. I must admit, the alcohol on a near-empty stomach was also having an effect on me. Lunch was late and the bleary haze of slight inebriation was making me doubt my conviction. No one would make up a pregnancy, surely? Least of all someone as relatively high-profile as Ris. It would be madness.

I tried to work my way back, logically. The recent announcement indicated a conception around January. That tied in with the second honeymoon she'd just referenced, custard tarts and Port tastings in consolation for another failed round of IVF. No sign of Miles in the holiday photos, but she seemed to think they'd both deserved the gorgeous five-star hotel after the trauma endured. So, dates-wise, at least, there was some opportunity, if not it seemed, much likelihood after such a long and fruitless journey.

I balanced this in my mental spreadsheet, taking a view, but as she drank more, my cynicism, if not my glass, was topped up. Why would a woman who'd dreamt of motherhood for so long risk her unborn baby's health in such a cavalier manner? Why didn't she care what I thought? Did she have so little self-awareness? Questions bubbled, but I held my tongue, whilst hers loosened.

She leant forward, her heavy head supported by a cupped hand, words slurred as she asked if I'd ever wanted children. I told her no, quite truthfully, I hadn't. I didn't see myself as a natural mother and kids had never been in my plan. I was a career gal, always had been. She nodded, as if that was a wise choice. Same when she asked if I'd been married and I explained I found relationships tricky. I was probably better on my own.

'But you must have had lovers, Gail? Men? Women? Both?'

She laughed at her disinhibition and poured another glass. With still no sign of the food, she was drunk. Her comments and their volume drawing stares.

I responded that, unfortunately, I was one of those people who found it hard to trust and besides, I'd had to look after my mother for years; it simply hadn't been possible. She didn't ask about Mum, which was probably for the best. I'd rather over-egged my role as her primary carer, but Ris wasn't interested in Mum, or me. She was working up to the question she really wanted to ask, which of course revolved around her relationship with *Hubs*.

'So, what would you do, if you thought your partner was cheating on you, Gail? Would you act? Or would you let it take its course? Hope he, or she, sees sense?'

I was contemplating my roasted chicken Caesar salad which had at last arrived. I'd placed my order first, otherwise I'd have followed Ris' choice of chipotle burger which looked and smelt incredible. Although a surprising selection given she was usually averse to red meat and carbs. She was already polishing off the sweet potato fries and onion rings, stuffing them in as she waited for my response. It amused me she thought I might be anything other than heterosexual, but I guess I must have taken too long in my consideration because Ris then startled me, and the woman at the closest table, when she said, her mouth thick with fried food, 'For fuck's sake, Gail! Isn't it obvious what I mean? I'm talking about Miles playing away, again!'

Thankfully, she then lowered her voice, leaning in conspiratorially and almost knocking her wine over as she added, 'I have reason to believe my husband is seeing another woman. But I am dealing with it, in my own way. So she can fuck right off, whoever she is! He has a family to think of now, doesn't he?' Then she patted the napkin shrouding her flat stomach and bit into her burger, medium rare red meat juices oozing out and running down her chin.

A chair scraped loudly across the tile floor beside us. I moved the bag containing my tissue-wrapped coat as the woman at the next table walked round and wrestled a baby from its highchair. I suppose she might have been the infant's nanny, but I assumed she was the mother. The child, a cherub, staring at us with dark piercing eyes. The woman then tutted loudly as she pushed past, as if her charge might have comprehended the F-bomb Ris had dropped and repeat it at will. Ris waved at the baby whose face immediately crumpled, its mournful wail obliterating my response.

Then Ris was on her feet and loudly telling anyone who wanted to know she was off to the bathroom.

I watched her push her way through the busy restaurant, hoping she'd make it in time – those jumpsuits are the devil to get out of – and wondering if I should follow. Offer some assistance. But then the waiter arrived and cleared our dishes, garrulously upselling dessert and coffees.

I dismissed him but he returned with a coiled slip of till roll on a saucer. I ignored his presence until he asked if I'd like to pay by card or cash. I requested he give us a minute longer and he bowed rather churlishly and left me alone.

When Ris eventually came back, falling into her seat, she seemed both more drunk and less amenable. She dropped a card on the saucer and the waiter was straight back. I enquired after her health as he took payment and she threw me such a look, even he noticed and grimaced in solidarity.

The second she'd paid, Ris was up again. I gathered our shopping bags and ran after her, afraid I might not find my way out without my guide. Although the dance she led us around that store, clearly disorientated, I might well have done better to make my own way home.

* * *

We returned to an empty house, Ris going in ahead of me, sobriety somewhat restored by the brisk walk home it seemed. I had been keeping pace by trotting most of the way, and I was laden with all the bags, and clearly not paying full attention as I slammed into her, almost toppling us both.

Ris had come to an abrupt halt just beyond the mat, the cause of her distress something foul-smelling that had spread across the rug and was still spiked onto her right stiletto. A thin black plastic bag, tied at the top, pierced by her high heel. The mess had exploded over both her shoes and then I'd walked through it too. The entire hallway stank. She swore and kicked off the shoes then ran upstairs, leaving me marooned in a sea of dog excrement.

Yes, the infamous dog-poop incident which of course the press always reference when I'd only mentioned it in passing, some even suggesting I might have been the person who posted it through, which is frankly ridiculous. Why would I do such a thing?

I have no idea who was responsible for that unpleasant delivery.

A disgruntled neighbour? Kids? If you believe in karma then perhaps it was to do with Ris' lies: cosmic payback. All I know is it was an extremely nasty thing to do and I was left to clear it up.

I washed our shoes first. In the kitchen sink, which Ris wouldn't have liked, but she'd gone upstairs, and I wasn't having that foul smell in my kitchenette; it would have stunk out the basement for days. It makes me gag just thinking about it. I threw the doormat in the laundry for the cleaners to deal with and scrubbed the rug then I made Ris a cup of green tea. As if she was the one traumatised. But you know, those were the dynamics we lived by.

When I tapped on her bedroom door, cup in hand, there was no reply. I edged in and the room was dark, blinds drawn, but the bathroom light was on. The room was so dark I wasn't sure whether she was asleep or in the lit en suite, but as my eyes adjusted, I noticed a lump in the bed. Ris was curled foetal on her side, and then I caught a flash of pink tabard in the bathroom. A lone cleaner, finishing up their duties. There had been no sign of the van outside. I would have deployed her for the clean-up in the hallway had I known. It must have been parked round the corner, no spaces outside. Ris had simply crawled, possibly still a bit drunk, into her bed.

I placed the cup down on her bedside chest and she propped herself up and thanked me for the tea. No mention of the dog shit I'd had to deal with. Just, 'Could you be a doll and get me some paracetamol? And tell that woman to get out, I've asked her twice but she just grins at me.'

The packet was by the sink, the cleaner coming out of the en suite as I went in, a tied white bin liner swinging from her wrist, her heavy cleaning caddy stocked with sprays and cloths held in two hands. Ris shouted through impatiently, and I called back to say I was just checking the tablets were OK for her to take, in her condition. 'Don't worry, Gail, I've checked and they are.' I pretended not to hear, running the tap and filling a glass from the shelf. I only had a moment. If that.

I found the blue branded box in the cupboard under the sink, pushed to the back. I crouched down and retrieved it, noting one end had been ripped open and counting roughly a third of the tampons were missing. I returned the box to where I'd found it and pressed a toe to the pedal bin, the lid flipping open, but as expected, it was empty, a fresh liner inside. It had just been emptied. There was a modicum of relief I'd been saved from the ignominy of witnessing my boss's used tampons, but also disappointment of course. The evidence removed only moments before. Ris had her period and the paracetamol were for that, same as the frequent visits to the loo. I was certain of it.

I'd have probably searched through the dustbin given the chance, but the cleaners took everything with them, the van gone by the time I eventually got back downstairs. I closed the cupboard door and handed Ris her tablets and the water. She was sitting up in bed, smiling. Although she looked a bit peaky. Hardly surprising after the best part of a bottle of wine at lunch.

'Gail, you're such a doll. And thanks for clearing up that mess. Who would even do that? It's awful. My money is on that snappy little dog at forty-two, they never pick up in the residents' gardens, it's disgusting!'

I agreed, it was disgusting, and asked if she was feeling better. She took a sip of water and swallowed the tablets before setting the glass down, and to my surprise she patted the bed for me to sit beside her. It was becoming something of a habit, these bedroom tête-à-têtes. 'I really shouldn't have been drinking at lunch, Gail, please forgive me. And lord knows what I was saying about Miles: madness. Hubs and I are soulmates. I just get paranoid, but please ignore me!'

She paused, I assume to allow me the space to agree, but I

didn't; I kept my counsel, waiting for her to fill the awkward silence, which she did.

'The thing is, Gail... I spend too much time on my own. But please, let's keep this... lapse... as our little secret.'

Not sure if she meant 'lapse' as in her drinking, or sharing confidences, maybe both? But I assured her she could rely on my discretion at all times.

I excused myself before I said something I might regret. Cleaning shit off her shoes had been a low point. I'd have loved to tell her where to shove her job and her lies. I've never enjoyed being patronised. There was no happy marriage. And certainly no soulmates. But more importantly, no baby. I had found the evidence I had been looking for, those missing tampons, and I would use it, judiciously and with stealth, to eventually fell my target. But only when the moment was right. The missing tampons were the closest I'd come to finding my evidence, but it still wasn't absolute proof.

And I knew my word alone would mean little to nothing.

What I needed was a greater groundswell of support. I would have to bide my time, and build my case. But I would get there. Of that I was now certain.

EMAIL SUBJECT: INTERVIEWS WITH GAIL FROST

DATE: SATURDAY 29 OCTOBER

Hi, I hope you are keeping well? It's turned rainy and cold here in autumnal UK. I guess you'd call it fall? Have you had a chance to listen to the latest interview recording I sent over? Sorry to chase, I know you're busy. Interesting if somewhat disturbing dynamic between Gail and Ris now developing, don't you think? Gail seems to be part confidante, part employee, part spy, part friend. The enemy within. How creepy to have someone who means you such harm living under your roof. I started out thinking this was a case of obsessed fan/conspiracy theorist/disgruntled employee, but I'm increasingly beginning to wonder if it's about something much darker than that: a personal vendetta? She's talked about planning to take Ris down; it's very chilling.
I really wish I could get hold of Ris. I'd love to explore her side of things: the hurt it must have caused, the betrayal after she welcomed this woman into her home, paid her, bought her a fucking Burberry coat. I'd also like to know she's OK. Because if it wasn't her who I saw behind the door picking up my business card last week, then who was it and where is Ris now? I've no idea when she was last seen. The last reported sighting I can find was at the book launch which was four months ago! Her baby was due this month too, but no announcement yet.

I've abandoned my search for flight crew called Becca. May not be any connection to Ris' troll anyway and it was taking up all my spare time. And no luck putting a name to this lover of Miles' either. All roads lead to cul-de-sacs right now.

When you get a moment, can you read the transcribed diary entry (attached). It's worth your time, that's all I'll say. Crazy stuff! Mind you, I think I'd also go a bit Alanis Morrisette if I was treated like that by a man almost twice my age who should be at home with his wife.

I'm profiling this Other Woman as in her twenties, and judging by Miles' 'type', tall, skinny, dark hair, quite harsh looking. Cabin crew. Up for a bit of fun! Beyond that, no fucking idea, excuse my French, other than (spoiler alert!) he tries to end their affair, which I guess is kind of to his credit, and she's not having it. It would also seem, at least according to the account he gave this Other Woman, if her diary entry is accurate, that he believes his wife to be pregnant. Which kind of discredits Gail's theory somewhat, doesn't it? As Gail said herself, the January trip to Porto fits in, dates-wise. That could well have been when the baby was conceived. Second honeymoon, stress of IVF over... it happens.

I'm going to interview some of the cleaning staff. See if they heard/saw anything that might provide a clue to The Other Woman's identity. Gail said she chatted to the cleaners when Ris wasn't around but doesn't know any names. They were all 'foreign-sounding' according to her and didn't speak much English!

I'm also planning a trip up to the Foxes' Cotswolds retreat in Gloucestershire – banking on the small chance he took The Other Woman there and one of his staff remembers meeting her, or even just to get some background on the marriage: how was it going, was Gail's perception it was failing an accurate portrayal or way off the mark?

Also, to go back to my Becca theory, maybe the diary and the trolling and the dog poop through the door are all connected? Gail can't be the only one who envies Ris. What if the heinous crime she alluded to isn't just in Gail's imagination; what if it's real? What if Ris was in danger from this love rival? I've got nothing on which to substantiate this theory, certainly nothing I could take to the police, but let's just say alarm bells are ringing... loudly. Ris and Miles have been remarkably quiet on the whole thing ever since the shit hit the fan the night of the book launch. Refusing to comment directly, even when Gail's claims about a fake pregnancy lit up the clickbait media.

What do you think? Should I be concerned about Ris? I think I'll go to Lexington Gardens again. Knock on the door until I get an answer or spot Ris and the baby, if they're in there. They must occasionally leave the house, surely? Don't babies need fresh air and checks and stuff, assuming it's arrived by now? It's just so hard finding time to get out there and do the day job and still see Gail every Sunday.

Best wishes,

Ax

DIARY ENTRY #3

We are in a different hotel bed, on this side of the Atlantic and a month after that first joyful time together in NYC. The 'love-in' as we have jokingly referred to those incredible twenty-four hours we spent together. The weeks since filled with longing and delicious anticipation of this reunion. His wife would never get that John and Yoko reference. According to Miles, she is humourless, dull, and has also been, or so I'd thought, rendered sexless after years of trying unsuccessfully for a baby he never wanted. I guess that must sound awful, but I've fallen hard for him, and I think I'm about to hit the ground with a thud.

'Wait, what?' I laugh, looking up at him, his face inches from mine. 'What did you say?' None of it computes with the fact he is still inside me. 'Is this some kind of joke, Miles? Because it's really not funny!'

He rolls away, the loss of him physical and now more profound. My thoughts spiralling. I can't equate this devastating piece of new information with how I'd been feeling only moments ago. Connected to him, deeply, more than I ever was with my ex. The desire I feel for Miles primal, so even when we were making love I wanted more, needed more. Will beg for it if I have to. But first, I'm angry.

I am on my feet now, naked. A deer in the field beyond our mullioned window catching my eye as the tears burn hot. I pull a sheet from the messed-up bed, wrap myself in it to cover my body, although I've been working hard to get myself in tip-top shape for this day and spent the last hour or so entirely without inhibition. He's also naked, seated on the side of the bed. And I still want him, so much I ache with it. He says nothing so I goad him to speak. 'Thought you'd fuck me first, before you told me, did you? Get what you want, did you?'

'I wanted to tell you in person, because what we've had this last month, it's honestly saved me.' He pushes past me to get up and pulls on his underwear.

'Saved you from what? Your frigid wife?'

He shakes his head as if I'm the unreasonable one. It's maddening because he's right. I should have read the signs, worked out what was behind his reluctance to meet up. He's been travelling a lot with work, but despite my availability – I've changed shifts, missed flights, literally made myself accessible whenever – this was the first time he'd been free. Diverting from a weekend spent with his wife, because he wanted to be with me, or so he said. He certainly didn't take much persuasion to fall into bed. Neither of us could wait to get our hands on each other, clothes scattered to the floor in the gorgeous suite he booked under a pseudonym. Yes, I should have read the signs. Seen what was coming. Realised this wasn't a reunion, not in the true sense. We are miles from anywhere. Discreet, but only an hour's drive out of London to the multi-million-pound home he shares with his bitch-faced wife. His pregnant wife.

I totally fell for the set-up. Great sex, no-strings, before heading into scans and nappies and playing at being the good guy. A great father. A loving husband. Bastard!

Panic rips me apart as I stagger around, unsteady, a hand reaching out to him. 'I love you, Miles! You know that, don't you? This isn't an affair. I don't do one-night stands, never have. I love you!'

'But I have to stand by her, you see that, don't you? It would be a terrible thing to leave when she's—'

'No! A terrible thing would be to waste your one life on someone you don't love. Is that what you're saying here? You're breaking up with me?'

I swallow, or try to, a dry sob escaping. The room is spinning although we haven't touched the champagne. 'You told me in New York you don't love her any more. That you'd been trying to get pregnant but were going to tell her it was over before it got complicated. But you've had sex with her, recently?'

'No, but yes, it has got complicated. I'm sorry. In different circumstances… But I never promised you anything.'

The possibility tortures me. 'In different circumstances.' Bittersweet. A very different outcome. The one I've dared to dream might happen for the past month. Not only to be with Miles again, but properly in his life. I cough, afraid the bile in my throat is about to erupt all over the bed. I imagine the bodily fluids the mattress conceals. Honeymooning couples. And tarts, like me. Fucked then dumped. My longest relationship ended just over a month ago. Marriage over. I'd thought fate had intervened when I met Miles. The best timing. I love you, Miles Fox. I hate you. I love you.

I sit on the bed and this time he crouches down in front of me, takes my hands. 'God, I'm so sorry, darling, I don't know what to say. This is not something I do regularly—'

'Regularly?!'

'You're the first and only, I promise.' He places a heavy hand on my shoulder, broad and tanned, and straightens up. He's not mine to love any more, but I grasp for him anyway. He pulls away, steps back. 'Like I said, if things were different—'

'So you weren't happy, but you were still sleeping with her?'

'She's my wife, what am I supposed to say?'

'You could have told her about me. How we feel about each other.'

'I should go.' He is pulling on trousers, socks, his shirt. He's slipping away from me.

'No!' I lunge at him, find the tail of his shirt, the fabric tearing.

'Fuck's sake, woman, have some pride!'

'I'm sorry.' It's getting messier. I need to change his mind, but he won't listen.

'I really don't want to hurt you, at least not any more than I clearly have.' His tone is cold, determined. 'I thought you understood my position, we're both married—'

'I'm not married, I'm separated... you know that.' I sink to the floor, no strength to fight any more. 'I've got nothing. No baby, no home, no you.'

'Look, you're in a bad place.' He's placed a platonic hand on my back. 'Maybe I can help, financially?'

'Is that what you think I want?'

'OK fine, suit yourself.'

'Do you love your skinny, hard-faced wife? Does she go down on you? Does she love you? Ever ask yourself that? She's guessed about the affair, hasn't she? Trapped you with this news.' I look up, warming to my subject now, a glint of hope creeping in. 'Do you know if it's true? I mean, have you seen any actual evidence?'

'Of course it's true.'

He's at the door as I scream, 'No one will ever love you as much as I do!' I hear it slam shut behind him, but I can't move, my eyes squeezed tight against the pain of him leaving me.

13

FIFTH INTERVIEW WITH GAIL FROST – SUNDAY 30 OCTOBER

The morning after I discovered the partially empty box of tampons, Ris was still leaning into the pregnancy lie, her social media posts attracting more and more congratulations as well as tips for morning sickness and other pregnancy-related ailments. I found the comments from women who were going through infertility issues particularly poignant. There was a lump in my throat as I sipped my filter coffee – finances having allowed an upgrade from instant – whilst seated at my half-moon table by the basement's patio doors. The loaned laptop was ancient and slow to update as I scrolled the endless admiring comments, but it was clear she was their inspiration. Their hope. I hated her then. Not only for me, but for them. The women to whom she gave a false expectation of a happy ending. Not everyone wants kids, but they did. What she was doing was wicked. The way she told them never to give up. Their support and love for her prodigious, although Becca's sardonic commentary provided a welcome contrast to the good wishes and gushing adoration. I had to smile at Becca's witty observations as she attempted to balance the books.

Becca2004xxx Literally cannot believe how things have turned around for you, Ris.

Becca2004xxx Amazing what you can fake these days, but surely there's a limit?

Becca2004xxx Just as you launch your book, perfect timing!

And Becca was bang on the money. Whilst I don't believe it to be the primary reason for the lie, the pregnancy announcement had undoubtedly improved Ris' chances in the upcoming duel with the rival *Lifestyle & Beauty Bible*, and with Ris' publisher making good on their hasty promise of extra content by announcing a new section entitled 'Mummas 2B', things were really looking up.

Along with a legion of new fans expressing their uncontained delight – a female demographic predominantly younger than Ris – Fleur was making the most of the 'uptick' in press interest and fandom, emails flying back and forth between her and Ris, and always cc'ing me in, detailing the coverage she was pitching for off the back of the 'great news'. You can't blame Fleur, of course. It was her job and she was doing it very well, but ultimately it would prove to be wasted effort all round.

At least it was Friday morning by then, so just one more working day to get through before I could regroup back here and work out my next move. It would be a relief to get away. Ris' drunken confessional over lunch the previous day had driven a wedge between us. She clearly regretted sharing her suspicions of her husband's infidelity, and despite the request for discretion, which I'd assured her was a given, she'd been keeping me at arm's length ever since. It was only my second week with her. I needed to keep my job. The weekend break would do us both good.

I found her curled on her side on the bed when I checked in

late-morning and offered my services. Not that she was at all grateful, reminding me it was her space and off limits unless she messaged to ask for something. I left her to it after that, concerned she might decide I was surplus to requirements, but I knew she was fine as she was on her Insta and Twitter feeds, commenting on and liking pregnancy-related stuff.

Ris had by then claimed to her acquisitive fans that she was twelve weeks pregnant in the Paris photo, which would mean she'd be twenty weeks, *supposedly*, by the night of the book launch party. How she would explain the lack of a bump by then puzzled me. She would be the focus of everyone's attention, not least because her book was now predicated on the fact she was a 'Mumma 2B'. I just couldn't fathom how she planned to get away with it when all eyes would be on her. The practicalities preoccupied me.

For instance, where was that twelve-week scan photo? It's a rite of passage on Insta, often posted at the point of an announcement, but Ris hadn't shared one. Very unlike her to miss an opportunity for bragging rights.

Except that Becca and I knew why the omission, and I was hoping Becca or someone else on social media would question that oversight, but other than a couple of 'Have you had your scan yet, hun?' comments, everyone was being extremely respectful. Frustrating, but nothing I could do except wait for Ris, or Becca, to show their hand. And nothing from *Hubs*. Not a single call. At least, none that I'd heard. Although I couldn't keep track of every conversation, not with two floors separating us. Even the keenest of eavesdroppers has to be careful.

I still had access to Ris' private email and naturally I was refreshing it constantly, but there was nothing of note.

It had been a long week and it was a long Friday.

When I tapped her door at five to say I'd be leaving for the weekend, she gave no response. Didn't even roll over in bed to acknowledge me. It was a crappy way to treat a valued member of staff, but clearly she had a lot on her mind. I left for Reading in a downpour, soaked through by the time the train left Paddington. Not sure I dried out all weekend.

It was the Sunday evening when the scan photo finally popped up. A grainy black-and-white image posted to Instagram and Twitter simultaneously. I recall my stomach dropping, the spoonful of cold beans I'd been about to eat dropped back into the tin. The sight of that 'evidence' sending me into freefall, as if I'd crested a hump-back hill and the lag had hit, my internal organs swooping. This bedsit is depressing enough, but a Sunday evening alone here and seeing that... definitely a low point.

Ris had taken the necessary precaution of redacting any identifying details before sharing the scan image. And yes, I agree you would do, for personal privacy, but that's really not the point. I'm as convinced as I can be it was a stolen photo. You can buy them; did you know that? There's a whole market for fake scans, but I believe Ris, very lazily, simply copied and pasted from Google images.

The one I matched it best to, although I don't pretend to be an expert, is from a woman who gave birth in South America two years ago.

Disappointingly, not one of the journalists who interviewed me in the furore after the launch party took up my suggestion to take the photos to an expert, or at least print the scan photos side-by-side for public comparison.

Afraid of the Foxes' legal team, no doubt. But the images are identical. Hundred per cent. Not that I worked that out immediately. I had a wobbly few hours down a rabbit hole of research into scams and scans before I was fully convinced, but I did at least have the comfort of *Hubs'* email response to his wife in the meantime. That arrived within an hour of the scan photo going up.

Two things to say about me reading Ris' emails. Firstly, people really should be more careful. We never think it will be us, until it is. So strengthen your password game, that's what I say. And secondly, those emails were barely a line or two long. Which is, wouldn't you agree, rather bizarre between a husband and wife? Not a justification for reading them, no, but if we set the ethics aside – agree to disagree – I can tell you they confirmed the Fox marriage was clinging on by an absolute thread. I don't recall the exact content, but the gist was *Hubs* was again furious she had posted personal stuff on Instagram without consulting him. There was also a reference to a previous conversation along similar lines, inferring he'd asked her to keep quiet until he'd at least had time to talk to his twins, which suggests he believed the pregnancy was bona fide. Then, and I'd almost forgotten this, a rather oblique request to allow him more time to take care of everything his end. It was all very guarded. Then, without any mention or prior agreement, the email exchange stopped.

Yes, I guess he might have been concerned the emails were hacked. A man of his wealth with a loose cannon of a wife was only of minor interest to the tabloids, but there's all that stuff about phone hacking, isn't there, so I suppose he could have been being cautious and therefore switched to a safer method of communication. But I know for a fact there was no hint of suspicion about me. I was a trusted employee.

Anyway, the scan photo was up there for all to see, even a cute video of her 'revealing' it. Although she revealed a bit more than she meant to. Her informed and eagle-eyed followers spotting that it was a boy. Something to do with the direction of the nub? And when this supposed scan took place I could not tell you. I'd only been away for two days, a Saturday and Sunday. I concede if you pay privately, you could, in theory, get a weekend appointment, but that photo was someone else's. Hundred per cent.

* * *

I returned to Lexington Gardens on the Monday to a much brighter version of Ris than the foetal one I'd left in bed. This perkier iteration greeting me in her study with a cheery, 'Good morning, Gail! So fabulous, you're here!' Then she took off her glasses and without a hint of concern added, 'We have a lot to organise between us, only a few weeks to pull together this book launch, but take the morning to catch up in the basement. I'll message when I need you.'

I couldn't settle, but did as instructed, only leaving the basement once or twice to see what was happening upstairs, which was how I heard her chatting on the phone to *Hubs*. I don't know who called who, and I wouldn't describe it as a row, but it was a serious discussion by the sounds of it. Unusually, he was doing most of the talking, Ris only interjecting occasionally with her contrite agreement. 'Yes, yes, I know, of course, I'm sorry.' Long periods of silence in between as I listened outside her closed study door.

I was desperate to know how much, if anything, Miles knew of Ris' deception, but without his side of the conversation I was working pretty much on supposition alone.

All I gathered was that he was still travelling with work, a Manhattan prime location hotel project keeping him stateside for weeks at a time.

It appeared that despite the huge risk she'd taken, Ris had not secured the future of her marriage.

The book stuff on the other hand, was more promising. The finalised cover looking lovely. The publisher had done a great job. A very flattering image of Ris. And a much bigger campaign planned in view of the extra pregnancy chapter, although pre-order sales still weren't great.

I checked on Amazon almost daily, and whilst it was of course impossible to know for sure until the competing titles were in the shops – both coffee table style books that would be more likely impulse purchases in physical bookstores, at least according to Fleur's encouraging emails – the two books' relative chart positions, filtered by genre, were very illuminating, even to the uninitiated like myself. Mind you, I had picked up some of the publishing lingo by then. Like I said, I was always copied in by Fleur and the *sell-in* to retailers was described as 'disappointing'. This news was carefully worded as if Ris were a fragile potted orchid who must be protected from the outside world rather than a woman of thirty-five, almost thirty-six, who claimed to be enjoying the easiest pregnancy on record. No sign of morning sickness or any other pregnancy-related ailments as she entered the early stages of her second trimester. Yes, I understand this is sometimes the fortunate case, but another indicator of her falsity in the ever-growing catalogue of evidence I was compiling.

Ris pushed aside the pregnancy issue as much as she could in those pre-publication email exchanges with Fleur, who did tend to mention it a lot. And I must say, it is disappointing it was such a focus. Women fall pregnant every day of the week, so why the big deal?

The gist was that it was a refresh of Ris' image, a change in the narrative that could play into a lot of emotive and very current trends: later motherhood, beauty expectations pre and post giving birth, modern parenting. And Fleur was right, of course. You only have to look at the magazines in the supermarket to see how a high-profile pregnancy is utilised to the full, every intimate detail discussed and dissected. Nothing off-limits with the influencers' #BestIsYetToCome signoffs. Not to mention the revealing of bumps, daily. Which Ris had notably, still not done, and for someone so keen to show off their body, that was picked up on in the weeks which followed.

And why not? That was the question, for Ris desperately needed the ongoing exposure, literally and figuratively. She was not a celeb. Not like her twenty-something rival who'd popped out her enormous fake boobs on prime-time TV and was dating a pop star which were apparently all the credentials needed to become the 'author' of an instant bestseller.

Ris hadn't written her book but she had at least *read* it. Which meant she was able to answer the inane questions posed at the few press interviews secured for pre-publication and all conducted on Zoom or by phone; as requested by Fleur, in deference to Ris' 'condition'. Ris had clearly hoped for more and she told Fleur this, but it made no difference. My guess is the remote interviews were the best on offer. Fleur was simply trying to spare Ris' feelings.

Meanwhile, Ris' following on Insta was steadily climbing. A fraction of what was to come at the height of the tabloid feeding frenzy, but clearly Ris felt it should have made more difference, PR wise.

The only printed book review I saw was buried in a London-centric freebie and was really rather underwhelming. Ris sent me out to find a copy and then threw the paper on the kitchen island and flounced out. I don't think her attitude did her many favours with the press, her reputation from the early days with Miles preceding her. But she simply wasn't as famous as she liked to think she was. And the book was very much, as the reviewer quite rightly said, 'Style over substance.'

There was one photo shoot for a prestige glossy magazine, about a month before the launch, stylists running around fifty-six Lexington Gardens, a gorgeously handsome photographer strutting in late, the same one she used for the launch, his assistant setting up lights and props in the sitting room. There was even talk of Ris being on the magazine's cover. Ris loved the attention, naturally, although she pissed off the poor stylist who'd dragged a rack of stretchy body-con dresses up the steps to the house, only for Ris to disappear to get changed in private, insistent she had to wear her own clothes, despite the lucrative brand endorsements on offer. Ris didn't need the money of course, but her immediate and definitive refusal to wear the close-fitting clothes raised a few eyebrows. Poor Fleur, she'd set the whole thing up thinking it would be a pleasant surprise, at a loss why Ris was being so stubborn. I shrugged my shoulders and raised an eyebrow in return, but of course I knew why. And it seemed finally there were others with a like-minded opinion. A small but growing number of comments on social media suggesting, in very subtle ways, that all wasn't as it seemed. Why wasn't she showing them her bump? The next scan was overdue, where was that? Why wasn't she talking about check-ups, supplements, mother and baby health? Birth plans? I'm sure Fleur must have noticed those comments too, and Ris most definitely would have, but other than vague replies about not wanting to jinx anything the charade continued during those weeks of April and into May, all of us complicit in as much as we kept our counsel. But what else could I do? I hadn't procured enough evidence to show my hand and she was so bristly on the matter. I daren't push it.

The feature was never printed, not on the cover or any page of the magazine. I'm not sure why. Lack of interest? There's a lot of luck involved in these matters, as I understand it. You would know more than I do.

And the book did very badly, of course.

It was pricey, and really not that informative.

And whether my press interviews affected sales or not, we will never know. But yes, ironic given the lengths Ris had gone to.

I bet she cried buckets over the loss of that cover. She'd spent hours studying the stills the magazine sent over, deciding which ones she liked the best. They were good photos too, bony splayed hand covering an imaginary bump beneath the loose-fitting tops she'd insisted on wearing. Long legs slippery with glistening bronzer, cherry-tipped toes pointed. Shame the beautiful photos portrayed such a heinous lie.

Oh, and I should have said, Ris' PT sessions were cancelled by then, the skin-tight leggings and crop tops replaced with more modest attire, folds and folds of fabric swamping her. Which meant the shape of our days also changed profoundly. No more Veronique and protein shakes, the build-up to the book launch taking precedence over everything as May marched on. My workload such that on occasion I would lose myself in my duties, the logistics of realising Ris' vision of the perfect celebration, proving an organisational nightmare. I'd go hours without even thinking about the absurdity of it all and then pause to shake my head and remind myself that everything was a sham: from the bump to the book... even me.

And yet, the necessary and incontrovertible proof still eluded me, the pretence increasingly hard to stomach. I even considered making an anonymous call to a newspaper or radio show, my attempts to walk in on Ris naked, camera phone ready, thwarted by the fact she was always covered up when in my presence, even when it was unexpected.

It was the smaller things that really began to eat away at me during that time, like the messages summoning me from the basement for the most ridiculous of reasons. On one occasion because she couldn't recall the rival author's name! I supplied it, although Google might have done the same without a woman in her fifties having to climb three flights of stairs.

And yet Ris still thought she was a cut above. Buying loyalty with an expensive coat, or a hefty tip, or a few insincere kisses on the end of an email or a comment. But despite my building resentment, this was also a period of relative calm. One that would last only a few days more. Because a new arrival was about to join us at Lexington Gardens, and the presence of that third wheel would change everything.

EMAIL SUBJECT: INTERVIEWS WITH GAIL FROST

DATE: MONDAY 31 OCTOBER

Thanks for the catch-up last night, really helpful to chat on the phone straight after the latest interview. You have no idea how bleak station platforms are on a Sunday night. Sorry if my frustration is showing. I'm as eager as you to get to the bottom of Gail's claims, and believe me I have pushed back, as hard as I dare. She's insistent she tells it her way, so I still think the best thing is to allow her to talk, and we are so close now. I can feel it.

I used the train journey into London to review the interviews she gave to a couple of tabloids in the aftermath of her dismissal. It's not as big a deal as she likes to make out, hardly front-page news, but yes, the photo of her running away in an odd hat is there, definitely use that, and a few details of her theories, which have been pretty much discredited, but I believe there's more to it than her being 'disturbed' as one reporter so tactlessly put it. Some of her points are well made, much more so than the articles would on first glance portray, and like she says, she was the only one there with Ris at the time.

In other news, I just had a great call with one of the cleaners who used to work for Ris, by the name of Harriet. (Not a 'foreign sounding' name at all!) I found her through the agency Gail described, pink tabards and a pink van; they were happy to name and shame some of the sacked contract workers who'd been on the rota at Lexington Gardens. Most of the names I was given slammed the phone down on me, if they answered at all, but Harriet listened to my explanation and though she was a bit nervous to talk, I got some of the story out of her. Awkward to chat whilst I was at work, but she's clearly got some issues with Ris. Harriet's a really bright kid, studying medicine and cleaning part-time to top up her student finance. Does not have a nice word about Ris. Called her an absolute c**t!!! She also told me Gail was a bit odd, but always polite and hardworking. Used to treat them like human beings, unlike Ris. And that Ris was an utter bitch to Gail who took it all without complaint.

Apparently, all of the cleaners who worked the contract at 56 Lexington Gardens were dismissed by the agency in the aftermath of Gail's departure. A real cull, with 'fabricated' claims of information leaks, stuff passed to the papers, nothing specific but they all lost their jobs, legal threats if they spoke. Intimidation from Miles Fox's lawyers, she believes. Harriet's kept in touch with some of the sacked staff, a kind of post-Ris WhatsApp support group, and I'm hopefully meeting up with a couple of them soon, including Harriet, who've agreed to talk off the record. I'm hoping, with Harriet there to encourage them, and the obvious resentment towards the woman who got them sacked, I might get some insider information about Ris' state of mind at that time, and also Gail's. A desperately needed outsiders' perspective.

I've also transcribed another diary entry, attached. Let me know your thoughts, but I don't feel Miles, quite rightly, comes out of this at all well. Could The Other Woman be our troll? Is she *Becca*?

I've done the obvious thing and sent a few DMs to Becca2004xxx on Instagram, but no response as yet. Please tell me it's always this hard right before a big breakthrough? Feeling downhearted. But better get back to the day job, I suppose. The boss is giving me death stares again!

Best wishes,

Ax

DIARY ENTRY #4

Leaving the hotel felt like an admission of defeat, so I stayed. In denial, I suppose, but also in despair.

Miles claimed he never meant to hurt me, just a coming together of two lonely people, a moment's comfort, and now he has to face up to his responsibilities. 'Please try to understand and allow me to move on!' But I know it was much more than that. I've never experienced before what I feel for him. And OK, there is a child to consider now, but why does that mean we can't be together? Only a few days ago I read an article about how you shouldn't stay together just for the kids. It damages them in the end. I'm prepared to wait for him until he feels the time is right. I understand, as he said, that it's complicated. I've told him all this in my messages. He's responded only twice.

The first time to apologise and repeat that he didn't mean to hurt me, but it's best if we make a clean break. He's made his choice. The second time, late last night.

I should have gone home, got ready for my flight. Instead, I rang work, feigned sickness, again. Then I ordered a bottle of wine to our, sorry, my room, second glass poured when his text flashed up. I dropped my phone and ran to the door. And there he was.

The journey home was endless. I've always been a bad passenger, goes with the job, easily disgruntled by any slips in the standard of service and ready to find fault, even on a train. I check my phone constantly, but nothing. He messaged me as soon we were parted in New York, as I was leaving Manhattan, so does this mean it's different this time? He said last night that he's tried to give me up, clean break, but couldn't. I believed him, but was that true? It felt so perfect again, before he left for a second time. No promises sought or made. I hoped he'd at least message me, after what we'd just shared.

My phone ran out of charge somewhere around Bath and I endured an interminable wait to get home and charge it again. I messaged Miles before I checked out of the hotel this morning to say I was leaving, but could we please meet up soon, talk things through properly? Our night together had been amazing, but we do need to talk. He still hasn't responded.

14

SIXTH INTERVIEW WITH GAIL FROST – SUNDAY 6 NOVEMBER

With each passing day and then week, the time bomb ticking ever louder, I fully expected Ris to take what would have seemed like the obvious route and either confess to the lie – she could have invented a breakdown, or blamed the pressures of 'fame', or some such nonsense to excuse her retraction – or claim that things had not worked out for this pregnancy. A tragedy that is unfortunately, I believe, far too common and where my mind absurdly went when I heard a scream in her en suite that Tuesday morning in late May, seven weeks into my employ.

Ris would have been, according to her own calculations, almost eighteen weeks pregnant by then and that is significant because the scream was in response to a campaign begun by Becca that morning on Instagram. A campaign which was tied to those pregnancy milestones. A crusade which although remarkably simple in its device – one themed post per week – was devastating to Ris, even on its first strike. The source of Ris' distress, not physical – all sorts going through my mind went as I sprinted up the stairs – but in response to the picture Becca had posted.

In fact, it wasn't just a picture, it was a GIF. You know what I mean by that? No words, just the moving image.

This first one was an animation of a hopping halved smiley-faced avocado with skinny legs and trainers.

Why an avocado? Because that was the size the foetus should have been at eighteen weeks.

Like I say, a simple but clever idea, which had very much hit the intended nerve. Although I did feel slightly guilty for my initial amused reaction when I'd noticed the dancing avo an hour earlier.

Listening through the locked en suite door to her genuine distress was humbling, but Ris was never one to play down the drama. At least where she was concerned. She could be very dismissive of everyone else's pain, barely noticing it. But Planet Ris was a hostile environment, the atmosphere volatile and often explosive.

I knocked in between wails and Ris finally unlocked the bathroom door then slid down the wall, her back against the tiles. Limestone, I believe. Very cold, hard to keep clean as they're porous. And ruinously expensive, of course.

She was wearing one of her monogrammed robes, hair in a messy bun, the shower running in readiness for her to step in. I guess she must have seen the GIF and changed her mind, that dancing avo triggering her reaction.

She didn't look up at me, my chest heaving from the dash to get to her, breaths loud. And when she spoke, it was quietly so I had to strain to hear above the clattering rain shower, her voice cracking as she stared at her phone screen, mesmerised by the dancing avo with its domed conker-brown stone stomach. 'What have I done to deserve all this, Gail? Tell me! All I ever wanted... all I ever wanted was...' She held it up for me to see, and I feigned surprise, then sympathy, although it could have been viewed as a supportive post, celebrating a milestone, which I tried to point out.

Ris clearly hadn't taken it as such, her consternation at it and then me wrought in her haggard appearance. She looked awful, make-up down her tear-stained face, long feet planted on the tile floor, back slumped against the wall. I've never been good in those situations. A pat on the shoulder the best I could manage, but I did my best to say the right thing. I suppose it was adequate as she was persuaded up and then back into bed. I switched the shower off, closed the bathroom door, and offered tea.

Speaking of which, would you like any?

No, I don't blame you. The mould is really getting out of hand in this damp weather now we're in November.

Anyway, where was I? Oh yes, the GIF.

Maybe I should have intervened at that prompt. Had a proper talk with Ris. Asked why she was so upset, used her distress as a way to tease out the truth. Maybe I could have put a stop to it then, demanded to know why it had upset her so much when it was ostensibly harmless? I might have suggested more strongly that the GIF was meant to be encouraging. Questioned why such a bad reaction. Although given Becca's trolling history, it would be fair to assume it was the reverse of supportive, which Ris obviously had. And frustratingly, that fluffy robe she wore covered all manner of sins. Her stomach, or lack of, buried beneath the overlapping edges.

Would a well-timed intervention at that point have been enough to deter Ris from the action she took later that day? I doubt it; the ticking was already too loud, those loyal followers banging the drum too loudly, the book's extra content already written, but believe me I have tortured myself with that particular What If. It was another turning point for us both, but it was Ris' choice entirely to take the next drastic step. Like I said, she had an easy escape route up to that point, maybe two; but she chose not to use them. And to understand why, you have to try to place yourself in

Ris' head, as uncomfortable a place as that may be to inhabit. Here's my theory...

Firstly, and on the most basic level, she relied on her husband for everything: money, status, home, validation... and in return she saw her role as a fairly traditional one. She felt, rightly or wrongly, that it was her side of the bargain to provide a happier marriage than his first one. Good sex, a wonderful life together, a new family, but none of that seemed to be happening, and she blamed herself for that. Their infertility was, in her own words, her punishment for taking him away from Trudy and the twins.

Not that Miles' ex-wife seems to have suffered any lasting effects. I'd imagine Trudy's very happy with her ginormous divorce settlement and her much younger hipster partner. But their grown-up twin daughters may have been affected more deeply. Parental neglect is of course, traumatising. An absent father never ideal. The girls certainly never visited Lexington Gardens to my knowledge and Ris didn't appear to have a relationship with them at all. There weren't even any photos of them around the house. But then again, *Hubs* was never there to look at them, was he?

Secondly, Ris posted #TheBestNews! post after Miles abandoned her on their Paris trip. Whether she pre-planned the pose or the hand placement was a fortunate accident, she used it to provoke a reaction, which it did. She felt rejected by her husband, imagined him in another's arms, and she retaliated, making him furious.

Thirdly, soon after that meeting with the publisher about her failing book, she made the choice to turn the provocative but ambiguous prank into a huge, shared lie by confirming the news, which no doubt made it much more complicated, if not impossible, for her to backtrack. But she still could have allowed 'nature', tragic as it can be, to provide an excuse. And yet she persisted.

I think we can reasonably interpolate from *Hubs*' curt emails that he was caught unwittingly in her web. She'd hoodwinked him as much as she had everyone else. He was trying to find a way to leave her, she was right about that much, but she was making it as tricky for him as she could. The suspicion of this 'Other Woman' taunted Ris, her insecurity feeding into every thought, every action. The madness and desperation of a woman who feared she would lose everything informing her increasingly crazy choices. She told him she was pregnant and he believed her. She then had to live with the consequences.

For all those reasons, Ris had created a juggernaut no one could eventually stop, even if they'd wanted to, which she clearly did not. Quite the reverse. She longed to be pregnant, and she loved the adoration it brought from her fans.

OK, let's, as you suggest, for argument's sake, say she was late for her period as she left for Paris, which would go some way to explain the packed tampons, yes.

And that despite evidence to the contrary after years of trying and failed IVF attempts, she hoped that her prayers had finally been answered and that's why she posed as she did on the Saturday and told *Hubs* the news, thinking that even though she wasn't certain it was true, it could be, and might be enough to change his mind about leaving early. But it still doesn't fit with her claim of being twelve weeks, does it?

No, it was a lie from the start and therefore as much of a shock to him when that photo and caption went up late Sunday night, as it was to us all.

Ris' motivation was always to entrap her husband into staying in the marriage. Miles was her ticket to the dream and she intended to make it a continuing reality – at all costs. Despite her period having already arrived – by early Sunday absolutely latest, I'd say judging by her crawl into bed when she arrived home that morning – she knew she had a photo that would change everything. So Sunday night, drunk and rejected, she made the rash decision to post it. Her plan to publicly ensnare a man who'd abandoned their romantic weekend to be with, as far as she believed, another woman. It was a bold move, but one I consider her more than capable of.

Where were the positive tests? The pregnancy symptoms? It was all make-believe.

What Ris lacked, however, and which was becoming an increasingly urgent issue, was a baby. Or more accurately, a woman who was eighteen weeks pregnant, give or take. A woman who, unlike Ris, or at least unlike the social media version, was not deliriously happy about her confinement. A woman who, with some encouragement, might be persuaded to give up that baby, a boy, at birth. A mother who, perhaps due to circumstance or misfortune might also be convinced, financially, to keep an illegal adoption private. It was a big ask, but remember, we are talking about Ris. A woman with access to very deep pockets and who was losing her grip on reality, her moral compass set well off course, even by that point.

* * *

It was at around two that same Tuesday in late May when Becca's avo GIF was posted, that Ris messaged me to say she was going out. A surprise after her previous distress and reluctance to leave her bed. I pelted up the stairs from the basement and caught her at the front door. I'd been worried about her all day, keeping an eye on Becca's dancing avo and wondering if Ris would publicly respond, which she hadn't. But it seemed I had worried in vain as Ris looked her usual polished self.

She was wearing a beautiful white shirt, cuffs turned back, and it was pleated at the back so it trapezed around her body, her thin legs ensconced in soft skinny jeans tucked into stiletto ankle boots. I asked where she was going and she said she was meeting a friend.

This was the first I'd heard of it. She never met up with anyone. She appeared to have disconnected entirely from her life before *Hubs*. No school friends, no cocktail waitresses she might show off her 'amazing' home to. I said something along those lines, hopefully diplomatically, expressing my surprise at this sudden assignation. I suppose I was concerned of the impact on me and my plans. I certainly had no concept of how awful the consequences would be, for all of us.

Ris became defensive, said it wasn't really any of my business who she was seeing, but if I must know they'd met in a chat room for pregnant mums, both a similar number of weeks pregnant, wasn't that nice? They were going to have a coffee – well, a decaf or maybe a juice.

It would be perfect, she said, to have their boys at the same time.

EMAIL SUBJECT: INTERVIEWS WITH GAIL FROST

DATE: MONDAY 7 NOVEMBER

Hey, hope all's good with you? Have you listened to the latest interview recording I sent over last night? Anyway, don't laugh, but I've taken the day off work to 'stake out' Lexington Gardens. Like some kind of psycho stalker! Been spending far too much time in Gail's company, clearly. But joking aside, I am really starting to worry about Ris. I'd parked Gail's talk of a 'heinous crime' and 'missing woman' – she's not the most credible of interviewees and she loves a bit of drama as much as she claims Ris did – but she mentioned something yesterday that I cannot shake. It came after the none too subtle hints of a third wheel supplying said baby, and when I asked her about who that was, hoping of course to get to the incident at the party and start to make a few connections, she clammed up and said best save that for next time. Then she said… 'But maybe we should talk again sooner rather than later. I have a theory regarding Ris' disappearance from public life.'

It's all getting a bit crazy, but I can't stop fixating on the idea Ris has come to harm. Where the fuck is she? All her social media accounts were deleted and they were her obsession, and no sign of her I've seen, although I haven't had much time to visit since I dropped that card through almost two weeks ago. It could have been anyone behind that door, picking it up, including a cleaner. But it all feels wrong.

Doesn't help there's tons of theories about Ris on Tumblr, if you want to fall down the same rabbit hole I did. 'She's being held captive' 'She was never pregnant' 'It was a psychosomatic illness' 'Miles is some kind of kidnapper/psychopath'. And the fake pregnancy stuff is huge, definitely an angle we should consider. Not just about Ris, either. Pretty much every wife of a celebrity, or boy-band girlfriend have been accused of faking it to trap their partner, according to the conspiracists in the chat rooms. There's a few bona fide media sites touting the same about Ris, with all kinds of disclaimers attached. And of course Gail is always cast as the mad old bat who started it all; it's pretty out there!

It's strange how every interview Gail gave to the tabloids ended up feeding the same narrative, even when it doesn't seem to fit. But can you imagine how the trolling and Gail's fake-bump articles in the press must have affected Ris? She was clearly struggling long before Gail turned up. Her marriage falling apart, infertility. God knows what all this has done to her...

Anyway, back to my stake out or I'll end up missing Ris if she sneaks out and that will be a wasted sick day! I'm in my car, few doors down. It's raining, which doesn't help, and there's a skip outside, blocking my view. Hope weather's still good for you. I'll transcribe another diary entry while I'm sitting in the car and send over. Spoiler alert: there's quite a bombshell at the end of this one.

Best wishes,

Ax

DIARY ENTRY #5

I should have cared a lot more than I did when the HR department at the airline called to say they'd scheduled a meeting to discuss my 'recent work performance'.

My main concern was to get to the head office at Heathrow ahead of time, but like everything is right now, it was such an effort. Not least moving to the new house. It's not that it's an awful a place to live – a similar size to the one me and my ex-husband just sold, two beds instead of three, a tiny patch of grass, single parking space – but the main difference is that I live alone, and it's rented, which stings. Or at least it should do. Everything feels surreal, the pain in my heart spreading over the last few weeks so I'm numb to everything but the loss of Miles. Broken-hearted is right. I feel as if I've been gutted and my organs are on show, heart bisected. The pain is physical. I need him.

But I did try to look presentable for the meeting. Freshly pressed uniform, make-up done, even washed and styled my hair. I was exhausted before I'd even left home, but thankfully the panic attacks have subsided. I couldn't have got in the car until a few days ago. No one can sustain that level of anxiety forever; it's physiologically impossible. Frightened flyers eventually settle, even if they're pathologically in fear for their lives as they board. I was on a transatlantic flight a while back where a man had a heart attack. Not sure why that's relevant, but the image of shocking his heart back to life haunts me. Won't be able to do that again.

Random thoughts like that keep crowding in. A minor miracle I got to Head Office in one piece. I contemplated swerving towards the central reservation more than once, oblivion waiting on the other side. But something stopped me from turning the wheel. That nugget of hope for the future that keeps me going on a straight path. Or maybe I was afraid it wouldn't be me that would die.

I passed through the same set of automatic doors I walked through for my interview all those years ago. I was eighteen at the time, but it feels like yesterday in some ways. Another life. I was so young, and drawn to the glamour of travelling the world. Of course, reality has been very different, but I've always loved my job. Now the only thing I know is that I love Miles. But I should have focused on the meeting. Today was important. I need a job, now more than ever. The money, the company, the normality of it. The house is so empty, so lonely. And then there's that other concern. The one I keep pushing down, pretending it's not there when I know in my gut it's true. I've been signed off sick for the last week, but I really should have pulled myself together for that HR meeting. Shit!

I usually grab something to eat in the café, use the lockers, shower before checking-in for a long flight. Instead, I decided to head for the admin area, figuring I would have time for a quick check. I chose my victim, the youngest there, and pleaded my case for using his desk, explaining I needed to print out my schedules, if that was OK? He was doubtful, but said he'd grab a coffee and be back in ten. Not long, but long enough.

I'm not sure what I was hoping to find.

I typed fast, scanning behind me for casual observers and catching the eye of Perry who I haven't seen since that First Class service to NYC less than two months ago. The flight where I met Miles. I closed down the social networking site and flicked to the flight info page I'd loaded, just in case, although I'd no shifts booked in.

Perry asked how I was doing, two-faced bastard, a smug look as he glanced at my screen and then over his shoulder at the head of HR. At least I knew then where I stood. He's the whistle-blower. I have no doubts. Reporting my lateness, and drawing unwanted attention to my recent sickness record, unblemished for years but admittedly patchy of late. I missed that flight back from Dubai a couple of weeks ago. That was a definite no-no.

I'm entitled to a union rep, but I waived that right. Why complicate things? Let's just get this over with, that was my thought. I had no appetite for a scrap. I explained my situation as best as I could, how I've been in a bad place, but I am feeling so much better now. They offered to accommodate me, but we all knew which way it was heading. I threw in the towel long before I needed to. My offer to resign snatched up with insulting enthusiasm. I left the meeting barely thirty minutes after it began. I didn't want to be there.

Better now I move on. A different life to lead. Realities to face and some hard choices to make. There are two of us to blame, and I will not shoulder the fallout alone. Time Miles is brought to bear for the consequences of his actions. You can't make someone a part of your life and then just cut them out of it. I will not allow it. His wife isn't the only one who's pregnant.

EMAIL SUBJECT: INTERVIEWS WITH GAIL FROST

DATE: MONDAY 7 NOVEMBER

Hey! Sorry to spam you with emails today, but the door to Lexington Garden just opened and out she fucking came!

Ris!!! Alive and well.

I have to say I was more than a little relieved to see her, and oddly, she seemed keen to see me too. Well, at first.

She said hi, and I fell into step with her, picking up on the conversation as she led it. She said she was a new mum, just going to buy something for her newborn who has colic. Said her husband would usually help, but he was away on business, bit trigger-happy with the excuses for Miles, and she also said the baby kept crying so she'd been on a forum and the stuff she'd been recommended was her only hope. We were bonding nicely; I said my nephews had colic when they were tiny and it was awful. My sister had almost lost her mind. Ris seemed genuinely happy to talk, but when I asked where the baby was she asked me who I was and when I admitted it was me who'd put the card through, she hit me with, 'No comment,' and ran ahead down the wet pavement. I chased after her, but she's pretty fit, running through the downpour. Clearly I spooked her. I tried to find her, went to two pharmacies, but no luck and I didn't see her come back. Must have missed that return.

I know I don't have kids so can't comment, but she has snapped back into her skinnies pretty fast. My sister was not that flat stomached so soon after giving birth, even the first time.
No sign of this new best friend Gail's mentioned either. Really need a name. I'm going to press Gail on that later, and that comment about a missing woman, because I can reassure her it's not Ris, if that's who she meant. Gail and I have another interview booked for next Sunday but as I said, I'm going to try and move that to tomorrow, work permitting.
Chat with Harriet and other sacked cleaners now delayed, annoyingly. Fingers crossed they won't be permanently spooked by the NDAs they signed. I'm working on it, but one got jittery and the fear spread like wildfire, so they all jumped like lemmings and who can blame them? They had decent jobs, worked hard, did nothing wrong and yet Ris has ruined their employment record and Miles' lawyers apparently threatened to sue the agency if they so much as expressed their disappointment at the termination of the contract, hence the last-minute wobbles about our chat.
And thanks for your voice note. I so appreciate your feedback on the transcribe, especially as you're mid-shoot, and yes, Miles is certainly spreading his legacy around at the moment.
What's the next stage with the script? I definitely want to be involved, please emphasise that in any negotiations.
Back to the day job from tomorrow, but I'm hoping to see Gail in Reading afterwards. I've never spent so much on train fares! Mind you, my sister lives on a big estate nearby so I often visit her and my nephews whilst I'm there. Small world, eh?
Best,
Ax

15

SEVENTH INTERVIEW WITH GAIL FROST – TUESDAY 8 NOVEMBER

You sure you won't have something to eat with me? You must be starving. No, I don't feel hungry either. Funny that, must be the time of year. Very melancholic. I woke up this morning with the most terrible feeling of... I don't know, as if something awful had happened overnight but everything is just the same.

And no, I didn't know the name of Ris' new friend, at least, not until after she returned from their coffee date. Ris had been very mysterious before she left, I suppose in case it hadn't worked out, but it had clearly gone well; her mood most definitely improved. A far cry from the state of distress she'd been in after spotting Becca's eighteen-week avocado GIF that morning. Even her slight annoyance at my probing questions in the hallway was set aside as she made us both one of her nice coffees – such a treat after the cheap stuff I was used to, even the ground coffee I'd bought was nowhere near as nice as her pods – and then she talked my head off about the fun they'd had together and how amazing it was to click with someone straight away like that.

Not my experience of making friends, I'm afraid. Maybe your generation connect more easily, but I find people stand-offish, especially as you get older, and if you tell them anything even remotely honest they look at you aghast, as if they hadn't requested a truthful reply. But Ris was enamoured with Mia.

Yes, that was her name, this new friend. Mia Chance. According to Ris, 'a wonderful girl'. Which I'm afraid to say was as far from the truth as it was possible to get.

* * *

I first met Mia just under a week later, the last Monday in May it was, but her name had been dropped with such regularity before that I'd begun to wonder if she actually existed, or whether she was another part of Ris' elaborate hoax, the exact reason for her invention unclear.

I'd returned from the dullest of weekends in Reading, two days of my own company and a few takeaways under my belt. In fact, funny thing, the usual notch was feeling a bit tighter on the train so I'd undone it and forgotten to refasten it again. The leather strap was swinging freely through Paddington's grand concourse as I marched across, the bear himself regarding my state of undress with amused incredulity when I stopped to adjust myself.

I was looking forward to returning to Lexington Gardens and my cute little basement quarters. My mood rather bubbly. It might seem strange to you, but I was proud of who I was and how far I'd come. I treated myself by hailing a taxi. My wages for that month paid into my account that morning, after a prompt by myself over the weekend.

I also had a key to the basement by then. I'd begged for one after the incident with the alarm and Ris had finally relented, so I took my case down the basement's steep outside steps and dumped my belongings just inside the door then I went up via the internal stairs to the hallway and smoothed my hair in front of the mirrored tiles, removing my coat and shoes and leaving them in readiness for the many errands I would no doubt be soon sent on.

The first I heard of them was Mia's laugh. The memory of it still makes me shiver: a hyena cackle that rises and falls and goes on so long you fear you might have to gouge out your own ears if it doesn't stop. They were in the kitchen, the door closed, Ris' voice just audible as Mia laughed again. I set my expression to a neutral smile and walked towards the nerve-jangling sound.

Mia, although I did not know her name by then, had her back turned as I went in, a stranger seated on my usual stool at the kitchen island. A tiny slip of a thing. If she'd have been wearing a pink tabard, I'd have warned her to skedaddle before she lost her job, which is ironic really as I did occasionally see Mia chatting with the cleaners. Anyway, Ris was seated beside her, and they were deep in conversation, their animated chat interspersed with Mia's hideous laugh, Ris' hand to Mia's arm as it had once been to mine. It was then I noticed something deeply shocking, the confirmation of that given as their stools swivelled towards me.

I honestly couldn't tell you what surprised me more. That Ris had brought such an uncouth and frankly scruffy companion into *our* home or the matching pregnancy bumps under their tight-fitting exercise wear.

They had come from some kind of pregnancy yoga class, Ris explained, hence the leggings and vest tops, but that's not what I was curious about. It appeared that in the space of a weekend, Ris had sprouted a bump.

I don't think I said much at all. I was dumbstruck.

And I know you shouldn't judge a book by its cover, but I could tell that girl was trouble from the moment I set eyes on her. I feel terrible saying that now of course. But she really did test a person, even someone who likes to give the benefit of the doubt as much as I do.

I was old enough to be her mother, and she was visibly pregnant, so it wasn't the most charitable reaction, but there you have it. I didn't like her. And whatever people might say about me, I am a good judge of character. My gut is very rarely wrong and I had my eye on that girl from the start.

I'd thought her to be in her early twenties, but she was actually nineteen and without all that cheap blusher and heavy eyeliner to age her up she could have passed for even younger. Chipped nails, dark roots, straw-like yellow-blonde hair held up in a lurid scrunchie, the peroxide clearly out of a bottle. I could almost smell the bleach on her. And the way she spoke! *Rough as old rope* my mother would have said. Definitely not a likely friend for social-climber like Ris, other than of course those matching bumps. And yes, I know we all make connections through circumstance, finding our transient tribes as we need them and shedding them again, but even so... the friendship felt very *off*. And that laugh: my God, I can still hear it.

Ris hopped down, a hand to support her newly acquired bump. I couldn't take my eyes off it, the evidence right in front of me. No more swaying smocks. It was out there for all to see, upending everything I'd held true since I'd found the opened box of tampons in her en suite. I'd only been in Reading for the weekend, but it did give me pause. Of course it did.

Had I jumped to a hasty and wrong conclusion? Maybe she was telling the truth? The tampons could have simply fallen out of the box or been stowed elsewhere for some reason after her return home. But it still didn't make sense. Why pack a sealed box, brand new, that according to the receipt was purchased only a week or so before? Especially as she'd claimed to be, by then, over two months pregnant. It wasn't like I'd seen the bloodied evidence in the bin, but surely proof enough? But as I say, I did question myself. I am a pragmatic, logical, mature woman. I ran every variable and at the end of that process I came to exactly the same conclusion as before. The pregnancy, and therefore the bump, must be fake.

Ris announced that Mia was just going, looking at her supposed new friend with one of her pointed stares. A very unsubtle directive. Which was rude if they were, as Ris claimed, such a good fit. Mia looked doubtful for a second, not moving, then that screeching hyena laugh erupted. She slipped from her stool inelegantly, the smallish bump and her petite height – she was probably only just five feet – hampering her. Her trainers were scruffy, her black leggings almost see-through. The crop top she wore bright-prink, exposing the top of the bump, whereas Ris' vest top, designer of course, was pulled tight to her hips and hastily covered by a matching zip-up top as she noticed me staring.

I waited an inordinate amount of time for Mia to make a move from the kitchen towards the front door. I couldn't see the joke they kept laughing at; there was none. Ris had a hand to Mia to guide her out, but Mia hung back and gave me a half-hearted wave, arms stick-thin and pale, her posture appalling as she called over her bony shoulder, 'See ya soon, Gay!'

I would have returned that cheeky look if I hadn't learned better in my fifty-plus years on this planet, but it's like my mother always used to say. 'Manners cost nothing, but you can't buy class.'

Ris did at least have the decency to mouth an apology behind Mia's back as she corrected her. 'It's Gail, Mia, and she is literally my right-hand woman, aren't you?' Ris beckoned to me and placed an arm round my shoulder, the bump touching my side, but annoyingly I could gain no sense of its fleshiness, or otherwise, under that zip-up jacket.

I asked Mia when she was due, Ris shooting me a glance. 'September,' Mia replied, rubbing her stomach mournfully as if she might will the contents away. 'Worst luck.'

I left them to their protracted goodbyes at the front door, Mia's hyaena screech setting my teeth on edge as I went back down to my basement flat, dragging the abandoned case into the bedroom to unpack. That's when I noticed the bed was unmade, having clearly been used over the weekend, a soiled tissue under my pillow containing a sticky mess of chewed gum. And the toilet hadn't been flushed, the yellow liquid greeting me as I walked into my shower room and recoiled.

They were still at the front door when I stomped back up, my anger barely suppressed as I interrupted their explosions of incoherent high-pitched chatter to demand who exactly had been using my bed. I sounded like a bad impression of the mother bear in Goldilocks, but I was bold with rage. The tissue held aloft between the tips of my thumb and forefinger as evidence.

'Oh, that would probably be mine,' Mia replied, raising her hand like a child accused of passing notes in class. 'I've got a bit of a snotty cold.' She then burst into fits of shrieking and snorts as she leant into Ris and nudged her into complicity. 'I crashed for the weekend, didn't I, Ris?'

I could have slapped Mia's stupid smug face as she grinned at me, but I do feel bad about that now. She was so young, you see. So vulnerable. It was bravado, some of it at least.

Ris, on the other hand, had no such excuse, the woman who had sanctioned this ingression offering only a half-hearted apology. It wasn't enough. The invasion of my personal space demanded a heartfelt admission of wrongdoing, by both of them. Ris claimed she'd told the cleaners to sort it out and blamed them for the misunderstanding. But the cleaners never changed my sheets or scrubbed my toilet bowl; I did it. If she'd asked them to, on that one occasion, then they'd have complied, no question. And she certainly hadn't checked it had been dealt with. But Ris was my boss. *Her house. Her rules.* Not that she said as much, but it was implicit in her lack of remorse. It was a betrayal, on top of many before that, and it hurt my feelings, of course it did, but I couldn't say anything other than, 'No worries.' And at least Mia was leaving.

* * *

I was in the process of expunging any evidence of Mia from my flat when I knocked over a jar of magnolia blossom I'd arranged by the bed, the soggy mess draining from the surface of the small one drawer chest to the carpet. I honestly could have cried at that point. But that's reminded me of something I'd completely forgotten until now.

I think I still have it, let me just have a scout round.

There you go! I knew I had it somewhere. Here, take it!

I was down on my knees mopping up the spilt water and flowers when I noticed it. Must have fallen behind the bedside chest, a glint of gold catching the sunlight that came in from the other room. I'd opened the patio doors to air the place out, having unfortunately caught the unmistakable odour of stale cigarette smoke, not something Ris would have sanctioned, the house strictly a smoke-free zone, and especially in Mia's condition.

As you can see, it's an old-fashioned locket and definitely not one of Ris'. No weight to it, and not a designer logo in sight. And Ris never wore yellow gold, said it was passé.

Press your thumb nail to the edge... that's it. The left-hand photo is definitely Mia, the eyes, and that cheeky grin. Even at that age, maybe nine or ten, I am certain it's her. Not sure about the other one. They're both clipped from a larger print I'd say, and poor quality. I suppose it could be Mia's mother? I think more likely a sister. Mia never mentioned her family, and sadly I never asked, but there's a strong resemblance I'd say.

Her accent? It was rather coarse, but if I had to pin it down... Essex? No, Estuary English. Greater London or Home Counties, but definitely nowhere posh like Belgravia. Although she copied Ris' pseudo-Sloane, or at least she tried to.

I took the locket upstairs with the intention of showing Ris before handing it back, further fodder for my outrage at Mia's unauthorised stay in my basement quarters, but the hallway was empty.

Ris was in her study, hair damp and scraped up into a topknot, the bump, or rather the lack of it I'd say, concealed beneath a baggy jumper. It was a warm day, clement enough for the study windows to be open, voiles blowing theatrically. Hardly jumper weather, but she did feel the cold and I suppose her hair was wet from the shower she'd just taken. Even so, the oversized cashmere was an odd choice, aside from the fact it swamped her. I'd planned to hand over the locket, as I said, but for some reason, I didn't. I kept it tightly coiled in my hand.

Ris looked up and said something about me being such a doll for taking care of the cleaning, which came across as insincere, as did her justification for inviting her newly acquired best friend to stay. She said Mia was sofa-surfing whilst she was between jobs and in her condition she could hardly say no to her, could she? 'We have so much space here, Gail, have to do my bit. And she has a nasty cold.'

Fair enough, but why *my* flat? It was evident Ris had felt obliged to help but not enough to unconditionally welcome Mia into her home. The basement was the compromise. Servants and underlings quarters. Plus, Ris was germ phobic.

What could I say? I was living there rent-free and was as much of an invited guest as Mia. I was certainly made to feel as such in that moment, and many others after Mia moved into the guest suite on the top floor. But again, what could I do? My position as Ris' right-hand woman in no way trumped the care of the very thing Ris lacked but needed most. That would be rammed home to me over the coming weeks.

But I couldn't resist saying something along the lines of if she could let me know in future, I would be sure to leave the place tidy? To which Ris, I felt slyly, replied that I always left everywhere tidy. 'Almost as if you haven't been there, Gail.'

It was a barb dressed up as a compliment, but I was too preoccupied by another concern to bite back, the sudden and disquieting thought of Mia having had access to my private space for the whole weekend sending a spasm of panic through me. Imagine if my filled notebooks had been found, or the loaned laptop? My search history alone! I needed to check, but I was fairly confident Ris had no idea of any wrongdoing on my part. She couldn't have suspected and still looked up as she did, dismissive and superior, but with not a trace of anxiety. However good a liar she is, she isn't that good.

And I had been careful. Everything I didn't take with me locked in the drawer of that bedside chest, the key with me at all times.

One worry was then superseded by another when Ris advised me, oh-so casually, that 'Darling Hubs' was on his way home.

Our paths hadn't as yet crossed. *Hubs'* business trips, as Ris had advised me at the interview, keeping him not only out of London, but out of the country. And whilst I'd known this day would come, I hadn't expected it so soon and at such short notice. I needed time to prepare. Mentally and in my personal presentation. Best foot forward and all that. I was already making my excuses to leave the study, Ris raising an eyebrow at my hasty exit, when she advised, 'He's not coming here today, Gail. We're rendezvousing at the estate in Gloucestershire this coming weekend.'

Google it!

I think you'll be as impressed as I was, and on that note... I always thought it strange Ris liked the Cotswolds house so much. It had been the family's country home when Miles was with Trudy and the twins, but Ris appeared not to mind, or if she did, she kept it to herself. Maybe she viewed it as another trophy she'd won in the war to claim *Hubs*.

Anyway, the plan was I should stay in London that coming weekend whilst Ris was away, so I could see to the launch party arrangements. The impending party was her all-consuming passion and, with under three weeks to go, all she talked of. As if getting that right would mean everything else would miraculously fall into place. And I was very happy to be trusted at Lexington Gardens rather than having to return here.

We ran through the day's diary and I was tasked with a list as long as my arm for the launch. It was very much like old times, thoughts of Mia set aside, although tellingly, Ris asked, *oh-so casually*, that if I were *by any chance* to speak to Miles before the weekend, would I mind not mentioning Mia? She wanted to tell him about her new friend herself.

She was clearly anxious enough to cover even the remotest possibility I might answer a call from *Hubs* and then somehow drop that name into conversation.

I asked why the concern and she said something about trouble with someone in the past, unspecified, but enough for him to be *jumpy* about people he didn't know coming to the house, so she'd rather tell him herself. Apparently, he'd wanted to interview all the potential EAs but hadn't been around to do so, and despite this, had not been best pleased when Ris presented my engagement as a *fait accompli*. 'Although we've proved him wrong, Gail, haven't we?'

I'm not sure what I thought about that, but I was relieved all seemed to be well with me being there, at least for the time being. You just never know, especially with someone as savvy as the head of an international hospitality business like Miles. He could have looked into my background, put two and two together and the jig would have been up, as they say.

But he wouldn't be home that weekend. And neither would Ris. They would be together, in Gloucestershire, me at Lexington Gardens, all the implications of that preoccupying me as I took my leave, feeling brighter than I had before our catch-up, but still out of sorts. My thoughts redirected from Mia's ingression to that marital reunion.

Would Ris wear the false bump for *Hubs*? And if so, was that an indication of their lack of intimacy, or not? Questions swirled. But our conversation had decided me on one thing, for Miles Fox was coming to the launch. So that would be the perfect moment to show my hand, with everyone there to witness Ris' long overdue unravelling, her precious *Hubs* included.

I ran back down to the basement to double-check the contents of the locked drawer, relieved to find they were undisturbed, as expected, but I took a moment then to update my notes. I had a lot to do before the party. And I don't just mean organising the catering. My plan was hurtling towards its denouement. I couldn't tell you if I was more excited than nervous.

EMAIL SUBJECT: INTERVIEWS WITH GAIL FROST

DATE: SUNDAY 13 NOVEMBER

An update! As you know, I'd shoved that business card through Ris' door with hope but very little expectation and after I'd chased her down the street last Monday, I assumed that was it. I'd blown it. Imagine my surprise and delight when she called me yesterday and after much debate – she sounded confused and upset, not sure if she wanted to meet or not – we agreed I'd call round this morning for an 'off the record' chat.

Naturally, I cancelled everything, the next planned interview with Gail included, and hot-footed it straight over to leafy Belgravia before Mrs Fox could change her mind.

Gail was right: the interior of the house is fucking amazing! Will make such a good setting, really aspirational. I can see the opening credits now. The drone shot of Lexington Gardens, then the impressive front door. I'm obsessed with credits! Gail was underselling it if anything and she loves that place. Mind you, compared to Gail's basement flat in Reading, anything would feel luxurious. But number fifty-six is incredible. The money Ris must have spent. And I don't agree with Gail: Ris has incredible taste. Designers need directives and approval. She's done an amazing job. It's like something out of an interiors magazine.

Although I do concur that it felt weird to be there. I mean, I'm not saying I know every detail like Gail does, but it was a bit like walking onto the set of a features spread. Felt eerie, to be honest. Strange vibe, despite the glamour. The courtyard garden is being landscaped, which explains the skip that was there last week, now gone. She said they'd let her down, mid-job, but the residents were very hot on the Facebook page about the road's appearance so she'd had the skip collected, although she was hoping to get the landscapers back soon to finish the work. Once the weather improved.

It was a tightrope with Ris. She was extremely nervy, kept saying she wasn't sure about the interview at all, but she felt she should clarify her side, seeing as I am talking to Gail who is 'a pathological liar'. I took it steady with her, as you advised. Main goal: build trust and get invited back, tick and hopefully another tick. She's clearly desperate to talk to someone, anyone. Just her and the baby knocking around that huge house. No sign of Miles Fox. As always, conspicuous by his very absence, and the temperature change when I first mentioned this friend Gail's started talking about. Wow! Could have cut the atmosphere with a knife. I swear Ris' hands started shaking when I dropped those three syllables: Mia Chance. Good job she wasn't holding Teddy, no sight nor sound of him. Not at first. And 'no comment' regarding Mia.

Gail's described her former boss's appearance a lot, and obviously I've seen photos, and social media posts before they were deleted, and the stuff in the papers, and I met her briefly in the street, but this was like meeting a different person. She's a new mum, I get it, but Ris is barely recognisable from her glory days. No make-up, greasy hair, trackies and a stained tee. She made me a black coffee, apologising she had no milk in the house other than formula. I do get it. It's pretty full-on looking after a baby, but such a contrast from the glamorous woman on Insta and the way Gail described her as this formidable, hard-faced bitch. She says Ris was obsessed with her look, but I saw no evidence of that today. To be honest, the woman I just met is a shell of the employer Gail has described to me at length. I think that duality would be a great visual cue for viewers, but you're the visionary so I'll leave that up to you.

Shame I couldn't film mine and Ris' conversation; I'd have liked you to see her. The defensive body language really speaks volumes, especially when I vaguely mentioned receiving some diary entries. I wanted to gauge her reaction by dropping that in, much like Mia's name, but she was so jumpy already it was hard to tell if she sent them to me or not. Although she didn't seem that shocked when I told her they suggest her husband's having an affair. She refused my offer to read them – interesting – but denied their claims. Said the tabloids were always making stuff up about their marriage, especially since Gail Frost had begun spreading her lies; that's why she deleted all her social media. I suggested she might want to put the record straight and she immediately backed off, said she couldn't do that; Miles would be furious. Which kind of begged the obvious question: why contact me in the first place? She wants to talk but is afraid to for some reason. She kept asking me to promise it was all off the record and anonymous, and no recording allowed. Not that she told me much. It was more a vibe I came away with.

Sleep-deprivation would make us all… skittish… but even so, something feels… as Gail would say… a bit 'off'. For a start, where is Miles Fox on a sunny Sunday, and why is he dictating his wife's silence?

Then the baby woke up. I was keen to get a look at Teddy, but she wasn't going to get him from the nursery until I'd gone, that was made very clear. The crying sounded really urgent and yet she ignored it, for like two, three minutes. It seemed to bother me more than her. But maybe Gail's got into my head? I have been spending a lot of time with Ms Frost. I asked to see the nursery and Ris said she'd rather not. Claimed she was trying to observe boundaries and she found it very hard to trust since Gail. The experience has scarred her, she claimed.

Let me know your thoughts when you get chance and best of luck, really hope pilot season goes well. Send me a bit of that LA sunshine. London weather is dreary in November, but I'm getting excited about this story; it's unravelling fast.

Best wishes,

Ax

16

EIGHTH INTERVIEW WITH GAIL FROST – MONDAY 14 NOVEMBER

I'm sorry, but this is too much! I welcome you into my home, which I know isn't much, but I let down my guard, trust you, and now I find out the reason you cancelled on me is you'd rather talk to madam than keep to our agreed schedule!

I thought we'd built a good rapport. I've entrusted you with so much in these interviews. Bared my soul piece by piece because you seemed like a decent young woman. Ambitious, as I once was, and nothing wrong in that as long as you're kind and honest, which I thought you were. But you're no different than every other journalist who promised to tell my side of the story, are you? Oh, don't bother with more silly excuses. You're not being balanced and nuanced, not now you've proved you'll drop me the second she snaps her fingers. You won't gain any 'perspective' as you put it, listening to her lies. Frankly, I'm staggered you'd waste your valuable time.

So what did she tell you? Scarred?!

She's scared, not scarred. Scared to death of the truth getting out, so she's covering up. Spinning you a tale, but it's hard to explain it all away, isn't it?

Was he there, *Hubs*? No, of course he wasn't. And the baby, did you see him?

This vow of silence of yours is becoming very tiresome. Give me something, I've given you enough, haven't I? You owe me.

Born a month premature, is that what she said? *Interesting*. And how very convenient. Mia's due date was September. A month before Ris'. I've scoured the announcements online but of course nothing. Teddy, you say she's called him? That's cute. He'd be roughly six weeks old now if he's Mia's. Shame you didn't get a peek at him. But I can see why. I recall Ris' expression so clearly when Mia let her due date slip. I don't believe Mia had the faintest idea of Ris' intentions at that point. She just saw an opportunity at Lexington Gardens. Then her greed quickly got her caught up in Ris' ridiculous plan. That's the trouble, you see. It's all a bit dazzling, that amount of displayed wealth. Covers all manner of sins. You should bear that in mind if you go back. Which I assume you will, now she has you in her thrall. And you should; to see that baby if nothing else.

And look out for signs of Mia if you do. She was always so messy: make-up, clothes, any plate or cup she used left lying around. And she smoked; you might have smelt it, or spotted a cigarette butt? She threw them down from the roof terrace which is accessed from the guest suite on the top floor, but I'm not surprised Ris kept you confined to the kitchen. She won't have wanted you snooping around, spotting clues. Did you hear any movement, either above or in the basement? She might well have asked Mia to move down there after I left, out of her way. There's a door from the hallway, but if it was closed, you won't have noticed it.

Landscaping, in the courtyard you mean? Oh, that's such a shame. I loved that little bit of outside space. I hope they haven't touched the magnolia. It's got pink flowers, but obviously not in

November... not important, but you remember me telling you it was magnificent?

What did Ris have to say about her new best friend then; did she explain Mia's absence? 'No comment', that's interesting.

Well whatever she says, Mia was still living at Lexington Gardens when I left in June, so if there was no sign, then something's up.

No, Mia never mentioned the baby's father to me and she definitely wasn't living with him. She was sofa-surfing before she moved in with us. It doesn't stack up, her leaving, does it? I'm even more worried about that girl now than I was at the start. I should have trusted my gut, intervened much sooner. The whole situation is very unsettling.

Mia drove me crazy, but beneath the swagger, she was still a child herself, only nineteen and clearly troubled. I don't know her background, but I'm guessing not great. The homelessness and lack of the baby's father as well as a general absence of manners would suggest as much. She seemed to have no one in her life to support her and no place else to be. And Ris... I knew how easy it was to fool her, how she wanted to trust people, be liked, and witnessing Mia take advantage as she did... I feared for all of us, to be honest. It was never going to end well.

The thing is, you don't go into something like that, whatever the arrangement between them was, unless you're desperate. And remember, this is coming from someone who was never Mia's biggest fan. I tried so hard to give that girl the benefit of the doubt, but she was awful. Truly awful.

I recall the creeping dread that overcame me when I heard that heavy case of hers, more battered than mine, being dragged up to the guest suite by Ris less than two weeks after I'd first met Mia. It was the second of June, two months into my employ, and very poor timing as it was also the day before Ris was due to go to Gloucestershire for the weekend and I'd have had free rein at Lexington Gardens. My heart sank when I saw Mia, grinning over her shoulder at me as she followed Ris up the stairs to the top of the house. A heads-up would have been nice, I thought, biting my tongue.

No, Mia was not an easy housemate – noisy, messy, and omnipresent. Sneaking up on me when I least expected it. Questioning my movements and motives. Why was I outside Ris' closed bedroom door? Why was I in the study, or kitchen, or anywhere but the basement?

There was no way I could check the en suite cupboard for tampons or look in Ris' bathroom bin. Not when Mia was only ever a few steps away, running down from the guest suite and challenging me, or attaching herself to Ris like a bloody limpet when we were working together, or trying to. Nothing better to do, I suppose. She clearly had a total crush on Ris. Not romantically, although I guess that's possible, but I mean in that way younger girls look up to established women, thinking they know everything and have it all sorted, which none of us do.

There was this one time, just after Mia moved in, when we were all three of us in Ris' study. It was a few days after Ris had returned from her weekend away in Gloucestershire, a week or so before the launch. *Hubs* had been a no-show for the planned weekend together and Ris was still not happy about it. Not that she said, but her mood was very low... I was busy emailing and calling the outstanding RSVPs for the book launch, although I have to say it was slim pickings. No friends or family, just people from the publishing house and her agent. The invited press had either declined or ignored the invite. I'd suggested she make up the numbers with fellow influencers and bloggers, a few chosen fans, but she'd shot down that idea in flames. There was clearly no desire to welcome them into her home, her followers not worthy of any in-person attention.

It had been a difficult meeting all round.

The photographer Ris wanted for the party, the same one from the cover shoot, was at least confirmed, and the themed cupcakes ordered. You know they can print a book cover on a sugar paste topper? Very effective, although I suspect most of Ris' cakes ended up in the bin and I never saw any of the 'official' party photos.

Anyway, Mia was there with us in the study, and unbelievably pestering Ris for yet more stuff. And I mean *really* pestering. Holding her fancy new phone right up to Ris' face to show her what it was she wanted this time, and then, when ignored, taking a selfie of the two of them and threatening to post it.

Mia, like me, was never mentioned in any of Ris' posts, which is extremely bizarre, don't you think?

Anyway, all Ris said was, 'Don't!' and held Mia's gaze long enough for Mia claim she was only joking about the selfie and return to mithering for a new party outfit. I thought Ris would tell her she'd bought her enough already, but then I'd thought the same about the new phone that had arrived the day before, and the multiple shopping trips they'd taken together that week already, and the brand-new Mac. It all seemed to happen so fast; one minute it was the two of us, then all of a sudden we were a three. Anyway, Ris looked up again, eventually, and said, 'How much?' Which means the skimpy designer outfit Mia wanted must have had a price tag of several hundred at least.

As a sidebar to this, I was 'gifted' a very old phone, screen scratched to pieces, and the laptop I used was also second-hand, whereas Mia had brand-new everything.

But despite Ris' generosity, Mia was still demanding something new to look nice in at the party. And it wasn't as if Ris hadn't bought her bags of clothes. They'd been shopping only the day before and come back with a ridiculous amount of stuff. But there was a limit to Ris' patience that day, and Mia had found it, because Ris had already decided what Mia was to wear. A demure and expensive, neck to calf, flowing dress, which Mia had tried on at Ris' request the night before to show me 'how lovely' it was. Mia's face had been a picture of petulant resistance. And in fairness, it wasn't lovely. It was like a tent on her.

I was jotting in my notepad throughout this latest back-and-forth, ostensibly adding to the list of checks for the book launch, but in fact recording the bullet points of their exchange. Because why was Mia even coming to the party? I'm sure Ris would have preferred her not to be there, parading that bump and her presence in Ris' life, not to mention home, but if she had to be on the guest list, it was best she was wearing the Cos smock dress.

I was carefully making my notes. Hand curved around the pad. A necessary precaution. With Ris not so much, but Mia was clever at spotting when I was up to anything covert, which was troublesome as I'd planned on another attempt to locate the fake bumps before the party. This was nigh-on impossible with Mia watching me 24/7 but I was onto Mia's lark. It was obvious what she was after, freeloader that she was. She didn't even try to hide her ill-gotten gains. The stained vest tops and ripped jeans by then replaced with expensive designer gear and none of it what I'd call maternity wear. She liked outfits that showcased her protruding navel and small but swelling breasts. Oh yes, Mia was definitely pregnant. The ensemble she wore to the launch left no room for any doubt whatsoever. It was quite something, although in the week leading up to that night, Ris did her best to suggest Mia might wear the more appropriate dress. Mia was tiny. It wouldn't have been obvious at all that she was pregnant, not in that tent.

It was also at this time that Ris began grooming Mia in other ways for the moment her friend and *Hubs* would finally meet, a program of improvement beginning in earnest with a trip to the salon a week before. Mia's dark roots and yellowing split ends dealt with by Ris' hairdresser, Patrice, who – no doubt at great expense and the sacrifice of Ris' much-coveted monthly appointment – turned Mia's brassy blonde to a flattering deep brown. And Mia had a conditioning treatment that smelt divine on their return. Yes, it was a complete transformation: subtle make-up, expensive clothes. Not that Mia wore those often, she still gravitated to her cheap tat, or pricier versions of the barely-there outfits, but the resemblance to Ris on the days they played dress-up together, particularly from behind, was uncanny.

It was an odd metamorphosis which mirrored the degree of Mia's intrusion into Lexington Gardens, and Ris' exceptional tolerance of her guest's 'ways' as she referred to them whenever I dared to question anything Saint Mia had done.

I've wondered since if Ris' influence over Mia's appearance was a subconscious way of justifying what she planned to take from the younger woman. Maybe it wasn't only that Ris was ashamed of her uncouth friend's dress sense. Maybe she felt guilty. Or like my raincoat, she simply couldn't stand to be in the daily presence of something so inferior. But mainly I think it was Ris trying to make the best of a bad situation, because Mia wasn't going to be hidden away. Mia was, to use her vernacular, 'Totally psyched' for the party.

Her excitement filled every floor of that large house, the heavy bass of her music pumping down through the floorboards, as did that horrendous laugh, detritus scattered endlessly in her wake as she refined her 'look' for the big night.

Make-up everywhere. Cheap crap at first, then replaced with the same brands as Ris', stroked on with expensive brushes in front of the mirrored tiles in the hallway, mimicking her idol's pout, the collection of Mia's 'stuff' growing as they took their daily trips to the beauty counters, returning with more and more bounty which I collected nightly and left outside the guest suite. I suppose I was finally accepting what I'd hoped was a temporary inconvenience had sadly become a more permanent arrangement.

After Ris' program of transformation was complete, Mia could have passed as the kind of young woman who might rightfully live in Lexington Gardens. Until she opened her mouth, that is. Because no amount of hard work or money could conceal the fact Mia was still *that* kind of girl. The kind who'd smoke and drink throughout pregnancy. The kind who felt she should share her opinion on everything. That awful, mangled accent of hers – a strange hybrid of common-as-muck and pseudo-posh – coupled with that ringing laugh, punctuating my every thought.

I recall Mia's presence being especially jarring during a painful final planning meeting two days before the launch party. I'd carried out Ris' exacting requirements to the letter. And yet there was Mia, such a recent and unwanted addition, nudging between us at Ris' desk and adding her ridiculous suggestions: 'We should order take-away pizza for the party; everyone loves a stuffed crust! Or cider? Fruit flavours are super-classy. What about a DJ?'

It was all so... *tacky*. Mia wanted a beer pong – I had to look that up – and shiny party bags filled with sugary sweets. As if Ris were, like her, a Frankenstein's monster of teenager, mother-to-be, and seven-year-old child. It was exasperating as hell.

But with hindsight, it was also sad to witness how much Mia worshipped Ris and yet know, or at least deeply suspect, she was being used as a walking womb. It was the only possible explanation. Ris wasn't being altruistic. She was the very opposite of that.

People like Ris assume money can buy them anything, and that, I believe, is exactly what has happened. Despicable and just plain wrong, but I fear it is the reality we now live with.

But even if... *even if* Mia was an enthusiastic participant in this illegal adoption scheme, giving birth weeks ago and then willingly handing over her child before she skedaddled with her pockets filled, I still want to know where she is now, don't you? Because until we establish she's safe and well, no ill effects from her ordeal... well, the alternative doesn't bear thinking about, does it?

EMAIL SUBJECT: INTERVIEWS WITH GAIL FROST

DATE: WEDNESDAY 16 NOVEMBER

Hey, just to update you, I met with Ris for a second interview this morning. It was easier to persuade her than I thought. I bit the bullet and sent her a text message now I have her number in my calls list; said I have some important new intel on Mia Chance and she asked me to go straight over to Lexington Gardens. I don't think she wanted me at the house, but I guess she can't leave Teddy, although she had left him when I saw her running to the pharmacy, now I think of it. Anyway, she was clearly desperate to know what I knew so I made an excuse and left work, headed for Lexington Gardens.

I got straight to Gail's claims about Mia's baby and as you might imagine, they did not go down well. Ris eventually calmed down after pacing her kitchen and ranting about 'that lying bitch', a flash of the old Ris I suspect, and then she admitted to meeting Mia online. Not that she could do much else when I showed her the screen grab.

The chat room thread was a lucky break. A few Google searches after Gail told me they'd connected on a website for mums-to-be around 24 May. There's more similar websites than you'd think but I went for the obvious one, and so must Ris because, bam, there it was! Ris' comment: 'Seventeen almost eighteen weeks, looking to make friends with anyone with a Sept/Oct/Nov-ish due date,' and Mia's reply, 'Hey babe, me! I'm a September!' They must have DM'd after that, a shrewd move, but it proves Gail got her facts straight about that much at least. But I cannot find any trace of a Mia Chance anywhere, at least not one that even remotely fits the bill (in that online chat, Mia was using the appropriate pseudonym, SofaSurfer, whilst Ris used the rather more identifiable, RisELFOX56).

By Gail's description, Mia was nineteen and her accent British: London or home counties. Not much to go on. But rules out any theory of her being an illegal immigrant. My guess is she's a runaway, maybe after falling pregnant accidentally, her reticence to post on Ris' social media also leaning me towards that, as well as no mention of the baby's father. It's a working hypothesis but seems to fit. So where the fuck is Mia Chance now? (I saw no sign of her at Lexington Gardens.) Come to harm, living rough, with or without her baby? Or sent off in the back of an Uber with a pile of cash? I'm with Gail in that I need to know she's all right before I can let it rest. And I'm aware this feeds into Gail's claims – adoption after a faked pregnancy – but even setting all that aside, it does seem like an odd friendship. Although, Ris is undoubtedly lonely and people do strike up the most unlikely of associations when they're desperate. Which is pretty much what Ris told me herself after I'd shown her the Mumsnet screenshot and asked where her friend was now. Aside from the rather lazy contraction of Ris' name and house number, her initial reaction gave it all away. There was no point denying RisELFOX56 was her, or that she'd known Mia. The 'no comments' had to stop.

Ris' explanation was this. She'd wanted a friend, especially with Miles away a lot, and as established by then, she found Mia through the chat room. At first, she thought Mia was great. Someone to share the pregnancy journey with, and despite the age difference, and other significant dissimilarities in their circumstances, they quickly became good friends. Too fast for her to question a few red flags. Mia was fun, but terribly needy. In every which way. Ris tried to help, offered her a place to stay, treated her to a few new clothes etc., but Mia took advantage, as people do when you're that rich, so she was forced to cut ties just before Teddy's birth. Miles was right: she was far too trusting. He'd advised her to say nothing on the subject publicly. She'd finally learnt her lesson. First Gail, then Mia. She was better off alone. Everyone let her down. She begged me not to quote her, on anything.

Sounds perfectly plausible, except I don't buy that Mia left as easily as that. She wasn't looking for friendship, even if Ris was. It doesn't fit with the fact she was constantly after more, bigger and better. Ris had admitted she bought Mia expensive things and put her up for a while in the guest suite; said she felt guilty she had so much when Mia had nothing and no one. So if Mia was onto such a good thing the question remains: why leave Lexington Gardens and all that was on offer? She was homeless and penniless before she latched on to Ris. Wouldn't she have milked that friendship for all it was worth? Especially as she was due to give birth. Wasn't that the very time she'd be most in need?

I asked all of this and Ris shrugged, said things got a bit strained between them. Nothing major, some inappropriate behaviour for pregnancy, and they were no longer in touch. That's all she would say.

It's easy to see what Mia saw in Ris, but the question is, as Gail has said, many times, what did Ris see in her? Was it Mia's baby Ris was after, as Gail contests? A paid adoption arranged once Ris had Mia installed at Lexington Gardens? If we go with that theory for now, it does make a lot of sense. They had nothing in common other than their close-ish due dates, which is setting off all kinds of alarm bells for me. Especially as Teddy did not look like a premature baby to me.

I got a better look at him today, finally. Not planned, but the baby monitor starting flashing bright red in the kitchen – she'd switched off the video – his cries hard to ignore. He's cute but does not seem a particularly settled or happy child and Ris is not a natural mother. That's maybe harsh. Don't mean to be, but that was my feeling as I watched her trying to get him to take the bottle. Also, comparing him to my nephews at that age I can confidently – well, fairly confidently – confirm he was not born a month early as Ris claimed when I asked when he arrived. He's a big boy already, which would make it more likely Mia's due date is the correct one. I mean, I'm not a mother, so I can't say any of this for definite of course… but I'd say there's some room for doubt. I asked how Teddy's colic was and Ris said not great. I commented it was good she'd had some childcare so she could get to the chemist the other day and she said it was time I should go. She couldn't wait to get me out the door and slammed it shut behind me.

As always, love to hear your thoughts. And any suggestions of what might be next steps from here? Shall I keep trying to trace Mia Chance, if that's her name? It's going to be a case of checking every hospital for births, and not sure I have time for that with the day job too. Plus, she might well have moved on by now. Any budget for some help with the dry research? I'm trying to get a first draft script done, but with everything else…

The money Mia may have been paid before she left, if we make that leap, could have been used to fund a better lifestyle, but what if it was spent on drugs? Gail said Mia smoked roll-ups but no evidence of that at the house, not that I saw, or smelt. If Mia was an addict, then I don't want to think what might have become of her or the child. Hopefully, they're both fine and Gail's got completely the wrong end of the stick. I'm not drawing any conclusions, not yet.

I've approached Miles Fox again, as you suggested, but that's a solid brick wall. I can't imagine I will ever get a comment, let alone an interview. Can't get past his assistant: male, by the way.

I threw another sickie yesterday and drove to the Gloucestershire estate, but there are fucking six-foot gates, cameras, dogs. It's like a prison the amount of security, but according to someone in the nearby village pub, old chap who looks after the estate, Miles Fox hasn't been seen there in months and plans to sell it. He also said Ris came down, more recently: early June, so not long before the book launch night. Big fuss to get the house and grounds ready, but Miles was a no-show. Although he does remember Ris was definitely looking pregnant. Seemed a pretty reliable source and it's a tight-knit community. Miles is not exactly a popular man by all accounts. Very 'brusque'. But surprisingly, given Gail's descriptions, this estate chap said Ris was 'very polite and thanked them for all their hard work to ensure the house and gardens were looking beautiful'. Gail said Ris was in a foul mood after Miles was a no-show. And it all ties in with the diary entry; attached.

Sorry it's taken a while to transcribe, but as you can tell, I've been pretty busy. And these pages were particularly battered so I'd been putting it off. This is the last one. Everything else is much of a muchness. I feel terribly sorry for The Other Woman. Two sides to every story. Maybe more. But even so…

I was thinking we could dramatise some of the backstory, maybe an episode five from her POV? It's emotive stuff. And as Miles has kids on the go everywhere I don't think his fertility can be in question.

Ris again denied all knowledge when I asked her if she'd sent the diary pages, but she would say that, wouldn't she? Although it is perplexing. Why would she send me The Other Woman's account of a love child rather than confront her cheating husband directly? Maybe she has and he's denied it? Perhaps she wants this woman exposed so she can discredit her? Or she's afraid of her husband and is highlighting his infidelity as a way out of an unhappy, maybe abusive marriage? Ris being controlled by Miles is, I believe, central to her motivation for sending the diary pages. Or have I read the situation wrong? She didn't seem that shocked when I showed her the entry I've attached here. More sad and disappointed. Then she gave the pages back after only a cursory look and claimed they were clearly the work of a sick and jealous liar. For a second I thought she might be about to provide the author's name, but she didn't. Lips pressed tight. Possibly she has no more idea than I do. Another motive for sharing them?

I've asked Gail before and she said Ris always had her suspicions he was seeing someone else, but Ris never said who The Other Woman was. Maybe I just confirmed something to Ris that she already knew. It must have been humiliating talking about her husband's infidelity to a stranger. And I'm wondering if they've separated now anyway, in which case maybe the diary share is to do with a potential divorce? There's no sign of him, or anyone else living there. Just Ris and the baby.

Many congrats on the new series. When is it out in the UK? Cannot wait to watch.

Best wishes,

Ax

DIARY ENTRY #6

I thought the days would drag after I lost my job, but it's been a month and I'm getting used to my feet being firmly and permanently on the ground. Flying has been my life since the age of eighteen. I couldn't have imagined not being cabin crew. But times change and I've had to adapt. It still makes me sad, though. Not to be flying. I sacrificed my marriage to it. Cabin crew life is incompatible with being a normal couple according to my ex. I called him after I lost my job, prompted by loneliness I guess; an awkward dinner for old times' sake where I spoke of little except Miles, which was tactless, I see that now. My ex said he worried about my 'fragile state of mind'. I couldn't really argue with that. I am mad with grief for an unrequited love. Obsessed with a man whom I continue to adore despite his apparent indifference. Whose wife is very much pregnant, as am I. A woman he apparently loves, if all reports are to be believed. Including his own, on the rare occasions he replies to my messages. Maybe I shouldn't have shared all that over dinner, or the fact I threw myself into my job because I've never found anyone I love as much as flying, until Miles. I was going to tell my ex about the baby, but he was angry by then.

'You need help!' were his parting words. And he is probably right. I think love is a kind of insanity; no point denying it even if there seems to be nothing at all I can do about it. Impossible to imagine I could feel this way after such a short time, but I do. I've never loved anyone properly before Miles, I know that now. That's why I'm keeping our child.

I went to Miles' house in Gloucestershire last weekend to tell him. I knew he was going there. He told me last time I messaged, warned me to keep away. Said he was seeing his wife.

Soon as his car drew up at the gates, I pounced. There was a moment of stillness between us, then I saw his expression and I ran back towards my car. He caught me easily, held my wrist, his grip firm, returning me to the moment we first touched. The turbulence that bucked the plane, the scent of his skin.

I told him everything then, finally. The feelings I've tried and failed to convey in my messages. The fact I'm carrying our child and have decided to keep it. He was hurt. Asked why I hadn't told him before what was going on. He would have helped if he'd known; didn't I know that? I didn't have to deal with all my problems on my own. He would make sure I was looked after.

We went somewhere private. Rekindled our love. Before we both left he said he'd be in touch, soon. I'm still waiting…

17

PHONE INTERVIEW WITH GAIL FROST – THURSDAY 17 NOVEMBER

No, not ideal talking on the phone, but I understand you're busy, what with the day job and all those chats with Ris...

I'm joking! I've actually made my peace with you talking to her. In fact, it might help. And no, I didn't want to wait until Sunday either. Too much time has passed already.

I'm annoyed with myself that I didn't make more of the time I was with Mia. I couldn't tell you a single fact about her that I haven't already. A missed opportunity. Mind you, what would I have said to challenge her presence, or warn her to be careful of Ris? 'I think she's faking her pregnancy and only pretending to be your friend so she can buy your baby.' Not the kind of observation you can drop into conversation, especially as we hated one another.

Mia was used to wheedling and petty theft, I can tell you that much. The way she extorted from Ris on a daily basis with those shopping trips and daily deliveries, but I don't believe she was accustomed to such high stakes. She was out of her depth and I should have looked out for her, made sure she was OK. We were never friendly, but why I didn't I open my eyes and take in more of what was right under my nose, I can't say. In my defence, Ris was running me absolutely ragged for that party, and Becca2004xxx was a distraction too, her campaign of GIFs like mini time bombs exploding without warning.

They still pop up occasionally on social media, ex-fans of Ris reposting, and speculating when Ris might reinstate her accounts. Screenshots of dancing avos or ripe mangos reminders of how each one was timed by Becca to match the point Ris' supposed pregnancy should have reached, and always accompanied by increasingly nasty comments. I don't recall them all but a red pepper is one that sticks out for some reason, I think that was posted just before the party. Anyway, as I said, I haven't made a note of the comments, they were deeply unpleasant, but I do recall the words 'fake' and 'bitch' were often featured and Becca's GIFs provoked Ris' increasing distress every time they landed. Yet she wouldn't block or report the vile troll.

Becca's observations spoke of someone with a deep-seated insecurity and self-loathing. Of herself, her body, her fertility, who knows... not someone I wish to be associated with, even if some of our views 'overlapped' as you so delightfully put it. Those keyboard warriors are generally unhappy individuals, aren't they? Small lives and small minds. Like road rage: a coward's crime. Not my style at all. Say what you will about me, but I am never snide.

And although Ris refused to block Becca, she did consider responding on occasion, or pretended to. It was all for show, crocodile tears and fingertips poised over the keyboard with no intention to type. And Mia's sycophantic support was hard to stomach. 'They're not worth it, babe!' It did make me wonder at the blatant charade. The hypocrisy and pantomime of it all. By them both, yes.

Are you still there? Good, I thought I'd lost you. Not great mobile signal down here. Are you at work? You're speaking very quietly.

And Becca certainly wasn't the only one casting aspersions.

There are many doubters still out there, if you look for them. It's a popular theory, this fake bump stuff. And not just aimed at Ris. She's one amongst many women in the public eye accused of strapping rubber prosthetics to themselves to give the appearance of being pregnant. Most are using a surrogate, at least according to the conspiracists, although I'm sure it's complete rubbish in most cases, but it did send me on a trawl of the internet when I first tapped into this world. Ended up in some dark places. Oh, you too? Fascinating, isn't it?

You can buy the latex bodysuits very easily online. I'm sure you saw that too. Actors wear them; that's the legitimate use. They come in different sizes and skin tones, but they're not cheap and you'd have to buy maybe three or four to mimic the bump's growth to full-term. I assume it was the first one I saw on Ris, the day I met Mia, which she must have bought from just such a site. Ris always signed for parcels herself, despite her aversion to most tasks involving any effort on her part.

Regarding the trolling, I have thought about this a lot and I believe, as far as Ris was concerned, it was a symbiotic relationship with Becca. Dysfunctional and co-dependent; but one certainly fed the other. For instance, Ris would post about the folic acid she'd taken, *For the bub*, then Becca would immediately respond with a line of vomiting emojis and ask something along the lines of why would a skinny bitch like Ris need them, which in turn drew the collective wrath of Ris' fans who held up their shields and surrounded her with kisses and hearts.

There was plenty of fodder for Becca's contempt in those weeks leading up to the launch, Ris' increasingly smug posts showcasing her newly acquired 'motherly' persona mocked mercilessly by Becca and the rest of the trolling brigade who'd jump on Becca's bandwagon and hitch a ride. It really ramped up, the comments more frequent and unpleasant in the extreme. I'm not saying the strained atmosphere at Lexington Gardens was entirely Becca's fault, but she certainly didn't help. The three of us – me, Ris and Mia – individually and collectively, in a state of high anxiety. Becca the naked flame to our pile of tinder.

I think of that period as another turning point.

If *Hubs* hadn't bailed on the Gloucestershire weekend, would Ris have still gone ahead with her plans to buy a baby? She'd only just met Mia by then, nothing could have been agreed. Maybe he'd have put a stop to it all had he known?

She seemed sad he'd let her down, again, but I think there was an element of relief too, which soon turned to resentment, pushing her to up the stakes further. So high, in fact, there was no way she could climb back down. Hard to say, isn't it?

But it's not surprising that tempers began to not only fray but spill over. The launch was something it seemed Ris was both anticipating and simultaneously dreading. A big night in many ways. Not least because *Hubs* was definitely coming. I also had mixed feelings about that fast-approaching deadline, my nerves sometimes getting the better of me. Whilst Mia was, in her own words, 'Ready to partee!'

But it wasn't only Mia testing my patience; Ris' usual disregard for my service had deteriorated further. Sometimes our exchanges lacked the most basic of manners. I only just managed to resist telling her where she could stick her job on more than one occasion. I didn't plan on quitting, especially when I was so close to what I hoped would be a successful conclusion to my plan, but tensions reached boiling point between Ris and Mia several times a day.

I recall one day, near the launch, I was seated at my half-moon table in the basement, patio doors open to the gentle sun, on hold to the caterers, from memory, when I heard them arguing. I closed the doors and crept up the basement stairs, edging the top door open to catch the tail end of a spat about Mia's spending on a loaned card. She'd bought herself, amongst other things, a bottle of vodka.

But mostly the disagreements were low-key and yet they rumbled on, the friendship tested at such an early point. Although I have to say, I agreed with Ris on most of her complaints. Mia's utter lack of regard for her unborn child, the smoking, her erratic and unhealthy eating habits, including excessive alcohol consumption, were reprehensible. They didn't think I heard them, but you can't share a house and not know what's going on in it, can you?

Then two nights before the party, I was woken past midnight and wrenched from a terrible nightmare, by their noisy return. An argument in full flow in the hallway above.

To put this in context, Ris and Mia had gone out for a late supper that evening, just the two of them. Miles was due home in less than forty-eight hours and I think Mia wanted to lay claim to Ris, or maybe it was that Ris wanted to set a few house rules before *Hubs'* return. Clearly Ris would have a *lot* of explaining to do.

Mia had chosen the restaurant and made the reservation online earlier that day, after reading aloud from reviews of establishments ranging from burger joints right up to Michelin-starred fine dining, all whilst pacing Ris' study carrying the brand-new Mac she'd recently acquired. Silver, but otherwise identical to Ris' rose-gold version and balanced on the top of Mia's burgeoning bump.

Like most of Mia's swag, the laptop was delivered in a brown box, the contents checked by Ris first then passed to Mia who seized on them and crowed about whatever it was until she started angling for the next purchase. The recycling bin was stuffed with cardboard. It was ridiculous.

Anyway, a pretentious restaurant was settled on – a trendy new sushi bar ruled out at the eleventh hour when it was pointed out, by me, that raw fish might not be the best idea for two pregnant diners – and a cab booked for a couple of hours' time.

Immediately, Mia was restless again, walking up and down from the study windows to the desk and then back. Ris and I were seated side-by-side, much like the recent but already long-forgotten days 'BM', Before Mia.

I'd taken the opportunity to discuss the numbers attending the launch, still disappointingly low, and suggested maybe she should reconsider inviting some family and friends. There must be someone she'd like to be there on her special night? She said the only person she needed was *Hubs* but she'd speak to Fleur again about it. I caught Mia's expression, which surprised me as it appeared to convey something akin to genuine sadness that she hadn't been mentioned as a person of import to Ris. The inference being, she and I were only there by default.

Anyway, it was likely going to be a small gathering. Only twenty names at most left on the list, and they were mainly people Fleur had co-opted from the publishing house after the invited press had defected to her rival's competing launch (it was at The Groucho and the goody bags shared online afterwards were amazing). Far from ideal, for any of us. A full house would make it much easier for me to speak with Miles in private, his arrival set to be a little later than hoped. Ris had looked so disappointed when she'd shared his intended tardiness with me. I mean, whatever your view, it was not by then a marriage, was it? They barely saw one another and it was her 'special night' as she kept telling us whilst simultaneously excusing her husband's apparent lack of priority for his wife's celebration. 'No biggie, Gail. He'll only be half an hour late.'

And throughout this lengthy and somewhat difficult exchange between myself and Ris, Mia continued to wheedle in the most irritating fashion. 'Maybe we should make a night of it, cocktails, dancing. Just us girls.' This from a *girl* who was starting to look like she'd stuffed a football down her top. A small compact football, I'll admit, but her bump was much more noticeable than Ris', which although swamped by clothing appeared unchanged from that first appearance a little over two weeks earlier.

The meeting broke up and sometime later the cab arrived and they left for dinner. With not even a goodbye. But I had the place to myself, at last, which was how I liked it. Play-acting I was the lady of the house. Silly really. But it also gave me time to get a few things sorted in readiness for the party.

But first I went up to Mia's bedroom, way up in the eaves.

The guest suite is so lovely, especially with the door to the roof terrace ajar at the top of the metal steps, a nice breeze coming down. I was brave and went up, just enough to poke my head out and see the views over London's skyline in the twilight. Incredible. Mia had trashed the gorgeous suite, of course. Cigarette butts flicked onto the roof terrace, dirty undies gusset side up on the bedroom carpet, toilet unflushed in the en suite, and it stunk of smoke despite the breeze circulating, but none of that was a surprise, or that interesting. What was, however, were the stack of notifications on Mia's battered old phone which she'd left charging by the bed. I leaned over the scratched screen and squinted, afraid to pick it up in case the view changed. I didn't have my glasses on, but the surname of the sender of the unread email was foreign: lots of consonants, few vowels.

No, not committed the name to memory, I'm afraid. To be honest, I was far too struck by the subject line, which I do recall.

Have you agreed to anything yet, babe?

Frustratingly, another email then came in and stacked on top of it, the ping making me jump. My chance to note anything down then lost forever. It wasn't even an interesting replacement. One of those clothing chains that exploit child labour. It seemed that glimpsed subject line on the locked screen was all I would get. But very illuminating.

Isn't it obvious? It was from the baby's father. That question: *'Have you agreed to anything yet, babe?'* referencing the proposed adoption.

I left the guest suite as I'd found it, a pigsty, so Mia wouldn't have known I'd been up there, then I went down a flight and into Ris' bedroom, and then another to the study, checking cupboards and drawers as I went. I was looking for a receipt, or even the fake bumps themselves. Ghostly torsos on hangers, or more likely stuffed in a drawer, but unfortunately I found nothing. Ris was hardly going to leave the evidence lying around, was she? And at least one bump was strapped to her; under the stretchy dress she'd changed into for dinner. Maybe that was the only one she'd bought by then? If so, my search was a lost cause before it began. But you understand why I had to try. I was running short of opportunities before the party, and I needed my proof.

Thwarted, I helped myself to some snacks and a glass of wine from the kitchen and went back down to the basement to update my notes with the tantalising email titbit. Then I washed my greasy hands (those olives, delicious but so garlicky) and tried on my party outfit before I went to bed. I was shattered, but too preoccupied to sleep. I must have though, as I was woken around midnight, as I said, by their noisy return from dinner. Clearly a humdinger of argument in full force as they fell through the front door.

I unlatched the basement door and crept up the internal stairs, peering through the sliver of a gap as I'd left the door open at the top. A long finger of moonlight slunk its way through the etched glass panel in the front door and slipped past me down the steep flight, but I couldn't hear exactly what was being said. I ventured out, but only after I was certain they had both stumbled into the kitchen, the bright LEDs switched on. The hallway was in shadow where the door was half-closed, but I could hear much better. Mia's voice was loudest, although it was Ris I heard most clearly. 'You're drunk, Mia! Fucking drunk, and in your state! Don't you care about your baby? We've talked about this.'

I know the advice to pregnant mothers changes, and I'd seen Ris pour a glass for them both before they left, but getting drunk was an entirely different thing. I was shocked, my hand over my mouth to cover a gasp as I pressed my back to the wall, my toes feeling along the edge of the rug. I was wearing just a thin nightie; I might well have shivered too.

The argument continued, Mia retaliating, 'Oh, fuck off, Ris! You're drunk too.'

I could hear the telltale signs of drink in Ris' ever-so-slightly slurred syllables as she responded. 'That's different, Mia. And you know it. How many shots did you have that I didn't see?'

Mia was definitely the much worse for wear and shouting again.

'You don't have to remind me that I'm a fuck-up, I already know!' I didn't catch Ris' response; maybe she ignored her. Then Mia's voice again. 'Well, I don't fucking want this baby! So why shouldn't I have a good time?'

I ventured closer, my hand glancing the vase on the console. Heart in my mouth, I steadied it, then tucking myself in the wedge of concealment betwixt the open kitchen door and the wall it almost met, ready to sprint back down to the basement if needed, I listened. I couldn't see them but it sounded as if Mia had her back to me. Ris was calmer and talking too quietly for me to fully catch her replies, but Mia was loud, unguarded and stumbling around, crashing into things. The bin, I think, and a stool, which toppled. Ris swore. I shrunk back, using the kitchen door as protection and concealment whilst Mia vented her true feelings.

'I fucking hate being pregnant! I've never wanted it, not from the start! And he doesn't want it either. All he wants is what he can get out of me, bastard!'

I heard retching, then running water: the kitchen tap. Then crying. Mia's. And just before I crept back down the hallway to the basement, the sound of Ris' voice, soothing.

I made my descent in almost total darkness, the top door pulled shut. Whilst above me I imagined Ris holding Mia's hair or enfolding her into her long arms. Like a mother might tend a sickly child. Their differences already behind them. It was not a pleasant thought. But I had heard what I needed to and I would not forget what it confirmed.

* * *

By the next morning, the cleaners had obliterated any signs of the night before, the kitchen gleaming and peace restored. It was as if nothing had happened. I went in search of Ris and found her in the study. Dark hair scraped back, glasses on, rose-gold laptop open on the desk. Much like the photo she'd asked me to take and promptly discarded. Then a hyena laugh cracked the silence.

It wasn't Ris.

Mia was wearing the sleeveless fitted dress Ris had worn for dinner the night before, bump sitting neatly in her lap, as if a small cat had crawled under the knitted fabric and curled up there. The bodycon dress was stretched to its limit, whereas it had hung off Ris. 'All right, Gay?'

I told her I was looking for Ris and she took great delight in the fact she knew where Ris was and I didn't. It had got that petty between us. Apparently, there had been some last minutes hitches with the book, flagged by Fleur, whom Ris was meeting at a café in Sloane Square. The extra chapter – Mumma2B – contained a horrible typo, an unfortunate line break between the first and second syllable of cocktail. They'd wanted to push back the pub date at this eleventh hour... 'blah, blah, blah,' as Mia so delightfully put it, then added, 'Keep your knickers on, Gay. Ris just messaged. They've decided to embrace the cock. All fine for launch.' Then she mimed a lude act with her tongue, poking it into her cheek, her fist pumping. I waited for her to stop or grow tired of her puerile antics when I gave no reaction. She exhibited no signs of a hangover, nor felt the need to offer any kind of explanation for her invasion of Ris' office, let alone the fact she was using Ris' laptop rather than her own, a shiny new one.

The only time I ever used Ris' Mac was when I'd logged on to pay Veronique's bill and my expenses that first weekend of my employ. I wasn't there to steal from Ris and I'm a moral person. I wouldn't do that. Anyway, even if I'd wanted to, Ris had changed the passwords, which was annoying. I was owed another chunk of expenses by then, as well as more wages, neither of which were forthcoming. Ris was so tardy with admin. But there was Mia with full access and presumably up to no good. She snapped the lid shut, but she was grinning like a Cheshire cat. No shame whatsoever.

I asked her what she was doing. 'Helping yourself? Haven't you had enough bought for you lately? You know the password is regularly updated?'

She removed Ris' glasses and gave me such a chilly expression of superiority the resemblance to Ris was uncanny. Mia was a jumped-up nobody, and yet she had the upper hand. And didn't she know it.

'You don't know the new password, Gay? No, I guess not. But I do.' And with that, she unplugged the Mac and stood up, holding it to her chest. 'Ris tells me everything. Literally, everything. You want to watch yourself: I've got your number, Gay.'

It reminded me of schoolyard scuffles over the affections of the coolest girl in the year. I have wondered since whether Mia and I were being played off against one another. A pleasant diversion from the growing mess Ris had got herself into. But in that moment with Mia, I was incapable of such measured thought. The red mist had descended. I marched towards her and grabbed Ris' laptop, the screen opening as Mia clutched the keyboard, her stubby fingers with bit nails clamping the edge as Becca's latest GIF was displayed.

I'd just seen that GIF myself: a green face in the manner of someone feeling nauseous, the animated emoji overlayed on the finalised book cover which Ris' publisher had asked her to promote. I honestly don't think Ris would have pushed the book as much on social media if it weren't for the obligation she felt towards the publishing house, and Fleur. And like everything else, the book had become about the pregnancy and the pregnancy about the book. Something Becca had clearly picked up on. Mia's swollen stomach behind the laptop only adding to my wretchedness.

I was outgunned in every respect.

Mia was a hundred per cent self-assured. And why shouldn't she be?

Despite her lack of education, and manners, she trumped me on just about every level.

Why?

Because she was carrying the one thing Ris needed more than anything else, which meant she was supremely confident in a way I was not and have never been. Probably never will be. So I did what every cornered animal does. I lashed out.

'It's you, isn't it, Mia? You're the troll!'

EMAIL SUBJECT: INTERVIEWS WITH GAIL FROST

DATE: FRIDAY 18 NOVEMBER

Hey, apologies for the oversight, thought I'd sent the Becca screen grabs ages ago. I'll get on to the GIFs later, trying to juggle the day job here, but a choice few comments below from Becca and a couple of others so you get the gist. I agree: fabulous to have some SM quotes on cards between scenes, or even in VO. I've only included the pre-pregnancy stuff for now, but maybe we could reproduce some of the fruit and veg pregnancy milestones Becca posted? The ones Gail's been talking about as mini bombs going off and unsettling Ris. If they're not in too poor taste, or copyright?
Catch up soon! Very dynamic situation here, I'll keep you in the loop when I can! Gail's now claimed Mia was the troll! We're catching up by phone again later.
Best,
Ax

Sample of Becca2004xxx negative Instagram comments:

Becca2004xxx If you believe the hype! Not sure I do. Fake bitch!

Becca2004xxx Think I buy into your fucked up world? Think again! Fake bitch!

Becca2004xxx Nice dress. Designer? Natch! How much though? (Link inserted as well as a photo of a starving child)

Becca2004xxx Hey, who takes a photo of themselves every fucking time they do… anything? Oh yeah, you do! Fake bitch!

Becca2004xxx Starve yourself, babe? Yeah, great example for the fans who have normal bodies. Eat normal food. Have a normal life.

Becca2004xxx 'You can't compete with the Kardashians, so you don't try.' Is that your vibe? Srsly?

Becca2004xxx Some girls have all the luck? Life isn't fair. Not for most of us.

Becca2004xxx No one's life is that fucking perfect. Fake bitch!

Becca2004xxx Hey, who's about to be the wrong side of thirty-five? Watch out for the next wife coming along… choo-choo! It's the truth and you know it. Your husband is a PLAYER!!!

18

PHONE INTERVIEW WITH GAIL FROST – FRIDAY 18 NOVEMBER

It was the obvious conclusion, wasn't it? Finding Mia on Ris' laptop with Becca's vomiting emoji on the screen. Mia was Becca! Mia was the troll. She denied it, of course. Hand on hip, Ris' Mac snapped shut and tucked under her elbow. She looked like a petite letter b in profile. B for bump. B for Becca. Becca2004xxx.

Then Ris appeared at the study door, returned from her meeting with Fleur and taking us both by surprise as she coolly asked what was going on. Her tone querulous, arms folded over what appeared to be a man's shirt. She looked exhausted, eyes puffy, dress sense clearly dictated by the need to obfuscate the lack of a swelling bump. Unlike Mia who was very much into flaunting or maybe denying her encumbrance; I was never sure. The shirt Ris wore was very large on her skinny frame and was presumably one of Miles'. It didn't do much for her. Such a lapse in Ris' previous standards. And as we all know, me most of all perhaps, once you let things slide, it's a very fast downwards trajectory. And for someone like Ris, always so glamorous, so put-together, it was shocking she'd made so little effort for her meeting. We women do tend to dress for one another.

Talking of which, where are you calling from? Sounds like a bar. Are you on a date?

Anyway, I explained to Ris that I had come into her study looking for her and instead found this doppelgänger, logging on to *her* Mac. I may have even accused Mia of stealing from Ris. I know I expounded on my theory that Mia was the troll. Of course, Mia denied it all and Ris chose not to listen to me. In fact, she went further and mocked me. 'Honestly, Gail, don't you have more important things to do than squabble with Mia? You're old enough to be her mother!'

I was angry, of course. Ris was my boss, but I'm also more than twenty years her senior, and that should entitle me to a little respect. I'd done a great job thus far, worked hard, by her own admission, and yet Ris dismissed me like a truculent child whilst insulting me for my maturity. But it was Mia's triumphant expression as I left the study that sent my blood pressure soaring. I closed the door but waited outside, listening to their conversation which resumed in a friendly manner, as if there had been no trespass on Mia's part. Not even a warning from Ris to use her own damn laptop, recently bought and no doubt at great expense. I retreated as Mia was telling Ris how she'd compiled a 'banging' playlist for the party. I tried to imagine what that might include, my eyebrows lost in my fringe, but I must admit tears were pricking.

* * *

They went shopping again that afternoon, Ris returning empty-handed whilst Mia was laden with purchases in the familiar Harvey Nicholls' black-and-white bags. Identical to the one I'd feverishly clutched with my Burberry coat inside. Mia held them up and told me she was 'spoilt for choice' what she might wear for the party. 'You got a new outfit, Gay?'

I told her I had dug something special out. The dress I'd selected and transported from here already hanging in the small closet of Lexington Gardens' basement quarters. A few spots of mildew beneath the yellowing polythene wrapping when I'd tried it on, but the sequins covered most of the damage and at least it still fitted, with the aid of some shapewear.

I tried everything on again that evening. Sparkly dress and heels, sheer tights. Nothing designer, but that outfit holds a very special place in my heart. Then I tucked the dress away, excited and nervous to wear it. The flapping butterfly wings returned to my tummy as I packed my suitcase with everything else I owned.

* * *

Sometime in the early hours of that last night at Lexington Gardens, unable to sleep, mind wakeful, it occurred to me I hadn't properly looked into Mia's background. A huge oversight, but she hadn't been my focus. I'd googled her of course, and checked social media, that goes without saying, but when I came up with a big fat blank I gave up, my antipathy towards her outweighing my curiosity. And as I say, my days were busy, any clandestine research confined to evenings and weekends. And Mia wasn't, unusually for her age, flaunting her new-found fortune online. No activity whatsoever. Unless she was posting under the pseudonym of Becca-2004xxx, which as you know was my working hypothesis. I tapped away into the dead of night, but still found nothing. All very curious. I was about to switch out the light and try to get some much-needed sleep when another thought occurred. Phone in hand, I cleared the search history (it was my work phone, so I often did that) and typed, *paid adoptions*.

Whilst Ris undoubtedly had the means at her disposal to fund any level of payment, and also therefore access to expensive lawyers who might draw up all manner of agreements, the law is the law. No one is above that. Mia would be the birth mother and therefore named on the birth certificate, not Ris. So unless Ris had worked out a way to eliminate Mia from the picture entirely, the paper trail would surely be problematic? Babies have to be registered, checked regularly, there would be hospital and surgery visits; what would happen with all that?

My best guess was, as I reached the point of exhaustion in the early hours, a tentative and no doubt illegal arrangement had been brokered between the two women, the drunken argument the aftermath of those early negotiations. Hence the father of the baby emailing in anticipation. Mia must have suspected Ris' motives and told him there was a possibility of a very large payday coming soon. He was clearly itching for his cut. Sounds like a lovely guy.

Mia was certainly using her leverage with Ris to the max. You only take those kind of liberties if you're sure of your position, or you have something so potentially toxic on the other person, so damaging, you can act without fear of the consequence. Mia had a get out of jail free card growing inside her day by day, the thought of which filled me with deep anxiety as I tried again to get some beauty sleep before the big day. It wasn't only going to be Ris' special celebration; it was mine too, even more so in fact.

But I couldn't sleep. I had to ensure I wasn't about to be outmanoeuvred by a nineteen-year-old. A teenager who had no money, no home, and a greedy, distant partner. All of which made her the *perfect* choice for Ris. What I couldn't work out was how Ris planned to co-opt *Hubs* into her mad scheme. Would she keep up the pretence at the party? The talk would all be of her pregnancy, and the emphasis on the Mumma2B chapter in the book only underlined that focus. Somehow, I had to get to Miles before Ris did, and tell him the truth of his wife's supposed 'pregnancy' the second he arrived. He'd be appalled, confront her and then she'd have to admit it all, publicly.

I switched on my lamp and opened my notebook, determined to work out exactly what I would do and say the moment Miles Fox walked through the door. Bullet points scored through and a script, of sorts, written, I switched out the light and was finally able to rest. But I may as well have ripped up that prepared speech for all it was worth when my moment finally came.

EMAIL SUBJECT: INTERVIEWS WITH GAIL FROST

DATE: SATURDAY 19 NOVEMBER

Shit!! So sorry to hear that. Ris must have got cold feet and told Miles she's spoken with me and he instructed that solicitor's letter be sent to you straight away. Sorry I dragged your name into it. I thought dropping a TV connection might help persuade Ris to talk more not less; she's so keen on the idea of fame. I get the sense he's controlling her to the point of being an abuser. Is that why she's so scared to publicly defend herself against Gail's claims?

Was hoping the interviews with cleaning staff, whom I've finally persuaded to talk (don't ask, let's just say my budget, non-existent, is stretched!) might have provided recollections of something a bit more substantial about that time, like used tampons, or not, but I've spoken to three so far and none had anything of interest to add. They came and went from Lexington Gardens, working on rotation to spread the load as Ris was so rude. Other than that, they said Mia was messy, occasionally chatty, but mainly she stuck to Ris who had nothing to do with 'the staff'. Gail was described as mousy but polite, and that was about it. Which corroborates someone called Mia Chance, pregnant, was there. But we knew that.

Clearly an odd dynamic between the three women, Mia, Ris and Gail, but could simply be a clash of personalities? Gail is a bit… prickly at times. I mean, I like her, but I can see she might be difficult. Her theories do worry me.

And I also share your concerns about the legalities, but if it's any help it won't put me off. That's part and parcel of investigative journalism and we're almost at the point of Gail telling me about the party, so I can't stop now. Going down to her place in Reading again tomorrow but hoping that will be the final time. Aside from the cost, it's a bloody health hazard that bedsit.

Sounds like Ris may be unreceptive to talking to me again, but I'll keep trying, in spite of that warning from Miles Fox's lawyers. See if I can tempt her to at least comment on the night of the party.

I imagine locating Mia Chance or uncovering the identity of our diarist – The Other Woman – or tracking down Becca2004xxx in real life will prove the key that unlocks the truth. Just need to catch a break!

Becca hasn't posted in a very long while and my DMs remain unread and unanswered, but you know, live in hope if not expectation. (God, Gail's voice is on a loop in my head!)

The threat of legal action makes me think there's something worth pursuing here. Something big. And if there is, I'll get there. Don't worry about that, or me.

Best wishes,

Ax

19

NINTH INTERVIEW WITH GAIL FROST – SUNDAY 20 NOVEMBER

Nice to have you back here in Reading; always better to speak in person, don't you think? I only wish it could be somewhere... well, nicer. And appropriate we should be together as we get to the part of my story you have been waiting for. The night of the party.

The day of the book launch began early, and appropriately enough with a scream. Not mine; it came from somewhere way above. A heart-lashing, blood-pounding shriek that ripped me from a dream-fuelled sleep, nightie hitched-up around my waist. I was on my feet in seconds. Then out the door and up the basement stairs, adrenalin making me race up the next two flights to the master suite where, breathing heavily, I listened at the closed door.

I heard laughter first. Ris', then the hyena's. Hysterical, uncontrollable, *maddening* laughter.

I knocked loudly and went in. Not that they heard me, a loud pop covering my entrance.

Mia screamed when she saw me, champagne all over the sheets as the uncorked bottle shed a spume of foam. A tableau I'd describe to you now as a mix of eighties album cover and Bullingdon Club debauchery. They were both in Ris' bed, Mia kneeling above the covers, tiny T-shirt barely covering the essentials, her swollen belly protruding like my father's beer gut had towards the end. Ris was more demure in her silk pyjamas, a throw hastily pulled over her stomach as she leant against the propped pillows. The look of alarm at my entrance had replaced Ris' laughter, but Mia was undeterred and began to chug the expensive fizz straight from the bottle. Extremely vulgar, not to mention the alcohol consumption in her condition.

However, no one wants to be the bad guy all the time so I tried my best to hide my feelings. Clearly not well enough as Mia said, 'Oh, don't look like that, Gay, it's only a bit of fizz!'

Mia held the bottle out to Ris, displaying the half-moons of her near-naked bottom as she leant forward, a red thong all that separated us from indecent exposure. It might have been the same pair of knickers I'd seen Ris in before Paris. I didn't want to witness those... cheese wires... either time, but I found it impossible to know where else to look. Finally, I mustered the words, 'What are you two celebrating, then?'

Ris frowned and said, 'The book is published today, Gail. Had you forgotten?'

I forced a smile, maybe even a congratulatory comment. I had forgotten, preoccupied with my own plans. That's when I caught sight of myself in Ris' dressing table mirror, a scowling expression on my face, but worse, the lawn cotton of my nightie was turned transparent by the piercing sunlight, blinds and windows flung open to greet Ris' 'special day'. If I tell you I do not ascribe to Ris' regime of waxing and that the triangle of evidence was there for all to see, you will understand my mortification. Never missing a trick, Mia smirked, my face colouring. I turned on my heel, but my hasty exit was stalled as Ris started firing off a list of last-minute arrangements for the party. She wanted everything double-checked and running like clockwork before 'Darling Hubs' arrived home. The thought of his entrance that evening sent shock waves through me. A flicker-book of how that moment might play out resurrected from an abandoned dream. I told her it was all in hand and left the room, but then I turned back, remembering something *I'd* wanted to double-check. Good job too or I would have missed the tail end of an exchange between them.

Ris' gaze had slid down her nose, chin to her bony chest as a look of reproval was sent Mia's way, a solemn nod given by Mia in response, the gist of which could be reasonably divined as a signal to modify their behaviour once *Hubs* was home. Given it's a lot to intuit from one quick look, but that's how it felt to me. A definite change in mood from the larking around I'd interrupted. A prompt to Mia to tone it down at the party. In other words, she had to behave herself or the deal was off.

Ris then tersely confirmed to me when I asked, that yes, *Hubs* was still due home at seven, half an hour after the party was due to start. No change there. She was clearly disappointed he hadn't arranged an earlier flight but told me we'd just have to make the most of it once he *was* home. I took my leave and changed into my work uniform of blouse and skirt, in readiness for what I knew would be a ridiculously busy day of preparations. Which proved to be a good distraction. Although, the butterflies in my stomach were fluttering so hard I'm surprised Ris didn't hear them when we crossed on the stairs later that day.

I'm not overly superstitious, but it *is* supposed to bring bad luck. My mother never stood for it, making me run back up if she saw me coming down. And I suppose it was a portent, of sorts. Not that I had time for that kind of reflection until much later.

Ris was in a robe, hair wrapped up in a towel. She didn't acknowledge me at first, then she doubled back and grabbed my arm. I thought I must have done something wrong, but she was grinning, telling me she couldn't wait for me to meet *Hubs*. It was all a bit manic, her voice breathy as she said, 'I really want you two to get along. The two most important people in my life. And I'm proud of you, Gail. I hope you know that.' It took me totally by surprise. So unexpected and, after feeling very much the third wheel whenever Mia was around, much needed praise. I thanked her, said it meant an awful lot. Then I assured her she didn't need to worry about anything today apart from herself, as I had everything planned down to the tiniest detail. Nothing had been left to chance.

Her smile was genuine, as was mine. It was a moment for just the two of us, Mia nowhere in sight. Then the mood was spoiled, as everything was, by the spectre of our house guest: Mia's music assaulting our ears. Ris raised an eyebrow and smiled, resigned, it seemed, to her friend's lack of regard. Then we both laughed and pulled faces as Mia began to sing along, her pitch terrible. I was soon quite hysterical. It took me a moment before I noticed Ris had stopped laughing and was staring at me. I reiterated my offer to take care of everything, eager to carry on up to the study where I'd left the receipt for the cupcake company whom I needed to chase, but Ris then said, 'Actually, do you think you might keep an eye on Mia for me? I was hoping she would be persuaded to keep a low profile tonight, but she's very keen to be at the party... and I need everything to be perfect, Gail.'

What could I say but yes? I could hardly refuse on the basis I had my own plans for the celebration. Plans I hoped would see a very drastic change in all our living arrangements. But I could see why Ris would want a close eye kept. I was the only hope of accommodating Mia without her presence ruining the celebration, not to mention Miles' reaction to his wife's bizarre 'new friend' in the midst of so much unknowable chaos. Ris would have to explain her presence, not only as a guest, but as a resident of his household, and that would be tricky. Clearly something she hoped to discuss in private, and once the party was over. 'It would be so appreciated, Gail.'

She pressed her palm to my sleeve, said I was 'such a doll', then we went our separate ways.

I had no intention of honouring that promise. It was in my best interests for all hell to be let loose, Mia exactly the diversion I needed to speak with Miles on my own.

* * *

In the hours between that moment and Miles walking through the door, I didn't have much time to think about anything other than a million and one prosaic demands on my time: missing drinks orders, catering staff calling in sick, a florist who hadn't fulfilled the brief – effortless chic those arrangements were not – and then the drama of a mislaid Mont Blanc pen which Ris *had* to have to sign books. I located the pen on her desk and sorted every other inconsequential detail, readying myself and the house for a celebration I neither wanted nor could wait to begin.

By six, I was ready to greet Ris in advance of the guests due at six thirty. It had been a last-minute rush for me, but I was happy with my look and Ris seemed genuinely surprised when she finally made her grand entrance, strutting into the kitchen at six fifteen and declaring, 'Gail Frost! Is that really you?'

I'd had twenty minutes to change whilst she'd been upstairs with 'Hair and Make-up' for almost three hours. And much as I hate to admit it, that discrepancy showed.

Ris was resplendent in a black structured mini dress, form-fitting and with enormous ruffles framing her tanned bare shoulders, legs slender and glossy, heels impossibly high, and most arresting of all, a bump to match the size of Mia's, or possibly outdo it. It was all I could do to lift my eyes from that... protrusion. It had doubled in size since the last time she'd worn anything vaguely revealing. Surely I hadn't missed that metamorphosis? Even hidden beneath the loose-fitting man's shirt she'd lived in for the previous few days, it would have caught my eye. You certainly couldn't help but notice it now, which was presumably her intention. I couldn't think what to say. I'd had no warning. The photos she'd posted of herself in varying states of preparation for the party – rollers in and tagging #makeupby #stylist – had all been of head and shoulders whilst seated at her dressing table in a loose robe. The reality of her at over six-foot in five-inch heels, with that featured domed stomach under the skin-tight dress, was breathtaking. How was that bump even possible? Surely foetuses grew slowly, not exponentially? The contrast to her previous preference to deflect from her confinement was stark, especially as she was constantly stroking and cupping her rounded stomach. She reminded me of a flamingo, her preening movements measured, the familiar ponytail replaced by a sculpted updo, which one hand air-skimmed as if she were afraid to spoil the effect of so many hours' labour with even the lightest touch, whilst the other hand circled the larger fake bump, round and round.

The caterers were milling about by then – canapés in and out the dual oven, and glasses of fizz being poured to offer on trays – all taking wide arcs to avoid Ris, as if there was an exclusion zone observed, to retain her aura of specialness. Whereas I was jostled and bumped regularly in the hot working kitchen.

Any satisfaction with my appearance vanished. I was dowdy, even in sequins and heels. A silly middle-aged woman in a too-short dress. I stuttered my admiration of every detail of Ris' finished 'look', except the belly, I ignored that, and she accepted my gushing compliments, smiling as if my observations were so obvious they didn't require a response.

Then she reached out and took a lock of my curled hair and

twirled it round a pointed, blood-red nail. 'Have you dyed this blonde, Gail Frost?'

I stuttered that it was just out of a box, not a fancy salon treatment like hers and Mia's, and she nodded, as if that made sense. She let go of the lock and said the colour had taken years off me as she stroked a palm down the front of my dress, loose sequins spinning to the kitchen floor. I stepped back and explained the ensemble was a favourite of mine, although I hadn't had cause to wear it in years. Twenty, to be precise. It was my dancing dress, those days long over, of course. I felt ridiculous, mentally surveying myself through her eyes, the harsh kitchen lighting and Ris' intense stare diminishing me further. I was burning up, sweating in the constricting shapewear and polyester tights which were rolling down even as we spoke. How could she compute that her invisible assistant had once been younger, and equally as desirable, when I too found it incomprehensible? She said something flippant about how I could still show her a thing or two on the dance floor no doubt, and she glided out, smile painted on to greet Fleur who had appeared at the open front door.

I took the chance to pop down to the basement and see to my descending tights, but mainly to check through my rehearsed speech for Miles' arrival. I'd been over and over it, but the words jumped around and I knew I'd never get them out in the right order.

There had been questions when I was younger of me having a 'condition', something awful which was never investigated because Mother was having none of it. Not that she was defending me, more offended by the inference of faulty genes, although I have wondered if my propensity towards anxiety and depression is connected to that. Anyway, my mind would not behave, and there was an awful lot to unpack with Miles, in what I suspected would be a very small window of opportunity. I'd just have to hope something coherent came out my mouth when the moment arrived.

I went to the bathroom, again. The shape knickers such a pain to take down I almost didn't make it in time. My bladder can be... sorry, TMI, as they say. You don't need to know any of that. All you need to understand is that the guests had begun arriving. More of them, by the sounds of it, than anticipated.

But there was only one person I was waiting for. I straightened my dress and applied the bright-red lipstick I'd borrowed from Ris' stash on her dressing table. A smile as I rubbed my teeth and checked the result. A woman I hadn't seen in over twenty years smiling back at me from the past.

20

NINTH INTERVIEW WITH GAIL FROST – SUNDAY 20 NOVEMBER

The hallway was filled with strangers as I emerged from the basement. The only person I recognised was Mia, a look of utter derision on her heavily made-up face when she took in my appearance. 'Fuck me, Gay, what are you wearing?'

I could have asked her exactly the same thing. I'm not a prude, but to my mind, pregnancy is not a fashion choice and Mia's exposed, swollen stomach was not an attractive look: the dome of flesh betwixt a tiny crop top and low-slung mini skirt bisected by a dark brown line from navel to pubic area. An increase in melanin I believe, and yes, as nature intended, as you say, but did we all need to see it? It was definitely something I could have done without in my jittery state, and hardly the look I knew Ris was hoping for the first public outing of her new friend. Not that Ris introduced Mia to anyone that night; she ignored her as much as possible and Mia accepted that without question, so I assume it was a pre-agreed condition of her attendance that she keep, as suggested, a 'low profile'. I guess she gave it her best shot, but it was never going to happen, not with that amount of alcohol at play. Her breath was neat vodka.

I referenced the demure Cos dress she'd been asked to wear and Mia pulled a face, the enormous gold hoops swinging as she shook her head dramatically then laughed. I dropped my gaze to take in the full glory of her stomach, eyes then drawn down to scuffed white boots with platform soles, so chunky I was surprised her spindly, fake-tanned legs could lift them. I suggested again she might like to change into the dress Ris had bought her. It was a half-hearted recommendation. I didn't care either way by that point, but it was a bonkers ensemble, especially as she took that moment to further condemn my outfit.

'Woah, didn't realise it was a themed party! Are we disco-dancing tonight, Gay?' She twirled a finger in the air whilst she wiggled her slim hips, almost falling over, then added, 'Looking se-xy!'

I suppose my outfit was a bit retro and maybe a tad young on me, but I was wearing it for sentimental reasons and I wasn't going to let that little madam ruin my night. I accepted the compliment as though it were meant, smiling as Ris wandered past with Fleur, the former frowning at us as Mia loudly explained how she'd helped Ris into the couture Valentino, which was 'quite the performance'. I should have asked Mia what she meant – had she seen what was underneath? – but she wouldn't have told me even if she had, and besides, I was distracted with thoughts of Miles' arrival, my eyes flicking to the open door.

It was certainly getting busier in the hallway, new guests arriving all the time. Fleur explained she'd 'rallied the fans' when I met her coming back in from a trip outside. She was with an underling, I believe, the younger girl at her heels and carrying two heavy tote bags filled with books. I suggested they set up in the sitting room and maybe direct people in there. I left them to it and joined Ris in the kitchen, Mia clamped beside her, of course. The three of us vying for space as the caterers arranged the cupcakes on stands, the island covered in emptied white cardboard boxes. I asked Ris if she liked the piled-up creations, a miniature version of her book topping each frosted cake. My efforts going unappreciated, as always as she commented on the lateness of their delivery.

Mia's ear-splitting laugh cracked the hot air in the confines of the busy kitchen and Ris grimaced, reaching for a cupcake from one of the glittery tiered stands. Mia was flirting outrageously with a red-cheeked waiter, the laugh for his benefit. Honestly, even if I'd tried, there was no controlling her that night. I smiled at Ris and then, to my enormous surprise, she took a huge bite of the cupcake she'd been inspecting; a swirl of gold and white frosting sticking to her lipstick and even a blob on the end of her nose where high-lighter had been artfully brushed. She swiped the stickiness with flexed fingertips, as if the blood red nails were still wet, the rest of the cake popped in straight after, mini cover included. It was the only time I recall Ris eating refined sugar. And she relished every bite; all two of them. Then she strutted out, licking her lips and holding her bump, the fans parting to allow her to move through them, their glamorous if distant host a whole head taller in her Louboutins as she swiped a glass of champagne from a passing tray.

Mia looked at me and shrugged, then she did exactly the same: cake then fizz, clomping after Ris in those hideous white boots. I took a cake from the display beside me, then placed it back. No stomach for it. But I took a sip of champagne, for courage. I was going to need it. It was almost six forty-five.

* * *

The books looked nice, scattered around the packed sitting room on side tables and lined up on the decorative bookshelf in the corner, the gold accents on the covers glittering under the enormous chandelier and reminding me of disco balls spinning, my dress similarly sparkly. *Being Ris* was an oversized hardback, Ris' face on the cover in soft focus and with foil lettering for the title. Very classy and much admired on the night. Wish I'd swiped one now. I do like a souvenir. I might have a look on eBay; you can probably get one cheaper on there, although I assume the majority went into landfill, or do they pulp unsold books? Maybe they are stored in a warehouse somewhere? There's none in my local Waterstones, I can tell you that. They said they could order one for me, but the price! Thirty pounds! It's not worth that to me, or many others it would seem.

The irony is of course that notoriety and scandal brought Ris many new followers, but the old adage of any publicity is better than none is clearly not always the case. At least as far as sales of aspirational beauty and lifestyle bibles are concerned. Fleur was literally giving them away on the night, which I assume was in lieu of the rival's goody bags and the reason 'fans' had been persuaded to come at short notice. The ones I spoke to seemed to only know of Ris in passing, and none were familiar with her 'Brand'.

I may have contributed to the negative press, that's true, but I wasn't the only witness to what happened that night. There were numerous photographs taken and shared, and videos. Neighbours came out too, attracted by the sirens. It was bound to invite press attention, that level of drama, especially given Miles' status and Ris' so-called fans' predilection for social media. Mine was just one voice amongst many, but I suppose my interviews dominated. Gangs of journalists and photographers waiting outside my flat from the very next day. Banging on the glass door so hard I thought it might break, and there's nowhere to hide in here, as you can see. Except the toilet I suppose, but I couldn't sit in there all day.

They would press their noses to the glass, the journalists, whilst I sat at this table or on the couch over there, hoping they'd get fed up and leave. I could feel their eyes on me the whole time, even when mine were closed. Impossible to ignore them. Goading me to open the door and defend myself.

And I wasn't arrested at the party as reported by some. That was a woeful inaccuracy and no, I was not a 'known stalker' either! Utterly ridiculous.

But if you're asking if I regret my decision to speak up, then no, not on balance. I only wish I had been more accurately quoted, which is why it remains so very important to me that this be a truthful account.

I sincerely hope I've placed my trust in the right person this time. I've been misled with promises of 'telling my side of the story' before, and then it's all salacious clickbait and trial by the below-the-line comments.

And that photo the papers used when I finally gave in and talked, the one of me in my charity shop coat and rain hat running down the road to the corner shop... I should have worn the Burberry, but I thought they'd finally given up and gone home. It made me look deranged when I was only trying to get some bread and milk. Soon as I saw that photo I knew no one would believe me, I'd lost all credibility. That's why I went quiet for a while, to regroup and plan, until our serendipitous meeting when the universe intervened and I decided to trust you with everything.

Where was I? Oh yes...

The launch kicked off proper at a little after seven. Miles was even later than promised and Ris had wanted to wait, but Fleur was concerned people needed to get going and suggested it would be best to do the speeches sooner than later. Ris looked deflated by the reality of it all, the actuality so different from her expectations, her ire directed at the official photographer who'd been following her around and capturing poses with those she deemed worthy of her time. The so-called fans were not included. None of those professional photos saw the light of day as far as I'm aware and she told the poor man to leave long before Miles arrived. He was eating canapés and looking bored when I last saw him.

But Mia was having a whale of a time. Chatting to the startled and sometimes amused guests and taking glass after glass from the generous amounts of champagne available. Then Fleur tapped her glass and held up the book, Mia whooping loudly.

Ris shot me a pointed look then glanced in Mia's direction. I dropped my gaze and pretended I hadn't noticed. I had no time for Mia's antics and nothing left to prove.

I recognised the editor I'd briefly met, Phoebe, who was clapping at Fleur's glowing praise of Ris whilst raising an eyebrow behind her raised flute. I checked my wristwatch as Ris 'said a few words' and tried to clap with a glass in my hand, then there was brief lull before Mia's playlist started blasting out profane lyrics and a thudding bass.

Mia's gyrations, her swollen stomach thrusting as she dropped a hip and raised a hand, caused quite the stir. A glass was smashed, champagne spilt on one of the pink velvet couches, and guests were jostled in the crowded room before the music was switched off.

Ris grabbed Mia's hand and dragged her towards me, ignoring the stares as she hissed under her breath, 'Get her upstairs, Gail, now! She's drunk.'

Mia leant into me and I somehow got her out the sitting room despite the fact she was not in the least cooperative. A few insincere expressions of concern for her welfare as we skirted guests and eventually exited the room. We paused in the quieter hallway, Mia slumped at my side, and it was then I saw a long, dark car pull up outside, the front door left open for any latecomers. Typical that I was saddled with Mia when I finally had the opportunity to catch Miles alone. Mia choosing that precise moment to look up from her boots, startled, and say, 'I think I'm going to puke, Gay.'

I dragged Mia into the kitchen and propped her by the sink. She'd gone very pale, but I wasn't focused on her, my attention entirely with that parked limousine. The driver of the limo had opened the door for his passenger, but the guests were starting to spill out of the sitting room, signed books tucked under their arms, their meandering goodbyes blocking my view. I was ready to abandon Mia and push my way past to greet Miles when Ris flew out the sitting room and towards the front door, high heels clattering, book bearers duly parting to allow her through.

Mia groaned.

I ran a glass of water and shoved it in her general direction before abandoning her to make my way through the crowd, my 'excuse mes' largely ignored. It seemed I wasn't the only one interested in Miles' arrival, the hallway now rammed as everyone followed Ris. I went up on my toes and saw our host had fallen into the arms of a distinguished man in a navy suit. A glint of his gold wristwatch as Miles held his cloying wife at arm's length, then a tantalising flash of his profile as he turned to the house. I couldn't make out his expression from that distance, at least a dozen excitable young women between me and the door, but I knew it was him.

It was all so frustrating, near and yet far, and by then I was too wobbly to move, the sight of him making me quite literally, weak at the knees. So much emotion bound up in that moment, and what was to come. Everything depended on how the next few minutes panned out.

And just to reiterate, unlike Mia, I wasn't in the least drunk. Other than a sip of champagne, I'd switched to sparkling elderflower in the hopes of a clearer head and looser tongue, but as

Miles walked towards the house, Ris' clawed hand leading him up the path, every word I'd rehearsed for months, years even, deserted me. Every thought, every hope, gone. My mind entirely blank. I couldn't have told you my name if you'd asked me. The shock of seeing him was even greater than I'd anticipated. I shrank from view and retreated to the kitchen as if to tend to Mia's plight. The older woman in the shadows, looking after the drunk girl. Always my role, it would seem.

Mia was leaning forwards over the sink, saliva drooling from her open mouth. I glanced back to the door and saw Miles had been waylaid in the hallway by the excited 'fans', the handsome new arrival much more of a draw than his supposedly famous wife. When I next stole a furtive look, he was being introduced to Fleur, and Ris' agent, a striking redhead, Miles leaning in to accept a double kiss from both young women. He was drowning in a sea of femininity, the only male presence other than the pubescent red-faced waiter Mia had flirted with. Even the lone journalist – whom Fleur had confided in me she'd 'persuaded' to come at the last minute – was indistinguishable from the young female crowd. I suppose that's why Miles felt he was the one who had to come to the rescue in the end.

Those final few seconds were the hardest to endure. Although it meant I had time to take in the greying hair, and a few new laughter lines, but mostly I was catching my breath. The years had taken their toll, but there's no escape from that for any of us, is there? The heavy march of time. However much we might want to live in the past, the days roll by. But our youth lives on inside us. Sometimes more real than the present. I don't feel much different than I did as a young woman, not inside. I'm still that girl in the sparkly dress.

Age is just a number, and few aches and pains, take my word for it. We still want the same things.

I guess he must have sensed my gaze, seeking his out. And it's a terrible cliché, but our eyes literally locked. It was as if everyone else, even drunk Mia, had melted away. A pull so strong I had to cling on to the sink with both hands to restrain myself from moving towards him.

I'd lived for that moment, planned and schemed and sacrificed so much towards it. Too many years lost in the shadows. Sometimes it was only the thought of seeing him again that kept me going. Lonely, broken-hearted, and yes, I'll admit to it now, jealous. Of course I was. Ris had everything I wanted. But I stood tall when I saw the recognition in his eyes.

He has beautiful eyes. Photos never do them justice. Steel blue. But they narrowed too quickly and I saw familiar anger flare as he shook off his wife's possessive hand and pushed his way past Fleur and the flame-haired agent, and too many other people I have no name for, shoving Mia aside so hard I thought she might topple. She certainly swayed dramatically and said something loud and incomprehensible which drew stares, Ris' included. Miles ignored Mia and pulled me towards him, holding me by both wrists, so close I could smell his cologne and his laundered shirt. I daren't look up. I felt faint, but in heels I was level with the triangle of tanned flesh where he'd loosened his collar.

The scent of his skin took me straight back to a hotel lift, the powerful memory stealing my voice, my breath, almost my consciousness. As he held me up, grip so tight it hurt, all I could do was silently plead with him to acknowledge the bond that can never be broken. Not by twenty years, or two wives and myriad broken promises and lost chances, too many to mention. Nothing can ever keep us apart, because we have something so precious, so important it is undeniable. We have a child.

Our beautiful son's name was the only word I could utter. Two quiet syllables.

I still don't know if Miles heard me. It was complete chaos in that packed kitchen. But I know he understood. I've always known him better than anyone. Right from the start when we met on a flight to New York and spent a magical night together, Miles has always said I am the only one who truly gets him. That's why our love has stood the test of time.

21

NINTH INTERVIEW WITH GAIL FROST – SUNDAY 20 NOVEMBER

I must say, I'm disappointed the possibility never occurred to you that I might be 'The Other Woman' as you so prosaically now call me. Especially after I shared the diary pages I wrote at the time; a prompt I assumed would nudge a clever young woman like yourself in the right direction. Maybe I overestimated your investigative abilities? I should have been more upfront, handed the pages to you myself. But allow me that small indulgence after the lack of control I've lived with all these years. I wanted to witness you working it out; see the moment you joined all the dots, the revelation written in your expression. And I must say, it's been worth it. You look... blindsided.

Plus, there was the consideration of sparing both our blushes. It's an intensely private and candid account. I wasn't even sure at first that I'd have the courage to share my most intimate moments by proxy, let alone discuss them face to face. Although I knew it would be necessary, to ensure I am viewed as a credible witness this time.

And in fairness, why would you or anyone else ever suspect me? I'm the least likely person to have a passionate affair with a handsome millionaire. Invisible and the wrong side of fifty in my dowdy raincoat and slightly odd hat. I'm actually older than him, did you know that? Only a matter of eighteen months, but I suppose I do rather buck the trend. You can't, even now, equate me with that younger version, can you? You're trying to fit the woman seated in front of you at this rickety table in this grotty one room basement in Reading with the glamorous flight attendant you pictured in New York who met a handsome millionaire in First Class and fell in love. You thought she was in the recent past. Maybe, as Ris clearly felt, an ongoing threat. You mixed her up with Ris' suspicions of a current affair. And we have a child. That's another shock, I can see. Although you knew The Other Woman was pregnant. A precious son. Grown now, of course, and equally as handsome as his father. It's a lot to absorb, I get that. But do close your mouth, dear, it's not an attractive look.

You simply need to adjust your perspective a little. Rewind the last two decades to when I was thirty-six and Miles thirty-five.

Not that anyone but Miles and I had a clue what was going on between us, his grip on me lost to everyone else in that crowded kitchen. Especially Ris, whose entrance then split us apart. 'Ah, good, I see you two have met at last. This is Gail Frost, darling.'

I could see Miles weighing up his options, even as his hands fell to his sides, a forced smile for his wife. I opened my mouth to correct Ris' inaccurate introduction, but as usual, words failed me.

Ris was looking bemused at Miles' similar lack of response, her frozen forehead managing to wrinkle despite the recent top-up of Botox. 'I told you about her, darling, she's my right-hand woman. My executive assistant.'

Miles is usually such a pragmatist, but I suppose he didn't have the luxury of thinking time, forced to make a split-second decision. It can't have been easy for him. My presence was so unexpected and Ris was confusing matters further, but it took me by surprise when he grabbed my arm and dragged me out the kitchen, past stunned guests and that reporter, who put a very negative spin on why I was, as she put it, 'forcibly removed'.

I stumbled down the steps, my right ankle turning over painfully in the high heels. I must have cried out, but Miles didn't stop, or look back at Ris who was calling after us. Then we were in the road, a van swerving round us, horn blaring. That poor driver, neither of us looking and emerging at speed from between parked cars. He only missed us by inches.

I had no idea where we were headed until we reached the gate to the residents' private gardens, Miles warning me through gritted teeth to shut up and say nothing when I pleaded with him to listen, his fingers digging in my arm so hard I had the marks for days.

The gate was locked, as it always is, but he rattled it several times, frustration leaking as he swore at me when I explained he'd need a key.

Ris was trotting towards us by then in those crazy five-inch Louboutins, the tight dress making her even slower and the fake bump looking frankly ridiculous. I laughed in spite of myself and Miles gave me one of his looks, but the party was spilling out the door and Ris was catching us up, so I had no opportunity to explain. No time to say anything except, 'She's lying to you, Miles. She's a fake. The pregnancy is a fake.'

His blue eyes narrowed and he asked, 'What are you on about?'

Ris' artful hairdo had come undone by the time she reached us, tears brimming from between false eyelashes, dark tracks lining her face as she pouted. 'This is my special night, Miles. What's happening?' Then she looked at me. 'What have you done, Gail?'

Typical she would assume it was my fault. But Miles was ignoring her, more concerned by the guests who'd followed her across the road. He held up a hand and smiled at them, saying it was OK, all being handled, eyes unsmiling. The onlookers who'd given chase duly hung back, but they were watching us, wary. I suppose that's why he then spoke under his breath but enunciating every word for his stupid wife. 'This woman is *not* called Gail Frost, Ris. Her name is Abi Green. You understand?'

Ris took a step back, but the penny still hadn't dropped. 'Abi Green? No, you're mistaken, she's called Gail Frost. Abi Green is the woman who...'

She surveyed me then, much as you did a few minutes ago. Reassessing everything she'd taken for granted. Adjusting her perspective. Not that she knew anything about the real me, not really. All she knew was that name, Abi Green, and that it contained a perceived threat. A name from her husband's dim and distant past who'd made him cautious about staff, about friends. Abi Green who'd supposedly frightened his previous wife, Trudy, when she was pregnant, so the first wife had taken out a restraining order. A ridiculous overreaction, as was Ris' step back from me.

Ris and I had lived together for over two months by then, and I'd never so much as laid a finger on her. Quite the reverse; I'd cared for her, seen to her every need, even when she'd pushed me to the point of exasperation. Why would she consider me a danger now? But clearly she did.

Her hand flew to her chest and she sucked in the cooling evening air, so when they came out, her words were breathy. 'No, you can't be her. I checked your references. You showed me ID. You're not the stalker Trudy was terrified of when she was... that woman had a completely different name. Abi Green.'

Ris looked down at her bump and began the absurd circling movement again. She really was very slow on the uptake.

Miles' voice cut through, making us both jump. 'You need to shut up, Ris!' He glanced at the onlookers, the journalist amongst them, camera phone held up. There were several people doing that, even as Miles smiled at them and asked for privacy. Then, through gritted teeth he said, 'You better have got her to sign a fucking NDA, Ris.'

Ris started to cry again and he snapped, 'Fuck's sake, Ris. I thought after all the trouble with the last one, you'd have learnt your lesson!'

A ripple of something akin to shock came from the gathered onlookers. Miles looked up and gave them reassurances it was nothing and they should go back inside, have more champagne. But he was right to be worried. The massive stateside deal he'd been working on for over a year fell through soon after. A buy-in to a family-run chain of hotels in America who said they were 'concerned' by the negative press surrounding the Fox name. All Ris' fault.

He'll bounce back though, he always does.

Anyway, the extent of the fallout was at that point unknown, but clearly he was doing his best to limit it, so I adjusted my response to match his, despite his wife's histrionics, and pointed at Ris' stomach, trying again to explain to him, calmly and quietly, that there was no baby in there, only foam.

That's when Ris exploded. 'You're such a fucking liar! Coming into my home under false pretences. My God, I trusted you with everything: passwords, personal information...' She glanced at Miles, realising how he would react to that and pre-empting his anger with her own. 'We should call the police, Miles. Have her arrested. You don't believe her, do you?' Ris' hand circled the fake bump. 'If she's who you say she is, she's a known stalker!!!'

There was a collective gasp from the crowd, a shift in the dynamic, the mob baying.

What happened next was a last ditch act of desperation, I suppose. But I never had any intention of... I would never want to hurt anyone. You believe me, don't you? You know me well enough now to know I'd never intentionally... I just wanted Ris to admit to her lies, but she clearly wasn't going to, and I was frightened, with threats of the police being called. I saw it as my only chance. I was a cornered animal. You understand how I was feeling? I wasn't thinking or acting rationally. Everything was slipping from me, and I couldn't allow that. I just couldn't.

They say the camera never lies, but it did that night, all those phones raised. That journalist's video was the worst. I didn't know it was the same woman when I gave her my side of the story a few days later. But I promise you, it didn't happen how that video made it look, or sound.

I was just trying to prove in my clumsy way that Ris wasn't worthy of Miles' love, or loyalty, because she was nothing. The pregnancy was a hoax to entrap him. A complete fake, like her. And the only way I could see to finally get through to him was to expose that mound of fakery strapped to her flat stomach. Incontrovertible proof that she wasn't pregnant and he was free to leave her and finally be with me. The only woman who'd ever accepted him for who he is. All his flaws. All his failings. I was fighting for him. The man I love. The father of my boy.

I'm not proud to admit this, but yes, I lunged at her; but not to hurt her. Only to try and rip that dress open and expose what was beneath. The fabric was stiff and too tight, I couldn't get a hold. But I didn't mean to push her to the ground. I lost balance, in those silly heels. And we fell together like a pair of skittles. It was an accident. I swear on my life.

But I can tell you one thing, I felt that bump beneath me as we landed, Ris on her back, me above, my knees ripped to shreds on the tarmac, and it was not a baby squashed flat between us. No, there was nothing but foam or silicone, or some other padding in there. Not that the baying crowd saw that, she was too quick, pushing me off before she rolled onto her side, then curling in as if she had to protect the baby when all she was doing was hiding the truth from all those potential witnesses.

Then my hands were pulled back and twisted behind me so painfully I almost passed out as Miles yanked me up and threw me against the locked gate.

He had no idea at that point of the extent of her treachery, and he's always been a protector of women in that... well, that supposed state, and we were all acting irrationally, good sense and decorum thrown to the wind along with my pride, but it was hard to understand in the moment why he was being so rough. I fell heavily, my back hitting the solid metal bars so the wind was knocked out of me and I landed in a heap on the grass verge. Ris was hysterically sobbing and shying further away from me and the fans she'd barely said two words to before were suddenly her best friends, helping her up. Whilst Fleur was looking at me as if I should be burned at the stake. I think one woman actually stood between me and Ris.

Miles was doing his best to diffuse the panic, saying it was fine, just a misunderstanding, and looking at me as if I were the root of the problem, then making light of it by claiming I'd had too much champagne on an empty stomach, but no one was listening until he rubbed his palm through his hair and called for everyone to pay attention.

Miles then spoke as if he was reluctant to do so which made it sound much more authentic. He placed an arm around Ris and explained that I was being fired for gross misconduct, which was news to me. Someone offered to call the police and he shook his head, said that his wife, should not, in her condition, have to deal with this kind of crap from staff, again, so if everyone could please collect their belongings and leave, calmly, he would call the police. The party was over.

The gathered crowd all duly turned to the house, Miles' authoritative tone ensuring their complicity, and I was pulling myself up too, when someone screamed.

I don't know who screamed first, but it was definitely Fleur who screamed loudest, grabbing Miles by the sleeve and pointing up at the roof of number fifty-six. Then people were running back across the road, congregating on the path and looking up, grabbing one another for support.

I dried my eyes and wiped my hand under my nose and looked up too, my blurred gaze sweeping quickly from the open front door, up past the sitting room window, the study, into the eaves, then right up to the steeply pitched tiles where a small figure in white boots was standing at the apex, waving at us.

And that was when Mia lost her footing and fell.

22

NINTH INTERVIEW WITH GAIL FROST – SUNDAY 20 NOVEMBER

In the confusion of my expulsion from the house, Mia had been forgotten. Then she had somehow, inexplicably, ended up sixty feet above us on the roof.

As she fell, the screams were universal, including my own, chaos below as people ran to see where she'd landed. Not, thank goodness, at street level, but caught on a narrow ledge just below one of the two windows on the top floor and howling in agony. Her pain ripped through me with each anguished cry. I was about to run to her aide when Ris kicked off her heels and darted inside, Miles right behind her. I ran too, but someone held me back, the door slammed before I broke free.

I'm guessing Mia must have gone up to the roof terrace for a cigarette and then for some reason I still don't understand – maybe her drunken state made her bold – clambered her way round to the front of the house and up onto the slate roof. I wanted to do something, say something, but all I could do was come back down the steps and watch the house, as we all did, and listen, for any sound or movement. Because Mia had, worryingly, fallen silent.

My knowledge of the narrowness of the ledge she was lying on made me feel sick. I'd leant out once when one of the cleaners was demonstrating how impossible it was to get the mop down there, shaking her head as I'd peered at the collected mulch Ris had apparently moaned about. The ledge is only a foot wide and there is no barrier. I thought of the baby then, squashed beneath Mia who'd fallen forwards. Not a mound of foam but a real child, in danger. Why had the screams subsided? If Mia had blacked-out, she could easily roll over the edge and then—

I stepped back into the road and shielded my eyes against the evening sun. A platform boot, chunky white, was now hanging over the edge. Then the window above opened and a hand was stretching down. If a mop couldn't reach the ledge, Miles definitely wouldn't be able to.

It was excruciating. Mia was right there, just below him, on a knife edge. But out of Miles' reach. He retreated. The helping hand gone.

We waited, rubbernecks folded back, a bigger crowd gathering on the pavement and in the road, cars forced to slow and swerve. I was slightly apart from the other party guests who'd congregated by the door, Fleur eyeing me warily from the steps. Her reaction saddens me. Fleur and I had built quite a bond over our shared frustrations with Ris. She'd even told me in confidence she was thinking of leaving PR and I'd suggested cabin crew as a good option for someone as sociable and vivacious as her. I really felt like we'd built trust. Anyway, she and others were clearly suspicious of me after the previous scuffle, so I took up a position at the back of the group, but I couldn't have left Lexington Gardens. Even though there was the opportunity to slip away and avoid the threat of police action. Not with lives at risk.

The other top-floor window then opened and Miles climbed out, his back pressed to the house, palms flat against the stucco as he edged towards Mia along the mossy ledge. I could barely breathe. He would never survive that fall. No one would. But it was impossible to look away.

God, it was awful watching him inch towards her. Some of the younger girls were hugging, shrieks when he would wobble, stop, steady himself and then start again, slowly sidestepping.

He eventually got close enough to crouch down and reach out, a muscular arm stretching, fingertips snatching at one of those awful white boots. Then the tortuous return journey as her body, inert, was pulled little by little towards the open window he'd climbed through. But it was far too risky, anyone could see that. Her arm slipping over to a collective intake of breath below. He sat beside her then, holding her hand, his bare feet dangling, and although I can't be sure, I think he closed his eyes. That's when I assumed she was dead.

* * *

Someone must have called 999 as blue lights came flashing round the corner only minutes later. In fact, now I think about it, they were so speedy maybe they had been called earlier by a 'well-meaning' but misinformed guest during the misrepresented fracas between myself and Ris.

Anyway, a police car arrived, followed by an ambulance, then a while later a fire engine. The whole street in chaos, blocked off at both ends, uniforms everywhere. We were held back, moved across the street. Lining up in groups, me on my own of course, in the lengthening shadows, the flashing lights dazzling so at times I could no longer see Miles that clearly at all.

Two officers and two green suited paramedics ran up the steps first and began knocking loudly until an unseen person, I assume Ris, let them in, then the fire crew mounted their rescue, clearing the area even further so we had to watch from the park gates, backs to the same railings I'd been winded on. A firefighter appeared at the window Miles had climbed through and persuaded him back inside, a glimpse of Ris as she hugged *Hubs*, then a roped fire-fighter emerged and inspected Mia's inert body with care. A stretcher was lowered and she was winched to safety. It was executed quickly and with relative ease, but she'd looked like a pregnant rag doll.

* * *

We waited outside for a long time after that. Mutterings of, 'Did anyone know her name, poor girl?' I heard a few suggestions bandied around, none correct. Then, as the warm evening fell away into a chillier atmosphere entirely, the mutterings changed to whispers about how unacceptable her behaviour had been. Was she a cocktail waitress as Ris had once been? Was that the connection? Someone else said they thought she might have been a relative; 'Ris' family weren't known to be the best'. Concern soon turned to condemnation. 'Fancy drinking that much when you're pregnant.' Then the coincidence of the pregnancies was debated. 'Maybe Ris met her at an antenatal class, that could have been what happened?' And then, 'Thank goodness Miles got to her, what a hero.' Then thoughts returned to Ris herself. How she was so brave running in without a thought, and in her condition too. Inevitably, all eyes turned to me as Fleur added, 'Especially after being attacked in the street by a mad woman.'

Maybe thirty minutes later, it felt like hours but can't have been, the front door opened and the stretcher was carried out. Mia was under a blanket and strapped in, but she sat up and called out something incomprehensible. It was oddly comforting, a good sign. The swear word I caught, particularly reassuring. Then the sirens took her away and it was quiet again. I thought about leaving then, but I hadn't waited all this time to see Miles again, only to walk away. I had to open his, and hopefully everyone's, eyes to the truth.

A female police officer came out the door to take names and contact numbers, offering assurances all was well with the 'girl on the roof', mother and baby unharmed other than a suspected broken wrist, but they'd whisked her away 'just in case'. No one would be allowed back in tonight unless they were family, coats and bags handed out on the doorstep. I tried to explain I lived there but was interrupted by Fleur who told the police officer what had happened, or her version of it. Someone else then very helpfully showed a video clip on their phone, I think the reporter, but who knows? I certainly didn't realise it was the same woman when I invited her into my home in good faith a few days later.

It was all a blur by that point in the evening. Twilight was falling, or maybe rain. It felt cold and that odd half-light that casts shadows. The party well and truly over.

* * *

I never made it back inside number fifty-six, guided instead towards a police car parked a little down the road. I asked what was happening, where were they taking me? The young officer charged with 'looking after me' seemed to have no more idea than I did. 'Just a few questions,' the female officer said when she returned with my belongings and threw them into the boot. I suppose it was fortunate that I'd packed everything as a precaution, including my notebook, observing that perennially true adage of 'Hope for the best but plan for the worst'. Or is it the other way around? No matter. Me and my battered case were leaving in a marked car, blue lights flashing. As if I were a criminal being arrested, which I absolutely am not.

So that's how I left Lexington Gardens last June. Tights ripped, knees bloodied, heart breaking, a shoe lost somewhere so I'd limped to the car, and still wearing a ridiculous sparkly dress, incongruous frivolity as the sirens began wailing, ghostly faces watching my ignominious exit as we sped the length of those white mansions and turned the corner, taking me away from everything I'd hoped could at last be mine. My dreams over, plans in tatters.

23

NINTH INTERVIEW WITH GAIL FROST – SUNDAY 20 NOVEMBER

They kept me at that police station for eight hours, asking me the same things over and over until my head spun. I was offered a solicitor, but I just wanted to get it over with. It was almost dawn as I emerged into a new day. Traumatised by the events at the party. The police wouldn't even tell me how Mia was, said she was being taken care of, and I shouldn't worry, but I couldn't help it. All they were interested in was the scuffle between Ris and I. Was it true I was stalking Miles Fox and had been living there for almost three months under an assumed name? It's all quite straightforward, as I kept telling them. And no, it wasn't an assumed name, it was my real name, they both were. Although, technically speaking anyone can call themselves anything they like, not an offence as far as I know.

* * *

Green was my married name. The one I was using when I met Miles in New York. Mrs Abigail Green. Feels like another life now that I've been Gail Frost again for the best part of what... six months. But you know, I quite liked the fact the change gave me license to be a bit different. That was all part of the performance, I suppose. Taking on a new identity, or in my case, resuming an old one. But as I also told those detectives, I'm not a stalker. That's completely untrue.

Frost was my maiden name and I hated it. It reminded me of an unhappy childhood. 'Abigail Frost, what on earth have you done now?' I'd gladly taken my husband's surname, Green, as soon as we were married, and even stuck with it after the divorce. He died a few years back, of a heart attack, I believe. We lost touch soon after the decree nisi, and we were already well into the process of separating when I met Miles on that flight to New York. An affair was the last thought on my mind. I was working. Our paths crossed. That was all. Although, I was immediately attracted to him, and I can't claim any impunity on the grounds of being broken-hearted about my husband and I parting ways. The marriage was long over, and I wouldn't term it a marriage at all. We were never in love. At least, I wasn't. 'Marry in haste, repent at leisure,' as Mum would say. As well as repeatedly reminding me, 'Lucky you didn't have any children, Abigail.'

She was right, in a way. But my husband was a good man and he gifted me a better name, which I'd kept.

So I was Mrs Abigail Green right up until I applied for the job as Ris' assistant.

Fellow cabin crew knew me as Abi, adopting the shortened version of Abigail without asking, and it fitted that perky persona expected of female crew, even if I didn't always gel with their idea of the role. It was party-party back then, and I was a career gal. Until I met Miles and fell in love...

He always called me Abs.

Like I said to those detectives when they lost patience with me, it's very simple really. Abi Green became Gail Frost. Because the best lies contain an element of the truth. Not that I said *that* to the police. Just that I was very sorry for what I'd done, and yes, I'd keep away from Ris and Miles in the future, although technically speaking I haven't violated the restraining order. It was years old and only applied to Trudy, Miles' first wife. Another very unnecessary overreaction.

I was very clear with the officers who interviewed me that my misdemeanours then and now were completely misrepresented, any 'threats' as they termed them were purely imagined. Although I was relieved when they told me they had decided not to prosecute and I was free to go. Anywhere except Lexington Gardens, they warned me. Said I should consider myself extremely fortunate, and that I'd had a very lucky escape.

I didn't feel in the least lucky.

I came back here, to Reading, and then the journalist from the party arrived, along with many others. They'd got hold of the story via social media. Videos and photos of a disturbance at a Belgravia party and an unnamed girl on the roof.

You know the rest.

I've few regrets, they're rarely worth it, but I have to say those terrible stories in the papers have done little to improve our son's opinion of me, or that photo of me running down the street. I've tried to keep him out of this as best I can, but it's proved impossible to convince anyone of the truth without referencing my past with Miles, and so I decided that I would have to find a better confidante and explain everything. I'm tired of our son being treated as if he never existed. Our child, well grown man as he is now, is proof of a bond that cannot be broken. Although he won't thank me for dragging him into it. He's got his own life now, and there's no space in it for his mad old mother.

I haven't told you his name, deliberately of course, but I'm sure you could find out. Please don't. Much like his father, he is a very private man. They share a lot in common, but the Fox name was never on offer. Not that he would want it. He has made it plain he has no wish to claim that dynasty. Yes, he's full of his own opinions. Two peas in a pod they are, despite whatever either of them may say. And yes, they know one another, extremely well. Estranged now, sadly, but as a boy he idolised his dad, and it was entirely mutual, I assure you.

* * *

Miles was in his mid-thirties when we met, and as I say, I was a little older than him, only by eighteen months but I think that's what made the difference. Miles always saw me as someone to look up to. To confide in. His rock, he called me. He was at the start of his empire-building. Trudy, his first wife, had funded a lot of the early investment in clubs and hotels, her wealth eclipsing his, although Miles came from money too. You could tell that as soon as you met him. A certain confidence, even swagger. It was very hard to resist.

They'd met at university and got married very young, tried to get pregnant for years, but it hadn't happened. By the time he and I met it seemed unlikely Trudy would conceive, despite medical intervention. He was relieved, he told me, because it would make it easier to divorce, a clean break. He didn't love Trudy. Probably never had. Their lives were enmeshed through circumstance, not love, but soon it got even more difficult.

You won't remember the days of having a text message allowance. I had such a basic phone. The Nokia brick. I believe it's collectable these days but I'll never part with mine, for sentimental reasons. Those early messages are so precious. We exchanged them incessantly, no thought to the cost; well, maybe a little for me, but I didn't care. And he pursued me, flowers and presents. But it wasn't lavish gifts I wanted; it was him.

You've read the rather painful account I wrote at the time of what happened next, so I won't go over that again. Suffice to say Trudy's unexpected news put rather a crimp in our plans. The IVF had worked.

I've never met the twins, but I gather they have survived their parents' divorce unscathed which is exactly what I tried to explain to Miles at the time. There is no point sacrificing your happiness for theirs, it doesn't work like that, but Miles was trying to do the right thing. He's always tried to do the right thing. That's what you should have read in the diary, but I don't suppose you were looking for his better qualities, were you? Any more than you were looking for me. You saw a woman scorned. A young, foolish woman. And a philandering husband who left his mistress pregnant and penniless. But see it from the other side for a moment. Think of the dilemma he faced, how there was no way that he could be with us both, not the whole time. There's only one of him and he had two families, to his great surprise. His sperm count and my maturity... I won't go into detail but it seems our 'connection' had conquered all. And he loved us all as best he could, for many years.

I don't have to justify myself, or Miles, to you, or anyone. But don't condemn without knowing the full story. Although you're right: his decision to marry Ris was the hardest to bear. After years of waiting for him to leave Trudy, and then when the girls were finally old enough, he ended up with *her*. I knew he'd live to regret hooking up with someone so beneath him and I told him so. That was the start of the rift, I suppose, but I had to say something. For him as much as me.

From the moment I saw those first photographs of them in the newspapers, I knew she was the wrong choice. Even setting aside my feelings of betrayal and anger, she was nothing but a glorified barmaid, and sleeping her way around London if you believe the gossip, which I do.

We fell out over Ris and Miles' visits to our lovely rented home in Reading ended, as did his financial support, but I knew he'd come to his senses eventually; I just had to be patient. Like I say, we all make mistakes. Some worse than others. I was prepared to forgive him.

But it was hard to just sit back and do nothing. Ris flaunted her ill-won good fortune on social media. And me, fool that I am, could not look away.

What even is an influencer? It's nothing, that's what. A made-up word for a made-up occupation. All smoke and mirrors. No wonder she was paranoid about losing him. She had no right to him in the first place, and he had so clearly fallen out of love with her, if he ever loved her in the first place. Lust is all-consuming, I know that, but what's left behind is what sustains a relationship through the good and bad times. And actions very much do speak louder than words.

You only had to look at her posts even a few months after they were married to see he was never with her. I had to do something. Like I say, for him, as much as me.

I suppose it all sounds barmy to you now. Why would I even want him after the way he'd abandoned me and our son? But if you think that, then you haven't been listening properly. He cared for us. He loved us, both. Yes, his visits stopped after he met Ris, but you don't switch off a love as strong as ours. I knew that bond hadn't been broken, not irrevocably. Miles and I share a son, but more than that, we have shared the very best parts of ourselves. We have been a family. From the moment I told him I was pregnant he was by my side, or at the end of a phone. He always called me back or messaged, even when he was busy. We understand one another in a way no one else can. I wasn't going to stop loving him just because he temporarily lost his mind. He wouldn't be the first or the last man to have a mid-life crisis. When you care that deeply for someone, you have to forgive them.

You think me a fool, and an old one at that. I can see it in your eyes. *She's deluded. Maybe even a threat.* That's how I was portrayed in the press. A mad woman stoking the conspiracist theories. And I admit that at the start, this was a plan to prove Ris unworthy.

Revenge? Yes, I suppose so, if I'm honest. At least, in part. But mainly I felt it beholden on me to open Miles' eyes to his mistake.

I never wanted to *be* her, as you put it, but replace Ris at Lexington Gardens, that was an attractive proposition. Of course. Who wouldn't want to live in Belgravia in preference to a bedsit that stinks of damp and a toilet that won't flush properly? I'd be lying if I told you I didn't covet that home, that lifestyle, but it wasn't ever about that. Cherry on the cake, for sure, but it was Miles I wanted. And I'd waited long enough. I'm a patient woman, but we all have our limits.

Anyway, that pipe dream is over now. I am a fool, and an old fool. That's painfully clear. But there is more than a broken-hearted woman's pride at stake here.

A girl was taken away in an ambulance. A pregnant young girl who seems to have vanished without trace. Not even when I got wise to the system and told the hospitals I rang round, the necessary but blatant lie that I was her distraught mother.

It's been five months since I left Lexington Gardens and not a day has gone by when I haven't thought about Mia Chance. Nineteen years old, pregnant, injured. Missing.

Which is why we need to go back, you and I, and find out exactly what's happened to that poor girl and her unborn son. We need to find Mia.

EMAIL SUBJECT: INTERVIEWS WITH GAIL FROST

DATE: MONDAY 21 NOVEMBER

Hi, great to have a quick call last night after I finally got back to London from Reading. So much to unpick. I was blindsided by that last interview. A twenty-year pursuit is something else. Even now we know there's a love child to consider, and that (according to Gail) Miles was in their son's life for the first seventeen of those years, Gail's bunny boiler quest is really not helping her credibility. Good shout to look for any press releases from Mr and Mrs Fox's legal team. Very cleverly handled by Miles' publicist. A neatly worded statement designed to debunk the wilder theories and defuse all the press and social media interest in the aftermath of the calamitous party. And minimal reference to the unnamed 'girl on the roof'. A professional cover-up if I ever saw one. And no mention of the restraining order Gail's told me about. Cannot see any reason she'd make that up, so clearly Miles didn't want any more publicity. Even Gail's questioning by police is glossed over with 'enquiries concluded and no further action taken'. Which could further indicate his desire to keep things quiet for the sake of his business interests. As Gail said, there was a Stateside hotel chain deal at stake, which still fell through, but is something more sinister than business interests being kept under tight wraps? Either way, his lawyers and publicist have cleared up what could have been a much bigger mess, passing it off as a party where too much booze flowed and things got a bit out of hand after a member of staff was dismissed for 'gross misconduct'. Even Gail's attempts to stoke the flames of conspiracy soon fizzled out, her account, such as it was after her story was reduced to sound bites and scrappy videos, widely discredited as the sour grapes of a mentally unstable sacked employee. I've put in a call with the journalist she spoke to who was at the party, but she's nothing to add. Clearly wrote up Gail as a nutcase and we don't want to ignite any competing interest in the story at this delicate stage of negotiations with interested production partners, I'm assuming?

The so-called 'fans' have disappeared back into the ether. Ris was only a big deal for a very short time and the fact she's deleted her accounts has killed all that. So I'm left with Gail's testimony which does match the facts, mostly. Although one party guest I DM'd, who'd posted a photo of the 'attack' on Instagram, described Gail as 'unhinged' and said she definitely saw her lunge at Ris.

I do share Gail's concern about Mia's whereabouts, particularly as I had a very interesting call from Harriet late last night. Remember her? The medic who was a former cleaner at Lexington Gardens. She contacted me to tell me about someone she's recently met on an office cleaning job in Holborn. Turns out this woman was a former friend of Mia's! Apparently Mia was also an office cleaner, briefly, just before she hooked up with Ris, but was fired from the job for stealing. Petty stuff, office supplies, but obviously not good, and Mia kicked up a huge fuss when caught, refused to leave the premises until threatened with the police. This woman told Harriet she felt sorry for Mia because she was pregnant and no sign of the father, but Mia told her not to worry and then she showed her Ris' Instagram profile. Said she was hoping to stay in this new friend's posh house in Belgravia, so they could stuff their shitty job. Interesting, but we know most of this, except Mia also told her she'd chosen a different name in this chat room for expectant mums where she'd made the friend, because foreign sounding surnames were 'off-putting' to some people (!!).

Mia Chance is actually called Amelia Koslowski.

I've found her on social media, not that she's posted in months, but I made contact with an Elise Koslowski last night, after finding an appeal for information about her missing sister, Amelia. Father is Polish, deceased. Mum works in a school. Nice if modest family home in Chelmsford, Essex. They officially reported Amelia missing three months ago, although they've been concerned about her for over six months when she left to 'travel' with a new boyfriend. But they had no idea she was pregnant or going under a different name, or that she was so close by. Only just over an hour from home by train or car.

Elise, older by five years, agreed to come to London and meet with me as a matter of urgency regarding her missing sister. Because Harriet also told me this office cleaner who wants to remain nameless – said she can't risk a visit from the police! – kept in touch with Mia for a while and was becoming increasingly worried about an 'arrangement' she'd set up with her rich benefactor. The last message gave the impression Mia was still living with Ris in Belgravia and that was this month, I think she said around the sixth, the day before I saw Ris rushing to the chemist for colic meds. Was Mia still there, looking after a baby Ris claims is hers? I could be adding two and two and getting five (a Gail-ism!!!) but you know… Mia was maybe still there? Which is in one way reassuring after the last known sighting of her was leaving in an ambulance back on 16 June.

In a series of late-night messages and calls up to 6 November, Mia told this cleaner friend she'd got in out of her depth with a plan she'd hatched with her boyfriend, who apparently was a druggy waste of space but had resurfaced when he got wind of Mia's new living arrangements. It was never specified exactly what the plan was, but the inference was a big payout was expected. This nameless woman told her to get out of there, she could stay at hers, find her a new cleaning job, but

Mia said she couldn't work, she'd broken her wrist and it wasn't mending well. The cleaner never heard from Mia again after that. Calls, messages, all unanswered.

I think, as Gail has said, we need to go round there ASAP.

I know this isn't entirely ethical, so totally on me, and take a deep breath... but Elise, Mia's sister, is with me now. We're waiting for Gail's train to arrive at Paddington and then I'm going to drive them both to Lexington Gardens to confront Ris with this new evidence.

Elise looks exactly like Mia, take a look at the family photos on Facebook, so her turning up should get a strong reaction, even if Ris slams the door in our faces. And Elise is wearing an identical locket, with the same photos in as the one Gail found.

Will keep you updated. Wish me luck. I need this to pan out as I think I may have lost my job. My editor was not happy when I called in sick again.

Best wishes,

Ax

CALLS/VOICEMAILS WITH GAIL FROST – MONDAY 21 NOVEMBER 3.00PM:

A: Gail, it's me, I'm here with Elise, we're back in my car round the corner from Lexington Gardens. I thought you were with us. Where did you go? We're going to drive back round, see if we can see you outside fifty-six. Call me when you get this.

A: Gail, can you call me back? And whatever you do, don't go into the house!

G: Hi, just to let you know, I'm in the house, and before you go mad, I don't think it's technically breaking and entering if you have a key, which I do, at least for the basement. I'll call you again once I've sorted the alarm. I'm hoping the code is still the same but if you hear it go off, come get me!

A: It absolutely is breaking and entering!!! Gail, get out of there, now! I'm going to drive round to fifty-six, meet me outside, or call me!

A: Gail, call me back. Or just come out. We're driving past now.

G: Missed your call again. But it's fine, I sussed the alarm. Code's been changed, but there was one of those tile-thingies, hanging on a hook by the door. Honestly, people are so lax with security. It's like they want to… sorry, got distracted there. It is very odd being back here. I'll hang up now and have a good look round. See if there's any sign of Mia. Call you in a min.

A: Gail, we're driving round again. Can you please answer your fucking phone or just get out of there!

A: Gail, thank goodness, I was just leaving you another message, you OK?

G: Yes, I'm fine, I'll put you on speaker. Think I just saw you drive by. Did you see me wave? I was in the study.

A: Gail, listen, this is not a good idea, you could be—

G: Yes, yes, I'm leaving. Although… I just had a thought. The suitcase, the huge one she took to Paris, I think she keeps it at the back of her wardrobe in her dressing room. I'll just check that again before I leave.

A: Gail? You OK? You still there?

G: I'm fine, just pulling the case out. Can you still hear me? My phone is… damn, the case is locked, interesting… Ris has nail scissors in the dressing table drawer. I'll grab those. Hang on!

A: Gail? You OK? Was that a scream?

G: Sorry, I managed to stab myself with the scissors as I tried to bust the lock.

A: Stabbed yourself?

G: Just a scratch, I'm more worried about opening the case than, although… there's actually a lot of blood. I'll get a towel.

A: Gail, are you OK? Gail?

G: Yeah, bit of a mess on the carpet, but I'll wrap it in a towel. Oh my god!

A: What? Gail? What's oh my god? Gail, are you OK?

G: I've just caught sight of myself in the bathroom mirror and I look a state, blood smeared all over my face! Anyway, got my hand wrapped up now and I also found some better scissors to prise the lock.

A: You might not want to open that case, Gail. How heavy was it? Human sized?

G: Don't be ridiculous! Hang on, this is going to take a bit of brute strength, I'll just put the phone down again. There! Cracked it!!! And I knew it!

A: Knew what? Gail?

G: Just like I saw on the internet, but they are freaky in real life. Like Russian dolls, but limbless and headless, one inside another. Flesh coloured, attached to stretchy–

A: The fake bumps?

G: Yes. I suppose I'd describe them as small, medium and large and I've bled all over them. Not that it matters now. This is our evidence, isn't it? Proof of what I've been saying all along.

A: Gail, take a photo and leave.

G: How can I take a photo?

A: On your phone?

G: Except I don't have a camera phone, remember?

A: For fuck's sake, the Nokia brick! That's all you have with you?

G: Yes, I had to give back my work phone as a condition of my release from the police questioning. Shit! I think I heard the front door open.

A: Gail, you need to get out of there. Can you get back down to the basement and out that way? Gail?!

Voice Note from A – Monday 21 November, 4 p.m.

Hey! Sorry to contact you again whilst you're on a shoot, but to cut a long story short, Gail let herself back in through the basement door of Lexington Gardens about an hour or so ago. She still has a key, so maybe it's not technically… anyway, she was disturbed, as in someone came home. We're in the car, Elise and me, parked a couple of streets away, been waiting for Gail to call, but I think we should leave now. Regroup at the hotel Elise is staying at and wait for news from Gail there. Feel really bad abandoning her, but not much choice. I don't think I should call the police either. Gail will be in all kinds of trouble, and if she mentions my involvement… realise that's totally on me, but Gail took matters very much into her own hands. Plus… hang on, just getting out the car a sec… Sorry, Elise is a mess, frantic about her sister and making noises about calling the police herself in case Mia is in danger. I need to put some distance between us, boundaries. Feel like I've royally fucked up. I'll call or message again soon.

* * *

Voice Note from A – 5.15 p.m.

Hi, I've dropped Elise at her hotel and decamped to a bar in Soho. Elise is going to call the police and I wanted to try and keep my name out of Gail's break-in, which she's promised to do. I tried to call you again for some advice, but I know you're mid-shoot. I'll call back as soon as I know more. Sorry!

* * *

Voice Note from A – 8.58 p.m.

Me again! You're probably sick of these messages, and I've completely lost track of which time zone you're on. It's late evening here but call me if you're available; you'll want to hear this. I've just got off the phone from Gail. She's fine, been sent to A&E to get patched up for a cut hand, but other than that, unscathed.
But there's news of Mia and Ris. Huge news. It's just awful. I can't believe what's happened. Anyway, can you call? Not something I want to

leave in a message. Not after the journey we've been on with these three women. Jeez, I wish this had gone another way.

Voicemail from Gail Frost – 9 p.m.

I tried to call you back, but you were on another call I think. Anyway, regarding your kind offer to take me to A&E and then a hotel, I've been to a chemist and got one of those wound dressings, so I'm heading home now. The last train to Reading is about to leave so I'll call you in the morning, explain it all then. There's not a lot more to say than you already know from our previous call, but I'll fill in the details tomorrow once I've processed everything, or begun to. It's been such a shock, as I'm sure you understand. I want my own bed tonight. It might not be much, but I need to be as far from Lexington Gardens as possible after what I witnessed there today. And there's nothing any of us can do for her now, is there? So very sad. I'll call you tomorrow. Bye for now.

Call with Gail Frost – Monday 21 November, 9.05 p.m.

A: Gail, where are you now?
G: As I explained in my message, rushing to catch the last train. And I cannot find which platform it's leaving from, so if you'll forgive me—
A: Don't leave London, Gail, please. We need to talk. You're in shock, it will help to talk it out.
G: I'm tired. And to be honest, I can't face seeing Elise. Great! Platform two, which is of course the furthest away!
A: You don't have to see Mia's sister if it's too much. We can go to a

different hotel. But we need to catch up. I have questions. Lots of them. Stay. I'll cover your costs.

G: I'm sorry, we will talk, but now I really have to—

A: Gail?

G: Fuck, I just missed the last train. Thought I might be lucky, but of course not!

A: OK, I'll book you an Uber now.

G: There's really no need, I can make my own arrangements.

A: There, done! It'll be outside Paddington in four minutes and I'll see you at the hotel in half an hour.

G: Thanks, I appreciate it, but could we save our talk until tomorrow morning? I'm exhausted.

A: Come on, Gail, you owe me that much.

G: OK, but maybe make it forty-five minutes. I need a shower. Wash the blood off.

24

TENTH INTERVIEW WITH GAIL FROST – MONDAY 21 NOVEMBER, 10 P.M.

Mum used to say there's not much you can't fix with a cup of tea, but of course she was very much mistaken. Not that she ascribed to her own advice, but yes thank you for asking, it is helping. As did a hot shower. What time is it? Left my watch by the sink and I like to be in bed by midnight at the absolute latest. I'm exhausted now, as I'm sure you can appreciate. But yes, maybe best to explain what's happened whilst it's fresh in my mind. Get it over with.

* * *

As you know, I used my key to get in via the basement after I gave you and Elise the slip. Sorry about that but you were so adamant I couldn't go in and... anyway, I glanced round the basement quickly, but I was in a rush to get to the alarm before it went off, and once that was sorted, I checked round the rest of the house, which was messier, baby paraphernalia everywhere, but no evidence of Mia, not as far as I could see. Then I was waylaid by investigating the suitcase, the one Ris kept at the back of her walk-in wardrobe, or as she always called it, her 'dressing room'. I'd checked the case before and found it empty, but the fact it was locked this time made me even more determined. Then of course I managed to cut my hand breaking into it.

Yes, it's fine now it's dressed, thank you, but it did bleed an awful lot which must have added to the shock when Ris found me sitting on the cream shagpile, also stained horribly with my dark claret, face smeared with blood, as were those freakish prosthetic pregnancy bumps which I had spread out around me. Weird things they were, three fleshy domes, small, medium and large, attached to nude vest tops. She must have been slipping them on under her clothes, which very much upholds what I've been saying all along, doesn't it?

Oh, it's fine, I'm not interested in apologies. Way beyond that level of vanity.

Ris screamed at the sight of me, dramatic as always – although I must have looked like something out of a horror movie – which roused Miles, who sprinted up after her and took in the same scene. They'd been to a private doctor in Harley Street for Ris, apparently, but I'll get to that.

There was a fair bit of shouting after that, some mine, I have to admit. I felt very much vindicated and therefore somewhat belligerent, but I tried to explain to them that I wasn't there to cause any trouble – half-hearted threats of the police and no second chances were being bandied about – I just wanted to talk to them about Mia and her baby. Establish they were both OK. Wasn't her wrist broken in the fall? Was she better? Where were they now?

Miles said as far as they knew, Mia was fine; she'd long moved on. I said I knew that wasn't true and Ris fell unexpectedly quiet as I explained I knew Mia's real name, and that I'd met her sister.

Oh, and to reassure you, I didn't say you were involved, or even mention your name at all, but I made it plain I had enough evidence to prove Teddy wasn't Ris', and that unless they could produce Mia that second, I would be going to the police and damn the personal consequences.

There was panic in Ris' eyes, pure panic, but she still hadn't said anything to dissuade me from my concerns. Leaving it up to Miles to try clear up her mess.

He did his best, claiming the police wouldn't listen to a word I said, which I know was for Ris' benefit, but even so... it did get my goat which is why I might have been a little... overwrought, shall we say. I explained I had access to screenshots of a chat room exchange linking Mia and his wife six months before, as well as a friend of Mia's who'd been in touch with her constantly up until just a couple of weeks ago when she was still living at Lexington Gardens. That's when Miles flashed his wife a look of disbelief and invited me downstairs to talk it through. Like adults. There would be a solution. We just needed to find one that suited us all. And I needed to calm down. He was most insistent about that. And he was right; I'd rather lost my cool.

* * *

It was all very civilised at first, Miles asking if I needed anything for my cut hand, the towel still wrapped around it, and offering sweet tea, for the shock. Ris and I went into the sitting room, Ris carrying Teddy who'd been left in the hallway in his pram but had woken and was crying. He's a very handsome boy, but so clearly not Ris' child. I said that to her whilst we waited for Miles to return with the tea, also observing I thought Teddy looked a couple of months old, at a guess, thinking back to my son at that age. She looked up from the baby and said, 'You told me you never wanted kids.' It was true, I hadn't. Not until I found out I was pregnant by the man I loved, but it was neither the time nor place to share that with her.

Mia was, of course, never far from my thoughts. I saw a resemblance in the baby, that Polish influence which Elise also has. God, poor Elise, how do you ever recover from news like that? How is she?

Of course, to be expected.

This is going to sound odd to you, in the circumstances, but it was so nice to be an invited guest for once, the chandelier twinkling above us and the softness of the pink velvet sofas as Miles brought in a clinking tray. It all felt very civilised. Although the colour palette wouldn't be my choice, or Miles' either. He prefers a homely place to come back to after his travels, a shepherd's pie in the oven and Lego all over the rug to build castles and ships with our boy, the simple pleasures... anyway, Miles poured my tea, no need to ask how I take it, and then inspected the cut to my palm, cleaning and dressing it with a wipe and plaster he'd brought on the tray. I took my first sip as he sat back down by Ris. Then he took her hand and said, 'OK, how much do you want this time, Abs? And this has to be it; no more!'

I was apoplectic. I have only ever taken what was needed for our son and not a penny more. Nothing forthcoming since he met Ris, which has not been easy; you know my reduced circumstances, but I have my pride and Miles knows full well it was never about his money. I almost threw my teacup at the pair of them. Instead, I set it down with trembling hands and said all I needed to know was where Mia was, then I'd leave.

Ris still said nothing, but I saw her hands were shaking too and Teddy was picking up on her mood, as babies do, and started grizzling again. Miles frowned and told Ris to take him upstairs, he couldn't hear himself think, which she resisted at first but when Teddy started properly wailing, she had no choice.

After they left the room, Miles explained Ris wasn't at all well. Postnatal depression. She wasn't thinking straight; he was getting her the help she needed, hence the visit to Harley Street. Might even mean a stay in a psychiatric unit. I asked if he meant one of those mother and baby places and he said maybe. Then he tried to pass off those false bumps as from a past 'episode' shortly after they gave up on IVF, and he reiterated he was happy to pay me whatever it took to ensure their future privacy and for my 'inconvenience', gesturing to the bloodied towel beside me. 'Name your price, Abs. I'm sorry it's come to this, but we all need to move on as best we can.'

I lost patience at that point, and as you know, that's usually my strong suit. Ris wasn't even in the room; he could drop the devoted husband act. But I suppose he was showing compassion to a woman who was so obviously not in her right mind. That's laudable, of course. And I told him so. Along with the fact I understood he was doing what he thought was right, but it really wasn't, not this time.

The trouble was, much as I tried to clear my head to make a lucid argument, I couldn't stop thinking about Mia. How she would lean over the side of the roof terrace and look down at me in the courtyard below, flicking ash or a cigarette butt down so I was afraid it would land in my hair or my coffee. And the night of the party, when she'd been up there, even higher in fact, and how she'd fallen. Landing on her wrist. Taken away in an ambulance. I asked him again if Mia was OK, looking up at the ceiling. He appeared confused, glancing up too as he asked what it would take to buy my silence, which frankly was making my blood boil. I'd been treated very poorly the night of the party, but I'd set that aside to ensure Mia was OK, and I would endeavour to do so again. Whatever Miles was going through with Ris would pass, and we would resolve any residual acrimony between us, as we always have, but right now this wasn't about me. It was about a vulnerable young girl of nineteen. Wild thoughts ran through my head and finally I was able to find the words I needed to demand answers. I had to know where Mia was. Was she still up there? Was

Ris keeping her quiet? He wasn't helping Ris by protecting her. She needed professional help. I had to know where that girl was.

Miles grabbed me at the door and held my wrist, preventing me from leaving the sitting room. I was right, he owed me the truth, that's what he said. Could I please let him explain? Then he raised my hand to his lips and kissed the dressing he'd so lovingly applied to my wounded palm. 'Please, Abs, you know I've always been completely honest with you. But what could I do? She gave me no choice. I believed her lies too, and by the time she confessed that you were telling the truth about the faked pregnancy, it was too late to do anything but try and limit the damage.'

It was exactly as I'd thought. An entrapment. I felt so sorry for him, history repeating itself.

He rubbed his forehead with his thumbs, leaning into me and resting his head on my shoulder before he pulled away again. He looked so defeated, not like the Miles at the party at all, but *my* Miles, the one who'd turn up at our lovely rented home in Reading with the cares of the world carried on his shoulders and I'd be there for him, with our son, making it all OK again.

I reassured him that of course I understood, taking his hands in mine. He was right, he must get Ris the help she so desperately needed, then we'd deal with our future. But I still had to make sure Mia was accounted for.

Ris came back then and we dropped hands. Not that she noticed, Teddy still in her arms, her eyes glazed with exhaustion. 'He wouldn't settle in his cot. He clearly hates me.'

Miles told her to sit down. If she was calm, Teddy would be too. But the baby wasn't pacified, not at all. I'm sorry to say she was right; he didn't like her. And although I knew it wouldn't help her state of distress, I had to press on with my questioning, for Mia's sake. That was why I was there, after all.

I'd popped on the locket to show Elise, as you know, and it occurred to me then that I could show Ris the photos inside. 'She's called Elise,' I told her, 'and she's nearby. Amelia is her baby sister. She's worried sick about her.'

That's when Ris started to cry. Quietly at first, shushing the baby as she got up and paced the room, but it got worse. Miles was trying to reason with her, but Ris was sobbing when she ran out, Teddy clutched to her, his head lolling unsupported. His cries cut through me.

Miles told me to stay where I was. In fact, he instructed me not to move, then he ran after Ris.

* * *

I stayed there a while, on the pale-pink velvet, shaken by Miles' angry command, the bloodied towel in my lap and a stain on the couch I doubt will ever come out. Although baking soda is supposed to be... Sorry, it's not that I don't care, just my weird wiring... anyway, I think it was that recurring vision of Mia up on the roof that made me brave. I knew she wasn't up there. Or at least I thought I knew. But it just wouldn't leave me alone. The What Ifs...

* * *

There was no sign of them in the master suite, just the carnage I'd left in the dressing room, fake bloodied false pregnancy bumps on display for all to see. I assumed Ris would have hastily tidied them away, as if they had never been there, but no. And the door across the landing was open, which I don't recall it ever being before, not when I lived there. I'd looked inside of course, and it was empty, but it had been filled with nursery equipment. A cot and boxes of nappies and clothes shoved in. Very messy.

The voices I then heard came from above, distant but more than one, and a baby was crying.

I flew up the next flight of stairs, my shoe catching on the top one, so I tumbled into the dark. My wounded hand grasping for something to save me as I fell into the guest suite. I felt around the bed, the white bedding stained red as the dressing came away. Not that I saw that until later, only the strung lights on the terrace to illuminate my way as I climbed up the rickety half flight of metal stairs and poked my head out to the windswept terrace.

* * *

Cold, damp air hit my face, Miles' white shirt the first thing I spotted as my eyes adjusted. Then I saw Ris and I gasped, almost losing my balance on the steep steps.

I've no idea how, as it was dark by then and it's a decent climb up and over the boundary walls that line the terrace, not to mention the spiked railings, but there she was, seated the other side, feet dangling as she stared at the London skyline. And most terrifying of all, Teddy was still in her arms. In fact, one arm, as the other hand was gripping the bars behind her, an awkward position to hold for long.

I must have screamed. I certainly ran towards them, not a thought for my vertigo, only that baby, and yes, Ris of course. Miles shouted at me to keep back, halting me a few paces out from the staircase. He wasn't much closer to Ris than I was and every step he took, she flinched. He stumbled by the first lounger and she looked so startled, I told him to stop. She would have to be persuaded to climb back over herself. *It's the only chance.*

A terrible faux pas. The inadvertent use of Mia's assumed

surname; Chance. She lurched at its mention, and for a second... God, I thought that was it, both of them gone. And it would have been my fault. Stupid Abigail Frost with her oddness. I could hear my mother's voice berating me for my clumsiness.

Miles spun round and shouted at me to back off. Which I did, of course, but I couldn't go back inside. Not whilst Ris and Teddy remained silhouetted against a navy sky. Those strung lights reminiscent of a New York rooftop bar. Nothing but fresh air between Ris and the cobbled courtyard far below.

I couldn't take my eyes off her, then Ris started talking. To herself, or maybe Teddy. I had to strain to hear her mutterings, dragged this way and that on the gusts which were really getting up by then, the rain heavier with each passing minute. Then Miles was reassuring her in his calm persuasive manner that he would fix this, but he was still marooned between the oversized loungers and afraid to move nearer. He'd promised her, he said, and he would make it better. She just needed to hand him the baby first, then she could come over too. His hand stretching out.

The wind took the strength from her voice, a stream of consciousness pouring out that I couldn't decipher, although I sensed her rising panic.

I had my phone, I could have called for help, and I did think of it, more than once, but would that be a good idea? Or would the sirens send her, literally, over the edge? The responsibility of that decision and its consequences paralysed me. Time passed; I have no idea how many seconds or minutes. Teddy was quiet. Ris was holding him to her, his face pressed to her chest, the little thing exhausted from crying. At least, I hoped that was the reason he was silent. Then the wind dropped and she and Miles were talking again, and this time I could hear them perfectly well.

Ris kept saying she was sorry, over and over. Her hair blowing over her face as she looked back at him. It was as if I was no longer there. They ignored me, Miles getting up and moving to the edge, their hands touching through the bars, the metal slippery with rain as would be the mossy brick she sat on. If Miles could grasp her, would he be able to save them both? Even if she had no intention of harming Teddy, one wrong move and he wouldn't stand a chance. And it was freezing, the temperature dropping as the unrelenting rain fell. Ris was only wearing leggings and a thin vest top and like I said, she's got so terribly thin. I edged a tiny bit nearer and saw she was shaking, violently, eyes wild as she looked at Miles and repeated over and over, 'I'm sorry, I'm so sorry. What have I done? What have I done? I should be the one... not her. I should be the one.'

They both discounted my presence, Ris' head down as she talked to Teddy. Miles was telling her it was OK; she didn't have to be so upset, it would all be dealt with.

He's a good man at heart, loyal. I know that might be hard to believe, but you barely know him. He's been between a rock and hard place for years.

Anyway, Ris started to shout at him then. 'Nothing is sorted. How can it be? It's all a nightmare.' That's what she called it, 'A fucking nightmare.' Then she started tipping forwards, hand still gripping the bars but arm straight so she was leaning out. I had to hold in a scream.

Miles moved fast, mounting the brick wall and grabbing her by the back of her top, both straps pulled into his tight grasp. He's strong, always has been, but I had no idea if the straps would hold her and the baby. Would the fabric rip? Would he lose balance in the driving rain? Would she drop Teddy? She looked up at Miles and he shouted, 'Do you trust me, Ris?' And she nodded and then he asked, 'And can I trust you?'

And she said, 'Of course, always.'

I inwardly begged him to pull her and Teddy to safety,

squeezing my eyes shut when I could no longer bear to watch. *Just do it, Miles. Before it's too late. Please, my darling.* Then he shouted at Ris, 'OK, let go!'

* * *

It was quiet. But I could hear something, leaves rustling. I imagined a soft bed of magnolia petals in the basement courtyard, cushioning the long fall. Fanciful, I know, but it was of some small comfort. I'd loved that garden so much. It was my sanctuary. Early morning coffee at the table beneath the beautiful magnolia tree. Such a contrast to that windswept roof terrace, blackness all that awaited in the void as the rain fell on my closed lashes, my hair running wet, my feet in a puddle.

I opened my eyes in time to witness Ris handing Miles the baby over the spiked railings, then she was climbing back over, nimble as she must have been to get there in the first place. It was shocking how frail she was, skeletal against London's night sky, but I knew she'd be fine then.

Miles thrust Teddy at me and pushed past, taking the metal steps back down at speed. He looked badly shaken.

Ris and I stared at one another, neither of us able to move, and both soaked through, as was poor Teddy, limp but thankfully unharmed as I held him tight. I tried to shut out my mother's voice, which was all I could hear and managed to for long enough to say, 'Why did you tell Miles it should have been you, not her?'

That's when she said the words I doubt I will ever forget.

'I promise it was an accident. You believe me, don't you, Gail? I never meant to hurt her.'

25

TENTH INTERVIEW WITH GAIL FROST – MONDAY 21 NOVEMBER, 11 P.M.

Sorry to break off mid-thought, but do you think we might order something a bit stronger from room service? I don't usually drink spirits, or much at all, but maybe a brandy? This tea is stone cold and a proper drink seems in order, to steady our nerves for the next part, don't you think?

It would have made way more sense to go inside in that weather, the loungers didn't even have their cushions on, a hard plastic weave, but I was afraid to break the spell. Not when Ris looked like she was about to tell me what 'accident' had befallen Mia. I took the other lounger, so close our knees touched, both of us shivering and wet, but that was the least of it by then.

Teddy lay bundled and asleep in my arms. I protected him from the rain and wind as much as could, hunched over him. He was warm, and mainly dry in my cardigan and I honestly think that's what saved me from a panic attack. That soft sleepy lump on my lap, depending on me for shelter from the elements as well as protection from the woman whom I now feared had taken his mother from him... for ever.

Nursing Teddy also reminded me of when my boy was a baby. How I'd sunk everything into loving him. Trying to be both mother and father when Miles wasn't around, and it broke my heart that Teddy wouldn't have a proper family.

I forced a smile and prompted Ris with reminders of Elise's desperate need to know what had happened to her baby sister, Amelia. Ris got upset again, then she told me she'd had a younger sister too, still did in fact, but they'd lost touch. She said they'd been best friends as kids, relied on each other, but now she had no idea where she was. I told her I was an only child, wished I'd had that bond. It was so important, wasn't it? Irreplaceable.

It felt as though I was getting through to her, but until the moment she began her story, I had no idea if she would tell me anything of what happened to poor Mia. And in many ways I wish she had saved it for the police.

'It was a little over a month after Teddy's birth when it happened,' she said. The 'accident,' as Ris continually referred to it. Although I'm not sure I would.

To fill in the background a little here. It would seem that after I'd left Lexington Gardens in the back of a police car the night of the party, back in June, Ris had been forced to address with Miles what had been going on during his extended absence. An explanation required of not only my appointment as her assistant, but also for the pregnant girl in hospital sleeping off the after-effects of a bottle of a vodka after a near-death experience on his roof. They had sat down in the sitting room, she and *Hubs*, and Ris confessed to everything: the faked pregnancy, her plan to adopt Mia's baby and pass it off as her own, the lot.

Please, now is not the time to address my vilification for speaking the truth, but yes, I was right all along.

Miles threatened to leave Ris then and there, but she persuaded him to stay long enough to help her out of the mess she'd got herself into. Well, both of them really. The fallout would be incredibly damaging for his business. The publicity horrendous. As I say, Miles is both a kind man and a pragmatist. He would want to help, but she had placed him in an impossible position with her lies and Instagram shares and the paraded false bump. Even then, as she fell on his mercy, she couldn't let go of the hope it might all somehow work out. Mia would still have to be paid off, couldn't they keep the baby as planned, be a family?

I could see the desperation in her eyes, even as she recounted her useless pleas. And as an aside, she explained she'd always had erratic periods and had done loads of tests leading up to the Paris reunion. None of them positive but she'd clung to the hope that maybe she was pregnant. Hence that hand to tum pose outside The Ritz.

I'm afraid I don't quite believe that. It was far too convenient. A plan already forming, I believe, to entrap the husband whom she suspected of having an affair and had announced he was cutting their romantic getaway short. She knew what she was doing in that photo and she knew she wasn't pregnant. She'd bought tampons and packed them. Her period came after the photo, she claimed, but either way, the pregnancy announcement was a deliberate and calculated ploy.

The arrangement decided between Mia and Ris was that the baby would be born at Lexington Gardens. Mia's recent medical treatment was a paper trail concern; she'd given her real name at the hospital so there was a chance she'd be traced by her worried family, which meant she'd have to lay especially low. After the home birth, Mia would hand over the baby in exchange for what Ris described as a seven-figure sum. Miles, disgusted to learn of this crazy scheme, also named his price.

The divorce he'd wanted for some time – again, as I had long suspected – would be granted without any further claim on him or his finances. They'd both move on, 'his reputation unscathed' as Ris put it. A trace of the old Ris in that phrase and the expression that accompanied it. To my mind, Miles was being more than fair. He could have thrown her to the wolves, disowned her, but he didn't; he offered to stay and help, despite the rising personal and financial cost. Because Ris was not well. Not well at all. Even I could see that and although I do pride myself on being a good judge of character, I also know that I'm not always that emotionally intelligent. I hadn't read the signs, taking her arrogance as just that, rather than the spiralling madness it clearly was. I'd ascribed the fake pregnancy to her attention-seeking nature and the pressure on her regarding the upcoming book, but predominantly as a way to trap Miles into staying. All of which were true, but it was evident the unsuccessful IVF attempts had been, for her, a crushing blow. She was obsessed with becoming a mother, despite previously declaring to her followers that their attempts to have a child were sadly over but she'd reconciled to that. She had in fact *never* given up hope, that most relentless of task masters, as I know only too well. For that, she has my sympathies. But not, I'm afraid, for anything else, especially what she confessed to next.

Mia came back to Lexington Gardens with her wrist in a cast, which Ris cut off for her after three weeks as it was 'filthy'. Miles also stayed, as promised, and other than a few business trips that he simply couldn't cancel, he was there to support both women as Mia's due date, 24 September, loomed. Three months of clandestine cohabitation that I cannot imagine were easy for any of them. But they got through it and Miles covered the costs of a very discreet home birth with a private midwife who was recommended by 'a business associate' of his. Miles has a few fixers like that. People who name their price and get a job done, discreetly. I'm sure many people at his level do.

Teddy arrived bang on time, much to Ris' disappointment as she'd been hoping for a late and small baby to cover the month's discrepancy in her publicly declared due date. But despite Mia's recklessness during the pregnancy, he was a healthy eight pounds. A perfect boy.

* * *

As the rain continued, Ris explained how she was heartbroken to discover that despite the arrival of 'their son', Miles still planned on leaving as soon as possible. She'd hoped having Teddy would make a difference to his decision, but of course he wasn't his son – or hers, for that matter – and it had hardly been the happy family home she'd envisaged, a screaming baby disrupting them all, Mia's presence in the house unsettling to say the least. They'd agreed Mia could stay a fortnight, to recuperate. Her wrist hadn't healed as it should, but they'd persuaded her not to go back for check-ups; it was too risky. Ris hoped things would settle down when Mia finally moved out. It was confusing for Teddy, his birth mother always being around, offering to help with feeds and changes. He could smell the milk.

The trouble was, after the agreed two weeks, Mia refused to go.

* * *

Miles, however, left fifty-six Lexington Gardens promptly, sometime during the first week of October, I believe, and moved into a suite at his Mayfair Hotel. The US deal had fallen through and he was losing patience with the situation at home.

Ris had moved Mia down to the basement, out of the way, but even that was an inconvenience too far, her music blaring, and Mia making the most of the situation, the credit card Ris had lent her used to the full online. The risk having her there was all too much to bear. Weeks passed and she still couldn't budge her.

Clearly Mia had no place better to go. And let's face it, Lexington Gardens is a very desirable residence, especially if you're living there rent-free and with all expenses paid.

Ris said she'd been terrified Mia would answer the door to someone and the game would be up. A health professional checking on her, a journalist pushing their card through the door. She'd nearly had a heart attack when she found Mia by the door, your business card in her hand. And then of course you turned up again, asking questions. Just before it happened, in fact. The very day of the 'accident'. Yes, I'm afraid you were almost in a position to... But no point going there.

* * *

Teddy was especially fractious that day. Colic, Ris surmised, after she'd been on the forums trying to get help as there was no way she could call a doctor. She was bone-tired, sleep deprived, out of her depth and crying as she carried him around the house, up and down the stairs, begging him to be quiet. In desperation, she'd gone down to the basement to ask Mia if she'd have him for an hour whilst she popped to the chemist to get the medicine he needed. Mia of course said she would be more than happy. That's when you saw Ris leave the house. Running away from you in the rain once she knew who you were. Mia inside, alive and well, with her baby.

Ris said she ran away from you in a panic, bought the medicine and ran back when the coast was clear, terrified that Mia might have answered the door to you, babe in arms. She also had other concerns. Ones she had tried to ignore, but it was obvious Mia loved the child. That was the real reason Mia hadn't left with her payout, but maybe given the chance to escape with the baby too, she would take it... Ris ran down the stairs to the basement, terrified they'd be gone. The small sitting room come kitchenette was empty, the courtyard too when she looked out, the doors open despite the rain.

They were in the bedroom, but Ris' relief soon turned to something else entirely.

Teddy, or Luk as Mia was calling him, was on his back on the bed, and Mia cooing over him, the baby looking more content than he ever had with her, the reason clear as Mia turned around, exposing the breast she'd fed him with.

Ris demanded Mia leave her house. She had outstayed her welcome. Time to pack her bags. They argued, violently, no holds barred, no subject off limits. Mia accused Ris of being a terrible mother to Luk, tucking the breast away. She hadn't thought she wanted him, but now she did. Luk was her child; anyone could see that. They had a special bond.

At this point in the story, Ris was talking fast. All her emotions tumbling out. Sometimes I could barely catch what she was saying, although we were so close I could feel her warm breath on my damp cheek, rainwater running down our faces. That's when I noticed Miles was back with us, in the shadows. I tried to catch his eye, but he was looking at Ris, hanging on her every word. His face reflecting exactly my fears. I think we both knew, deep down, there was only one way this was heading. I hugged Teddy and waited for the rest.

* * *

Mia started to pack up some of the stuff she'd accumulated in her short time there, but remained insistent she was taking Luk with her. Ris said she pleaded with Mia to see sense. Begged her. Where would she take him? What sort of life would he have? No home, no father. Imagine everything he'd have with her and Miles as parents. He'd want for nothing. Mum, Dad, money. The argument went up another gear then, and fast.

Mia claimed Miles was having an affair. It was obvious, the way he was never there. He'd clearly moved out permanently this time!

Ris hadn't noticed Miles was with us on the roof terrace, her spittle flying at my face as she told me it was lies, all lies. Miles loved her, always would. She just needed Mia to go then everything would be fine again. He'd come home.

Mia claimed Miles was a ruthless bastard; he'd dropped Ris like a stone, and anyway, Luk was her baby. Ris was incapable of looking after him; he was crying all day every day. Did Ris know her milk poured for him; her breasts painfully engorged before she'd been able to feed him? Mia even asked Teddy, or rather Luk, if he was a happy boy now he'd filled his tum with milk from his 'real' mum.

'It was horrific,' Ris told me. 'I hated her so much, but I swear I never meant to hurt her.'

Ris had snot running from her nose by then. I had to look away, catching Miles' eye as Ris said she'd offered Mia more money, as much as she wanted. She'd never have to worry, Miles would pay an allowance, buy her a house, she could even have Lexington Gardens if she wanted? Name her price. Anything. But Mia said some things were priceless, not that Ris would appreciate that. And the house wasn't hers to offer, or the money. Ris would be homeless herself soon when Miles got his divorce papers signed. She'd heard them arguing. She knew the marriage was over.

Mia had finished packing by then, Teddy still on the bed, but she was worrying about a locket she couldn't find. Said it was precious, and she'd been looking for it for ages. Maybe it had fallen down the back of the bedside cabinet from when she'd first stayed? Mia got down on all fours to look but her wrist gave way and Ris took the chance to snatch Teddy off the bed and run out.

Ris was halfway up the stairs with Teddy when Mia grabbed her and pulled her down, so hard Ris said she fell back and was covered in bruises. She'd only been concerned with saving Teddy, not herself.

Ris looked at me then and said, 'That proves I was a better mother than her, doesn't it, Gail?'

* * *

I suppose what you need to understand here, before I tell you the rest, is that Mia was so much smaller than Ris, a whole head height, and Ris had, until recently, religiously worked out every day. She'd got thin, but that muscle memory was there. And the basement is very confined. The sitting room is tiny, the half-moon table, a small sofa, that's it. Plus it had been raining for days on and off, the patio doors open to the elements and the step muddy where Mia had traipsed mud back through after she'd been out there smoking. The landscapers had started the job of redesigning the garden, cutting down the tree and then they disappeared. I'll explain the significance of that in a minute.

Anyway, Ris said she put Teddy back down on the bed very calmly and then she wheeled round and hit Mia as hard as she could.

Reeling from the slap, Mia lost her footing and fell out the patio doors, landing softly in the freshly dug over mud the other side. Or so Ris thought.

I know it's the least of the casualties here, but I really loved that tree and I told her that. Asked her what the landscapers had left of it and she said nothing... well, almost nothing.

Ris admitted she'd wanted the magnolia gone the moment I left, knew how I'd loved it, spiteful of her, but Miles had persuaded her it was far too risky to have anyone in the house whilst Mia was living there. After he'd moved out, she'd gone against his wishes and booked the landscaping company who made a start. There for two days, cutting down the tree and digging over, the branches and the wide trunk taken outside to the skip, along with the table and chair I'd also liked so much. Then they'd buggered off and never finished the work.

The plan had been to create a pleasant outside space, Ris told me. Perfect for a romantic escape of an evening with a glass of wine, Miles shaking his head in the shadows as his deluded wife talked of providing a replacement for any foreign trips, as they couldn't get Teddy a passport, for obvious reasons.

It was clearly a pipe dream on Ris' part but, like the launch party, it had provided a focus. If only she could make that courtyard perfect, then Miles would move back in, because she was his wife, and Teddy their child, and fifty-six Lexington Gardens was their perfect home. She had designed every inch of it. It wouldn't be the same without her. She just needed to prove that to him again.

And yes, I hear the irony, but our situations, thankfully, are entirely different.

But the garden was a mess, the tree hacked down, the ground a quagmire. And that's where Mia landed, in soft mud. Or so Ris thought.

I saw Miles recoil, a hand to the wall to steady himself as Ris recounted the sound of Mia's skull cracking against the exposed tree stump – a sickening thud – but she convinced herself Mia would get up, eventually. She just needed to shake her hard enough. Snap her out of the sick joke she was playing on her.

Another flash of the old Ris as she looked to me as an ally again. Her right-hand woman.

'It was a freak accident. No one's fault.' That's what Ris kept repeating. Over and over. To me, herself, then finally Miles as he stepped out the shadows. 'An accident, Gail. You believe me, don't you? You know me, we're friends.'

Maybe it was the fact Mia had a broken wrist, maybe she could have saved herself if not for that recent injury. Who knows? Best ignore the If Onlys.

It was the magnolia, or the lack of it, that made me cry in the end. I'd loved it so much. I walked to the edge of the terrace, brave in my shock, after Miles had guided Ris down the ladder, and I saw with my own eyes that the tree was gone. Hacked down because it reminded Ris of me. Mia's tiny body concealed somewhere below that dug earth, her skull cracked like an egg. Hard to imagine it. Any of it. Mia had filled Lexington Gardens. Her laugh, her energy. Every floor bounced with her presence and I felt it again, one last time. Heard her again.

* * *

Mia's belongings were concealed in the skip out front, at least, I think that's what I overheard Ris tell the police later, but please, like I said, don't torture yourself with If Onlys. You weren't to know to look in there, and it wouldn't have made any difference. We can't blame ourselves, not you, me or Miles. There's only one person who is responsible for taking Mia's life.

I should have been crying for that poor young mother, but it was the loss of the magnolia that broke my heart. Teddy still in my arms and soaked through – not just rain; his nappy was heavy. I carefully climbed down the slick metal ladder with my precious cargo and, shaking, went into the nursery where I cried and cried. It just poured out of me.

Teddy kicked his feet on the changing table, happy again, poor lamb. A dry nappy and warm clothes, that's all it took.

* * *

Ris was in the kitchen when I came down with Teddy, Miles beside her at the island. I asked her to hold Teddy, or Luk, I wasn't sure which name to use, but she wouldn't. She warmed some formula and followed me around with her eyes as I jiggled him up and down. He suckled hard on the bottle, sated. I offered to stay, as long as needed, to look after him, but Miles said he'd promised Ris that he would take good care of the baby and he would. 'The boy' would want for nothing.

* * *

They separated us, the police, as soon as Miles let them in. Miles and Ris were in the kitchen, me in the sitting room, Teddy taken away from me by a social worker soon as she arrived. Detectives everywhere, issuing instructions to cordon off the courtyard garden, you know with that fluttering tape across the stairwell to the basement. I asked to use the bathroom and as I went up to the master suite I paused on the stairs and caught bits and pieces of what Ris was telling the police about the skip. How she'd had it removed after Mia died, and that she'd used a spade the landscapers had left behind to dig a shallow grave.

I leant over the banister and caught a glimpse of Miles' face before he got up and closed the door. It was usually tanned, but he looked grey and pasty as he briefly met my eye.

Ris was bundled into the back of a police car and taken away soon after. I thought we might talk, Miles and I, but like I said, they kept us apart. I told the detective who spoke with me in the sitting room that I was good with the baby. I could maybe foster him, just for a while, if Miles couldn't cope. She looked at me as if I was off my head and said I should go to A&E, about my hand. It was bleeding again, the dressing gone; not that I'd noticed. They offered a lift, but I just wanted to get out in the fresh air. As far as possible away from... well, I suppose it was a murder scene, wasn't it? Gosh, I feel like I've been talking for hours. What time is it?

Five to midnight?! Really? You should go. Yes, now!!! And please, give this locket to Elise. She should have it, not me.

EMAIL SUBJECT: INTERVIEWS WITH GAIL FROST

DATE: FRIDAY 25 NOVEMBER

So lovely to get your email this morning, after what has not been the best of weeks. Poor Mia, or rather Amelia. Elise was... well, you can imagine – inconsolable when the police told her. Not that I was there. She called me afterwards. I hope I sounded shocked. I still am, so I imagine I did. And then losing my job at the magazine, which I know is not the worst of it, but kind of a big deal to me.

It feels perhaps a little disrespectful and definitely incongruous in these sad circumstances to therefore feel incredibly excited about 'our news', but multiple interest in a limited series sounds very promising. I really want to take ownership and bring Gail, Ris, and most importantly Mia's story to the world as soon as we can. There's been so much press coverage in the days since Ris' arrest. I'm sure you've seen it, hard to miss, even in LA. All over the front pages here and the buzz on social media... let's talk soon. Maybe lunch when you're in London? And thanks, for everything. It's been quite the journey so far. I realise this is only the beginning, but to have those names potentially attached to a six-part dramatised version of the story is bloody awesome. Couldn't have done it without you, quite literally! Guess I better get on with writing the script now? Not much else to do! I've been working on the scene of that hotel interview with Gail on Monday night, but there's something really troubling me about it. I need to speak with her, but she will not reply to my calls, messages, emails.

I even went to her grotty flat yesterday, now I'm a free agent, but no sign of her there either. The landlord said there were loads of reporters hanging around Gail's door after the news of Mia's death broke, and the last one only just left. Oh and that 'Abi' is owing a month's rent. Maybe that's why she's made herself invisible.

I really want to help her out if we can. And on that note, any chance of the expenses I put in being paid sooner than later? I know nothing is anywhere near signed as yet, but I had a lot of costs putting up Gail and Elise last week. Only a couple of basic rooms for the night, but you know London prices and it seems Gail made the most of room service after I left. Sorry to have to chase, but my credit cards are totally maxed out and with Christmas only a month away and now I've lost my job… don't want to fall into the Christmas lull without a bit of a buffer.

And thanks for the heads-up re the podcast interest. As you say, great to start building the buzz nice and early. Do you think they'll pay me? An ex-colleague also said they'd love an exclusive, so let's get our heads together soon and see what we're happy to share and what we need to keep back, at least until we're green lit. Then we can go out guns blazing with a proper announcement on *Variety* and *Deadline*. Woo-hoo!

I've requested a visit with Ris. She's on remand, so not sure how that works, but even a call would be useful. Surprised she was refused bail – she pleaded guilty to involuntary manslaughter – but Miles isn't exactly throwing money at her legal team judging by that jackass representing her who keeps popping up on the news. And there's already rumours flying around (pun intended) regarding a new love interest for Mr Fox. I know!!!

Gail said Teddy has been taken into foster care, so if Miles did promise Ris he'd look after him, he's gone back on that agreement. Unless he had no choice? Gail worships the ground he walks on, but I'm not so sure that's deserved.

Fingers crossed I hear from her soon. I swear I saw Miles Fox going into the hotel Gail was staying at, just as I left at midnight. Hardly his usual haunt, a Premier Inn. I only wish I'd challenged him at the time, but that bloody traffic warden was slapping a ticket on my car. The last thing I needed in my impoverished state – hint, hint!

Best,

Ax

WHATSAPP MESSAGES – MONDAY 28 NOVEMBER

G: Sorry I haven't been in touch this last week. Not ignoring you, just had a few things to sort out. Can we meet up, one last time? You were right to think there's more. I'm ready to share. Gx

A: Gail, great to hear from you! Love to meet up, when and where? Name your place! Ax

G: Tomorrow? Lexington Gardens. You'll see why when we meet. Around 3?

A: Maybe better to meet on neutral ground? I'm not sure you are allowed back there, Gail, or should I say, Abi?

G: Gail's fine, and we won't go near the house, I promise. You'll see why when you get there. Around 3? Has to be well before dark.

A: OK, if you're sure. See you then. Ax

26

FINAL INTERVIEW WITH GAIL FROST – TUESDAY 29 NOVEMBER, 3 P.M.

Don't look so worried; I told you, we're not going anywhere near the house. The gate to the gardens is just along here. It's locked, residents only, but... sorry, can you hold my bag? It's nothing sinister inside, I promise. A blunt instrument for a very important – but I assure you benign – task. All will become clear. No, nothing illegal either, trust me. Well, I don't think it is! There, we're in.

Funny story about the key. I'll explain in due course. Head towards that bench opposite number fifty-six. Then we can take a pew and I'll catch you up on everything.

* * *

Do you recall me telling you about a young woman with a tiny dog, the one I saw when I first came here on the day of my interview? I bumped into her again. Just a few days before the party. I'd escaped the house for a breath of fresh air. It was a powder keg up there, in Ris' study. Mia wheedling for this and that, Ris demanding all my time and energy for the arrangements when all I wanted was to think about the moment Miles arrived and what he might say after almost three years of separation. So I came here, to the residents' garden, and the same young woman, a teenager I suppose, was crouched down outside the locked gate, hunting in the grass. I thought at first she was picking up dog poop, the mutt beside her looking vaguely guilty, ugly thing, but no, she was already holding a full bag, so it wasn't that.

I helped her look for the lost key. She said that her mum would kill her, but I have to say for someone in so much trouble, she gave up the search very quickly. I waited until she'd moved on and then lifted my foot.

Rather a neat bookending of my time living here, wouldn't you say? And a much pleasanter memory than the terrible events that brought me back here a week ago, which brings me to the contents of the shopping bag.

Can you hold the trowel whilst I wrangle this rather sad, but I'm assured will be magnificent, bit of twiggy plant which incidentally cost me a small fortune. Shall we get planting? Then we can walk this key back to number forty-two, the home of not only the rightful owner of the key but also the benefactor of the dog shit posted through Ris' door, if I'm not very much mistaken. My research, as always, coming up trumps.

I found that nugget of gold the other day, when I was unable to sleep, another of my random thoughts sending me off on a tangent. A complaint on the Lexington Gardens residents' Facebook page, which I'd occasionally dip into, but not in a very long time. This comment was dated just after my appointment as Ris' EA, when it has to be said I was preoccupied with other matters. A gripe about owners not always picking up after their dogs in the park, hardly my priority. Guess who posted the complaint?

It's funny though, I can only think fondly of that version of Ris.

The one who took no prisoners and railroaded her way through life, despite everyone's utter disregard for her. No wonder she collected followers like badges of honour. They were her fans. Such a contrast to the woman I think of now, up on that roof terrace, soaked through, trembling. Broken by it all. Or more recently on the end of a phone, begging me to see justice done as she cannot bear the sounds of the prison at night.

Yes, we've talked, and it's fair to say it's complicated how I feel about her, but it's not hate. Never has been. And that brings me to why we're here today. Do you want to start digging, or shall I? The ground looks quite hard. Maybe you? You're younger and fitter than me.

* * *

What do you think? Not much to look at now, but give it five years...

The man at the garden centre said it can take a decade, maybe more, to grow to the height of the one so cruelly cut down in the basement garden, but a fitting tribute don't you think?

Oh, don't look at me like that!

I do realise planting a magnolia tree in memory of Amelia is a little... eccentric. I get the irony and so would Mia. I can even hear that laugh of hers. She'd probably say something like, 'Gay, you're such a crazy old girl.' Then she'd cackle and I'd have to place my hands over my ears and grit my teeth. She was such a firecracker; I still can't believe she's... anyway, I want her to be here, by my favourite bench. Except it's hers now. I shan't visit. But I'll hold her in my heart.

I've got a flask of tea in my bag; shall we make a toast and then I have a train to catch.

* * *

I'd sit on this bench for hours some days, imagine myself up there, with Miles, scratches over my arms from scrambling through a gap in the hedge. Mind you, I was a dab hand at blagging my way through the gate. Played many parts over the years. A gardener, or a visiting Granny who'd been locked out, even a Russian oligarch's wife. Whatever it took to convince someone I belonged.

I'd often see Ris, running in and out, or in her study on the third floor. And I suppose I envied her, but of course all that has changed.

Strange to think there was a time I was beside her, at the glass desk, literally her right-hand woman. I know it can't be, but I like to think that in some parallel universe, me her EA, she promoting her bestseller, we *are* friends. Lunching and shopping. Equals. Because I liked Ris, I really did. Surprising as that may sound. I just didn't like her behaviour at times. Although I understand it a little better now. Ris and I have much more in common than I ever realised. This last week has certainly been an eye-opener.

Did you see this morning's post on Insta? No, not Ris! 'The Replacement'. That's what we call her, well I do.

You know they call him 'Air Miles' on account of this new one also being cabin crew? Oh yes, he has a type. The waitress type. Such a turgid inevitability to it all; I'm not surprised it's become a joke on social media, despite the darker themes of this story. No sign of Teddy on the trip, which I'm assuming was arranged long before he was caught up in Mia's 'accident'. You'd have thought it might have put a crimp in his plans, but Miles can be very... single-minded.

I don't suppose some random woman's baby fitted into Charlotte's – LottieLou to her devoted followers – plans either. A romantic weekend away for her engagement announcement. Pretty poor taste after what's just happened. Barely a week between one wife and the next-in-waiting. Patience clearly not this one's strong suit. And I'm assuming there was an overlap in Miles' 'affections', if we can call them that.

That's not even the real joke. Neither Ris nor I, and dare I say, not even LottieLou, will ever win the great prize of Miles' everlasting devotion, because the only person Miles is faithful to is himself. Are you picking up on my new-found cynicism? Sadly it's taken me a long time to get here, but better late than never, eh? That's what I've tried to tell myself over the past week. It's been an emotional journey and you'll be relieved to hear I am finally coming to terms with the fact I've wasted the best years of my life on a very underserving recipient. Which is a bitter pill to swallow. But I will not tarnish my happy memories, not entirely. I have my son, or at least, I hope one day I will have him back in my life. Bridges are being built, one girder at a time. Is that the right word? You get my meaning.

Did I tell you we went on a proper family holiday once, the three of us? A remote cottage Miles found on the coast; it was lovely. A whole week together. Best holiday ever. Oh, and there was a day in London, sightseeing. An open top bus. We all loved it. Miles bought me that little Harrods' bear I had on my bed in Reading; you remember it?

I've left that awful bedsit, even that level of rent beyond my current means. Please don't pity me. I can see it in your eyes, and I don't need your money. I know you're being kind but allow me some dignity. I'm nothing if not resilient. I've had to be.

There's a theory it's the purest form of love we ever experience: the unrequited variety. I used to kid myself with that one. As if I'd lit a candle and had to keep the flame alive, whatever the storm that raged, but we all have our limits.

It's funny how once your perspective has been reset by a shocking piece of information, the scales fall from your eyes and you can see everything so clearly for the first time, and then of course, it all makes perfect sense.

It's taken me years, unfortunately, but these last few days have been a game-changer. I needed time to square everything away in my own mind, but I cannot wait any longer. There is a terrible miscarriage of justice that must be addressed. And I'm the only one who can do that. Well, actually it has to be you, but I must tell you first.

Gosh, I had no idea it would be so hard.

No, I'm fine, it has to be done. Aside from the moral obligation, I know from bitter experience how months of indecision and delusion can turn into years. If I don't say it now, then maybe I never will and I do have that train to catch.

I was on my way to the hotel last week, in the Uber you booked me, my hand cut and head still spinning from Ris' confession, when Miles called. He said the police had finally left the house and he needed to talk it all through, could he see me? He sounded awful. I told him yes, of course. I was staying the night in London, he must come over. Just give me an hour or two. I'd make sure I was ready by midnight. He had no idea I was talking to you. I thought it best to keep it that way and thank goodness I have. I hate to think what might have happened to you if... Anyway, Miles was in a contemplative mood when he arrived. Moments after you left, in fact. I was afraid you might have seen him in the foyer and to be honest, I was questioning my decision to talk to you at all by then. I was so thrilled to have Miles to myself at last, despite the tragic circumstances. We clung to one another that night, both shocked to our core by what had happened. It was like old times back in New York, and then the lovely hotel in the Cotswolds; that was where we made our son. Not that there haven't been numerous times since, but not in a long while and I was giddy, young again, inventing all sorts for our future. I'm sure you can imagine the ridiculous fantasies I had that night. And we got very drunk on the best champagne a Premier Inn could offer. It was all very... inappropriate after what had happened and I'm sorry it was all charged to your card. But death and passion are often linked, aren't they? Faced with our own mortality, we grasp at chances. That's what I thought it was, at first.

We were in bed, must have been three or four in the morning by then, when Miles started talking about how scary it had been, rushing home after a panicked call from Ris, to find her hysterical, watching over Mia's body in the mud. Ris hadn't mentioned to me that Miles knew about Mia's accident, let alone that he had been in any way involved in the cover-up. In fact, from what I overheard, she gave the police a very clear account of her burying Mia's body, then using the skip to dispose of all her belongings.

I wasn't sure what to say or think. But I suppose, if I'm honest, I was flattered he'd trusted me with such a huge confidence, but of course I was stunned he'd known about Mia's death and not reported it. I recall nodding and saying yes, of course I understood whilst still trying to make sense of it. Was he a loyal if misguided husband? Maybe.

He thanked me for my loyalty, kissed me again, said he knew he could count on me. I'd certainly proved that over the years, and he squeezed my hand so tight it hurt.

I think I could have lived with him being complicit in covering up what was a tragic accident. It would have been awful, but given the things I've forgiven in the past, I might well have excused that. What difference would it have made? Mia was dead, the culprit arrested. I needed Miles and so did our son, and so would Teddy. I could have easily been persuaded by that kind of twisted logic. But that wasn't the full extent of it, not by a long shot and my skin goose-bumped as the reality of what he was telling me sent a shiver down my back, even as he wrapped me up in his arms; the only time I've ever wished him away as he whispered, 'It's OK, Abs, I took care of everything.'

* * *

He'd arrived home after a mad dash across London following Ris' frantic call. 'Something terrible has happened, Miles. You need to come home.'

Mia was lying on her back in the mud, eyes closed and unresponsive, and sinking into the ground as the rain poured down. He took charge, got his distraught wife back inside, told her to get cleaned up and to deal with the baby who was screaming on the bed. He went back out into the courtyard, looking up at the ten-foot-high brick walls, and wondered how on earth he was going to move the body, and where to. Then he spotted the spade in the corner. He picked it up and was about to start digging when Mia opened her eyes.

He said he was sure I could appreciate how *inconvenient* it would have been if she'd lived. 'We were all in it up to our eyeballs, Abs. I had to sort it out. Sometimes you have to be the fucking saviour, don't you?' Then he said, 'But if she was dead... the problem was buried with her. You see that, don't you?'

His expression as his eyes pleaded for clemency reminded me of a little boy caught in the act, but not our boy. He, thank God, is only like his father in appearance. I suppose it was that thought that gave me away. Miles' expression turning cold, a familiar flash of anger which I've always feared but denied, replacing the previous contrition. 'I can count on you, Abs, can't I?'

It was as though someone had walked over my grave. A wave of terror scythed through me. The man I had loved all those years, who only moments before, pardon my candour, had been inside me, now terrified me. I could imagine him taking care of me as an inconvenience too, the pillow smothering me, or my skull caved in on the hard tile bathroom floor, much as Mia's had been by that spade.

I asked how he managed it, as if I was proud of him, and he mimed smacking her hard, several times. She was little more than a child, weighed nothing, lived for fewer years than I'd loved this monster. I thought I was going to throw up. I excused myself to the bathroom, leant over the sink, called out to him I was fine when he banged on the locked door. But I didn't throw up, I let him in. He would have ripped the sliding door off its hinges otherwise.

He pushed me up against the wall and then threw me in the bath, smacking my head back down when it bounced up. I thought I was going to die, but thankfully my screams summoned a young member of staff who was mortified by Miles' explanation of 'raucous sex', the champagne bottle upturned in the bucket and on full view. I cowered in the bathroom whilst Miles excused our behaviour and the embarrassed porter left, but it was enough to save me. Miles calmly got dressed and left soon after, but not before extracting a promise of my enduring silence.

I still have the bruises on my neck, and wrists, hence the roll-neck jumper. No, not just because of the cold. And I think I may still have a concussion, but please, no fuss. I'm not the victim here. Although, I must admit I have felt like one this past week, moving from place to place and changing my phone after all these years. I guess that will be the way of things until I hear he's been arrested. Although, he's clearly moved on, hasn't he? Romantically, I mean. But I can't trust him not to... come after me, I suppose.

I'll leave that responsibility with you then. If that's OK? I'll drop you an email, corroborate everything, but there's an imperative to address Ris' situation sooner than later. We will both be very much depending on you. I've spoken with her, today, so she is aware of what's on the horizon. That's all that's keeping her going, knowing she isn't to blame. At least, not of murder. Don't leave her there long without hope.

Oh, and talking of Ris, she did tell me one thing I'd like to share with you before I go. Not exactly important, but seeing as we won't be seeing each other again... you recall the troll who made Ris' life such a misery... Becca2004xxx?

Guess who?

Yes, I know! It's utter madness! Totally counterintuitive. Ris posting all those GIFs and emojis and hateful comments about herself. Hard to make sense of it, as you say, but she explained it simply as a way to create content and engage followers. I think there was more to it than that. A therapist would have a whale of a time pulling it apart, the conscience manifesting itself as an alter ego or some such. I for one will be keeping offline from now on.

Shall we walk to the end of the road together? As I said, I do have a train to catch.

* * *

I suppose this is it then? Goodbye for the very last time.

And I must apologise for leaving such a burden on your young shoulders, but from the moment I read that piece you wrote about how we women are often so cruel to one another and we should value difference, embrace our uniqueness rather than conform, I knew I'd found the right woman for the job. And you being a Reading gal, like me.

Coincidence? Our meeting on the train you mean? Oh no, I

don't believe in those. Planning is the key. A regular train route shared on your Facebook page, a photo with your gorgeous nephews most Sundays.

Social media is such a gift these days, isn't it?

LEXINGTON GARDENS

PILOT SCRIPT – FIRST DRAFT

FADE IN:

EXT. LOCATION #1 – A GRAND LONDON STREET IN BELGRAVIA – 1 APRIL – DAY

A line of icing sugar Georgian townhouses of grand proportions shimmers in the spring sunshine, a light dusting of unseasonable snow making them glitter. The camera pans down the street until it lands on the number 56 painted in neat font on a white pillar of a house near the far end of the exclusive street, then up to the glossy black front door where a mature woman's hand tentatively lifts the polished brass door knocker and releases it. We don't see her, just the hand, devoid of rings, the skin aged, a slight tremor detectable.

NARRATOR V.O

It was late 2022 when I first met Gail Frost. An unremarkable woman. Eccentric even, in that great British tradition. Socially awkward, prickly, defensive, but I was soon sloughing off my preconceptions which were purely superficial and based mainly on her unkempt appearance and reduced circumstances, as well as those terrible photos printed of her and salacious headlines. I interviewed her in the dank bedsit she was renting in Reading. An awful place, mould on the walls. She was lucid, intelligent, and entirely compelling throughout the lengthy interview process.

The camera watches the grand door as the unseen woman waits for it to open, her breaths ragged, sounds of her clearing her throat, then the camera looks up to the very top floor and a roof terrace, lingering there until it snaps back to the door. She knocks again, louder this time and then we hear sounds of footsteps approaching from the other side. A figure is visible through the small sliver of obscured glass, someone is unlocking the door.

NARRATOR V.O

Gail and I were to meet many times over the following weeks and then months. I quickly set aside the opinion I had formed of her based on what I'd read in the tabloid press. I would ask you to do the same. Come to her story with fresh eyes. Come to her story with compassion. As this series airs, I would ask you again, Gail, to be in touch. We care about you. We want to help you.

SCREEN FADES TO BLACK AS GAIL'S QUOTE TYPES, ONE WORD AT A TIME...

"We are rarely brought down by a nemesis exacting revenge. Those scenarios exist only in stories, bad ones at that. No, the dispiriting but prosaic truth is… we are our own worst enemies."

Gail Frost November 2022

SCENE ONE

The large front door to Lexington Gardens opens... we see the two women meet face to face for the first time.

ACKNOWLEDGMENTS

There are two women without whom *The Assistant* would not be the book it is. My agent, Hannah Todd, who helped me develop the idea and then supported me with tireless enthusiasm and endless wisdom. I have found the best home for my writing with Hannah and the team at Madeleine Milburn. And my editor, Emily Yau, whose vision and passion for this book have been an inspiration. Thanks to Emily and the Boldwood Books team for their professionalism and author care.

To my fellow authors and friends, Kate Riordan, Hayley Hoskins, Nikki Smith, Anna Mazzola and all the Ladykillers, thank you for listening, reading, providing laughter and a place to share the good and bad days.

To Louise Dean and the wonderful team at The Novelry, thank you for welcoming me and sharing your knowledge so generously. Mentoring is a symbiotic relationship, and it's an honour to learn from my colleagues and the writers I coach.

My family who support me with grace and good humour, thank you all and especially Chris, Beth and Dan, Mum and Dad, and George.

A final note to my faithful furry companion, Scout. There for every word.

Amanda

MORE FROM AMANDA REYNOLDS

We hope you enjoyed reading *The Assistant*. If you did, please leave a review.

If you'd like to gift a copy, this book is also available as an ebook, hardback, large print, digital audio download and audiobook CD.

Sign up to Amanda Reynolds' mailing list for news, competitions and updates on future books.

https://bit.ly/AmandaReynoldsNews

ABOUT THE AUTHOR

Amanda Reynolds is the bestselling psychological suspense author whose debut novel, *Close To Me*, was adapted as a major six-part TV series for Channel 4 in 2021. Previously published by Headline, her books have been translated into multiple languages. Amanda lives near Cheltenham.

Visit Amanda's website: https://www.amandareynoldsauthor.com

Follow Amanda on social media

 twitter.com/amandareynoldsj

 instagram.com/ajreynolds2

 facebook.com/amandareynoldsauthor

Boldwood

Boldwood Books is an award-winning fiction publishing company seeking out the best stories from around the world.

Find out more at www.boldwoodbooks.com

Join our reader community for brilliant books, competitions and offers!

Follow us
@BoldwoodBooks
@BookandTonic

Sign up to our weekly deals newsletter

https://bit.ly/BoldwoodBNewsletter

Printed in Great Britain
by Amazon